DATE DUE

BRODART · Cat. No. 23-221

THEMES IN DRAMA

An annual publication
Edited by James Redmond

10

FARCE

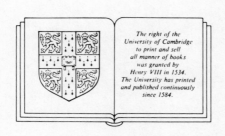

The right of the
University of Cambridge
to print and sell
all manner of books
was granted by
Henry VIII in 1534.
The University has printed
and published continuously
since 1584.

CAMBRIDGE UNIVERSITY PRESS

CAMBRIDGE

NEW YORK   NEW ROCHELLE   MELBOURNE   SYDNEY

Published by the Press Syndicate of the University of Cambridge
The Pitt Building, Trumpington Street, Cambridge CB2 1RP
32 East 57th Street, New York, NY 10022, USA
10 Stamford Road, Oakleigh, Melbourne 3166, Australia

First published 1988

Printed in Great Britain at The Bath Press, Avon

British Library cataloguing in publication data
Themes in Drama, 10
1. Drama – History and criticism – Periodicals
809.2'005 PN1601

Library of Congress catalogue card number 82–4491

ISSN 0263–676x
ISBN 0 521 353475

Contents

Themes in Drama volumes and conferences

The first twelve volumes in the series *Themes in Drama* are

1   *Drama and Society*
2   *Drama and Mimesis*
3   *Drama, Dance and Music*
4   *Drama and Symbolism*
5   *Drama and Religion*
6   *Drama and the Actor*
7   *Drama, Sex and Politics*
8   *Historical Drama*
9   *The Theatrical Space*
10 *Farce*
11 *Women in Theatre* (1989)
12 *Drama and Philosophy* (1990)

Papers are invited for the following volumes, and should be submitted in final form to the Editor before 1 August in the year indicated (potential contributors are asked to correspond with the Editor well in advance of these dates):

13 *Violence in Drama* (1989)
14 *Melodrama* (1990)
15 *Madness in Drama* (1991)

Themes in Drama conferences, 1989

Annual conferences are held at the University of London and at the University of California. The subject each year is that of the volume in preparation. The 1989 conferences will be on 'Violence in Drama'. Details of the conference in California may be obtained from *Themes in Drama* Conference, University of California, Riverside, Ca. 92521. Details of the conference in London may be obtained from the Editor.

James Redmond, Editor, *Themes in Drama*, Westfield College, University of London, London NW3 7ST

Contributors

Christopher Balme, *Institut für Englische Philologie, Universität Würzburg*
Michael Booth, *Department of Theatre, University of Victoria*
Victor Castellani, *Foreign Languages and Literatures, University of Denver*
Jim Davis, *Department of Drama, University of New South Wales*
Gregory Dobrov, *Classics Department, Cornell University*
Peter Holland, *Trinity Hall, University of Cambridge*
Richard L. Homan, *Department of Fine Arts, Rider College*
W. D. Howarth, *Department of French, University of Bristol*
William Hutchings, *Department of English, University of Alabama, Birmingham*
Albert E. Kalson, *Department of English, Purdue University*
Andrea G. Labinger, *University of La Verne*
N. J. Lowe, *Department of Classics, Westfield College, University of London*
Douglas M. MacDowell, *Department of Greek, University of Glasgow*
J. Paul Marcoux, *University Theatre, Boston College*
Jeffrey D. Mason, *Arts and Sciences, California State College, Bakersfield*
Gabrielle Robinson, *Department of English, Indiana University at South Bend*
Maya Slater, *Department of French, Westfield College, University of London*
John Swan, *Crosset Library, Bennington College*
David Wiles, *Department of Drama and Theatre Arts, RHBNC, University of London*

Illustrations

Editor's preface

This is the tenth volume of *Themes in Drama*, which is published annually. Each volume brings together reviews and articles on the theatrical activity of a wide range of cultures and periods. The papers offer original contributions to their own specialized fields, but they are presented in such a way that their significance may be appreciated readily by non-specialists.

Each volume indicates connections between the various national traditions of theatre by bringing together studies of a theme of central and continuing importance. The annual international conferences (see p. vii) provide an opportunity for scholars, critics and theatrical practitioners to exchange views, and many of the papers in the volumes are revised versions of papers read and discussed at the conferences. The present volume reflects the range and quality of the 1986 conferences on 'Farce'. Contributions are invited for volumes 13, 14 and 15; they should follow the style of presentation used in this volume, and be sent to

James Redmond
Editor *Themes in Drama*
Westfield College
University of London
London NW3 7ST

PREFACE

Clowning and slapstick in Aristophanes*

DOUGLAS M. MacDOWELL

The chief character of Aristophanes' *Wasps* is an old man named Philokleon ('Love Kleon'), who has a strange passion for sitting on juries. His son Bdelykleon ('Loathe Kleon') is trying to cure him of this passion, or at least prevent him from indulging it; and at the beginning of the play he has shut his father up in their house to stop him going to the lawcourt. The door is barred; nets cover the windows. The time is early morning. Two slaves, Xanthias and Sosias, are on guard, or are supposed to be on guard, outside the door; they have been dozing off at intervals, and also chatting so as to make the situation clear to the audience. Bdelykleon, the son, has been sleeping on the flat roof; from there, when he gets up, he has a bird's-eye view of the whole establishment, including the yard and the kitchen, which are at the back of the house, out of sight of the audience. At line 136 he stands up on the roof and calls down to the slaves on the ground outside the door.[1]

> *Bdelykleon.* Hey, Xanthias! Sosias! Are you asleep?
> *Xanthias.*   O-o.
> *Sosias.*   What is it?
> *Xanthias.*   Bdelykleon's getting up.
> *Bdelykleon.* Look sharp there, one of you, and run round here.
>   My father's just gone out into the kitchen.
>   He's crouching down and scuttling like a mouse: 140
>   He'll get out through the waste-hole of the sink!
>   You, lean against the door there.
> *Xanthias.*   Right you are, sir.
> *Bdelykleon.* Good heavens! What's that noise the chimney's making?
>   Hey, who are you?
> *Philokleon.*   Me? Just a puff of smoke.
> *Bdelykleon.* You, smoke? What wood are you from?
> *Philokleon.*   Syco-more.[2]   145
> *Bdelykleon.* Oh yes, that *is* the sharpest kind of smoke!
>   Go back in, won't you! Where's the chimney-board?
>   Get down! I'll put a log on you as well.

* A draft of this paper was read at the *Themes in Drama* International Conference held at the University of London, Westfield College, in March 1986.

2 *Farce*

There now! You'll have to think up something else!
But really, I'm the unluckiest man alive: 150
People will say that I'm the son of Smoky!³
Philokleon. Hey, boy!
Xanthias.   He's pushing at the door.
Bdelykleon.   Press hard
And strong against it; I'm just coming too.
And take care of the fastening and the bar:
See that he doesn't gnaw out the locking-pin!   155
Philokleon. What are you doing? You scoundrels, let me go
To try Drakontides,⁴ or he'll get off!
Xanthias. Would that upset you?
Philokleon.   Yes! The oracle
At Delphi once predicted that, if I
Let anyone get off, I'd shrivel up!   160
Xanthias. Apollo save us! What a prophecy!
Philokleon. I implore you, let me out – or else I'll burst!
Xanthias. Never, not on your life, Philokleon!
Philokleon. Well then, I'll gnaw the net through with my teeth.
Xanthias. You haven't any teeth.
Philokleon.   Oh, woe is me!   165
How shall I slay thee, how? Give me a sword
Without delay – or else a sentence-tablet.
Bdelykleon. Malice aforethought, that's what this man has!
Philokleon. Oh, not at all. I want to take the donkey
And sell it, with its panniers as well.   170
It's market-day.
Bdelykleon.   But I can go myself
And sell it, can't I?
Philokleon.   Not as well as I can.
Bdelykleon. Much better.
Philokleon.   All right, take the donkey out.
Xanthias. What an excuse, real disingenuous,
To make you let him out!
Bdelykleon.   He didn't catch   175
A fish this time though; I saw through his trick!
I'd better bring the donkey out myself,
So that the old man can't peep out again.
Why are you crying, Neddy? Just because
You're being sold today? Gee up! Why grumble?   180
Unless you're carrying an Odysseus!⁵
Xanthias.   Blimey!
He *has* got someone underneath, down here!
Bdelykleon. What! Let me see.
Xanthias.   There.
Bdelykleon.   What on earth is this?
Who are you, sir?
Philokleon.   No-man.
Bdelykleon.   No-man? From where?
Philokleon. From Ithaka; son of MacRunaway.   185
Bdelykleon. No-man indeed! You'll get no joy from that!

Pull him from under there at once! The scoundrel,
To get down there! He looks to me as if
A summons-witness[6] had produced a foal!
Philokleon. Leave me alone, or else I'll fight you for it!   190
Bdelykleon. Fight us for what, then?
Philokleon.   For a donkey's shadow.[7]
Bdelykleon. A bad'un, you – far gone in skill, no chicken!
Philokleon. Me, bad? No, I'm in prime condition now!
Can't you tell that? You will, though, when you taste
An undercut of an old juryman!   195
Bdelykleon. Get back indoors, you and the donkey too!
Philokleon. Help, fellow-jurymen and Kleon! Help!
Bdelykleon. We'll shut the door, and you can shout inside.
Here, you, pile lots of stones against the door,
And put the locking-pin back in the bar,   200
And when you've got that on the door, look sharp
And roll the mortar up against it.
Xanthias.   Ow!
Where did that clod of earth fall on me from?
Bdelykleon. Perhaps a mouse just dropped it down on you.
Xanthias. A *mouse.* Not likely! It's some animal   205
Under the tiles up there, a jury-roofster!
Bdelykleon. Oh dear! The man's converted to a sparrow!
He'll fly away! Where, where's my bird-net gone?
Shoo! Shoo! Get back! Shoo! It would be less trouble
To guard Skione[8] than to guard this father!   210

(Aristophanes, *Wasps* 136–210)

This scene, like many scenes in Aristophanes, is a compound of several elements, each of which will repay study. First, there are the elements of plot and character, and the contribution which this scene makes to the development of the play as a whole. The main theme of *Wasps* is the conversion of Philokleon; and this scene is vital to its development, because it is here that his character before conversion is first displayed to the audience. Secondly, there are the literary allusions, especially the parody of tragic fury (line 166). Thirdly, there is the verbal humour, such as the puns in lines 145 and 189. Fourthly, there are the topical allusions, including references to well-known individuals who were probably in the audience when the play was performed, such as Kleon (line 197) and Drakontides (line 157). In this paper I am leaving aside all those aspects of the scene in order to concentrate on a fifth one, the comic movements and activities of the characters.

This is in some ways the hardest one to study, because of the lack of evidence. The preserved texts of ancient plays have (with very few exceptions) no stage directions. They tell us what the actors said or sang; they do not tell us what the actors did. No doubt the director of the performance (who in most cases was the author himself) gave the actors oral instructions about their movements, but no written record of them survives. That of course is the reason why the stage action of Greek drama was largely ignored until quite recently. The texts of Greek plays have been carefully studied by classical scholars ever since the Renaissance, but they have generally been studied as poetry, for their linguistic and literary qualities. In the twentieth century more attention has been paid to their content, moral or religious or political or social; but it is only in the last twenty years or so that they have begun to be analysed from a theatrical point of view. Such analysis is, we now see, essential for a proper understanding of the plays. Greek dramatists wrote their plays for performance. They were not writing for readers; they intended their work to be heard and seen, and at certain points in a play a dramatic effect may be obtained by action rather than by words. That applies sometimes even in a tragedy: for example, the mere appearance of Medea in her dragon chariot shows her triumph far more effectively than any of the words that she speaks from it. But it applies much more often in a comedy, and most of all in a farcical scene like this passage of *Wasps*.

The main point which Aristophanes wishes to convey to the audience in this scene is that Philokleon is a lively old man whose energy and ability are misdirected and hard to suppress; and Aristophanes wishes not merely to make this point clear, but to make it funny. The point is stated in words, certainly; but in performance it is the action which makes it most forcibly and most effectively. The audience *sees* Philokleon trying to get out, and Bdelykleon and the slaves making frantic efforts to keep him in. Most people take things in through their eyes more immediately than through their ears; and so an audience understands the point of this scene primarily from watching what the characters do, and only secondarily from the words which we now have in writing. It is the activity which is dramatically the most important part of this scene, and also the funniest part, and which makes it a brilliant piece of farce.

As readers, then, we must try to reconstruct the activity. First, at line 137, the two slaves, who have been sitting or lying on the ground, have to jump up and rush about when Bdelykleon shouts to them; this draws the audience's attention and creates a sense of urgency and expectancy. Sosias at line 141 rushes away to the back of the house (and does not reappear in this scene);[9] Xanthias at line 142 rushes to the front door and leans against it as if he can hardly keep it shut. We expect to see somebody bursting out of the door, but what happens? Instead of popping out of the door Philokleon pops out of the chimney, pretending to be smoke. Bdelykleon, on the roof, rushes over to the chimney, pushes Philokleon back inside, puts a chimney-cover on top of him, puts a piece of wood on top of that – and immediately Philokleon is starting to burst out of the door again (line 152). Xanthias rushes back to the door, and Bdelykleon starts coming down from the roof (after line 155); but before he reaches the ground, Philokleon has already left the door and is looking out of the first-floor window (line 156). We can tell from the text that he must be looking out of the window, because his egress is obstructed by the net covering the window (line 164); and we know the window must be on the first floor, not on the ground floor, because in a later scene, when he actually does get out of the window, he has to let himself down by a rope (lines 379–80).

So far we have a type of activity which I call 'jack-in-the-box clowning'. A man pops up into view, is pushed back, and immediately pops out again. Putting a lid on someone is a very effective type of clowning, and in this connection Aristophanes' idea of using the chimney-board is brilliant. A chimney-board was evidently a lid put on top of a chimney to keep out the rain and the wind when the fire was not alight. When Bdelykleon puts this lid on top of Philokleon (line 147), and then puts a piece of wood on top of that (line 148), that gives a physical and visual impression that Philokleon is being squashed down into the house bit by bit.

But there is more to it than this: it is not just straightforward jack-in-the-box clowning, because Philokleon does not always pop up in the same place. This adds an element of surprise, because you never quite know where he is going to be next. First he is out of sight at the back of the house (line 139); then he is rattling the front door (line 142). Where will he be next? The window seems the most obvious other place; but no, he's popping out of the chimney (line 144). Well, surely the next place must be the window – no, he's back at the door again (line 152); that caught you out, because you didn't realize he might try the same place twice. If he's going to and fro like that, the next place ought to be the chimney again – no, now at last he is at the window after all (line 156)! All this movement from one point to another means that the audience is kept in a continuous state of suspense and expectancy, wondering just where Philokleon's next appearance is going to be. It also means that Bdelykleon and the slaves, instead of standing still, are continually rushing about, so that the stage picture presented to the audience is not a static but a lively one.

Next follows the passage with the donkey. Philokleon urges Bdelykleon to take the donkey out to market (line 173). The donkey is evidently kept in the yard, or in a stable opening off the yard. The door of the house, which the audience can see, is the door from the street into the yard (the rooms of the house being grouped around the yard); so this door is the one by which the donkey must be brought out. At the end of line 178 Bdelykleon and Xanthias unbar and open the door. Bdelykleon goes in, and immediately comes out again leading the donkey.

The first thing to notice about the donkey is that, in performance, it is not a real donkey; it is two actors inside a donkey costume. This must be so, because it has to bray on its cue to prompt Bdelykleon's question 'Why are you crying, Neddy?' (line 179) and a real donkey could not be relied on to do that.[10] So it is a 'pantomime donkey', and that by itself would look grotesque and laughable. But it is not by itself; it is carrying Philokleon, who somehow or other is clinging to its underside.

How can a man cling to the underside of a donkey? I suppose Philokleon may perhaps have his feet through the donkey's harness at the front end; with his hands he holds on to the panniers on each side; and his head hangs back, so that he looks upside down between the donkey's back legs. That, or something like that, seems to be the way in which he could hold on. In this position he conducts the polite conversation of lines 184–6. His position is quite exceptionally awkward and uncomfortable; but he has to stay there, because if he did not he would ruin his plan of escape. So the funniest aspect of this passage is not the dialogue (though the parody of the Homeric joke about No-man is quite amusing) but the appearance both of the donkey and of Philokleon, involving two types of clowning: actors dressed up in a grotesque costume, and a man stuck in an awkward position which he can't get out of.

Philokleon is pulled away from the donkey and pushed back inside the house (line 198), but after that he makes yet another attempt to escape by slipping under the tiles of the roof. But this is not just another instalment of the jack-in-the-box clowning which we saw earlier in the scene. The emphasis is different, because after line 198 the audience does not see Philokleon. Visually the centre of attention is Xanthias, who is bombarded first with orders and then with dirt. He is told to collect some stones and pile them up against the door (line 199). He starts out to do that, but before he has had time to do it he is told to put the bar and pin back in place (line 200). He stops in his tracks and comes back to do that, but then he is told to go and fetch the big mortar to set against the door (line 202). Before he has had time to do that, he has been hit on the head by a lump of dirt (line 203). The fun here is in seeing Xanthias rushing about, first one way and then another, achieving nothing at all, not knowing where he is going, what he is doing, or what's hit him. Bdelykleon all this time is just standing by doing nothing, with his hands (so to speak) in his pockets. He shows no sympathy at all, even when Xanthias has been hit on the head: 'Perhaps a mouse just dropped it down on you' (line 203). The clowning which we have here is in fact another instance of a man in an uncomfortable situation. Philokleon underneath the donkey was in an uncomfortable static position, from which he could not move; Xanthias is uncomfortable because he is made to run this way and that and suffers aerial bombardment too; but in both cases it is the character's unenviable situation which makes the audience laugh.

By line 207 Bdelykleon and Xanthias can apparently both see Philokleon: they say that he is creeping about under the tiles of the roof, that he is turning into a sparrow and is going to fly away. The audience cannot see him though. We can be sure of this, both because he is specifically stated to be under the tiles, not on them (line 206), and also because he speaks no lines at this point; if Philokleon were in view, we may be sure he would not keep his mouth shut. So all that the audience can see is Bdelykleon and Xanthias gaping upwards. Bdelykleon calls for a bird-net, but of course nobody brings him one, so that he and Xanthias just have to wave their arms about and shout 'Shoo! Shoo!' If the audience could see Philokleon this might be quite amusing, but it is funnier when all that the audience sees is two men excitedly waving their arms about and shouting 'Shoo!' at nothing at all. A perfectly normal and reasonable action looks funny if you remove its object. So here we have yet another type of clowning, the type in which a man solemnly devotes a great deal of attention and energy to something which isn't there.

So far all my comments have been directed at one scene, and I have been trying to show that even a single scene may contain clowning of several distinct types. Now I want to fit this scene into a wider context by alluding briefly to some scenes of clowning in other plays of Aristophanes, and by making some general comments about the types of clowning which he uses.

The commonest and most basic type of clowning in Aristophanes is hitting. There is hardly any of his plays in which someone does not at some point beat someone else. In *Clouds*, for instance, Strepsiades attacks one of his creditors with a goad (lines 1297–1302). In *Frogs* there is a scene in which Aiakos flogs Dionysos and Xanthias alternately to discover which of them feels pain (lines 635–73). In *Birds* Peisthetairos beats up a whole series of intruders into Cloudcuckooland. Besides the passages of straightforward hitting there is a nice variation at one point when he is bothered by two intruders simultaneously, an inspector and a decree-seller; whenever he beats and chases away one of them, the other reappears behind him, so that he has to keep dashing from one side to the other, beating them each in turn (lines 1044–55). When we read these scenes, or discuss them in a lecture-room, they sometimes seem unfunny or even coarse. But in performance there can be no question about their power to amuse an audience. Later drama too has found hitting an effective ingredient of comedy, all the way from Shakespeare (for example, Falstaff getting beaten on Gadshill in *1 Henry IV* II, ii) down to the Punch and Judy show, which contains a great deal of hitting and has been popular for a very long time. But why is it effective? Why does it amuse people to see someone hitting someone else on a stage?

This is a psychological question, and an interesting attempt to answer it has been made by Eric Bentley in *The Life of the Drama*. He refers to Freud's explanation of jokes, and he propounds a theory of what he calls 'comic catharsis', by which he means a release from inhibitions. Farce, he says, 'offers a special opportunity: shielded by delicious darkness and seated in warm security, we enjoy the privilege of being totally passive while on stage our most treasured unmentionable wishes are fulfilled before our eyes'.[11]

It is easy for a classicist to shoot a few holes in this description. In answer to the comment about delicious darkness and warm security, one may point out that all the plays of Aristophanes were performed in an open-air theatre, at a cold time of year (either the winter or the early spring), in broad daylight, so that the spectators could see one another as well as the actors. More importantly, the term 'catharsis' in this context is vague and misleading. 'Catharsis' means 'cleansing' or 'purgation', and, as everyone knows, it was first used in connection with drama by Aristotle, who says that tragedy produces a purgation of pity and fear. What Aristotle wrote about comedy is lost, but from later Greek writers who probably followed his views it seems likely that he said that comedy produced a purgation of enjoyment and laughter.[12] There is no evidence that Aristotle associated this with a release from inhibitions.[13]

Nevertheless, if we leave aside the expression 'comic catharsis', Bentley's theory that farce gives the audience a release from inhibitions is a valuable one. I should rephrase it like this. In ordinary life we (that is, normal adults) have learned to restrain the expression of our feelings, especially aggressive feelings and sexual wishes. For example, we should like to hit people who have power over us, because they are officials, or because they are our creditors, or because they are experts in a field in which we ourselves are ignorant; we should like to hit them, but we do not, we inhibit ourselves. In a farce we can see such hitting being done on the stage: we see Peisthetairos beating the pompous officials, and we see Strepsiades beating his creditor, and this relieves our feelings, so that we do not need to behave like that ourselves. If we did behave like that in real life we should feel guilty, but when we know it is only a play we need not feel guilty. We have no qualms about the outcome, not only because the actors are just pretending, but also because in a farce the characters are never seriously hurt. A man who is knocked down in real life may break his leg, but a man who is knocked down in a farce just bounces up again like a ping-pong ball.

But although this theory of release from inhibitions seems plausible when applied to scenes in which one character hits another, there are other types of clowning in Aristophanes which it does not fit so well. Take the prologue of *Peace*: Trygaios sitting astride a flying beetle, suspended in mid-air by the stage machine, wobbling precariously. He seems about to fall off at any moment; but in fact he does not, he lands safely. This is a splendid piece of clowning, which many people find the most memorable incident in the whole of that play. But here it is hardly convincing to say that we laugh because the sight releases our pent-up feelings of aggression. To meet this kind of case the Bentley theory must be, if not entirely abandoned, at least drastically modified.

Perhaps we may seek an explanation along these lines. In ordinary life we sometimes find ourselves in difficult or unpleasant situations, either because of circumstances beyond our own control or because we ourselves have done something stupid. In a farce we see other people in such situations. This makes us feel comfortable, and superior, and pleased that we are not in that situation ourselves. 'Thank goodness *I've* never had to balance in mid-air on the back of a beetle!' And so it is with several other well-known Aristophanic scenes. In *Clouds* we see Socrates suspended in his basket to look at the sun: we may say to ourselves 'Thank goodness *I've* never been so silly as to do that!' Dionysos, in *Frogs*, tries to row Charon's boat, gets into a muddle, and sits on top of his oar: 'Well,' says the spectator to himself, 'I may not be a rowing blue, but at least I'm not *that* incompetent.' This kind of clowning is effective because it gives the audience a feeling of comfortable superiority.

Some of these scenes get their comic effect not so much from the activity of the characters as from their appearance when stationary; and, as another aspect of comic appearance, it is worth noting that a comic dress can make an important contribution to clowning and to farce in general. Aristophanes probably made much use of comic costumes. One great asset which he could exploit was the Athenian tradition of animal choruses and characters.[14] An actor dressed as an animal can very easily produce an absurd effect. I have already mentioned Philokleon's donkey in *Wasps*; a later scene of the same play has leading parts for two dogs, and there is another donkey in *Frogs*. Then there are all the bird characters in *Birds*, and the chorus of frogs in *Frogs* – at least, I think so; some editors maintain that this chorus is only heard from behind the scenes, but I am convinced that the frogs were actually visible, clumsily hopping about, and that this was a major element in the comic entertainment.[15]

For farcical purposes, however, the more significant kind of dressing-up is the kind by which a human character changes his appearance in the course of the play. It may signify that the character himself changes in some way; thus Philokleon in *Wasps* puts on expensive and luxurious clothes when he gives up his old way of life as a juror. More often the change of costume does not mark an actual change in the character, but is a deliberate disguise: he wants people to think he is someone else, and a farcical situation develops because his behaviour does not fit his appearance and the disguise is a hopeless failure. The two best examples are the cowardly Dionysos dressed as the fearless Herakles in *Frogs*, and the old man dressed as a woman in *Thesmophoriazousai*.

It is also possible for a character to change his appearance without changing his costume. This brings me to another type of clowning which has always been very popular, one that I call 'custard-pie slapstick'. This is the type in which one character throws at another something harmless, soft, and messy. It is not necessarily a custard pie; it can be anything liquid or splodgy. The essential thing is that it drastically changes the appearance of the victim, and leaves him looking very uncomfortable, without doing him any actual injury.

The Athenians did not have custard. They did have some milk products fairly similar to custard, but at the time of the Peloponnesian War I suppose those were too scarce and expensive to be thrown about. Nevertheless there is one scene in Aristophanes which does clearly contain clowning of the custard-pie type. It is a most interesting example, not least because it is performed entirely by the chorus, not by individual characters. It is in *Lysistrata*, and it is the chorus's entrance scene, the *parodos*.

The chorus of *Lysistrata* is a divided one; half of it consists of old men, the other half of old women. First we see the old men. They come trudging along, carrying logs of wood and fire in braziers. They explain, in song and in conversation with one another, how they have heard that a gang of women (brazen hussies!) have occupied the Akropolis and barricaded the Propylaia. The younger men presumably are all away at the war, and so instead these old men have come to burn down the wooden doors of the gateway and force the women out. They put down their logs and start trying to set light to the doors. But then along come the old women, carrying buckets of water. They know that the younger women have occupied the Akropolis, and now they have heard that the old men are intending to set fire to it; so here they come to the rescue! With water slopping out of their buckets as they struggle along, they totter into and across the *orkhestra* until they come face to face with the old men. And the following dialogue ensues, with, I imagine, one man and one woman speaking on behalf of all the rest.[16]

Men. Well, here's an unexpected thing appeared on the horizon:
   A swarm of women, don't you see? They're coming to the rescue!
Women. You've got the wind up have you? Why? You ain't seen nothing so far!
   There's more of us to come, you know – ten thousand times this number! 355
Men. Here, Phaidrias, shall we allow these women's noise and chatter?
   I think someone should wallop them, and break his stick upon them.
Women. We'd better put our buckets down, and stand them on the ground here.
   If someone's going to start a fight, we'll need to have our hands free.
Men. What they shuld have is two or three good slaps on all their faces,   360
   Like Boupalos[17] once got, remember? That would stop their talking.
Women. All right then, someone, hit me! I'll stand here and let you do it.
   When next a bitch meets *you*, she'll find you've got no more virility!
Men. You hold your tongue, or with my stick I'll knock out your senility!
Women. Just take one step and touch Stratyllis with your little finger – !   365
Men. What if I smash her with my fist? What damage will you do me?
Women. I'll use my teeth to reap a crop: I'll bite your lungs and guts out!
Men. Of all the poets on this earth, Euripides is wisest:
   There really is no creature quite as shameless as a woman!
Women. I think it's time we picked our water-buckets up, Rhodippe.   370

Men. And why, you fiend, have you thought fit to come up here with water?
Women. And why have you with fire, you tomb? To get yourself cremated?
Men. My purpose is to light a pyre and burn up your companions.
Women. *My* purpose is to quench your pyre; this water's meant for dousing.
Men. You think you're going to douse my fire?
Women.   You'll soon see what will happen.   375
Men. I shan't waste time; I've half a mind to take this torch and roast you.
Women. Have you some soap by any chance? I'll go ahead and bath you.
Men. You're going to bath me, you old hag?
Women.   Just like a blushing bridegroom.
Men. You hear the brazen things she says?
Women.   I'm just as free as you are.
Men. I'll make you stop this shouting now.
Women.   You're not on jury service.   380
Men. Set fire now to the woman's hair!
Women.   It's your turn, river-water!
Men. Oh bloody hell!
Women.   It wasn't warm?
Men. What, *warm*? Stop! What are you doing now?
Women. I'm watering you, to make you grow.
Men. I'm shivering and withering!
                                                                    385
Women. How lucky that you've got a fire! Just what you want for warming.
(Aristophanes, Lysistrata 352–86)

The dialogue here makes the action quite clear. After a steady crescendo of abuse, the women pick up their buckets, they say they are going to give the men a bath, the men bluster and advance, and then – sploosh! and the men are wet through, with their clothes clinging to them, and water trickling from their hands on to the ground, howling and shivering.[18]

The sight of a man who is soaking wet is funny. It is funny because he is obviously very uncomfortable, and yet we know that it is not going to do him any serious harm, especially in a sunny climate, where he will dry off in a few minutes. Water in fact is a very suitable substance for custard-pie slapstick. There are plenty of modern films in which it is used in this way. In a modern indoor theatre water is more inconvenient to use, because it may leave you with puddles on the stage for the rest of the play with no sun to dry them up. Still it is used in modern theatres sometimes, for instance in Henry Livings' play *Eh?*, in which the chief character empties a bucket of water over his wife.[19] In *Lysistrata* it is the other way round: the women throw water over the men. And this perhaps is better; the men are physically stronger, and it is more satisfying to see the weaker party getting the best of it. If you have ever secretly wished to empty a bucket of water over some pompous blustering person, you will get great enjoyment and satisfaction from seeing it done at a performance of *Lysistrata*. And since the main theme of the play is the women's rebellion against the men, this scene is a clear example of a piece of slapstick used not just to provide incidental amusement, but to convey visually an important dramatic point.

There are of course many other passages of clowning and slapstick in

Aristophanes which I have not mentioned; this paper is not to be taken as a comprehensive account of the subject. But even from these few examples I think it is possible to see how it may be studied and analysed. The aim of Aristophanes was to entertain and impress his audience; and when he included some clowning or slapstick in a play, he did so because he believed that it would have that effect. If we ask why it was effective, that is a psychological question about the audience. Strictly it is a question about the ancient Athenian audience; but in this matter I see no reason to suppose that there was any great difference between an ancient audience and a modern one, and I believe that we can attempt to answer the question by observation of modern audiences, including ourselves when we go to see a farce.

Clowning or slapstick always involves someone having an unpleasant experience, and Aristophanes, it has been said, is a master of comic suffering.[20] But the nature and cause of the suffering vary. It may be inflicted on him by another character, who hits him or squashes him down (jack-in-the-box clowning) or throws something at him (custard-pie slapstick). Alternatively he may bring the experience on himself by his own clumsiness or stupidity, by putting on inappropriate clothes or by mishandling some physical object (like Dionysos making his incompetent attempt to row the boat) or by getting into a precarious location (like Philokleon hanging on to the donkey). The spectator laughs out of a sense of relief and superiority, because he is not in the uncomfortable situation himself. When the unpleasant experience is inflicted by another character, the spectator may feel a sense of identity with the aggressor, and so feel a release from the inhibitions which generally repress his own aggressiveness (by what Bentley calls 'comic catharsis'); but that cannot be true in the cases in which there is no aggressor. What is true in every case, however, is that the victim does not suffer any lasting harm; a victim who did suffer lasting harm would evoke sympathy rather than laughter. These are features of clowning and slapstick in modern plays too; and the fact that we find them already present in Aristophanes justifies us in calling him the father of farce.

NOTES

1 The translation is based on my own edition of the Greek text (Oxford University Press, 1971). A few different readings are adopted in the edition by A. H. Sommerstein (Warminster: Aris and Phillips, 1983, with a prose translation), but they do not affect the matters discussed in this article. Comment on details of the scene may be found both in my edition and in Sommerstein's. On the demands made on the actor playing Philokleon, see K. McLeish, *The Theatre of Aristophanes* (London: Thames and Hudson, 1980), pp. 115–17.
2 The Greek is a pun on 'fig-wood' (σύκινος) and 'sycophant' (a mercenary or

malicious prosecutor). The translation 'syco-more' is taken from H. Van Daele's French translation of the play in the Budé series (Paris, 1924).

3 'Smoky' was the nickname of an earlier comic dramatist, Ekphantides.

4 Drakontides was evidently a man awaiting trial in 422 BC, but his identity is uncertain.

5 Lines 179–85 parody the myth of the escape of Odysseus from the Cyclops, best known from Book 9 of the *Odyssey*.

6 The Greek is a pun on κλητήρ, meaning both 'donkey' and 'summons-witness'.

7 'A donkey's shadow' was a proverbial phrase for something not worth arguing about.

8 Skione, a town in northern Greece, was at present being besieged by the Athenians.

9 I assume here that it is correct to attribute to Xanthias all the lines in 142–210 which are spoken by a slave. This cannot in fact be proved. There are many passages of Aristophanes in which the attribution of lines to speakers is problematical, and often a problem of attribution is entangled with a problem of staging. If Sosias should be thought to reappear here (after line 155, for example), that would affect details of my reconstruction but not the general principles.

10 Cf. P. D. Arnott in *Greece & Rome*, 6 (1959), 178–9.

11 Eric Bentley, *The Life of the Drama* (London: Methuen, 1965), p. 229.

12 See especially the *Tractatus Coislinianus* (in *Prolegomena de Comoedia*, ed. W. J. W. Koster, Groningen, 1975, p. 64): κωμῳδία ... δι᾽ ἡδονῆς καὶ γέλωτος περαίνουσα τὴν τῶν τοιούτων παθημάτων κάθαρσιν. Cf. Richard Janko, *Aristotle on Comedy* (London: Duckworth, 1984), pp. 143–4 and 156–60.

13 Purgation of anger or hatred was probably regarded by Aristotle as a function of tragedy, not of comedy. Cf. Janko, *Aristotle on Comedy*, pp. 160–1. The best attempt to apply the notion of 'comic catharsis' to Aristophanes is that of D. F. Sutton, *Self and Society in Aristophanes* (Washington: University Press of America, 1980), pp. 69–82.

14 Cf. G. M. Sifakis, *Parabasis and Animal Choruses* (London: Athlone, 1971).

15 I have discussed the appearance of the chorus of frogs in *Classical Review*, 22 (1972), 3–5. A different opinion is maintained by R. H. Allison in *Greece & Rome*, 30 (1983), 8–20; cf. also D. A. Campbell in *Journal of Hellenic Studies*, 104 (1984), 163–5.

16 The translation is based on V. Coulon's edition of the text in the Budé series (Paris, 1928). The metre is intended to represent the iambic tetrameters of the original.

17 Boupalos was a sculptor at Klazomenai in the sixth century BC, lampooned in the poems of Hipponax. The reference here is probably to one of those poems.

18 There is no doubt that all the men get soaked, not just their one spokesman; that is clear from lines 399–402.

19 Henry Livings, *Eh?* (London: Methuen, 1965), p. 81.

20 E. Olson, *The Theory of Comedy* (Bloomington, Ind.: Indiana University Press, 1968), p. 75.

The dawn of farce: Aristophanes

GREGORY DOBROV

In his 'Note on Farce' J. D. Hurell remarks that, 'farce, having once been relegated to the lowest level of the series headed by tragedy, has continually been taken for granted as something if not actually beneath criticism, at least beneath the need for critical discussion'.[1] This attitude can be traced from the present (G. B. Shaw, L. J. Potts[2]) back to Aristotle.[3] Modern scholarship is surprisingly conservative in its uncritical condemnation of farce as 'vulgar', 'base', 'primitive', etc. Considering the fact that even well-intentioned studies of the subject[4] have made little progress towards defining 'farce' (much less explaining its relation to other aspects of comedy), the received attitude which does not reflect an empirically or theoretically coherent approach to drama appears especially unenlightened. Somewhat unexpectedly, the plays of Aristophanes – themselves the target of the first and most influential negative criticism of comedy – offer a unique point of departure in the study of farce, chronologically and definitionally. Besides being the first fully attested dramatic genre in western literature involving farce, Aristophanic comedy naturally identifies and isolates a set of practices comprising a dramatic sub-genre that serves well as an unambiguous definition of 'farce' and which bears an organic relation to comedy as a whole. In this paper I will first review the Aristophanic 'definition', and then discuss the diachronic and synchronic roles of this sub-genre in Greek drama.

INITIAL OBSERVATIONS

As C. Segal observes, 'it has often been remarked that the works of a long-established art-form are the most complex towards the end of its evolution when the form itself is on the verge of disappearing or undergoing a radical transformation'.[5] The mature, not to say overripe, form of Old Comedy was highly unstable even in the hands of Aristophanes and, as we see from the late plays, began to undergo a great transformation which was to result eventually in the form known as the New Comedy represented by playwrights such as Menander and Plautus. A significant aspect of the Old

Comedy's complexity is the integration of traditional (pre-dramatic, popular, and, ultimately, religious/ritual) elements with the artifices of individual literary craft. The scholarship on the origins of Greek drama is vast and has been ably surveyed elsewhere.[6] For our purposes it is necessary only to bear in mind that a great deal of the actual performative 'stuff' of the Old Comedy is clearly an inheritance from boisterous religious revels and less complex cult drama.[7] What is of the greatest interest, however, is the phenomenon peculiar to the Old Comedy of self-referential and seemingly devious criticism, especially in the so-called Parabasis (where the chorus, divested of its animal/fantastic identity speaks for the poet). The literary aspect of the comic art form raises its head, as it were, and deprecates its non-literary, 'primitive' counterpart (i.e. farce). This technique, in which the intellectual voice denounces the allegedly primitive and vulgar, is a subtle (if artificial) stratagem by means of which Aristophanes, by apparently opposing, actually integrates the rollicking, performative side of his show with the more poetic, literary 'Comedy of Ideas'. I submit that it is precisely what the 'literary voice' denounces that we have come to call farce.[8] Before turning to the relevant passages, however, it is important to say a few words about the nature of the Aristophanic *parabasis*.

Old Comedy can generally be said to be bipartite, the first 'movement' consisting of an *agōn* ('contest', 'conflict'), the second being a sort of revue play. The first part carries the action; the second is a series of 'sketches' illustrating the success of this action. In the first half, the chorus plays the part of a real actor, in keeping with its fantastic identity; in the second, it is little more than the mouthpiece of the author who attacks various contemporaries in satiric song. The Parabasis, or 'stepping forth', marks a transition between 'movements' and is unique in that it functions on two levels at once: as an element within the given play and as an extra-dramatic forum for self-expression on the part of the playwright. The spirit of contest, or *agōn*, informs the Parabasis on both levels. Thus, at *Wasps* 1060ff the identity of the old jurors is explained in an extended metaphor to the significant advantage of the 'wasps' over their rival, Bdelykleon. On the extra-dramatic level, Aristophanes competes with his rivals for the favor of the spectators and judges. The literary passages of the early Parabases, especially, are slippery, even downright baffling, unless viewed within their agonistic context.

One of the most striking features of Old Comedy is the diversity of elements that comprise the whole. The volatile synthesis included broad slapstick, ritual abuse, ceremonial wedding and feast scenes, metrically sophisticated choral song, extended word-play, literary parody, borrowings from tragic form (prologue) etc. Taking the comic performance as a whole, it would certainly be inaccurate to judge the so-called 'intellectual' aspects (the 'plot', paratragedy) as somehow favored by the poet and accorded a priority over the popular elements such as clowning and profane banter. If anything, the 'vulgar' comic features predominate, as one would expect, having even a general idea of the antecedents of the Old Comedy.[9] To the few critics such as C. T. Murphy who suggest that Aristophanes merely borrowed material from popular comedy 'to season, so to speak, his literary comedies and make them more acceptable to the "groundlings" in his audience',[10] I would reply in the words of Henri Fluchère, who, dismissing a similar cliché about Shakespeare, says that we need not assume that this poet 'alternates high poetry and farce in order to please *successively* the Court and the Pit. The Court equally with the Pit required clowning of him, and the Pit . . . appreciated, as did the favorites of Elizabeth and James I, Hamlet's soliloquies, the precious verbal fencing of Rosalind and Orlando, and the lyrical outbursts of Romeo.'[11] The foregoing remarks would not be necessary were it not for the odd posture assumed by Aristophanes in the Parabases, where he ridicules his rivals for a number of popular-comic practices, exalting himself and his work as somehow more 'intellectual' and edifying. The contradiction between claims made in the early Parabases and Aristophanes' actual practice deserves a closer look.

THE PARABASIS: ARISTOPHANES ON FARCE

In the Parabases proper ('anapests') of the early plays Aristophanes places a premium on *dexiōtēs*, 'cleverness', and on originality. His comments at *Wasps* 1009ff seem to be, to quote Douglas M. MacDowell, 'a striking example of the indignation of the *avant-garde* intellectual dramatist at the failure of unintellectual audiences to understand the merits of the work (here, *Clouds*)'.[12] In the *Acharnians* Aristophanes repeatedly recommends himself as a 'teacher' and champion of justice. He even 'quotes' the King of Persia to the effect that he, Aristophanes, is an indispensable 'adviser' of his native city-state. He promises to 'teach (the Athenians) many good things, so that they might prosper' (*Acharnians* 655–6). He alone, it seems, 'dares to speak just words' (*Knights* 510) and soars above his contemporaries in originality and refinement (*Clouds* 545ff, *Peace* 747ff). Examples of such boasting could be multiplied endlessly, adding little to our appreciation of Aristophanic comedy. The key to understanding the Parabases, I believe, lies in what might be called their 'contractual' nature.

'Primarily and essentially', W. B. Stanford reminds us, Aristophanes 'wanted to make his audience laugh and to win the prize.'[13] Complaining of the failure of *Clouds*, the poet says:

Τοιόνδ' εὑρόντες ἀλεξίκακον τῆς χώρας τῆσδε καθαρτήν,
πέρυσιν καταπροΰδοτε καινοτάτας σπείραντ' αὐτὸν διανοίας,
ἃς ὑπὸ τοῦ μὴ γνῶναι καθαρῶς ὑμεῖς ἐποήσατ' ἀναλδεῖς·

(Having found in him [i.e. 'me', Aristophanes] such a purifier, a deliverer from
evil for Athens, you betrayed him last year in spite of the novelty of the ideas he
set forth. These, in fact, you rendered fruitless through your failure to
acknowledge them.)[14]

(*Wasps* 1043–45)

The festivals of the Lenaia and City Dionysia were a contest between dramatists, and Aristophanes' literary comments have an agonistic 'spin' that
might be expressed as follows: 'I'll give you a good performance and praise,
you (the audience) give me victory (first prize).' In striving to excel in the
deeply traditional genre of comedy, the poet, naturally, isolates and emphasizes these features of his work to which he can lay personal claim, that
are uniquely his own. The competitive context filters out, as it were, all that
is conventional, inherited, and held in common by all practitioners of the
craft:

ουδ' ὑμᾶς ζητῶ 'ξαπατᾶν δὶς καὶ τρὶς ταῦτ' εἰσάγων,
ἀλλ' ἀεὶ καινὰς ἰδέας εἰσφέρων σοφίζομαι,
οὐδὲν ἀλλήλαισιν ὁμοίας καὶ πάσας δεξιάς·

(I'm not trying to deceive you by using the same material two or three times;
rather, in my clever craft I'm always introducing new forms (fashions) which
are unlike anything else and ingenious, all of them.)

(*Clouds* 546–8)

Aristophanes bids the Athenian audience, in the future, to especially
'cherish and support those poets who strive to say and invent something
new' . . . 'store up their ideas', he advises (*Wasps* 1051ff). Conversely,
Aristophanes' rivals are censured as repetitive, rude, and unimaginative:

Ὅστις οὖν τούτοισι γελᾷ, τοῖς ἐμοῖς μὴ χαιρέτω·
ἢν δ' ἐμοὶ καὶ τοῖσιν ἐμοῖς εὐφραίνησθ' εὑρήμασιν,
εἰς τὰς ὥρας τὰς ἑτέρας εὖ φρονεῖν δοκήσετε.

(So, whoever laughs at such things, may he not delight at all in my work! But if
you are pleased with me and my inventions, you will be thought intelligent in
the years to come.)

(*Clouds* 560–2)

What then does Aristophanes deprecate, having assumed the 'intellectual'
posture in order to advertise his work as deserving of unique recognition
and honor?

At *Peace* 748–51 Aristophanes says the following:

Τοιαῦτ' ἀφελὼν κακὰ καὶ φόρτον καὶ βωμολοχεύματ' ἀγεννῆ
ἐποήσε τέχνην μεγάλην ἡμῖν κἀπύργωσ' οἰκοδομήσας

ἔπεσιν μεγάλοις καὶ διανοίαις καὶ σκώμμασιν οὐκ ἀγοραίοις,
οὐκ ἰδιώτας ἀνθρωπίσκους κωμῳδῶν οὐδὲ γυναῖκας,

In Rogers's translation:

Such vulgar contemptible lumber at once bade from the drama depart,
And then, like an edifice stately and grand, he raised and ennobled the Art.
High thoughts and high language he brought on the stage, a humor exalted and rare,
Nor stooped with a scrurrilous jest to assail some small man-and-woman affair.

What he means by 'vulgar contemptible lumber' can be gathered from the Parabases of *Clouds* and *Peace*. Aristophanes recommends the first of these plays as *sōphrōn*, 'chaste', 'sober' and says:

'Ὡς δὲ σώφρων ἐστὶ φύσει σκέψασθ'· ἥτις πρῶτα μὲν
οὐδὲν ἦλθε ῥαψαμένη σκυτίον καθειμένον
ἐρυθρὸν ἐξ ἄκρου, παχύ, τοῖς παιδίοις ἵν' ᾖ γέλως·
οὐδ' ἔσκωψε τοὺς φαλακρούς, οὐδὲ κόρδαχ' εἵλκυσεν,
οὐδὲ πρεσβύτης ὁ λέγων τἄπη τῇ βακτηρίᾳ
τύπτει τὸν παρόντ' ἀφανίζων πονηρὰ σκώμματα,
οὐδ' εἰσῇξε δᾷδας ἔχουσ', οὐδ' ἰοὺ ἰοὺ βοᾷ,
ἀλλ' αὑτῇ καὶ τοῖς ἔπεσιν πιστεύουσ' ἐλήλυθεν.

(Observe her purity: no appendage of leather, red-tipped and gross, to arouse adolescent laughter; no jeering of baldheads or obscene *kordax* dances; no pantaloon punctuating his lines by poking his neighbor to cover bad jokes; no flying torch-bearer, shouting 'iou! iou!'. She has come confident in herself and her words.)

(*Clouds* 537–44)

Censured are the following features of the comic performance:
(1) use of a red-tipped leather phallus sewn onto the garments;
(2) mockery of the bald, old man (*senex stupidus*);
(3) use of the sensuous dance, the *kordax*;
(4) scenes in which a man beats another to cover up the ineptitude of his own jokes;
(5) torch scenes: actors running on stage with lighted torches, perhaps originally used in Dionysian revelry as an apotropaic device.

The prologue to *Wasps* (lines 54ff) includes a warning to the audience not to expect 'any jokes stolen from Megara':

Φέρε νυν, κατείπω τοῖς θεαταῖς τὸν λογον,
ὀλίγ' ἄτθ' ὑπειπὼν πρῶτον αὐτοῖσιν ταδί,
μηδὲν παρ' ἡμῶν προσδοκᾶν λίαν μέγα,
μηδ' αὖ γέλωτα Μεγαρόθεν κεκλαμμένον.
'Ἡμῖν γὰρ οὐκ ἔστ' οὔτε κάρυ' ἐκ φορμίδος
δούλω διαρριπτοῦντε τοῖς θεωμένοις,
οὔθ' Ἡρακλῆς τὸ δεῖπνον ἐξαπατώμενος,
οὐδ' αὖθις ἐνασελγαινόμενος Εὐριπίδης·

(I must tell the spectators the situation – after a short preface. Don't expect anything too grand from us, no jokes stolen from Megara. We don't have a pair of slaves to scatter nuts from a basket to the audience, no Heracles cheated of his dinner, no stale jeering at Euripides.)

So, we add to the list:

(6) throwing nuts to the audience perhaps to make a pun on the word *krithē* meaning both 'barley' and 'penis'.

(7) bringing on a comic version of Heracles who is ravenous and ready to eat anything.

None of this, asserts Aristophanes, will you find in his work: 'My Comedy's a modest girl: she doesn't play the fool . . .' (*Clouds* 537; trans. A. Sommerstein). In the Parabasis of *Peace* (lines 739–47) he further boasts of his service to comedy by forcing his rivals to abandon the following low tricks:

(8) jeering at rags and fighting lice;

(9) slaves running away, deceiving their masters and being beaten – a vehicle for stale humor;

In the poet's words:

> Πρῶτον μὲν γὰρ τοὺς ἀντιπάλους μόνος ἀνθρώπων κατέπαυσεν
> εἰς τὰ ῥάκια σκώπτοντας ἀεὶ καὶ τοῖς φθειρσὶν πολεμοῦντας·
> τούς θ' Ἡρακλέας τοὺς μάττοντας καὶ τοὺς πεινῶντας ἐκείνους
> τοὺς φεύγοντας κἀξαπατῶντας καὶ τυπτομένους ἐπίτηδες,
> ἐξήλασ' ἀτιμώσας πρῶτος, καὶ τοὺς δούλους παρέλυσεν
> οὓς ἐξῆγον κλάοντας ἀεί, καὶ τούτους οὕνεκα τουδί,
> ἵν' ὁ σύνδουλος σκώψας αὐτοῦ τὰς πληγὰς εἶτ' ἀνέροιτο·
> «Ὦ κακόδαιμον, τί τὸ δέρμ' ἔπαθες; Μῶν ὑστριχὶς εἰσέβαλέν σοι
> εἰς τὰς πλευρὰς πολλῇ στρατιᾷ κἀδενδροτόμησε τὸ νῶτον;»

(He was first to stop his rivals from jeering at rags and warring with lice. He was first also to banish from the stage in disgrace the ever needy and greedy Heracles as well as those slaves who always are busy with plans to escape or deceive and who are beaten only to be brought on for mockery: 'say', a fellow slave would ask, 'what happened to your hide? Did the whipcord invade your back with its ruthless army?')

The opening of *Frogs* (lines 1–23) has Dionysus forbidding the stale scatological jokes of Aristophanes' rivals:

> Νὴ τὸν Δί' ὅ τι βούλει γε, πλὴν «Πιέζομαι.»
> Τοῦτο δὲ φύλαξαι· πάνυ γάρ ἐστ' ἤδη χολή . . .
>
> Μή νυν ποήσῃς· ὡς ἐγὼ θεώμενος,
> ὅταν τι τούτων τῶν σοφισμάτων ἴδω,
> πλεῖν ἢ 'νιαυτῷ πρεσβύτερος ἀπέρχομαι.

(By Zeus, do what you will except that 'I'm hard-pressed routine'; Stay away from that, it's nauseating! . . . Don't do it! Every time I have to witness one of those 'brilliant inventions', I feel myself age a full year.)

So, we add (10) the 'shit joke' to the list of comic practices explicitly censured in the extant plays. Interestingly enough, these features have a striking common denominator: they are largely physical, violent, improvisatory, and mechanical in nature, i.e. what has come to be called 'farce' in the later dramatic tradition. The texts of Aristophanes' plays are, of course, readily available and we have little trouble appreciating the poet's intellectual powers. Farce in Old Comedy is more elusive. Judging from Arisophanes' own testimony, it would seem that he has banished it from his work altogether. A perusal of the plays reveals however, that, far from being ostracized from the realm of the 'intellectual', 'original', and 'clever', farce is alive and well in Aristophanic comedy; in fact, every practice criticized by the poet is attested, often widely, in his own plays. Thus, point-by-point:

(1) Abuse of the phallus: to begin with, the phallus was most likely the stock-in-trade of Old Comedy. Phallic jokes abound in the extant plays. Thus, in the *Acharnians* Dikaiopolis insults the 'Odomantian host' by asking:

> Ποίων 'Οδομάντων; εἰπέ μοι, τουτὶ τί ἦν;
> Τίς τῶν 'Οδομάντων τὸ πέος ἀποτεθρίακεν;

(What do you mean 'Odomantians'? Tell me, what's this here: who clipped their penises?)

(Acharnians 157–8)

Taunting the *miles gloriosus*, Lamachus, the same character says:

> Μηδαμῶς, ὦ Λάμαχε·
> οὐ γὰρ κατ' ἰσχύν ἐστιν· εἰ δ' ἰσχυρὸς εἶ,
> τί μ' οὐκ ἀπεψώλησας; Εὔοπλος γὰρ εἶ.

> (Forget it Lamachus!
> That's way beyond your strength. If you're really tough,
> Why didn't you peel my foreskin right off? You're well
> Equipped for *that*, you know.)

(Acharnians 590–2)

At *Wasps* 1342 Philokleon, newly rejuvenated, addresses the girl on his arm:

> 'Ανάβαινε δεῦρο, χρυσομηλολόνθιον,
> τῇ χειρὶ τουδὶ λαβομένη τοῦ σχοινίου.
> Ἔχου· φυλάττου δ', ὡς σαπρὸν τὸ σχοινίον·
> ὅμως γε μέντοι τριβόμενον οὐκ ἄχθεται.

> (Come here, sweet thing. Take hold of my 'rope' and
> Hold on for dear life. Careful! It's a bit worn . . .
> Nevertheless, it doesn't mind being rubbed and stroked.)

Similarly, when Mnesilochus in *Thesmophoriazousae* is discovered and his female disguise removed, the language suggests that the actors had a little fun undressing him and noting 'how stiff and stout "she" is! And, by God, no tits like ours' (lines 639–40).

(2) The 'destruction of the Old Man' is most evident in the thorough-going deception of Demos in the *Knights*. The poet has some fun with the notion of baldness at *Peace* 767ff where he seems to be referring to his own appearance:

> καὶ τοῖς φαλακροῖσι παραινοῦμεν
> ξυσπουδάζειν περὶ τῆς νίκης.
> Πᾶς γάρ τις ἐρεῖ νικῶντος ἐμοῦ
> κἀπὶ τραπέζῃ καὶ ξυμποσίοις·
> «Φέρε τῷ φαλακρῷ, δὸς τῷ φαλακρῷ
> τῶν τρωγαλίων, καὶ μἀφαίρει
> γενναιοτάτου τῶν ποιητῶν
>   ἀνδρὸς τὸ μέτωπον ἔχοντος».

(Each bald-headed man should do all that he can
That the prize be awarded to me.
For be sure if this play is triumphant today,
That when you recline at the feast or the wine,
Your neighbor will say,
'Give this to the bald-head, give that to the bald-head,
And take not away
That sweetmeat, that cake, but present and bestow it
On the man with the brow of our wonderful poet!')

(3) The *kordax* was the characteristic dance of the Old Comedy and was usually associated with drunkenness and clowning.[15] Here is how, for instance, MacDowell describes the final dance of *Wasps*:

> Some of the dancing may have been accompanied by music without words, and so the passage may have lasted longer than the time it would take to sing the words straight through. Most of the time was no doubt taken up by an expert display given by the sons of Karkinos. Philokleon must have taken some part; perhaps he did some clowning with much falling over and picking himself up again, in between dances by the sons of Karkinos.[16]

To imagine the Old Comedy without the *kordax* would be like imagining a Cossack show without the *pris'adka*.

(4) Beating scenes are almost too numerous in Aristophanes to cite. The opening of *Knights* is an example, as is the following exchange between the sausage-seller and Paphlagon in the same play (lines 364–70):

ΑΛ.   Ἐγὼ δὲ κινήσω γέ σου τὸν πρωκτὸν ἀντὶ φύσκης·
ΠΑ.   Ἐγὼ δέ γ' ἐξέλξω σε τῆς πυγῆς θύραζε κύβδα . . .
ΠΑ.   Οἷόν σε δήσω ⟨'ν⟩ τῷ ξύλῳ.
ΑΛ.   Διώξομαί σε δειλίας.
ΠΑ.   Ἡ βύρσα σου θρανεύσεται.
ΑΛ.   Δερῶ σε θύλακον κλοπῆς.

(*S*. I'll rip the lining from your rear to use for sausage casing!
P. I'll grab you by your rump and drag you off, bent double . . .
P. I'll stretch you on the rack.
S. For cowardice you'll get the sack.
P. I'll tack your hide to my bench.
S. I'll make a thief's purse from your skin.)

(5) Torch scenes are not uncommon in Aristophanic comedy. Thus, at the end of the *Lysistrata* one of the 'Athenians' asks:

'Υμεῖς, τί κάθησθε: Μῶν ἐγὼ τῇ λαμπάδι
ὑμᾶς κατακαύσω; Φορτικὸν τὸ χωρίον.
Οὐκ ἂν ποήσαιμ'. Εἰ δὲ πάνυ δεῖ τοῦτο δρᾶν,
ὑμῖν χαρίζεσθαι ταλαιπωρήσομεν.

(What's this? You're sitting down? Shall I singe you with my torch? That's vulgar! O, I couldn't do it . . . Yet if it would gratify the audience, I'll mortify myself.)

(*Lysistrata* 1217–20)

Similarly, at *Thesmophoriazousae* 655ff the women decide to light their torches and ferret out any men that might remain in their midst. The most striking example of a 'fire finale' is the conclusion of *Clouds* where Strepsiades burns down the 'think tank', or *phrontistērion*:

καί μοι γενοῦ ξύμβουλος, εἴτ' αὐτοὺς γραφὴν
διωκάθω γραψάμενος, εἴθ' ὅ τι σοι δοκεῖ.
'Ορθῶς παραινεῖς οὐκ ἐῶν δικορραφεῖν,
ἀλλ' ὡς τάχιστ' ἐμπιμπράναι τὴν οἰκίαν
τῶν ἀδολεσχῶν. Δεῦρο, δεῦρ', ὦ Ξανθία,
κλίμακα λαβὼν ἔξελθε καὶ σμινύην φέρων,
κἄπειτ' ἐπαναβὰς ἐπὶ τὸ φροντιστήριον
τὸ τέγος κατάσκαπτ', εἰ φιλεῖς τὸν δεσπότην,
ἕως ἂν αὐτοῖς ἐμβάλῃς τὴν οἰκίαν.
ἐμοὶ δὲ δᾷδ' ἐνεγκάτω τις ἡμμένην,
κἀγώ τιν' αὐτῶν τήμερον δοῦναι δίκην
ἐμοί ποήσω, κεἰ σφόδρ' εἴσ' ἀλαζόνες.

(Advise me: shall I sue them, or what's the best course? – Ah, that's good advice! No lingering lawsuits, but at once I'll burn the chatterers' house down. Here, Xanthias! Bring a ladder and a hoe, climb up the Thinkshop, dig up the tiles, if you love me, until their house tumbles. Bring me a lighted torch someone, I'll pay them out for all their grand pretensions.)

(*Clouds* 1481–92)

(6) Tossing food to the audience is attested at *Peace* 960ff where Trygaeus says:

σὺ δὲ πρότεινε τῶν ὀλῶν,
καὐτός τε χερνίπτου παραδοὺς ταύτην ἐμοί,
καὶ τοῖς θεαταῖς ῥῖπτε τῶν κριθῶν.

(Bring the barley, you; I'll hold the basin while you wash your hands. Now throw the grain [*krithē*] among the audience.)

This contrasts interestingly with *Plutus* 794ff:

ΓΥ. Εἶτ' οὐχὶ δέξει δῆτα τὰ καταχύσματα;
ΠΛ. Ἔνδον γε παρὰ τὴν ἑστίαν, ὥσπερ νόμος.
     Ἔπειτα καὶ τὸν φόρτον ἐκφύγοιμεν ἄν.
     Οὐ γὰρ πρεπῶδές ἐστι τῷ διδασκάλῳ
     ἰσχάδια καὶ τρωγάλια τοῖς θεωμένοις
     προβαλόντ', ἐπὶ τούτοις εἶτ' ἀναγκάζειν γελᾶν.

(*Wife*. Then won't you take the welcoming gifts I bring?
Plutus. Yes, by the hearth within, as is the custom.
So too we escape the vulgar tricks of farce.
It is not fitting, with a Poet such as ours,
To fling a shower of figs and sweetmeats out
Among the audience, just to make them laugh.)

(7) At *Birds* 1574ff Aristophanes brings on a classic 'hungry Heracles' whose main interest is to get started on lunch. In all the excitement of Cloudcuckooland he seems most concerned about the fact that the birds 'found guilty of an oligarchic plot' (lines 1583–5) are being cooked with too litle oil!

(8) *Clouds* furnishes some examples of 'jeering at rags and fighting lice': In the *phrontistērion* Strepsiades has difficulty learning because of a bedbug problem (lines 707–15):

ΣΤ.   Ἀτταταῖ ἀτταταῖ.
ΧΟ.   Τί πάσχεις; Τί κάμνεις;
ΣΤ.   Ἀπόλλυμαι δείλαιος· ἐκ τοῦ σκίμποδος
         δάκνουσί μ' ἐξέρποντες ὁ Κορ — ίνθιοι,
         καὶ τὰς πλευρὰς δαρδάπτουσιν
         καὶ τὴν ψυχὴν ἐκπίνουσιν
         καὶ τοὺς ὄρχεις ἐξέλκουσιν
         καὶ τὸν πρωκτὸν διορύττουσιν,
         καί μ' ἀπολοῦσιν.

(*St*. Ouch! Ouch! Ouch!
Ch. What's the trouble? What ails you?
St. I'm murdered! From the sack
Fierce Corinthians crew to attack.
My ribs they chew,
My blood they suck,
My testicles pluck,
My rump they excavate,
They'll leave me inanimate!)

Much fun is made of Euripides' arsenal of rags in a famous scene of the *Acharnians*: Dicaeopolis needs an outfit appropriate to a pathetic speech. He appeals to the tragedian and together they enumerate various figures of the Euripidean stage, each more sorry than the other, until the perfect one is found, Telephus, 'frightful even to mention' (line 429).

(9) Two slaves planning their escape are seen at the opening of the *Knights*. They have had enough punishment, and one gets the other to utter the desired *automolōmen* 'let's defect' by the old trick of supplying him with both parts of the words and then having him utter them in quick succession (lines 26ff).

(10) It hardly need be pointed out that the 'shit joke' is a staple of Aristophanic comedy. This category involves more than mere verbal humor; some scenes include easing oneself on stage. For example, at *Ecclesiazusae* 311ff Blepyros soliloquizes:

Τί τὸ πρᾶγμα; Ποῖ ποθ' ἡ γυνὴ φρούδη 'στί μοι;
'Επεὶ πρὸς ἔω νῦν γ' ἐστίν, ἡ δ' οὐ φαίνεται.
'Εγὼ δὲ κατάκειμαι πάλαι χεζητιῶν,
τὰς ἐμβάδας ζητῶν λαβεῖν ἐν τῷ σκότῳ
καὶ θοἰμάτιον. "Οτε δὴ δ' ἐκεῖνο ψηλαφῶν
οὐκ ἐδυνάμην εὑρεῖν, ὁ δ' ἤδη τὴν θύραν
ἐπεῖχε κρούων, ὅδε Κόπρειος, λαμβάνω
τουτὶ τὸ τῆς γυναικὸς ἡμιδιπλοίδιον,
καὶ τὰς ἐκείνης Περσικὰς ὑφέλκομαι.
'Αλλ' ἐν καθαρῷ ποῦ, ποῦ τις ἂν χέσας τύχοι;
'Η παντι·'γοῦ τοι νυκτός ἐστιν ἐν καλῷ·
οὐ γάρ με νῦν χέζοντά γ' οὐδεὶς ὄψεται.
Οἴμοι κακοδαίμων, ὅτι γέρων ὢ ἠγόμην
γυναῖχ'. "Οσας εἴμ' ἄξιος πληγὰς λαβεῖν.
Οὐ γάρ ποθ' ὑγιὲς οὐδὲν ἐξελήλυθεν
δράσουσ'. "Ομως δ' οὖν ἐστιν ἀποπατητέον.

(It's almost morning and she's nowhere at all. Here was I taken short in my own bed, and I groped about to find my cloak and shoes but I couldn't find a stitch, and all the while the pain kept banging hard at my back door, and so I wriggled into this chemise and stuck my toes into these flapping slippers. O where O where is a good nook? or is any spot in the dark a good enough one? No man could see me if I squatted here, I'm sure. O what a damned and utter fool I was to go and get married in my old age; I ought to be walloped, I ought. For it's not likely she's gallivanting at this time of night out of pure goodness, O but I can't wait!)

Other examples are found at *Peace* 175ff, *Birds* 65ff, and *Frogs* 479ff, to mention a few.

In a much-cited passage[17] Athenaeus adds a few stock themes that he knew from the Spartan farceurs or *deikelisthai*:

(11) theft of food or fruit;
(12) foreigners speaking dialect.

Both, naturally, occur in Aristophanic comedy: *Acharnians* 809–10, *Knights* 1193ff, and *Acharnians* 729ff.

Finally, one could add many instances involving clowning and farce-like action which, however, are not explicitly censured by the poet, owing perhaps to the limited number of comedies surviving from the fifth century (e.g. transvestism in the *Ecclesiazusae*, jack-in-the-box clowning in *Wasps*, and other slapstick routines).

From the explicit, artificially negative testimony of the comedies of Aristophanes, then, we can form a fair picture of the farce element in Old Comedy. Many aspects of what has come to be called 'farce' in the later dramatic tradition are present: rebellion, the destruction of authority, the mechanical, tit-for-tat, deception, the violent, the festive, the 'inflexible mind-set', and the absurd. The hungry Heracles of *Birds,* the jack-in-the-box routine of *Wasps*, the bedbug war in *Clouds*, the beetle-feeding scene of *Peace* are but a few examples of timeless farce that could easily be imagined in later drama from the *commedia dell'arte* to Woody Allen. Still unexplored, however, is the relationship of Greek comedy (as a genre) to farce. Beyond Aristophanes' agonistic bias discussed above, the peculiar treatment of farce in the comedies points to a deeper feature of the poet's art, namely, *mythopoesis*, a process in which comedy consciously and deviously retraces the union of ritual and myth in tragedy.

FARCE AND COMIC MYTHOPOESIS

In a synthesis of ritualistic theory from Frazer to Burkert, R. Friedrich has persuasively argued that in the evolution of tragedy from its ritual origins, the latter must have first developed into cult drama of some morphological complexity.[18] The decisive step out of the 'precincts of Dionysian ritual,' he says,

> was the replacement of the Dionysian myth by stories taken from the body of heroic myths. This must have developed in successive stages. One will remember that heroic myth, shaped as it was by the Homeric epic and imbued with the spirit of Olympian religion, was originally alien, if not antagonistic, to the religiosity of the Dionysus cult. In order to be integrated into the worship of the Olympian gods, the ecstatic Dionysus cult had first to be tamed; as a result of this process, the Dionysus myth came to be connected with the body of heroic legends.[19]

This 'decisive step' involved a severance between the *sacer ludus* and Dionysian myth. 'The point was reached,' says Friedrich, 'at which any myth suitable for forming a dramatic action could become the plot and thus take the place of the Dionysus myth.'[20] Heroic myth was thus a powerful 'secondary motivation' that dissolved the static sequence of ritual into its components and then recombined these 'to cohere about a new centre: no longer a natural cycle to which tribal ritual ultimately binds human life, but the actions of men, conscious of themselves as ethico-political beings'.[21] The birth of tragedy – the fusion of myth and ritual – involved not only the 'taming' of ritual by myth but, more importantly, the *making sense*, by myth, of the nonsense of ritual. 'The defect of ritual, in a human society,' writes Burkert, 'is the apparent nonsense, inherent in its redirection activity, the 'as-if' element; here a tale may supply a plausible context and fill the vacant places.'[22] Myth is summoned when ritual is 'in danger of being attenuated into folklore, or disappearing entirely, and is therefore in need of a new *raison d'être*'.[23] Although the complex of myth and ritual in tragedy was a relatively balanced union of traditional 'Dionysian' and 'Apollonian' elements, in comedy the picture is quite different.

It has often been noted how, in comedy, the ritual element seems much more prominent and less altered. 'The very freedom of the comic plot,' says Cornford, 'left standing the old scaffolding which Tragedy, bound to its epic sources and itself requiring the utmost internal coherence, was obliged to break up.'[24] This fact owes its explanation not as much to the inherent durability of ritual as to the very nature of the comic creative process which, I submit, is an artistic metaphor of the genesis of tragedy. Whereas in tragedy authentic, traditional *mŷthoi* were fused with ritual, in comedy the individual poet, in 'making sense' of the ritual inheritance, created his own *synthetic* myth. The pre-existent tragic *mŷthos* was successful in 'taming' and restructuring ritual by virtue of being, as Burkert points out, 'a structure of sense'[25] (as opposed to 'sign' or 'reference'), an instance of non-factual story-telling for which the given author disclaims responsibility: *ouk emòs ho mŷthos*. 'A myth, qua tale, is not identical with any text,' he notes; 'the interpretation of myth, therefore, is to be distinguished from the interpretation of a text, though both may evolve in a hermeneutic circle and remain mutually dependent on each other'.[26] The synthetic myth of comedy, on the other hand, being the creative product of an individual poet is, in fact, referred to as *lógos*, and is in every instance identical with a specific text and a specific comic performance. Citing *Wasps* 54, 64, *Peace* 50, and *Lysistrata* 119, Cornford says that 'the proper term for the comic plot is not *mŷthos* but *lógos*. The term seems to mean the "theme", or "idea" of the piece.'[27] Comic mythopoesis, then, as a metaphor of the union of genuine myth and ritual in tragedy, involves the application of a unique synthetic myth – the comic *lógos* (from *legein* 'to collect', 'put together') – to the vestigial ritual material that formed the basis of comic action. The 'Apollonian' logos of comedy was clearly less powerful in taming and making sense of the inherited ritual material, a fact evident in the relative prominence, structurally and proportionally, of ritual in the Old Comedy as opposed to tragedy.

We have traced the conflict, in Aristophanic comedy, between the allegedly intellectual *lógos* and a class of Dionysian activities corresponding to our notion of 'farce'. The close correspondence between the farce elements listed above and ritual is certainly no coincidence. As Cornford notes,

the physical violence and horseplay of the Old Comedy, like the elements of
personal satire and the obscenity, is to be explained as part of the inheritance
from the crudities of folk-drama . . . Since two of them – the personal invective
and the indecency – are admittedly traceable to the phallic origin of Comedy, it
seems likely that the third (i.e. physical violence) is also derived from a motive
which we have seen to be altogether in place in any dramatic form of the same
ritual of the expulsion of evil and the induction of the powers of fertility.[28]

Thus, scholars have connected the beating and expulsion motifs with the
phármakos (scapegoat) ritual, the scattering of food to the audience to the
katakhúsmata characteristic of wedding celebrations and sacrificial ritual,
and the final revels of the comedies to the *hieròs gámos*. Citing Herodotus
5.82, Cornford traces the stock-in-trade invective of Old Comedy to the
ritual custom in the fertility cults of Greece of 'two or more companies of
worshippers engaging in a set match of abuse'.[29] The connection between
phallic processions and the Old Comedy has been discussed since Aristotle
who notes that 'comedy originated with the leaders of the Phallic songs
which survive to this day as institutions in many of our states'.[30] The
passage of Athenaeus cited above contains further discussion of the
phallophoric antecedents of comedy.[31] Similarly, among the various
theories[32] concerning the relation between the Parabasis and the *agōn* is the
suggestion that they differentiated out of a 'ritual conflict between two
parties, each with its own champion'.[33] Finally, many other farce features of
the Old Comedy such as the *alazōn* ('impostor', 'intruder'), 'doctors
speaking dialect', and food theft are clearly traceable to earlier ritual
practices.[34]

The striking fact of comic mythopoesis is that the *lógos* of the playwright
(the synthetic myth), lacking traditional momentum and depth of authentic myth, fails to wholly subdue and restructure the Dionysian 'deep
structure'; it fails to fully 'dissolve the static sequence of ritual into its
components and then recombine these to cohere about a new centre'. Farce,
I submit, is that most tenacious element of the ritual inheritance that
refuses 'to be made sense of', that the comic *lógos* cannot tame. As we have
seen, the Aristophanic *lógos*, though largely successful in making general
sense of ritual material, simply cannot make sense of this most violent and
ecstatic ritual core that yet remains an indispensable feature of the comic
performance and is, therefore, isolated and artificially ostracized. In
metaphorical terms, we might say that farce, a small but powerful core of
vestigial Dionysian ritual, is, paradoxically, the *phármakos* (scapegoat) of
comedy. Unsuccessfully or imperfectly expelled by the rational poetic *lógos*,
it lingers and returns ever to haunt comedy from its birth onwards.

'Aristophanes,' writes Cedric Whitman, 'created a myth of his own
times, a myth which simultaneously required and transcended the
methods, however devious, which contributed to its making.'[35] Plato, in the
Symposium, represents this process by imitating it: having asked

Aristophanes to define love, he receives for an answer a 'myth' 'mingled of Empedocles, impertinence, and hiccups, yet embodying a wistfully hilarious image of human desire'.[36] The fusion of ritual and synthetic myth is undeniably a great achievement of the Greek dramatic mind. The vast distance separating tragedy and comedy is clearly a reflection of differing geneses, as well as differing creative processes. Whereas in tragedy authentic, pre-existent, and traditional myth powerfully restrained and restructured Dionysian ritual ('made sense of it'), the weaker, synthetic myth (*lógos*) of comedy succeeded only imperfectly in harnessing the ritual energy without actually suppressing or fully transcending it (*pace* Whitman). The rebellious Dionysian *phármakos* of farce refuses to be integrated into a 'structure of sense', to 'be made sense of', and remains a volatile and constant presence in comedy that, in the words of J. M. Davis, 'enshrines the element of unreason' and 'permits the indulgent regression to the joys and terrors of nonsense'.[37]

NOTES

1 J. D. Hurell, 'A Note on Farce', *Quarterly Journal of Speech*, 46 (1960), 426. Cited in J. M. Davis, *Farce, The Critical Idiom Series No. 39* (Bristol: Methuen, 1978), p. 6.
2 See Davis, *Farce*, pp. 6 and 21ff. The works discussed are L. J. Potts, *Comedy* (London: Hutchinson, 1949), and G. B. Shaw, *Our Theatre in the Nineties*, vol. II (London: Constable, 1932). Davis notes that 'as long as it is viewed as existing in symbiosis with 'richer' forms of comedy, farce can only be characterized by negatives – the more exaggerated characterizations, the cruder coincidences and the grosser pieces of joking belong to farce, while the more sophisticated elements of plot, character, and theme are those of comedy proper' (*Farce*, p. 6).
3 *Poetics* 1449a, 1451a, 1453a; *Nic. Ethics* 1128a 22.
4 In addition to *Farce* by J. M. Davis, the following studies have been useful: A. Caputi, *Buffo: The Genius of Vulgar Comedy* (Detroit: Wayne State University, 1978); A. Bermel, *Farce: A History From Aristophanes to Woody Allen* (New York: Simon and Schuster, 1962); C. T. Murphy, 'Popular Comedy in Aristophanes', *American Journal of Philology*, 93 (1972), 169–89.
5 C. Segal, 'The Character and Cults of Dionysus and the Unity of the *Frogs*', *Harvard Studies in Classical Philology*, 65 (1961), 207.
6 See, for instance, R. Friedrich, 'Drama and Ritual' in *Themes in Drama Vol. 5: Drama and Religion* (Cambridge University Press, 1983), pp. 159–223.
7 See especially in this connection A. W. Pickard-Cambridge, *Dithyramb, Tragedy and Comedy* (Oxford University Press, 1927), pp. 329ff; F. Cornford, *The Origins of Attic Comedy* (London: Edward Arnold, 1914); P. Mazon, *Essai sur la composition des comédies d'Aristophane* (Paris, 1904), and 'La Farce dans Aristophane et les origines de la comédie en Grèce', *Revue d'Histoire du Théâtre* (1951), 7–18; H. Herter, *Vom dionysischen Tanz zum komischen Spiel* (Iselohn, 1947). An especially useful review of Cambridge Anthropologist bibliography is found in Friedrich, 'Drama and Ritual', notes 1–6, pp. 212–13.
8 On the derivation of the term Davis (*Farce*, p. 7) says: 'Indeed, its name is

actually derived from the Latin *farcire*, "to stuff", and the word "farce" remains in both French and English a rather old-fashioned name for a stuffing for meat and other foods. Its first connection with the drama seems to have come by absorption of the verb-form into ecclesiastical usage. In the period between the ninth and twelfth centuries, the Latin liturgy of the Church underwent a process of musical and verbal enrichment by the addition of tropes, or embellishing phrases. Those phrases and their musical accompaniment which were inserted into parts of the Mass, such as the Kyrie and the Sanctus, were often called *farsae* or *farsurae*. The term was also used for the reading of Lessons and Epistles which had been "farced" in this way. In French and Italian cathedrals by the beginning of the twelfth century these *farsurae* were often composed in the vernacular, as a gloss on the meaning of the Latin passages being chanted to the congregation from the scriptures set for a particular day.'

9 See below the brief discussion of the various ritual antecedents of the Old Comedy such as the Dionysian phallic songs, the *phármakos* ritual, the *hieròs gámos*, ritual abuse etc.

10 Murphy, 'Popular Comedy in Aristophanes', p. 169. Murphy qualifies this statement by adding that 'the possibility, however, cannot be ruled out that he used this type of material because he himself enjoyed it and thought it funny'.

11 Bermel, *Farce: A History*, p. 94.

12 Aristophanes, *Wasps*, edited with commentary by D. M. MacDowell (Oxford University Press, 1971), p. 262. See also T. Hubbard, 'Parabatic Self-criticism and the Two Versions of Aristophanes' Clouds', *Classical Antiquity*, 5, no. 2 (1986), 182–97.

13 Aristophanes, *Frogs*, edited with commentary by W. B. Stanford (New York: St Martin's Press, 1963), p. xvi.

14 The examples presented in this article are based on the Coulon text of Aristophanes: *Aristophane*, texte établi par Victor Coulon et traduit par Hilaire Van Daele, Dixième Tirage Revu et Corrigé (Paris: Société d'Edition 'Les Belles Lettres'). In preparing translations of the examples I have consulted the Bantam edition of Aristophanes, edited by Moses Hadas (London: Bantam, 1962). The translations in this edition are the work of M. Hadas, B. B. Rogers, R. H. Webb, and J. Lindsay.

15 The scholiast on *Clouds* 542 explicitly refers to Aristophanes' use of the *kordax* in *Wasps*. Cornford in *The Origins of Attic Comedy*, p. 180, refers his reader to Schnabel's work, *Kordax* (Munich, 1910), devoted exclusively to the subject of the comic dance; cf. Stanford (ed.), Aristophanes, *Frogs*, p. xiv.

16 MacDowell (ed.), Aristophanes, *Wasps*, p. 330.

17 Athenaeus, XIV, 621ff, cited by Murphy in 'Popular Comedy in Aristophanes', p. 174.

18 Friedrich, 'Drama and Ritual', p. 185.

19 Ibid., p. 186.

20 Ibid., p. 187.

21 Ibid., p. 189.

22 Ibid., p. 183, quoting W. Burkert, *Structure and History in Greek Mythology and Ritual*, Sather Classical Lectures, 47 (Berkeley, Los Angeles, London: University of California Press, 1980), p. 56.

23 Friedrich, 'Drama and Ritual', p. 184.
24 Cornford, *The Origins of Attic Comedy*, p. 199.
25 Burkert, *Structure and History in Greek Mythology and Ritual*, pp. 2, 5. See also note 11.
26 Ibid., p. 3.
27 Cornford, *The Origins of Attic Comedy*, p. 199.
28 Ibid., p. 83.
29 Ibid., p. 110.
30 *Poetics* 1449a.
31 See Murphy, 'Popular Comedy in Aristophanes', p. 174, and Cornford, *The Origins of Attic Comedy*, pp. 183ff.
32 See Cornford, *The Origins of Attic Comedy*, pp. 122ff, and Mazon 'La Farce dans Aristophane et les origines de la comédie en Grèce'.
33 Cornford, *The Origins of Attic Comedy*, p. 129.
34 Murphy, 'Popular Comedy in Aristophanes', pp. 174–5; and Cornford, *The Origins of Attic Comedy*, pp. 100–2, 152ff, 180.
35 C. Whitman, *Aristophanes and the Comic Hero* (Harvard University Press, 1962), p. 14.
36 Ibid., p. 14.
37 Davis, *Farce*, p. 23.

Greek stagecraft and Aristophanes

N. J. LOWE

In one sense, text and performance in the ancient theatre have never seemed so far apart. The two most important currents in Greek dramatic criticism in English over the past decade appear almost polarized between word and action in their views of the text's essential nature. One tendency, prominently represented on either side of the Atlantic by Charles Segal and Simon Goldhill, has pursued textuality to new limits, in a unique marriage of European theoretical models with the traditional philological rigours of classical textual scholarship. Over the same period, however, a second movement, whose most vigorous spokesmen have been Oliver Taplin and Michael Walton, has emphasized the essential theatricality of classical dramatic texts. For better or worse, this rather diffuse movement has found a badge of identity in the proliferation of books on the tragedians with the vogue word 'stagecraft' in the title:[1] not with the force of a technical term, but in acknowledgement of the seminal position for such work of Taplin's study on Aeschylus. It is, in fact, a term of considerable looseness, in danger of meaning bewilderingly many things to different writers and readers. *The Stagecraft of Aeschylus*, *Vision and Stagecraft in Sophocles*, and *Stagecraft in Euripides* turn out to be respectively concerned with exits and entrances, the imagery of sight, and certain formal patterns of dramatic sequence. Yet although only the first can claim the kind of exhaustive coverage suggested by its global title, there is nevertheless an important unity of approach behind these and other recent studies: the insistence that their special topic is not the archaeological curiosity it has often appeared from earlier discussions, but part of the integral meaning of the performed text. To an extent, the diversity of the themes covered in these and other related works simply reflects the large field of analysis opened up by their shared approach, whose key principles may be summarized as follows.

Greek tragedy, in this fresh paradigm, is not simply, even not primarily, a verbal medium. Around the spoken text, it draws on a complex and highly sophisticated system of visual meaning to communicate thought, emotion, and narrative movement. This visual text is as integral to the play as the dialogue script itself: the roles of scriptwriter and director were not generally distinguished in the creation of fifth-century tragedies, and as the great majority of plays were composed for a single performance the reconstruction of that performance is an essential, not a peripheral, task in understanding the play. Moreover – and this is perhaps, for the classical mind, the more revolutionary discovery – this process of reconstruction can be to a large extent an unproblematic, even rigorous, procedure, owing in particular to three unique features of Greek tragic performance. First, the surviving texts were all, or nearly all, performed in a single theatre still explorable today, whose production conditions and resources are on the whole reasonably well understood from archaeological, artistic, and literary evidence despite some inevitable lacunae and obscurities. Second, the very large scale and probably imperfect acoustics of the auditorium forced an especially close collaboration between text and action, significant visuals being generally highlighted in dialogue and climactic verbal moments underlined by visual reinforcement. It is this that enables Taplin's important contention that all truly significant action in a Greek tragedy is recoverable from, but not reducible to, the words alone. And finally, precisely because of the unusually dependent compositional relationship between text and actual performance, the dialogue scripts brim with casual information about space, movement, props, sound, costumes, gestures, design, despite the near-total absence of formal stage directions in the transmitted texts.

A ground assumption of stagecraft explorations to date has been that different Greek dramatists speak essentially the same theatrical language, and that the practice of one playwright can be validly illuminated by the scripts of his rivals. Since these discussions have been confined to fifth-century tragedy, this premise has not seemed problematic. The trio of represented poets clearly exhibit distinctive dramatic styles and interests that cannot be explained by a simple evolutionary model, but that they deal in the same range of performative meaning and expression cannot seriously be denied. Nevertheless, only a few narrow aspects of tragic 'stagecraft' could now be considered fairly understood: the use of props, spatial conventions, the blocking of actor movement might perhaps be claimed, but even these topics remain to be investigated in detail for the majority of scripts. Above all, the task of applying the recent lessons from tragic stagecraft to texts outside the genre – satyr-play, Old and New Comedy – remains largely unattempted.[2]

In fact, when we examine the special case of Aristophanic comedy a surprising picture emerges. Fifth-century tragedy has clearly evolved a system of conventions for the communication of non-verbal meaning that remain to a large extent constant between different playwrights and genres. Moreover, this theatrical *koine*, or mildly variant dialects thereof, is broadly shared by the New Comedy of Menander and his contemporaries as well, in so far as we can generalize from the sparse extant evidence, as the critically elusive genre of fifth-century satyr-play.[3] Only for Aristophanes – contemporary of the tragedians, and grandfather of New Comedy – does the model resoundingly fail. While fifth-century tragedy and satyr-play share with fourth- and third-century comedy a basic core of assumptions, held in common between play and audience, about the way stage action is construed, Aristophanic comedy seems at first sight almost uninhibited by rules of any kind. Not surprisingly, therefore, even a cursory application of the tragic stagecraft model to fifth-century comedy turns up next to nothing of the techniques of theatrical significance common to Aeschylus as to Menander. Is it possible to explain the essential differences, and their implications for the evasive concept of visual meaning as applied to Old Comedy?

These are, of course, large questions. It may seem bold to address them armed with anything less than a full analysis of the genre's range of dramatic convention (itself a term of almost impossibly broad application), coupled with that Grail of comic criticism, a convincing theoretical model for the evaluation of meaning in comedy. Yet it may be possible to chart a few of the major differences that separate Aristophanic comedy from its neighbour genres in the non-verbal communication of dramatic meaning: first with reference to the available resources of convention and production unique to the genre, and then with closer attention to the dramatic requirements of genre and audience. One early clarification may be in order here. 'Non-verbal' is a cumbersome term to use of those aspects of the performed text that are not confined in the words, and it is habitual to speak of these aspects under the general heading 'spectacle', in perhaps misleading acknowledgment of Aristotle's *opsis*. But the stagecraft of Greek drama familiarly encompasses techniques of significance not strictly visual in themselves – sound, silence, imagined action, articulative patterns of sequence and event. In the absence of a suitable global label and of clear reasons for preserving the finer distinction, I occasionally follow convenience in extending 'visual' to these and other performance-related areas of textual enhancement not primarily verbal or musical. If this seems a more diverse area of discussion than has sometimes been the case under this label, I hope it will nevertheless help to tighten rather than diffuse the focus of the general problem.

External indications might suggest that Aristophanes was a comparatively unstagely writer. Unlike, it seems, the tragedians, Aristophanes did not regularly direct his own scripts for the stage; of forty-four plays attributed in antiquity at least one-fourth (*Banqueters, Babylonians, Acharnians, Wasps, Proagon, Amphiaraus, Birds, Lysistrata, Frogs, Cocalus, Aeolosicon 2*) were known to have been directed by his collaborators Callistratus, Philonides, or Araros, and only one of his five known vic-

torious plays was produced *suo nomine*. Other data support this image of
Aristophanes as more of a writer than a theatrical all-rounder. The
surviving *Clouds* is not a theatre script at all but a revision of the text for
book publication, while the close verbal parody of tragedies often a decade
or more old suggests an unusually literary immersion in the theatre. There
is some evidence to suggest that Aristophanes was not a unique figure in his
generation – that Old Comic poets in general went further in the separation
of writer and director than was normal for tragedy.[4] Are we entitled to
demand the same collaboration of text and image that we find in scripts
whose visual text is more regularly evolved with the words?

The answer must surely be yes. It would be rash to deny that
Aristophanes is deeply aware of the visual text of theatre, in others' work as
much as his own. In fact, Aristophanic parody is an important source for
the non-verbal language of fifth-century tragedy. He highlights Aeschylus'
distinctive visual trademark of extended silence and immobility, and gives
us our only account of the choreography of the astonishing music-theatre
finale of the *Persians*; he recreates daring Euripidean coups of staging with
parodic subversion of their central visual elements; and he caricatures the
choreography and musical style of both tragedians with a subtlety only
distantly appreciable in the extant script.[5] To observe an ancient dramatist
truly devoid of stagecraft, one has only to compare the tragedies of Seneca:
highly visualized in their way, and clearly marked by the conventions of
genuine Roman theatre practice, yet so deficient in the basic accommoda-
tion of word to action that only a tiny minority of scholars would now accept
them as authentic theatre scripts. By contrast, all the extant Aristophanes,
irrespective of dates and directors, clearly exhibits a consistent attention to
the visual reality of the spoken text – perhaps more fully even than
Aeschylus, and despite the radical differences in convention.

We must be clear what we intend by 'convention' in this context. On the
one hand, there are the formal patterns of action and sequence that help to
shape the movement of a play by defining it against an understood
background of traditional structural elements. Halleran's work on
Euripides has most recently argued the importance of an awareness of such
formal conventions for the creation of a dynamic sequence of anticipation
and surprise, and there are certainly moments in fifth-century drama, such
as the false *ekkyklema*-formula at *Medea* 1314, where the subversion of formal
convention is a major stagecraft technique. But this order of stage convention is not, on the whole, a lead instrument in the orchestration of dramatic
meaning. It is doubtful, for example, whether a close analysis of the
variations in metrical patterning of middle Aristophanic parabases would
tell us very much more about the meaning of the text than we would
understand from simply reading the words. Of surely greater importance
are the *representational* conventions that allow an audience to translate the

sights and sounds in the performance space into a coherent analogue of experience, because it is only through the manipulation of these agreed signs that dramatic meaning can be expressed at all. And it is in these representational conventions, and the opportunities they offer for the communication of dramatic purpose, that we can appreciate the most radical differences in stage technique between fifth-century tragedy and comedy.

Fifth-century tragedy strives to be consistent in space, time, mode, and milieu. Of these the most important for *opsis* is consistency in space: the requirement for the same set to designate a single segment of dramatic geography for the duration of the play. The essential layout of this performance space is moreover fixed by the unalterable design of the theatre structure, and the conventional range of spatial representation possible in tragedy is therefore closely constrained. A permanent stage building behind the acting space is only rarely disregarded in the text or identified as something other than a human structure with an entrance to an interior; two side gangways at left and right almost always serve opposing offstage spaces of imagination. Changes of scene in the course of a tragedy are rare, and signalled when they do occur by a unique and unmistakable convention, the creation of an empty stage in mid-play by the temporary exodus of chorus and agonists. Nearly every extant tragedy, therefore, assumes a setting outside the door of a building, sited on a road leading from an urban centre to an outside world. Offstage locales are restricted in the main to three, accessed by each of the three routes off stage: the two side exits leading into town and out of town, and the single doorway into the interior of the house.

This design compels a spatial setting, broadly constant between plays, with three essential dimensions of significance. The available spatial oppositions are inside and out, left and right, and to a more limited degree up and down; and this spatiality grows rapidly after 460 BC to articulate a cluster of thematic polarities basic to the genre's concerns. Thus the skene door becomes the interface between the private space and the public, concealment and exposure, the family and the community, the secluded space of women and the daylight lives of men. The opposed parodoi articulate a spatial dichotomy between home and abroad, the polis and the wild, the familiar and the alien, civilization and the savage outside; and the vertical displacement between the theatre floor and the roof of the skene offers a vehicle for the separation of human and Olympian worlds, rarely if ever bridged by direct passage. In traversing this symbolic space, the human figures map the action on to a visual framework of meaning that reaches beyond the literal representation of place.

In a similar way, Greek tragedy strives for consistency in the representation of time, in the evocation of epoch, and in the maintenance of illusion.

Offstage time is covered by a naturalistically congruent elapse of onstage action, with dramatic attention artfully diverted from any unavoidable temporal lacunae. Some elasticity of the time dimension is permissible across a choral ode, but here too at least the illusion of consistency is pursued. Dislocations in dramatic mode – breaches of the dramatic 'illusion' – are rigorously excluded from fifth-century tragedy,[6] even at the comparatively innocuous level of acknowledgement of audience in the spoken text, in spite of a highly-developed convention of face-on audience address in expository prologues; while inconsistency of epoch, in the form of anachronistic intrusions into the heroic universe of prehistory, is with few exceptions banished from the world of tragic representation.[7]

These vivid and specific consistencies lie at the root of tragic stagecraft as we are currently coming to understand it. Exits and entrances, the visual composition of tableau and movement, and the sequencing of actions on and off stage in dramatic time are now recognized as key terms in the vocabulary of the visual text of tragedy, and their usage is determined above all by the principle of consistent representation. The significance of the concrete – space, props, gestures – can only be sustained in a perform- ance medium where the concrete literality of the visual text is rigorously and consistently upheld by representational convention. And it is the conventions developed to sustain consistency, and the non-verbal devices for the communication of meaning evolved to exploit those conventions, that form the basis of the stage technique and performance expression, not just for classical tragedy and satyr-play, but for that comedy regarded in antiquity as the classical phase of its genre. Consistency of mode is not rigid in Menander, though metatheatrical lapses of illusion are still tightly constrained by convention; while the epoch has migrated from the heroic past to settle (consistently) in the here-and-now. But the fundamental conventions of space and time, and perhaps more remarkably the thematic polarities they have grown to express, are at least as rigorously observed in Menander as in the Euripidean tragic theatre from which they finally derive.

Only for Aristophanes, contemporary of the tragedians and grandfather of New Comedy, does the model resoundingly fail. In Old Comedy, paradoxically the most *opsis*-conscious of the fifty-century dramas, the four essential consistencies give way to an appearance of boundless lability. Once again the most significant field is the spatial. The scene of Aristophanes' earliest extant play, the *Acharnians*, glides from the Pnyx in the centre of Athens (lines 1–173) to Dicaeopolis' house in the country (lines 201f; twelve miles to the north of the city, if he lives in his registered deme of Cholleidae), and from there to the house of Euripides (lines 394– 479: on the island of Salamis, according to some accounts), then back again for the duration of the play to line 1096. The difficult scene that follows seems to suppose that the house of Lamachus is part of the set, and this is made explicit at lines 1174ff. The *Peace* opens on earth, follows Trygaeus on his adventure to heaven and descends to earth (by a route left mysterious in the text, line 726) across the break in the action supplied by the parabasis. More strikingly still, the first third of the *Frogs* is an extended tour of the underworld, whose imagined setting shifts continuously while the two travelling characters remain onstage throughout. At line 35 the skene represents the house of Heracles on earth; Dionysus and Xanthias set out at line 165 and by line 181 have already arrived at the lake infernal, which Dionysus crosses in Charon's boat. On the far side they pass through the purgatorial swamp of dung described by Heracles at lines 145–51 to the sunlit realms of the initiates. The skene then crystallizes into Pluto's palace, which remains the setting thereafter. Similar discontinuities of space across continuous stage action occur at *Knights* 751ff and 1326, *Lysistrata* 245, and *Thesmophoriazusae* 277 (with a curious stage direction in the manuscripts, 'the shrine is extruded'). The settings of the *Wasps, Birds, Ecclesiazusae, Plutus* and perhaps *Clouds* maintain a superficial constancy, but at a high cost in logic and naturalism and with the identity of the setting sometimes deliberately allowed to fade from the forefront of audience awareness. Scene changes are signalled not by the elaborate tragic convention of emptying and recreating the set, but by casual identification of doors and surroundings at an appropriate point in the dialogue. Many scenes, especially when crossing between locations, are set in an anonymous, spaceless limbo; and even the very physical skene can find itself generalized into an anonymous 'inside' when its functions as propstore and extra-dramatic nullspace are uppermost.[8] Clearly the conventions of Old Comic performance assume a space that remains empty of concrete identity until and unless one is specifically supplied, and in which continuities of location and their attendant associations may slide from existence as soon as they stop being invoked in the stage action.

As on stage, so off stage: Old Comedy presupposes no consistency or continuity of offstage space, beyond a broad acceptance of the basic spatialities distinguishing indoors from out and up from down. Even the *Birds*, the one comedy of the extant eleven to make sustained and significant use of opposed offstage spaces, is unable to identify these consistently with the spatially opposed boundaries of the playing space. In the astonishing sequence of quick-change character sketches at lines 859ff a series of eighteen new characters, all but one played by the same two actors in a rapid succession of masks and costumes, interrupts the hero's sacrificial preparations. The first sequence, to line 1057, is composed of terrestrial characters, types of the vices and pretensions Pisthetaerus has fled Athens to escape. Each in turn is chased from the stage only to be succeeded immediately by a new encounter, and the script makes it close to certain that both parodoi were used, new characters appearing while Pisthetaerus' attention is occupied with chasing the previous invader out the other side. (There seems no other interpretation of the climax of the routine, a series of momentary, lapped reappearances at lines 1047–55 that finally drives Pisthetaerus, and his sacrifice, 'inside' to escape the invasion – a necessary exit to cover the sacrifice of the animal, as at *Peace* 1020–2.) In this scene, therefore, both parodoi must lead to Athens, the human world, and civilization; but at lines 1122–1312 one and probably both parodoi are used by arrivals from the new-built city in the sky, and the parodos-entry of Prometheus at line 1494 appears to arrive straight from heaven. Once more, the audience is expected to make no assumptions about the identity or consistency of the represented space except as the script and action explicitly prompt.

Inevitably, this means that Old Comedy cannot depend on the uniform conventions of space and meaning available and exploitable in contemporary tragedy. It is not that Aristophanes is less concerned than the tragedians with the oppositions between god and mortal, male and female, civilization and the wild; the *Clouds, Lysistrata*, and *Birds* offer reflections on these axes of Greek self-definition at least as complex and sophisticated as those in tragedy. What Old Comedy lacks is a consistent system of spatial shorthand for the visual representation of these polarities, which must therefore be expressed in other, more fluctile theatrical terms. Thematic polarities are if anything more pronounced and more integral to the dramatic structure of Old Comedy than is ever the case in tragedy, with formal debates a fundamental structural device of enormous traditional prominence and sophistication, and antagonistic divisions in the chorus a powerful medium for the visual expression of polarizations of judgement. But the lack of a consistent bedrock of spatial expression means that the stagecraft of Aristophanes, the use of visible action to articulate meaning, has little use for the fundamental tragic resource of significance in exits, entrances, and offstage spaces.

With dramatic time, too, Old Comedy is uninhibited by pressure towards consistency and naturalism. Offstage action is traditionally compressible in tragedy, but the plays of Aristophanes are much freer in their tolerance of interruptions and illogicalities in the flow of dramatic time. In the *Acharnians*, Amphitheus runs to Sparta and back in the space of forty-five lines; and at some point in the action the date bounces from December (line 202) to late February (line 961). At *Lysistrata* 706ff an interval of days turns out to have elapsed across the choral altercation following line 613; and at lines 626–7 of the *Plutus* a night passes without even a choral break in the manuscript text. Tragedy's illusionistic treatment of time permits the development of a system of temporal motifs in rich thematic scope and dramatic versatility;[9] ideas of destiny, change, cause and effect are central to the tragic analysis of experience, and the plays are full of the language of *kairos, telos, aitia* and similar untranslatable terms expressing a teleological view of human time. The very movement of tragic action towards and across a peripety, a fulcrum of human change, is a consequence of its tightly conventionalized temporal frame. Within its traditional single span of daylight, dramatic form compels two things to be contained: first, a dynamic process of discovery or change guiding the action towards a theatrical climax of understanding or disaster; secondly, the closure of a pattern of meaning built up from actions on a scale of whole lives, nations, or generations. Not surprisingly, such a theatre will be driven to focus on the ironies of time and humanity's attempts to understand it, and even in New Comedy the language of time is thematically prominent.[10] But the looseness of Aristophanic time excludes any conventionally-enforced temporal dynamic. There are no pre-agreed constraints on the shape of the play's action in time, and even the basic dramatic processes of tension, movement and resolution have therefore to be established *ad hoc*. Only in middle Aristophanes do we first find comedies (*Lysistrata, Thesmophoriazusae, Frogs*) the terms of whose final resolution are signalled in the first scene and systematically postponed to the last; the plays of the 420s tend to resolve early and follow the parabasis with a series of confirmatory sketches (*Acharnians, Peace*) or an ironic shift of direction (*Clouds, Wasps; Birds* offers a flamboyant hybrid of both patterns, with the sketches dextrously interleaved with the divine-blockage continuity). Without a preset structure, time in Aristophanes is forced to mean something different, both as a thematic motif and as a technical resource, from its use in the theatre of Menander and the tragedians.

Above all, Old Comedy differs from its neighbour genres in its permeability of epoch and illusion. The bedrock of tragic stagecraft is the consensus that the universe of the play is both contained and self-contained: a re-creation in performance of the epoch of the Homeric epics, never allowed to acknowledge in words its own theatricality. Anachronisms of technology, political organization, and intellectual culture may obtrude in a limited way from the external world of the fifth-century audience into the internal world of heroic prehistory, but the non-violation of epoch remains a ground assumption. This is not to say the barrier of epoch is not constantly crossed in the practical experience of tragic theatre: the very act of watching a play performed in one age and set in another establishes a channel of communication and meaning across the interface between worlds. The heroic past is after all constructed by the present, and its experience articulates the major concerns of the contemporary polis. But the shared pretence of a distant epoch is essential to the function of tragic myth as simultaneously a mirror of the contemporary world and a microcosm of the human universal. Tragedy's espousal of the heroic epoch is

useful in a number of ways: it dignifies the medium and characters by
association with the seriousness of the Homeric epics; it permits allusive
access to a wide corpus of narrative beyond the immediate scope of the
action; and it commands an extra investment of emotional participation
from its network of cultic, geographic, religious and genealogical links to
the present. Equally, it is important to the theatrical effect of tragedy that
all action should be *confined* within its legendary epoch in order to retain an
intelligible, naturalistic, and emotionally gripping sequence of cause and
effect. The pretence can be highlighted, the likeness of the image enhanced,
by ironic narrowing of the gap between worlds; but such references must
remain oblique, and sustain rather than fracture the barrier of epoch. So
Melanippe speaks with the voice of Anaxagoras, Prometheus in the rhetoric
of Ephialtes, but the names are never named; and when Euripidean gods
trace *ex machina* the link between prehistoric myth and contemporary cult it
serves not to annihilate but to accentuate the reality of the invented world.
Early in the century, Phrynichus and Aeschylus experiment with tragic
action in a contemporary epoch, but significantly the dramatic setting is
distant in space from the audience's direct experience and the experiment
proves, in the immediate term, short-lived.

Old Comedy, however, remains stubbornly native to the epoch of late
fifth-century Athens, even when its action is purportedly located in heaven,
hell, or the age of Homeric myth. A major imbalance in our extant comedy
is the loss of mythological comedies such as the Aristophanic *Amphiaraus*,
Anagyrus, *Daedalus*, *Danaides* and *Phoenissae*; but the fragments show that
even these heroic burlesques included anachronistic references to contemporary individuals and events. The *Dionysalexandros* of Cratinus used a
mythological travesty (in which Dionysus impersonated Paris, judged the
goddesses, abducted Helen, and set off the Trojan War) for a sophisticated
topical allegory (Dionysus/Paris : Helen : Trojan War :: Pericles : Aspasia :
Peloponnesian War). Where in tragedy consistency of epoch is a fundamental of stage convention that can be teased but never breached, Old Comedy
flaunts absurdity and anachronism with such subversive abandon that
situational tension is difficult to sustain, when the action is always open to
absurd displacement of cause and effect. By the age of Menander, comedies
which depend on tension and resolution for their emotional manipulation of
audience find themselves confined to the contemporary epoch in order to
sustain consistency of convention in other respects – the illusionistic
treatment of space and time, and a dramatically credible representation of
causality.

Moreover, Old Comedy can invoke temporary, ironic, and generally
incomplete suspensions of genre, by lapsing selectively into the language
and convention of tragedy. Sometimes the whole stage action follows the
generic detour, as at *Thesmophoriazusae* 688ff, and sometimes one character

or more may prove fatally resistant to the shift, as Critylla at lines 855ff of the same play. Such displacements of genre logic, even when dextrously managed and clearly signalled, leave basic questions of motive and meaning unaskable. It makes no sense to inquire what the tragic fictions of *Thesmophoriazusae* 855ff are intended by their participants to achieve (to baffle the captors into letting the prisoner go? to persuade Critylla and the Scythian that they are watching a tragedy, and that the In-Law's escape is merely a theatrical exit? to smuggle him away by physical force alone?). It has been claimed that 'character' in tragedy is sometimes sacrificed to the immediate dramatic needs of the situation. Yet the reason this view has never widely convinced is surely that the conventions of tragic performance implicitly invite the audience to make psychological sense of stage characters' behaviour, however outwardly contradictory it may appear. (Hence Aristotle's shrewd recommendation that even an inconsistent character show an underlying pattern of consistency to make their oscillations of behaviour intelligible.) In comedy, where the very parameters of epoch and genre are liable to slip at the poet's will, psychological intelligibility is not always a prerequisite for dramatically intelligible action.

Most of the tragic consistencies outlined so far have occasional exceptions in the surviving scripts. The *Eumenides*, *Ajax*, and *Rhesus* allow changes of scene and (in the former case) a major discontinuity of time. The satyric *Cyclops* contains mild contradictions in the topology of its set and the hour of its setting.[11] Aristotle criticized the celebration, in the fiction of Orestes' death in the Sophoclean *Electra*, of the Pythian games in the legendary past.[12] Yet one anachronism never, as opposed to seldom, admitted in surviving tragedy is spoken reference to the theatre – and, *a fortiori*, metatheatrical acknowledgement of the context of performance. In itself, this is not a surprising find: a medium barely a century old could hardly be projected back into the Homeric age without grotesque disruption of the historical texture. What is perhaps more remarkable is the range of techniques that implicitly acknowledge the spectator: the prologue soliloquy, the entrance announcement, the evolution of the aside, the ironic challenging of convention. We might look for a modern analogy in the way a highly self-conscious period film drama like *The Draughtsman's Contract* is free to distort historical verisimilitude in language, dress, and attitudes; to compose and edit action in a way that highlights rather than disguises the cinematic artifice; and in general to ironize about its medium in every way short of an explicit (as opposed to ambiguous) dialogue reference, which is somehow perceived as piercing the illusory historical texture in a more fundamental and irreparable way.

In Old Comedy, however, illusion itself is constantly subverted by connivance across the boundaries of medium.[13] Explicit audience address is frequent, particularly in choral routines and from characters whose role in the action is expository or subversive. Snacks can be thrown into the audience as a cheap device to win approval; references to props, machinery, and budgetary constraints can subvert tension with bathos, and the seating arrangements in the Theatre of Dionysus allow even passing allusions to civic and religious officials to be directed at the target in the audience. Once more there is nothing intrinsically surprising in this, or in the continuance of this metadramatic conspiracy between actor and audience even in Menander, whose acceptance of tragic illusionism is otherwise close to total. Serious drama tends by nature to illusion, comic drama to collusion: the subversion of the distance between performer and spectator is not merely a powerful device for the abrupt introduction of incongruity, but a technique essentially disruptive of narrative tension by shifting the rules while the game is in progress.

Apart from these central differences between fifth-century tragedy and comedy in their essential vocabulary of performance convention, there are besides important differences in the character of permissible stage *opsis*. To begin with, the production values of Old Comedy are generally higher than in the average tragedy. The comic chorus is twice the size of its tragic counterpart, a difference apparently reflected in the typical production budget associated with a comic and a tragic *choregia*;[14] and its appeal to the eye is heightened by the old-established tradition of fantastic characterizations and, we must imagine, costumes for its members. Most of the extant Aristophanes was produced for festivals for which, for different reasons, the available resources for theatre production may have been limited, but the *Birds* offers an instance of how fantasy choruses may have been costumed in more extravagant days, with each *choreutes* apparently dressed to represent a different species (lines 267–304).

The extra visual resource of a double-size chorus is an important element in spectacle, and on occasion the scripts give us glimpses of choreographic novelties to exploit the visual possibilities. The *Lysistrata* is by far our most revealing text here, since it counterpoints its sex-war plotline with confrontational odes between symmetrical half-choruses of twelve old women and twelve old men to match them. Strophic responsion between the musically and choreographically identical verses sung by the men and women in turn reveals clear instances of stylized action in the songs' performance. Thus, the epirrhematic syzygy at lines 614ff is marked by metrically respondent exhortations by each side to its fellows to strip for action[15] (lines 615, 637; 661, 685 – a gesture finally inverted in the reconciliation at 1021ff) and culminates on each side with a kick to the enemy's face (lines 635, 657). More elaborately, at lines 796–804 = 821–8 each side in turn threatens the other's face, is repelled, aims a kick and in doing so inadvertently displays a view of the genitals; this is then ridiculed by the opponent chorus, and the kickers stoutly sing the defence of their bristling pubic apparatus. Mimetic dance remains a relatively unexplored area of Greek stagecraft, but the tragic scripts give no indication of choreographic flourishes at this degree of detail, and the more energetic character of Old Comic dance is well attested in and outside the texts.

A second consequence of the higher production values in comedy is the greater dependence on supernumerary actors and non-speaking extras. Of the eleven plays extant only *Knights*, *Peace*, and *Ecclesiazusae* seem bound throughout by the tragic restriction to three speaking actors, though the fourth actor is very sparingly used and five-handed scenes are, with one doubtful exception, not found. More remarkably, Aristophanes is curiously fond, especially in his prologues, of crowd scenes that seem to assume a substantial background presence of non-speaking extras: so at *Acharnians* 40ff and 155–72, *Clouds* 184–95, *Lysistrata* 65ff, *Ecclesiazusae* 41ff. Since all these crowds disperse before the parodos the most economical inference is that they were composed of the *choreutai* prior to their appearance in choral costume, but even this would imply a substantial expenditure in rehearsal and extra costumes. Some tragedies (Aeschylus, *Seven against Thebes*; Sophocles, *Oedipus Tyrannus*) seem to explore a similar form of crowd prologue, but with significantly less movement and (in accordance with the briefer compass of tragic prologues generally) for much shorter scenes.

Similarly, the range of props and visual extras assumed by the Aristophanic scripts implies a substantially freer production budget. A form of comic routine used repeatedly in the earlier plays (*Acharnians* 432–70 and cf. 1097–1126; *Wasps* 798–862, *Lysistrata* 916–47, cf. *Ecclesiazusae* 730–45) involves a rapid series of forays into the skene propstore to accumulate a preposterous catalogue of special equipment, the comic momentum deriving either from a cumulative visual absurdity or from the harassment of one involved character by another. In tragedy, animals appear on stage only in the special context of chariot entries;[16] but comedy seems to make a point of bringing live sheep or donkeys on to the stage (*Peace* 956–1022, *Birds* 848–1057, *Frogs* 1ff; doubtfully *Wasps* 173–96), and develops a stock routine of preparing at great length an animal sacrifice that the audience knows perfectly well cannot be enacted live on stage, finally producing an ingenious excuse for shepherding the action indoors. Interestingly, this pattern of visual *coup* survives in Menander's *Dyskolos* (lines 393–426), though without the metadramatic joke at convention.

To complete the catalogue, we should note the freedom with which Old Comedy seems to extend or redecorate the stage building itself for special visual impact or stage effects. The form and appearance of the skene in this period are subjects of sharp controversy still, particularly over the number of doors in the skene front and the nature and extent of *skenographia* or set-decoration,[17] but it is clear from the texts that Old Comedy is consistent in admitting uses of set, however they were staged, that were not acceptable in tragedy. Two doors seem assumed by the text of *Acharnians* 1096ff, *Clouds* 92ff and 132 with 125, and *Ecclesiazusae* 977ff; opening windows at *Wasps* 379ff and *Ecclesiazusae* 877ff; abnormal uses of the roof at *Wasps* 143–8, 202–9 and *Clouds* 1485ff – though the latter is a revised passage in our text, and perhaps not valid evidence for practical stage options. Some opening tableaux seem to refer in dialogue to unusual details of set-decoration: in *Wasps* the skene is covered by a net (perhaps painted?), in *Birds* the desolate landscape around the Hoopoe's cave seems to be represented in part by visual decoration (lines 1, 20, 54). Interestingly, these are both plays in which consistency of space is observed, at times against what seems the natural direction of the action. An anonymously-decorated skene is clearly easier to reidentify than a highly specific, visually unusual set.

Curiously enough, the use of stage machinery is not easy to establish in Aristophanes outside passages of obvious paratragedy. The only non-parodic *mechane*-scenes are the suspension of Socrates at *Clouds* 218ff and the descent of Iris at *Birds* 1197ff; while the *ekkyklema* is only textually indicated in two routines involving visits to a tragedian's house (*Acharnians* 408ff, *Thesmophoriazusae* 95ff), and both developing the same conceit of an assimilation of life to art such that the artist lives in a house designed like his plays. Dearden argues for frequent unsignalled use of the *ekkyklema* for the extrusion of additional backgrounds and properties, but the proposal has not found wide favour, and we are left with the surprising finding that mechanical effects are not a part of the normal repertoire of comic convention. One possible explanation may be that stage machinery is by its nature a concrete, illusionistic effect, and the very looseness of spatial representation in Aristophanes might tend against the use of machinery specific to the traversal of rigidly observed spatial boundaries in tragedy. The *ekkyklema* does not simply bring the indoor to exterior view; it blurs the distinction between them, and post-*ekkyklema* dialogue scenes drop the pretence that the figures on the trolley are still inside the house. Similarly the *mechane* seems – and we are hampered here by the poverty of evidence for the device in extant tragic texts – to have been used for exits and entrances involving passage between earth and sky or heaven, a function that no doubt encouraged its fourth-century use for divine epiphanies. The freewheeling fluidity of Old Comic space makes such elaborate transitions incongruous and unnecessary, except in contexts like the Iris scene where the tragic spatiality has exceptionally been established.

Finally, alongside these differences in production values, there exist striking differences between the visual resources of tragedy and comedy in their range of tolerated stage action. Physical violence – manhandling, injury or death on stage – is rare in tragedy[18] but widely tolerated in comedy. In particular, no character in extant tragedy strikes a blow to or inflicts pain on another in view of the audience, a practice frequent in

Aristophanes. Costume changes and visual transformations, normally kept off stage in comedy as in tragedy, are admitted on the stage when they amount to a variant form of physical abuse (*Lysistrata* 599–607, *Thesmophoriazusae* 213–68). Such scenes are not gratuitous discharges of dramatic energy: most are linked to an unfolding fantasy of power and subversion, and establish a relation of dominance by the physical violation of an intruder's person. Once the victim has been so abused, his credibility as a figure of authority is null, and the victims of beatings generally disappear from the play. Perhaps surprisingly, visual obscenity is rare. The distinctive costume of the comic actor allows ribald clowning with the costume phallus (as *Wasps* 1343, *Lysistrata* 981–92, *Thesmophoriazusae* 843–8), but any more graphic sexual or scatological activity seems generally confined to the language. Male nudity, interestingly, is avoided, despite or perhaps because of the aesthetic importance of the male body in Greek culture; it remains unclear whether unclad women were actually produced, either directly[19] or, bizarrely, played by padded male performers. Titillating female characters are frequent towards the end of plays (*Acharnians, Wasps, Peace, Birds, Lysistrata, Thesmophoriazusae, Frogs*); but deictic references in the text to female genitals (e.g. *Acharnians* 767–82, *Wasps* 1374, *Lysistrata* 89, 1158) do not invariably seem to indicate visual exposure.

These substantial departures from the tragic model are to an extent mitigated by the common constraints imposed on both genres by the theatre itself. Action and language are still closely interwoven, and the essential spatialities are still respected, even if their specificity is reduced – interior scenes are still never played on stage, and nobody leaves by a parodos and re-enters by the skene door. Above all, the comedies themselves do admit the firm inference from the extant dialogue script of necessary non-verbal action that must be credited as integral to the play as composed. There are scenes (such as *Clouds* 200–2, *Lysistrata* 1216–24, *Frogs* 1504–7) where specific interpretation of the necessary stage action must remain uncertain, but these support rather than undermine the general rule of approach. It remains possible that the visual text was compounded by some essential elements – portrait-masks, for instance, assigning visual identities to the slaves in the *Knights* – to which no reference is made in the dialogue; but in a theatre without opera-glasses, where the distance between actor and spectator can dwarf even the most ample movement, one would expect verbal underlining of significant visuals to be the norm rather than the exception.

But there is perhaps a more fundamental reason why significant non-verbal action in Aristophanic comedy cannot be assimilated to its tragic equivalent, and that is simply that 'dramatic meaning' is bound to be a far more elusive concept in Aristophanic comedy than it has ever been for fifth-century tragedy. The stagecraft vogue in Greek dramatic criticism is, after all, in some ways a ruthlessly reactionary movement. At a time (the late seventies) when the mainstream of critical thought increasingly favoured the autarky of the text and a plural, open-sided model of meaning, here was a way to read Greek poetry that reverted instead to the intention of the text and the experience of the original audience. Of course, there is no essential contradiction here. If the audience must imagine a text, it is because the text imagines an audience. But for tragedy, though not for comedy, we have lived two thousand years with a powerful and massively influential critical model that has built its evaluation on precisely this criterion, of the audience's experience of the text in performance. It is perhaps not wholly accidental that the stagecraft movement has been paralleled by a resurgence of interest in Aristotle's *Poetics*. A commonplace of stagecraft criticism is that approaches to Greek tragic meaning have been subtly warped by the influence of Aristotle, who notoriously rates *opsis* lowest of the elements of tragic composition. In recent years it has been increasingly recognized that Aristotle, far from offering a historically or intellectually privileged model of interpretation, is in some ways a highly idiosyncratic spectator: a philosopher and antiquarian, personally fixated with the theoretical modelling of abstract chains of cause and effect, who has read many more plays than he has watched in the theatre. It is only to be expected that such a critic will put extraordinary stress on plot, text, and formal evolution at the expense of transient performance values. Yet paradoxically one central contention of the Aristotelian model has emerged to new respect with the stagecraft movement in tragic criticism: that the primary meaning of Greek tragedy is emotional (and not, for example, intellectual, political, religious, or metaphysical).[20] Arguably Aristotle's boldest critical achievement was to argue that efficiency in the emotional manipulation of audience, far from being inimical to intellectual and theatrical complexity, was a necessary and sufficient criterion of excellence in tragic drama; and the *eleos-phobos* theory of tragic meaning has remained an extraordinarily elegant and powerful critical model, besides being by no means as inhospitable to *opsis* as some passages in the *Poetics* suggest.[21]

But whether or not the model is accepted, no such reductive or uniform definition has been found acceptable for comic 'meaning', in the sense of the text's teleological manipulation of its imagined audience in a context of performance – least of all perhaps for the case of Aristophanes. A comic analogue to the *eleos-phobos* principle would understand the whole function of comedy as reducible to the efficient provocation of laughter; but this is clearly not a helpful view. Not everything that is significant in Aristophanes is funny, even in the indirect sense of preparing a foundation for humorous effects to come; it defies intuition, for one example, to explain how the uncomfortable exchange at *Lysistrata* 587–97 contributes anything whatever to the audience's hilarity. Equally impoverished, however, must be a contrary approach which would perceive Old Comedy as meaningful only in so far as it makes a serious political or moral appeal to the intellect, relegating to a pejorative category such as 'slapstick' any overt address to the proper emotions of comedy. In fact, classificatory distinctions such as comedy/farce have never made much sense of Aristophanic theatre. We must, I think, recognize the irreducible diversity of dramatic purpose in these plays. Aristophanes himself advertises that Old Comedy entertains by (i) the provocation of laughter and (ii) engagement with issues of concern. But equally important in the appeal to audience, and scarcely dismissible as means to these first two ends, are (iii) the fulfilment of narrative, (iv) the attractive (but not necessarily funny) production of novelty, and (v) the gratification of fantasy, especially fantasies of power and subversion. Only the fifth of these is without a clear counterpart in tragedy; but the relationship between the other levels of appeal is surely of a different order in the two genres. The Aristotelian model of tragedy would subsume (ii) and (iii) under (i) and dismiss (iv) as a gratuitous distraction. But in comedy (i) and (ii) are presented as at least superficially antagonistic to one another; while (iv) is clearly more important as a general element in Old Comedy than it usually is in tragedy. Whereas it remains arguable whether any tragedy – even *Prometheus* – ever uses spectacle for its own sake, Aristophanes is under visible pressure to sustain a momentum of sheer theatrical energy. One can perhaps detect an awareness of the power of spectacle in the patterning of the play as a whole. Most plays open with a visual teaser to engage the audience's curiosity, with the initial dialogue withholding the meaning of the action for a carefully-elaborated climax of exposition. The parodos is later than in tragedy, perhaps again to protract expectation of this spectacular moment, and generally has to wait until the central scheme has already been set ticking. The parabasis provides perhaps twenty minutes of continuous, energetic choral action; the second half of the play is particularly characterized by scenes of violence and rapid movement, and the traditional *komos*-ending closes the action on a sequence of pure theatrical fireworks, often with minimal significance to the plot.

In the light of this, we should perhaps be wary of traditional categories such as 'visual humour'. Even 'pure' visual gags such as the costume of the diplomatic envoy returned from Persia and the visual pun involving the King's Eye (*Acharnians* 64, 94–7) are verbalized to the audience by exclamations from the cue-figure of Dicaeopolis. Moreover, both visual jokes are thematically linked to the narrative and argumentative logic of the scene: that the makers of Athenian foreign policy, with their far-fetched diplomatic schemes, show disdain for the interests of the working class they profess to serve (but in fact exploit to their own profit). Even visual ironies to which no explicit verbal attention is drawn, such as the travesty of Euripides' *Helen* in which the role of the legendary beauty is taken by a

priapic middle-aged transvestite, can generate verbal repartee acknowledging the continuity of motif with the rich network of sexual inversions
that underlie the play's thematic structure. The partition between visual
and verbal, humour and seriousness is a mostly arbitrary construct that
makes little sense of Aristophanic stagecraft in detail or as a whole.

Any attempt to define the aims of Old Comedy in performance, and
thereby the kind of meaning communicated by verbal and non-verbal
theatrical techniques, must surely acknowledge at least these five
simultaneous ends to which Aristophanes strives to affect his audience. To
polarize this diversity of functions into a simple tension between humour
and seriousness, and thence a division between 'sophisticated' and
'popular' or 'high' and 'low' comic techniques, is wilfully to eliminate
everything that makes Old Comedy complex. But this very complexity
leaves the 'meaning' or 'effect' of Aristophanic stagecraft a particularly
difficult topic to address in anything but a piecemeal, *ad hoc* way. This need
not discourage the attempt – the most successful applications of stagecraft
criticism to date have in any case tended to be those which follow texts
rather than systems and methodologies. But it does suggest the interpretation of Aristophanic stagecraft will have less to do with the unravelling of
convention than with the interpretation of Aristophanic texts in their
totality. The special value of Aristophanic comedy has always been felt to
reside in some way with the sheer diffuseness and diversity of the form: its
linguistic versatility, its astonishing range of comic techniques, its breadth
of thematic and imaginative canvas, as well as its dizzy flexibility of
theatrical idiom. But these plays' richness is not simply quantitative; their
artistry lies in the simultaneous pursuit of these different dramatic ends in
an organic and exciting linear performance. We will best understand
Aristophanic stagecraft if we can understand the semantics of comic drama
itself; but that too could take time.

NOTES

1 O. P. Taplin, *The Stagecraft of Aeschylus: The Dramatic Use of Exits and Entrances in
Greek Tragedy* (Oxford University Press, 1977); id., *Greek Tragedy in Action*
(London: Methuen, 1978); J. M. Walton, *Greek Theatre Practice* (Westport and
London: Greenwood Press, 1980); id., *The Greek Sense of Theatre: Tragedy Reviewed*
(London and New York: Methuen, 1984); see also D. J. Mastronarde, *Contact and
Discontinuity: Some Conventions of Speech and Action on the Greek Tragic Stage* (Berkeley
and Los Angeles: University of California Press, 1979), pp. 19–34; David Seale,
Vision and Stagecraft in Sophocles (London and Canberra: Croom Helm, 1982);
Michael Halleran, *Stagecraft in Euripides* (London and Sydney: Croom Helm,
1985).
2 For discussion of stage conventions in Old Comedy generally see A. W. Pickard-

Cambridge, *The Dramatic Festivals of Athens*, 2nd edition (Oxford University Press, 1968); C. W. Dearden, *The Stage of Aristophanes* (London: Athlone Press, 1976). Two distinguished critical studies with an important theatrical element are C. F. Russo, *Aristofane autore di teatro*, 2nd edition (Florence: Sansoni Editore, 1984); K. J. Dover, *Aristophanic Comedy* (London: Batsford and Berkeley; Los Angeles: University of California Press, 1972).

3 Stage conventions in Menander are discussed by E. W. Handley (ed.), *The Dyskolos of Menander* (London: Methuen, 1965), pp. 20–39; T. B. L. Webster, *An Introduction to Menander* (Manchester University Press; New York: Barnes and Noble, 1974), pp. 79–94; on the debt to tragedy see especially A. G. Katsouris, *Tragic Patterns in Menander* (Athens: Hellenic Society for Humanistic Studies, 1975). On tragic conventions in satyr-play see D. F. Sutton, *The Greek Satyr-Play*, Beiträge zur klassischen Philologie 90 (Meisenheim am Glan, 1980), pp. 141–5; R. Seaford (ed.), *Euripides: Cyclops* (Oxford: Clarendon Press, 1984), pp. 16–18.

4 R. L. Hunter (ed.), *Eubulus: The Fragments* (Cambridge University Press, 1983), p. 13.

5 *Frogs* 911–20, 1028f; *Acharnians* 326–51, *Peace* 82–178, *Thesmophoriazousae* 688ff, 855–928, 1015–1135; *Frogs* 1264–1363.

6 D. Bain, 'Audience Address in Greek Tragedy', *Classical Quarterly*, NS 25 (1975), 13–25; id., *Actors and Audience: A Study of Asides and Related Conventions in Greek Drama* (Oxford University Press, 1977); O. P. Taplin, 'Fifth-Century Tragedy and Comedy: A Synkrisis', *Journal of Hellenic Studies*, 106 (1986), 163–74.

7 P. E. Easterling, 'Anachronism in Greek Tragedy', *Journal of Hellenic Studies*, 105 (1985), 1–10.

8 See K. J. Dover, 'The Skene in Aristophanes', *Proceedings of the Cambridge Philological Society*, 192 (1966), 2–17: pp. 4–5.

9 J. de Romilly, *Time in Greek Tragedy* (Ithaca: Cornell University Press, 1968).

10 Notably in the *Dyskolos*: e.g. lines 271–83, 769 Sandbach.

11 P. D. Arnott, 'The Overworked Playwright', *Greece & Rome*, NS 8 (1961), 164–9; Sutton, *The Greek Satyr-Play*, pp. 102–3.

12 *Poetics* 1460a31, on *Electra* 681f; Easterling, 'Anachronism in Greek Tragedy', pp. 7–8.

13 W. Gorler, 'Über die Illusion in der antiken Komödie', *Antike und Abendland*, 18 (1973), 41–57; F. Muecke, 'Playing with the Play: Theatrical Self-Consciousness in Aristophanes', *Antichthon*, 11 (1977), 52–67; G. A. H. Chapman, 'Some Notes on Dramatic Illusion in Aristophanes', *American Journal of Philology*, 104 (1983), 1–23.

14 Lysias xxi.1, 4.

15 For the significance of this choreographic motif see G. M. Sifakis, *Parabasis and Animal Choruses* (London: Athlone Press, 1971), pp. 103–8.

16 Taplin, *The Stagecraft of Aeschylus*, pp. 74–9.

17 Dover argues for a two- or three-door skene as standard by the 420s ('The Skene in Aristophanes', pp. 6–17), against the more popular view of a single door at least to the *Ecclesiazusae*. On *skenographia*: N. C. Hourmouziades, *Production and Imagination in Euripides* (Athens: Hellenic Society for Humanistic Studies, 1965), pp. 35–43; A. L. Brown, 'Three and Scene-Painting Sophocles', *Proceedings of the Cambridge Philological Society*, 210 (1984), 1–17.

52 *Farce*

Walton, *Greek Theatre Practice*, pp. 135–6 lists the main instances, mostly scenes of physical struggle or restraint.
U. von Wilamowitz-Moellendorff (ed.), *Aristophanes: Lysistrate* (Berlin: Weidmannsche Buchhandlung, 1927), pp. 186–7.
See especially W. B. Stanford, *Greek Tragedy and the Emotions* (London: Routledge and Kegan Paul, 1983).
Aristotle's position on *opsis* is defended by R. Janko, *Aristotle on Comedy* (London: Duckworth, 1984), pp. 228–9.

Plautus versus *Komoidia*: popular farce at Rome*

VICTOR CASTELLANI

Taking materials from sophisticated Greek 'New' and (perhaps) the earlier 'Middle' Comedy but recomposing them in keeping with his own likely background and to please his *Roman* audience, and recasting them for the very different conditions of performance at late third-century to early second-century Rome, the Italian playwright we know by the name 'Plautus' created a new theatrical genre that, at its liveliest and best, can only be regarded as *farce* – in fact the earliest purest specimens thereof in western literature.[1] How he used – and abused – those foreign materials and what was his background, what were the evident standards and expectations of the Romans he entertained successfully for a quarter of a century or more, and what was the nature of festival 'theatre' in the Rome of the Scipios are the closely related subjects of this paper.

First it may be helpful to sketch out the history and nature of Greek Comedy from its 'Old', even its 'pre-Old' beginnings to the third century BC. Although other popular and traditional practices may also have influenced its development, its origin seems to have been twofold.[2] *Group play* with animal and other impersonation by means of masks and costumes, with song and dance, and marked by ritual humor, all in honor and under the supposed influence of the fertility god Dionysus, by a process we do not understand coalesced with *topical and/or satiric humor* (or, more accurately, 'invective') in the traditional medium of a particular colloquial verse type (iambic) to yield that 'Old Comedy' we know from nine surviving works by Aristophanes (c. 445 to c. 385 BC). Despite much fooling that we must recognize as 'farcical' (for example, Philocleon's disguise as smoke in *Wasps* and most of the avian business in *Birds*), the underlying subject of all his plays until near the end of his long career and therefore the unmistakable *purpose* of Aristophanes and (so far as we may judge from titles and fragments) of his older colleagues in comedy was *political*, whether in the narrow sense (concerning war and peace, operations of the radical democracy and its demagogue leaders) or in a broader one (concerning the

* A draft of this paper was read at the *Themes in Drama* International Conference at the University of California, Riverside, in February 1986.

entire literary, musical, and intellectual culture of the city-state). Fantasy
and wit were the old comedians' means to the end of seriously-meant
warning or exhortation.[3] Already in his last years, however, after Athens'
defeat in the great war he had so valiantly opposed, Aristophanes turned
away from specific Athenian issues to much more general concerns (in the
Congresswomen, a caustic satire on utopian scheming, and in *Plutus* – that is,
'Wealth' personified – on post-imperial social and economic problems of a
large class of Athenians, though not without some Aristophanic whimsy).
This is the beginning of 'Middle Comedy'. Satire (sometimes using the
medium of divine or heroic myth, other times figures from Athens' past
such as Socrates and Euripides) and humorous treatment of ordinary
people's rather ordinary problems seem to have been major trends in this
so-called 'Middle Comedy' during approximately the first three quarters of
the fourth century. Most of this period is, in fact, not at all well known or
understood.[4] *Only* titles and fragments remain, plus, probably (to the
uncertain extent to which we can reconstruct them), the Greek models of
Plautus' *Persa* and *Amphitruo*.[5] At the end of this 'dark age' emerges
something better known because far easier to know, the bourgeois 'New
Comedy' of Philemon (c. 360–264/3), Diphilus (c. 355–c. 300?), and, most
famous of all, Menander (342/1–293/2). Besides through the routine titles-
and-fragments we think we know something about Philemon from two or
three plots preserved in Plautine comedy, something about Diphilus from
another two.[6] Menander, already discernable behind four comedies by the
Latin playwright Terence, has been revealed in our century by extensive
papyrus fragments that include one early play almost complete (*Dyskolos* or
'The Grouch', that came to light only in the 1950s).[7] Notwithstanding
differences of emphasis and, perhaps, of preferred plot mechanisms, the
'New' comedians all worked very much in the same vein.[8] Their subject was
domestic relations among various typical characters, bearing typical
names, wearing typical (and soon standardized) masks and costumes.
Most often the plot involved the difficulties in love of a young man who
could neither marry (if she was free) nor purchase (if she was a slave) the
girl he loved. Blocking his success could be his parents, her parents – or her
owner – or a rival lover. Sometimes it was simply his poverty. By intrigue or
by the fortunate discovery that she was a long-lost cousin, or at least the
long-lost daughter of a family friend, boy almost invariably got girl, though
seldom before learning an edifying lesson or two. Characters and their
behavior were, it is true, often comically exaggerated (for example,
Knemon, the 'Grouch' of Menander's play); and yet all, or almost all,
persons and actions were plausible and (at least for Menander) *sympathetic*.
Moreover, particularly though not uniquely in Menander, female characters – slaves, prostitutes, young girls, and older, married women – played
major roles and were treated with respect and psychological subtlety. (In

this regard *Dyskolos* is *not* a good example of Menander's work; much better are a couple of the more fragmentary plays, most notably perhaps *Epitrepontes* and *Samia*, and two plays Terence adapted after Menandrian originals: *Andria* and *Eunuchus*.)[9] Overall, the genteel *humanity* of Menander and the other 'new' Greeks stands out in equal measure with their gentle humor. They were capable, to be sure, of satire and cynicism; but overall they seem to have been philanthropic (in the original sense of the word) and optimistic about the ethical development of the people whose typical characters they explored with increasing sensitivity and insight. Few, if indeed any, were two-dimensional 'bad guys' in this genre; for the playwrights seem to have attempted to think their way into *all* their important characters with an understanding that would in turn instruct their audience.[10] Finally, in the construction of their plays they practiced good Aristotelian sense, making the principal events of plot plausible in terms of their characters' motives and (often) their state of ignorance about important facts. Although frequently the dénouement depended upon a startling coincidence, that coincidence would be so esthetically *and emotionally* satisfying that the viewers were ready to overlook its unlikeliness. After all, as Aristotle wrote, it is likely that some unlikely things will happen.[11] *Tyche*, 'Chance', in an age that had begun to worship her more than many of the old gods of the city-states, plus the optimism of the poets – or the wishful thinking of their audiences – and the convention of the happy ending (often suggesting the *gamos* or sexual union that figured already in Old Comedy), brought the characters' problems, after amusing complications, to a pleasing and convincing solution by compromise, by discovery, or by sheer good luck.[12]

In Plautine adaptation, however, this decent, urbane and humane genre was quite metamorphosed – in his best plays, into *farce*. The Italian's campaign against the very nature of his model material marched (he was very fond of military metaphor) on four fronts that I shall call plot destruction, caricaturization, humorishness, and disillusionism. Before we examine, with examples, how he deployed his Latin forces against the construction, characterization, humor, and staging of the Greeks, however, I must try to explain *why* he would do so. Some of the reason must have to do with his 'barbarian' audience but much else has to do with his own background.[13]

Before the first translation–adaptation of Greek comedy was staged at Rome (in or about 240 BC, when Plautus was, we believe, in his early teens) the Romans probably had for festive entertainment at the *ludi* or 'games', where comedy later came to dominate, two forms of theatrical fun: mime and *fabula Atellana*.[14] Mime is a familiar enough term. Maskless, barefoot actors impersonated (often, it seems, quite improvisationally) a wide assortment of characters in situations taken from daily life or from mythology, but exaggerated to absurdity. From the titles of later, literary mimes of the first century BC it appears that their matter and imaginary setting were mainly urban. There were words (only pantomime was wordless) but likely not, at that early stage, a true script. If anything was written at all, it was almost certainly at most a scenario – and perhaps only a title. There was musical accompaniment; but the flute player, too, quite likely improvised. The second form of entertainment, *fabula Atellana*, requires explanation. The word *fabula* is used for all kinds of Latin drama (for example, in *fabula palliata*, 'drama in Greek dress', which is the standard name for the genre of both Plautus and Terence). *Atellane* drama was a particular kind of rustic farce imported to Rome from the Oscan town Atella near Naples. Originally performed in the Oscan dialect, it was early on done in the Romans' own Latin as well. Its features in the earlier period (before it, too, like mime, became literary) seem to have included the following: stock characters, wearing conventional masks, fooling one another, often by ridiculous impersonation-upon-impersonation. Though the stock *personae* may have numbered more, and presumably other characters were available as well, four masks/characters clearly predominated: the gullible old man 'Pappus' or 'Pop', the braggart – or alternatively the glutton – 'Bucco' or 'Big Mouth', the sly trickster 'Dossennus', which may mean 'Hunchback', and the stupid yokel 'Maccus', 'Clown'. The last of them is doubly important. For one thing, he seems to have been the most popular of all, lending his name to several titles from Atellane farce such as *Maccus Virgo* or 'Clown the Maiden', *Maccus Copo* or 'Clown the Innkeeper', and *Maccus Miles* or 'Soldier Clown'. In the first place, this all should suggest the sort of entertainment to which Romans in the mid-to-late third century were accustomed. Secondly, the figure Maccus has a name suspiciously like the Roman *nomen* or middle name (the 'gentile' or clan name) of the non-Roman playwright Titus *Maccius* Plautus, to whose career we must now turn.

Born at Sarsina in Umbria, Plautus, we are told upon ancient authority, made money at Rome early in life *in operis artificum scaenicorum*.[15] If only we knew precisely what this means! The adjective *scaenicorum* clearly refers to some sort of theatrical business; and one interpretation has it that 'in work for hire of scenic artisans' Plautus was a stage carpenter or the like. But since there were professional theatre companies at Rome from an early though unascertainable date, it is also very possible that he was involved in the creation and/or performance of some sort of drama.[16] The amusingly invented name 'Maccius' hints that this may have been Atellane farce rather than Greek-style *tragoedia* or *comoedia*. Complicating the matter further is our author's last name or *cognomen*, *Plautus*, which can mean either 'Dog-eared' or 'Flat-foot'. The latter would be synonymous with *planipes*, which is a common term for the barefoot performer of *mime*. One scholar has even held that Plautus can have had experience acting in both farce and mime.[17] George Duckworth (p. 50) finds this 'rather unlikely', but himself concludes that it is 'extremely likely that [Plautus] had personal experience on the stage as an actor before he turned to the writing of plays based upon Greek models.' I add the thought that his background in *successful* popular entertainment in one or another of the sillier genres farce and mime, the experience of earlier Roman writers and his own experience so far as we can follow his development to the known late works *Pseudolus* and *Casina* brought Plautus into open warfare against the norms of high comedy *and made of him an ally to the very different norms of farce*. He, like Naevius before him, seems to have learned what Terence would learn painfully a generation or so later, namely, that a close imitation of humane and earnest Greek comedy would not hold a Roman audience. In fact, under the likely conditions of performance at Rome, with no enclosed theatre and with citizens passing freely from one festival event to another, it was necessary to attend more to the part than the whole of the play, and to keep everything as entertaining as possible for the immediate moment.[18]

Plautus' attack on the genre whose material he pirated was, as already stated, fourfold. He de-structed many of the Greek plays' finely constructed plots; he reduced some, exaggerated others of the nicely drawn characters of Menander and of Menander's contemporaries and followers into caricatures; he substituted for or superimposed upon the elegant humor of his models his own more vigorous, more simply ridiculous foolery in action, in statement, even in language; and, on occasion at least, he discarded the relatively plausible theatrical space of the Greek theatre. All this will be demonstrated through examples from his funniest plays in the remainder of this paper.

First let us consider plot destruction. A re-writer could impair the neatness of a Menandrian, Diphilan, or Philemonian comic plot by truncation, by syncopation, by apocopation, or by interpolation. Plautus used all four methods with malice and with success. Truncation, that is, removal of the beginning, rendered what was presumably a complex double plot in a play by Menander entitled *Adelphoi* or 'Brothers' (a different one than Terence's model for his play of the same name) into a series of casually connected scenes from somewhere in its middle and from its end, with special attention on low-life characters such as the 'parasite' Gelasimus and some slaves.[19] The principal free characters, the brothers of the play's Greek title and their wives, are reduced in importance – the brothers especially – and all but forgotten at the end. One of the slaves, Stichus, not unfittingly gives his name to this Plautine wreck of a comedy whose most hilarious – and most farcical – musical sections he guides.

A better-known play exemplifies internal shortening of a plot or what I call syncopation, the *Aulularia* or 'Pot of Gold'. All who have read or seen staged a translation of this work will likely not forget the miserly old man whose fortunate discovery of a jar of gold brings him so much misery. They may even remember his name, Euclio. But how many can remember the male 'romantic lead' character by name or by predicament? His name, in fact, is Lyconides and he has decided to marry the girl (Euclio's only child) whom he raped nine months earlier and who is now about to give birth. We do not remember much about him because of damage to the plot of an unknown Greek new comedian by accident (the last part of the play, where he had a major part, has not been preserved in the manuscripts) *but also by Plautus*. Plautus' elaboration of some satirical business between the young man's mother and bachelor uncle but especially amplification of the role of Euclio in a number of scenes that contribute absolutely nothing to the progress of the romantic plot have reduced Lyconides' importance in the middle portions of the play considerably – and have, moreover, removed the poor daughter of Euclio from the stage entirely.[20] (The audience only *hear* her voice, invoking the goddess Juno Lucina in pain as she bears Lyconides' child off stage at lines 691–2.) The Roman comic writer just was not interested in her feelings (which were most likely treated in his Greek model) nor in her rapist-suitor's new found conscience and love (which we may be quite certain Menander or whoever had explored in some depth). He did need the young man for a very funny scene (lines 727–807) in which he and old Euclio are at first confused over what Lyconides is apologizing for (he means the rape of Euclio's daughter, while Euclio thinks he means the theft of his gold), but otherwise Plautus had very little use indeed for the protagonist of the play!

A very late play, *Casina*, gives us perhaps the most extreme possible example of Plautine apocopation or shortening of a plot by suppressing its *end*. The romantic leads here are named Casina (the girl who gives the play its title) and Euthynicus. But neither appears on stage during the course of this mutilation of an original by Diphilus. We see instead only a *false* Casina, the male slave Chalinus dressed up in her place for her 'wedding' to another slave (who is, in fact, surrogate for Euthynicus' father Lysidamus in a sordid rivalry between father and son); and we are told in the prologue (part of it is post-Plautine, but this much is not) that we must not wait for the young man: 'He will not return to town today in this comedy; Plautus didn't want him, he broke a bridge that was on his way.'[21] Nevertheless, we know, from the same prologue, that Casina, believed to be a slave, turned out to be free born and presumably could then marry Euthynicus, so they could both live, as usual, happily ever after – but not in Plautus, who cared not a whit for either of the lovers, for their problem or for its solution. Scenes among slaves and scenes involving the dirty old man Lysidamus are what preoccupied our author in this play, composed in what we think was the last year of his life and thus very possibly his very last work.[22]

Finally we have interpolation to consider. To be precise, there are two sorts. In one, for which we have learned the quasi-technical verb *contaminare* from the prologues to two of Terence's plays, a Roman playwright would combine material from two or more different Greek originals.[23] In the other, he would simply insert massive material of his own invention. In both, of course, there need be no detriment to the logic or the smooth progress of a play from problem through complication to solution. With Plautus, however, and his most un-Aristotelian disregard for integrity of plot, interpolation of both sorts typically interrupts or confounds the action to increase the *fun*. Although there are equally good examples in less familiar plays, let me cite one of the most popular comedies by Plautus, the *Miles Gloriosus* or 'Braggart Soldier', as a probable example of 'contamination'.[24] During this eventful play, Plautus' longest, there are in sequence two quite distinct intrigues to win the girl Philocomasium from her owner, the soldier Pyrgopolynices. First, a hole is broken in the wall between the soldier's house and that of a neighbor who colludes with her lover Pleusicles. When a slave of the soldier sees her at the neighbor's an amusing pretense about a twin sister prevents discovery of the dangerous truth. A good guess is that *this* intrigue was the typical stopgap which preceded a solution by recognition, that the girl was a free-born Athenian (or Ephesian or something), possibly even daughter or niece of the collusive neighbor, and that the soldier could therefore no longer hold her as a slave. But instead the action, set not at Athens but at Ephesus, takes a very different turn, thanks to the brilliant and complex scheming of the slave Palaestrio. He sets an elaborate trap for the braggart. A prostitute pretends to be a wealthy married woman who is madly in love with the soldier and woos him with gifts. He is induced to release Philocomasium to an Athenian sea-captain (in fact her lover Pleusicles) who is supposed to return her to her mother. Thereafter he is caught by his neighbor in (he thinks) adultery with the prostitute, suffers a beating – and is threatened with much worse (see below pp. 66 and 67). This second part of the action nicely fits the rather unusual non-Athenian setting since, under the laws of the Greek states, free birth at city A did not prevent lawful enslavement at city B. A citizen of A held as a slave at B could, of course, be ransomed (that is, bought) there and returned to freedom at A; but a more ingenious (and more economical) method would be to get him or her onto A'an territory or at least onto an A'an ship on the high seas – what Palaestrio and Pleusicles accomplish, with parting gifts from the soldier to boot! It appears that Plautus has conflated the plots of two plays, both perhaps involving a soldier and a free girl held as slave, but each neater and smoother by itself. He joins the two, it seems, to double the foolery and to amplify the role of the cunning slave Palaestrio. Any serious feeling of the lovers – or, originally, of the *two* sets of lovers and quite possibly of the mother of one of the girls – is sacrificed so that Palaestrio and his cohorts may hilariously deceive first the soldier's stupid slave Sceledrus, then the even more stupid soldier himself.

For an example of a purely Plautine interpolation we may turn to perhaps his funniest play of all, *Pseudolus*. In the first act of this long play action stops so that the young man in love (a helpless fellow named Calidorus) and the slave Pseudolus can overhear the pimp/slave-owner Ballio give elaborate instructions, spiced with many threats, to his stable of prostitutes (who include Calidorus' beloved, Phoenicium). Today is Ballio's birthday and he expects lavish gifts from the girls' regular customers. The scene, a hundred verses long, is animated and indecent – and utterly non-Greek, for the ancient Greeks simply did not celebrate birthdays with gifts as the Romans did.[25] Plautus seems to have built up a minor character from his model by an unknown Greek into a pimp to end all pimps by adding this long, memorable, yet completely inconsequential musical number (most of this scene and of the one that follows being in lyric meters) – which is, moreover, an improbable eavesdropping upon what would, of course, be an indoor conversation. The Italian playwright therefore sacrificed progress of plot and even human probability to exaggeration of a character (to whom we shall return below) by means of a major 'interpolation' of Plautine scurrility.

To conclude our discussion of mangled plots let me remark that another popular play, the *Mostellaria* or 'Haunted House', shows syncopation, apocopation, *and* interpolation. It is, in fact, extremely difficult to reconstruct a likely Greek plot *because Philolaches and Philematium, the romantic leads, disappear for good after line 405, a scant third of the way through the play.* Furthermore, two of the early scenes in which they *do* appear seem to be Plautine interpolation, whether 'contaminated' from other models or his own free composition: act i, scene iii, most of which is a very long eavesdropping scene (indeed the longest in Plautus) where Philolaches overhears his girl and a worldly-wise older woman who is dressing her; and act i, scene iv–act ii, scene i, which is a sequence of carousing by Philolaches and his girl and a thoroughly soused friend of his, Callidamates, and *his* girl into which Tranio irrupts with the dreadful news of the father Theopropides' untimely return to Athens. Some of this is musical (presumably with mimetic dancing by the drunk), and much is in horrible taste (Callidamates evidently passes out, then later almost vomits); and *all* of it prevents the audience from taking Philolaches' urgent problem very seriously. In fact, Tranio urges him not to worry and, far from sending away the embarrassing visitors, sends both couples inside the house to continue their debauchery. Inside, of course, is where such business belongs in any case – which may suggest that nothing much like this can have occurred in a more realistic Greek model. The whole role of Callidamates may well be Plautus' anti-plot invention, since, rather than bring back Philolaches for the expected solution to his problem at the end of the play, the poet brings *Callidamates* back for a splendidly implausible offer to repay Theopropides all his son has squandered in exchange for complete pardon and even license to continue his wanton ways – to which deal Theopropides perhaps even less plausibly consents (lines 1153–80).[26] Indeed the play ends with attention upon Tranio, probably only a minor character in the Greek. The slave urges Theopropides to grant Callidamates' plea – for today, since surely he will offend again tomorrow and can then suffer punishment for everything at once (lines 1178–9). Plautus was, as we have already seen repeatedly above, simply not interested in the romantic plot or any serious exploration of character or motivation, but only in fun – the fun of an old woman's cynicism, of young men's drunkenness, and, above all, of a shameless slave's cunning.

This brings us now to our author's characterization, or, rather, to what I have already called his *caricaturization*, his simplification and exaggeration of personalities to where they lose both psychological subtlety (for which Menander was famous) and ethical import. In the same process, moreover, the Roman playwright also often – and cheerfully – sacrificed the *sympathy* his characters could have had from the viewers in exchange for at most a kind of rooting interest. For we seldom care what happens to the young men or the old men of Plautine comedy at its best, or even what happens to the tricky slaves who usurp the stage and revise the plot; we care only to see 'games', *ludi*, in exactly the sort of trickery that was the substance of Atellane farce and between characters almost as *devoid of* substance as Dossennus and Bucco, Pappus and *Maccus*.[27]

Plautus routinely disfigured characters of every type we know from the remains and from ancient discussions of Greek New Comedy: old men and young men, women of diverse status and age, persons of assorted specialist vocations; while, as we have observed already, he repeatedly magnified slaves to become several plays' virtual protagonists, who drew to themselves that 'rooting interest' of the Roman audience. Let me be specific, with examples as before.

First, I shall treat old men. Doubtless there were some unattractive traits among the Greek comedians' *gerontes*. An example is easy to find in Menander's violently anti-social misanthrope Knemon. We believe, however, that such characters (again like that 'Grouch') invariably possessed redeeming features as well and were good 'deep down inside', having acquired their less pleasant exteriors and an endemic Attic parsimony from life's hard knocks or from too severe an upbringing. We also believe that, though they might not be brilliant, they were not blockheads, that they could be fooled only by plausible deceptions that played upon their foibles (for example, upon their pride over having brought up – they thought – well-behaved sons or, of course, upon their constant eagerness to make an easy drachma). We do *not* believe that any of them can have closely resembled either of Plautus' funniest two *senes*, the monomaniac miser Euclio who sleeps with a pouch over his face so as not to lose any breath (*Aulularia* 303–4), or the dirty old fool Lysidamus, whose lust after his wife's slave Casina is certain enough to come from Diphilus, but not his ridiculous slips of the tongue, his dirty jokes, or his humiliation by the false Casina, the male slave Chalinus, in 'her' bridal bed.[28] Moreover, many of the more standard *senes* in Plautus seem to have lost the moral earnestness, not without occasional all-too-human hypocrisy, that we see in most of the old men in Terence (who modelled them closely after Menander himself and the Menandrian Apollodorus). Examples include the fathers Theopropides in *Mostellaria*, who, as we have already seen, much too readily condones his son's extravagance, and Simo in *Pseudolus*, who pays no attention at all to another profligate son who has bought an expensive slave-prostitute. Even the anonymous *senex* in Platus' *Menaechmi* seems to be debased, so that, instead of sympathy for his daughter who has been gravely dishonored by her husband Menaechmus of Epidamnus, he gives her an amusing hard time before he does his duty of supporting her against the perplexed Menaechmus of Syracuse. His first reaction (that is, to accept his son-in-law's philandering without censure) brings us, in fact, to another type of old man that Plautus probably found adumbrated in New Comedy but reduced to silliness in his own plays: the amoral ally of the romantic young man and/ or of the tricky slave.[29] The old bachelor Periplectomenus who allows a hole to be broken from his house to the soldier's and then makes possible the second intrigue in *Miles Gloriosus* is one example; another is Callipho, who roots for and even wagers upon the success of the slave Pseudolus. Only Daemones, a very sympathetic and moral old Athenian exile reunited with his long-lost daughter in the *Rudens* or 'Rope' and bitter yet understandable Hegio in *Captivi*, 'The Prisoners', are likely to follow their Greek models rather closely – and do so at the expense of the amoral hilarity the Romans of the late third and early second centuries so obviously preferred.[30]

The *young* men in Plautus are perhaps even further removed from their New Comedy precursors – that is, when they have not been entirely or largely removed from the Roman plays, like Euthynicus from the *Casina*. The *neaniai* of Menander and the other Greeks were, to be sure, morally doubtful in important behavior. To begin with, they were in case after case guilty of rape or seduction, or at least of scandalous and costly whoring. Further, their problem was typically a conflict between honorable action, on the one hand, often in obedience to social or legal norms or to a parent, and love, on the other, whether or not they also owned a sense of moral responsibility to their girls. In contrast, Plautus' plays are full of the most delightfully irresponsible *adulescentes*, of whom we have already met two 'good' examples. Neither Philolaches in *Mostellaria* nor Calidorus in

Pseudolus contributes anything but a sort of mooning helplessness to those plays. Other young men who do contribute to the solutions of their own problems are often little 'better', whether in an ethical sense or a theatrical. Pleusicles, the young lover of the soldier's slave-girl in *Miles Gloriosus*, merely plays a 'bit part' in his slave Palaestrio's intrigue – and almost gives the game away by betraying affection for the girl he, impersonating a gruff sea-dog, is supposed to escort to his ship. No wonder, then, that Plautus was ready to mangle plot in order to reduce or even quite to eliminate such bland, passive, and (by his own design) non-sympathetic roles. Only in such moderately-funny or unfunny plays as *Rudens* and *Captivi*, or in utterly unmemorable *Trinummus*, do we find relatively serious young men, or under extraordinary circumstances such as those in act IV, scene ix of *Aulularia*, where Lyconides must act as straight man to the manic Euclio, who, as we have seen, misunderstands what 'treasure' of his the young man has seized.[31] Plautus' own preference, we can only surmise, lay rather with that one *adulescens* whom I have suggested he himself invented – the drunkard sponsor of debauchery in *Mostellaria*, the filthy rich playboy Callidamates (see above pp. 6of).

The women who were so psychologically and ethically interesting to Greek New Comedy come off a little better – sometimes. Even Plautus would not immoralize a free-born woman, whether young and marriage-able or older and already married. Such characters when he found them were simply reduced in importance on stage. It seems almost as if, since there evidently was no stock *female* character in the traditional cast of Atellane farce, neither Plautus nor his audience had much understanding of theatrical *mulieres*. Older ones, it is true, were occasionally useful as 'straight women' to more or less ridiculous old men, for example to the old lecher Lysidamus his wife Cleustrata in *Casina*, to the pompous aging bachelor Megadorus in *Aulularia* his sister Eunomia. (Even the latter's *name* suggests stuffy probity, meaning as it does something like 'Good Govern-ment'). And an *absent* wife, like that of Theopropides' old neighbor Simo in *Mostellaria*, can receive what looks like stock (and tasteless) criticism (*Most.* 690–9 and 702–10).[32] Younger married women could be awkwardly serious characters, with complaints against their husbands that the husbands' outrageous behavior would certainly justify. We see this in Alcumena of a unique 'tragicomedy' (as Plautus' prologue itself calls this play), the mythological *Amphitruo*, but also in the poor dishonored wife of one of the brothers Menaechmus. Some of Plautus' most tasteless joking comes at their expense.[33] Young unmarried women, on the other hand, especially slaves, were good for much direct fun. We may well suspect that Plautus sometimes purposely apocopated or otherwise altered plots so that girls discovered in the Greek originals to be free-born citizens were known to the end of *his* plays as slaves or foreign prostitutes, for such were capable of the gleeful deceptions that characterize, for examples from the *Miles Gloriosus*, not only the professional *meretrix* or courtesan Acroteleutium but also Pleusicles' beloved Philocomasium. Alternatively, he could leave a free-born girl relatively serious but add to the cast a slave-girl attendant to crack jokes, as I believe he did in the case of Ampelisca, the kidnapped citizen girl Palaestra's companion in the *Rudens*.[34] The Roman Plautus also happily appropriated the many prostitutes he found as important characters in Greek comedies, though he exploited them for what appears to be stock joking rather than (as Menander and after him Terence did) either for serious censure of 'better' people's morals or for the sometimes pleasing, sometimes cloying 'heart of gold' *topos*.[35]

We have come now to a third category of characters with which the *meretrices* overlap: the professional types. The more farcical bits of New Comedy involve parasites and cooks at least, probably also soldiers, moneylenders, pimps/slave dealers and the like. We do know that these types and more appeared, but do *not* know how ludicrous they were, in Menander's and the other Greeks' works.[36] Ludicrous they certainly are in Plautus', where several become dominant figures at the expense, temporary or permanent, of serious domestic comedy. The preposterously vainglorious soldier Pyrgopolynices in *Miles Gloriosus*, the grandly self-unrighteous pimp-slaver Ballio in *Pseudolus* add much fun where Plautus has removed much seriousness; while in plays where the seriousness remains, in *Rudens* another vivid, implausible pimp named Labrax, and in *Captivi* the parasite Ergasilus add vigor and unsubtle type-humor.[37] Such type-humor seems to have been native to Italy even before the importation of New Comedy, as titles of old Atellane farces suggest: recall that one was '*Soldier* Maccus'.[38] By mere exaggeration of Greek type-traits to Latin caricature Plautus made of these widely assorted figures at least minor characters to keep the action ridiculous, at most stage-stealing personalities like Ballio whose name became a byword for generations of Romans.[39]

By far the most important of Plautus' characters, however, are the cunning slaves, the Tranios and Trachalios, the Palaestrios and Pseudoluses who take charge of the action and who take to themselves as well the 'rooting interest' of the audience. Probably the best feature of Eric Segal's lively study *Roman Laughter* is its extensive treatment of the bold social inversion that makes slaves confident bosses, and masters either meek and stupid 'yes-men' or dour and equally stupid dupes – types, that is, from the popular native farce as we understand it.[40] It is one remarkable fact that intrigues were apparently few in Greek New Comedy and almost non-existent in Menander; and a second, even more remarkable, that, though male slaves were often treated with sympathy and respect on the Athenian stage, they seem seldom, if ever, to have given their names to plays and *never* to have been leading characters.[41] Indispensable they no doubt were, and frequently they must have solved their young masters' problems; yet no evidence suggests that the Greeks enjoyed or knew the likes of Tranio, who manipulates every other character and even (as we shall see below) the flexible imaginary space of Plautus' *Mostellaria*; of Palaestrio, who imperiously leads his 'troops' to glorious victory over the *Miles Gloriosus*; of Chrysalus, the 'double deceiver'-plus-one who controls information, persons, and action in the *Bacchides* (see n. 42 below); or of Pseudolus, arguably Plautus' greatest creation, who brings off a unique intrigue that ensnares three super-cautious adversaries: a soldier's lieutenant and (both of them forewarned that Pseudolus will trick them this day) his old master Simo and the arch-pimp Ballio; of Pseudolus, who is the subject of the farcical 'recognition scene' that may be Plautus' most hilarious pages (Ballio recognizes him by means of his clownish big feet); of Pseudolus, who commands old Simo to join him and *not* the *spectatores* for a deep drink at the end of what is truly *his* play.[42] Other plays, too, depend for much or almost all of their liveliest humor upon slave characters. To the largely serious *Rudens* a pair of male slaves, the fisherman Gripus and the protagonist-lover's attendant Trachalio, contribute two very funny scenes in act IV: a megalomaniac song by Gripus who has hauled in a flotsam chest, which he believes to contain wealth enough for him to found a city Gripopolis; and a long and ridiculous argument between the two slaves over possession of the same trunk where with the rope of the play's title they engage in a tug-of-war, and where Trachalio behaves inconsistently with his character in the rest of the play (and presumably throughout the Greek model by Diphilus); while two slave types, Sosia and his divine counterpart and impersonator Mercury, contribute virtually all the laughable lines and actions to the tragicomic or melodramatic *Amphitruo*.[43] Slaves, therefore, like other Plautine characters but even more so, detract from the seriousness and the very plausibility of the several plays' action, an action that these exaggerated clowns influence or, often, quite control, even as they contribute to the familiar and farcical tone and antics that Plautus' contemporary and posthumous audiences sought from Roman *ludi*.

The third front of Plautine attack on his Greek models, what I call 'humorishness', could take a dissertation to demonstrate.[44] With carefully selected examples, however, it is possible in a couple of pages to demonstrate how for the warm humor and the natural, lively, and often witty diction of Menander Plautus substituted slapstick and scurrility, sub-comical word-play and verbal violence.

There is not a single play in which we do not find actual or at least threatened violence of a sort we believe to be alien to all or most of New Comedy.[45] Gratuitous Plautine additions to two largely serious plays, *Rudens* and *Amphitruo*, most probably include in the former the long arrest scene where the pimp Labrax is threatened, taunted, and beaten (expanded, certainly, from whatever slapstick Diphilus used) and in the latter (a) a beating that Mercury, disguised as Sosia, gives the real Sosia and (b) in a fragmentary section the dousing by Mercury, still in disguise, of Sosia's master Amphitruo with a potful of fluid from the roof of Amphitruo's house. Equally highbrow and equally likely to be Plautus' *addition* to a play from which he subtracted so much, the *Casina*, is that scene where two slaves, Olympio and Chalinus, punch each other under the instructions respectively of Mr and Mrs Lysidamus. Furthermore, it is hard to believe that in *Menaechmi* act v the Italian playwright has not elaborated, if he has not indeed added, the near-violence between Syracusan Menaechmus and Epidamnian Menaechmus' father-in-law, the real violence of the local Menaechmus, aided by his unknown brother's slave Messenio, against the father-in-law's slaves; or that the beating and threat of castration given to the *Miles Gloriosus* at the end of his play is Hellenic. These few instances of gleeful and/or malicious violence – or even of, alas, Roman *cruelty* – will suffice, though examples could be multiplied from every surviving play of Plautus.[46]

Scurrility in the sense of violent insult, with or without a sexual content, is likewise pervasive in Plautus. It especially affects those sorts of roles which we have seen our author to have hyperbolized: pimps, prostitutes, soldiers, *et al.*, and, above all, slaves. A particularly memorable example is in the first act of *Pseudolus* where Pseudolus and his young master call Ballio every bad name in the book – and several others that occur nowhere else in Latin – all to his own shameless delight (lines 360–9); others are in the exchanges of taunts, each anticipating the other's sufferings, between the slaves Grumio and Tranio at the very beginning of *Mostellaria* (lines 1–73) and Olympio's anticipation of the physical and emotional pain he will inflict upon his fellow slave Chalinus in *Casina* (lines 117–40). Predictably dialogue between or with slaves is in general very rich (if 'rich' is the right word) in such untasteful Plautinity, as, for example, during several scenes of *Miles Gloriosus* and part of the Gripus–Trachalio sequence in *Rudens*.[47] Masters in particular, especially the old ones, are ever ready to threaten their slaves, even the most cunning and confident ones, with horrible tortures that would surely have revolted a Greek audience *and to taunt them for their impotence to resist.*[48] One might also cite the punishments with which Ballio threatens his girls.[49]

On the subject of word-play it must be granted that the greatest masters of comedy have never been immune to the temptations of punning and other figures of sound with or against sense.[50] Nevertheless, some such abuse of language is at best 'sub-comic', perhaps not so bad as to call for a groan, yet not good enough as wit or humor to allow a sensible person more than the most fleeting smile. Alliteration such as *mali, maeroris montem maxumum ad portum modo conspicatus sum* (*Mostellaria* 352–3) or etymological jumble like *memorem inmemorem facit qui monet quod memor meminit* (*Pseudolus* 940), though they are extreme examples, show what Plautus was capable of, even incongruously through the mouths of relatively dignified characters like the honorable old exile Daemones in *Rudens*, like Amphitruo and even the great god Jupiter in the one mythological play, like the household god who delivers the prologue of *Aulularia*, or like the divine star Arcturus who speaks that of *Rudens*.[51]

Punning is, of course, harder to demonstrate for general readers; yet two striking occurrences will give a correct impression. Each constitutes a sort of triple reference that is surely Plautus' own perverse ingenuity at play. The slave protagonist Tranio in *Mostellaria* says that he will 'make games' for the old man Theopropides, what *won't* happen when he is dead.[52] *Ludos facere* here can refer to *funeral* 'games', but also to trickery, for the same phrase can be translated 'to make sport or fun' – what Tranio certainly has done and will continue to do to his master. But there is a third possible understanding as well. The slave stage-manager of this plot-mangled farce *also* refers to the 'play' he will 'make' over the next several hundred verses.[53] Even less subtle but quite as complicated is a long sequence of puns on the word *testis* and several cognates thereof near the end of *Miles Gloriosus*.[54] The soldier Pyrgopolynices is threatened with loss of *testes* – that is, with castration. But there are legal meanings as well, related respectively to our own words 'testament' and 'testimony', that make it necessary to translate words in this passage like *intestatus* and *intestabilis* two or three times into English – 'castrated' but also 'dead without a will', 'castrated' but also 'legally disqualified to bear witness', 'castrated' but also 'without witnesses to an injury'. After the Greek this is not, high comedy this is not; but it *is* indecently funny in the Roman way and quite typical of Plautus.

Likewise typically Plautine are assorted ludicrous word formations such as unique denominative verbs, absurd diminutives and superlatives, and compound words, many of them Greco-Latin bastards. These have been admirably exemplified elsewhere.[55] It is, however, appropriate to cite, again as an extreme yet characteristic example, the remarkable, supposedly Persian name that the disguised slave Sagaristio assumes for the intrigue that gives the little known play *Persa* its title: Vaniloquides, Virginesue-donides, Nugiepiloquides, Argentumextenebronides, Tedigniloquides, Nugides, Palponides, Quodsemelarripides, Numquameripides. The compound names parody, of course, the Grecian forms of tragic and (often) of comic names in Greek drama, yet all the elements before the '-ides' suffixes save one (i.e. '-epi-' in the third part) are telling *Latin*.[56]

Fourth and finally we come to Plautus' innovations concerning the theatre – or, rather, the *non*-theatre – for which his *fabulae palliatae* were designed, what I call disillusionism.

When we teach, read, or even just think about Plautine comedy what do

we visualize? Before 55 BC the actors' companies who played the dramas
both tragic and comic at Rome had to use temporary stages and perhaps
only the most minimal indications of an architectural backscene (see n. 18).
Taking just one play for example (though any of several others would do
almost as well) let me attempt to show just *how* minimal the set can have
been.

The *Mostellaria* is a work of uncertain date that was quite possibly
produced not at the state games but at someone's funeral and so lacked the
resources of the aediles' or the censors' 'budget', and that will therefore
show the ingenuity by which the playwright seems to have turned this
disadvantage into a resource for his comedy.

The norm for Plautus' set seems to have been a façade for one, two, or
occasionally three houses or other interiors. Internal evidence suggests that
sometimes the same sets were used for successive plays, and that the stage
building, though temporary, was on some occasions quite sturdy. The
Prologue of *Menaechmi* tells us that 'While this play goes on this city is
Epidamnus; when another one is acted it will become another town; even as
the households regularly change – now a pimp lives here, now a young man,
now an old one, poor, penniless, or a king, a parasite, a priest.'[57] In
Amphitruo we find a scene (lines 1021ff) where Mercury, disguised as
Amphitryon's slave Sosia, taunts and (evidently) douses the frustrated hero
from the roof of his own house – which must therefore have been a
substantial structure.[58] In several plays really violent banging on doors,
moreover, suggests that those doors and their door-frames were reasonably
solid.[59] Though *Mostellaria does* contain two 'knocking scenes', things are so
unusual in this play that we should probably understand them very
differently than elsewhere. I would argue, in fact, that there is a nice joke in
Theopropides' impatient question at *Mostellario*. 462: 'How could I knock if
I didn't touch [the doors]', because, as I imagine this scene and this
extraordinary play to have been staged, there was no house, there was no
door to touch![60] Likewise at line 988 we may find special humor in the
remark of one slave to another who has been banging on the 'doors': 'Why
knock on those doors where there is no one inside?'[61] Invisible house,
invisible doors, and rather obvious emptiness 'inside' them would have
given the audience an extra laugh – with Plautus himself – at the convention
of imagination he can have used in this play.

As mentioned above, there are hints that *Mostellaria* was performed at
some funeral games. These are a pair of jokes at the expense of
Theopropides, the owner of the supposedly haunted house. At lines 427–9
the slave Tranio says to himself (and the audience) just after his old
master's exit: 'Today I shall stage games here for an old man still alive and
among us – what I don't imagine he'll get when dead.'[62] Perhaps we have
here only an allusion to the custom of having drama among other public

entertainments to mark the passing of the great. But the joke gets much more point if it is topical – if, that is, the funeral of Roman So-and-so celebrated by this comedy becomes the 'funeral' of Theopropides, who will be 'killed' by eventual discovery of what has happened to him and his household. In any case a second joke picks up the 'funeral-of-Theopropides' theme, during conversation between him and his neighbor Simo. Asked if anything was happening downtown, in the forum, Simo replies that in fact something was, saying 'I saw a man's funeral.' Theopropides groans. Simo repeats and elaborates, with sarcastic reference to Theopropides, who has just begun to understand the tricks Tranio has been playing on him: 'I saw a man recently dead carried out for burial; only a short while ago, they said, he was still alive.' Theopropides' angry response shows that he gets the point: 'Go to hell!'[63] There is, it appears, further point for *us*. We should connect this with the earlier remark of Tranio already quoted. Moreover, if my thesis is correct that *Mostellaria* was acted as part of a funeral celebration, we find here a clever allusion to the occasion of the performance, and possibly even an indication of where this minimal play was performed; for the best guess about where *ludi funebres* were conducted, plays and all, is *the forum*. Certainly the hypothesis that this play was part of a private festival and not a state one would open for us the possibility of its having been done 'on a shoestring', with minimal if any architectural set, with no fancy costumes or expensive props. For the *state* festivals funds for materials and carpentry were evidently available from the censors or out of the pockets of wealthy and ambitious holders of the aedileship or praetorship.[64] Not every mourner who held funeral games, however, can have had the means of a Scipio Aemilianus, for the funeral of whose natural father Aemilius Paulus two plays of Terence were performed that clearly require a scene-building, or the loot of a Mummius, who, for his triumphal celebrations in 145 BC, had a wooden theatre built.[65] Some bereaved families, noble but honorably land-poor, must have had to do with as little as I suppose Plautus used so shrewdly in his adaptation of (probably) Philemon's *Phasma*, 'The Ghost'.

Although many of its characters and events will already be familiar, a summary of the play's action will help to make the issues clearer. It opens with two slaves arguing over what has happened to the household of Theopropides during his absence abroad. One of them, Tranio, the play's star, as we have seen above, emerges from whatever house of Theopropides there is and is ever after inextricably associated with it. Philolaches, the master's son, has run up enormous debts to support lavish partying but also to purchase his girlfriend Philematium. We meet him, her, and some rowdy friends of theirs in the next scenes. There will be hell to pay if and when old Theopropides ever returns, which, of course, he does, even before his son's present 'symposium' ends. He must be kept away and in the dark about

Philolaches' misbehavior as long as possible. Tranio puts him off by a brilliantly improvised story about a haunting of the house, whose very doors, he says, it is dangerous to touch. Theopropides exits in frightened consternation. When he returns a bit later Tranio has yet another problem: the usurer Misargyrides arrives at almost the same moment, to demand payment on the wayward son's debts. Tranio improvises again: Philolaches, he explains to the *very* inquisitive old man, has had to borrow money to make the down payment on an underpriced house he had the opportunity to buy to replace the haunted one. Which house?, Theopropides reasonably demands. The neighbor Simo's, Tranio says, since he must say something. That is fine with Theopropides: his son got a bargain at the price Tranio mentions. The old man will be happy to pay his son's debt. When he wants to see 'his' new house, however, he is at first delayed; then, after Simo is given the story that Theopropides wants to get some ideas for improvement of his own house from a look into Simo's *and* after Theopropides is warned not to say anything about the 'sale' of the house (to which Simo is still supposed to be sentimentally attached), Tranio gives his old master a guided tour of 'their' new home. Eventually, of course, the game is up. Theopropides learns what has really been going on and reacts with appropriate rage. (It is at this point that Simo taunts him about his 'funeral'.) Tranio barely escapes to an altar for asylum and is saved, barely and just for this day, by Callidamates, sober now and (however implausibly) willing to pay in full for his friend's misbehavior. This unusual play, its plot radically mutilated as we saw above (pp. 6of), is not about a love affair, really. Rather it is about the comical ingenuity and boldness of Tranio's 'tale of two houses' – and, I believe, also about the *theatrical* ingenuity and boldness of Plautus and his cast.

The open-minded reader will find five features of the *Mostellaria* (a couple of them already mentioned in other connections), which make better sense as comic theatre if we suppose that Plautus staged it in an open area with a number of movable props and, at most, open door-frames than if we assume Greek-style architectural scenery: a monologue by the young man Philolaches, a dressing scene on stage, a drinking party on stage, a sequence of unusual, and unusually many, stage silences, and description of a house that cannot be the scene-building in Plautus' theatre.

(1) *Philolaches' monologue comparing a person's upbringing with the building of a house* (lines 91–148). This memorable extended comparison – fifty-eight lines in length not counting later allusion to it – uses tectonic detail and describes events befalling the house that (a) could not possibly have been realized on the simple, temporary scene-building of Plautus' time, but that (b) might be nicely indicated by broad gesture against empty space. (It is worth noting that Philolaches' entire speech, lines 84–156, uses *lyric* meter and was not only sung but probably danced as well.) Moreover, if

Philolaches does indeed 'build' a house of air the business is wholly appropriate to his morally unsubstantial character (*nihili sum*, 'I'm worthless', is his own admission at line 156).

(2) *Philematium's toilette* (lines 157–292). Not only is this amusing scene between Philolaches' girl and her cynical maid Scapha unnaturally set out of doors but an essential part of the fun is the commentary by Philolaches in the longest eavesdropping sequence in all Roman comedy (136 lines). Two premises of this scene, namely that an intimate conversation between the two women could take place in our sight and hearing, and that Philolaches can hear *and see* them unnoticed for so long are wholly implausible if they speak within an approximation of real space, viz., before visible housefronts. If, on the other hand, there are no walls, no illusion of a true inside and outside, the scene plays more easily, as does the next –

(3) *The drinking party* (lines 151–386 or so). This rowdy scene, in which Philolaches and Philematium are joined by their drunken friend Callidamates and his girl Delphium, is likewise easier to take if we ignore for a while any difference between inside and outside. Several mentions of *reclining* suggest that couches were suddenly produced and we must imagine the action to take place in a triclinium or some such *interior* room.[66] This impression, though, is not allowed to remain at the end of the scene, where we find explicit direction to Philolaches and his friends to go inside and remove 'this stuff'.[67] The conventional understanding of the sequence has it that all this is a rather awkward effort to bring an inside scene onto the stage and then move it back where it 'really' belongs. My proposed understanding removes the awkwardness and finds in this scene an amusing play with empty and thereby perfectly flexible space.

(4) *Stage silences in act III*. At the beginning of act III, there enter in quick succession the moneylender Misargyrides (line 532) and (at 541) Theopropides, presumably from opposite sides of the playing area. Despite the fact that both are headed for Theopropides' house Tranio is able to keep them apart for about sixty-eight lines – that is, for a matter of several minutes' real time. Later, in the second scene of this same act, Tranio manages to keep the old men Theopropides (who has remained on stage) and Simo (who enters at line 686) away from one another for about 118 lines! He does this, moreover, even though Theopropides wishes to see Simo's house and Simo emerges from it. These events, which allow one character to be ignored for such long stretches while Tranio is busy flattering and misinforming *another* character, are simply implausible if we are to suppose them as taking place in anything like real space.[68] My solution to the implausibility is to posit an open, unreal and thereby utterly *fluid* space in which a character *like an entire house* can pass into and out of our awareness as audience.

(5) *The description of Simo's house* (lines 817–42). At the end of act III

Theopropides wishes to inspect the house of Simo, because he believes his
son has purchased it. Simo invites him to have a look: 'He [Tranio] told me
you want to see inside this house.' Says Theopropides, 'Only if it's all right
with you.' Simo answers, 'But it's fine with me; go inside and have a look.'[69]
Almost needless to say, Theopropides does no such thing. Rather, after
some further assurance that it *is* all right with Simo and asides to and from
Tranio on Simo's supposed sadness over the sale of the house, he is given a
sort of 'standing tour' of the place while remaining on stage. Tranio points
out first 'this porch and covered walk at the house's front' – which, of
course, was hardly visible to the audience even if I am utterly wrong about
the staging and there *was* a scene-building. Then he invites his master to
admire 'the door-posts, how solid and thick they are.' Theopropides says
that he has never seen any more beautiful. He does, however, find fault with
the expensive doors, eaten at the bottom by woodworm.[70] Next Tranio calls
his master's attention to *coagmenta in foribus*, which is probably best taken as
the tight fit between the double doors. Finally, he points out what he
describes as 'a painting in which a crow makes fun of two vultures'. This
Theopropides cannot see – because, of course, Tranio is the crow and the
two *senes* are the vultures, as the slave's bold irony makes clear. He says,
'Look this way toward me to see the crow.' And later, 'Then look in your
own direction, since you can't see the crow, if maybe you can spot the
vultures.'[71] After more fooling and after Theopropides refuses a guide from
Simo's household, Tranio is about to escort him 'inside' when there is some
further business about a bitch in the doorway. This, too, like the birds and,
I maintain, like the whole house, is invisible and yet thematically telling.
Tranio is the one who notices it and at first cautions Theopropides to hold
back. When, however, Simo assures them that the dog is gentle *and mentions
that he is going to the forum now* Tranio repeats the assurance and tells his
master that it is all right to go in. He declares, 'Why look at her, how
peacefully she lies there.' Tranio has, it appears, been afraid that Simo, the
brighter of the two old men, might 'smell out' his trickery; but the dog
without her master will, of course, smell out nothing. She can be disregarded – returned, that is, to the nothing which (for the audience) she really
is. Throughout this amusing and unusual scene, therefore, Plautus, Tranio,
and the audience have enjoyed a nice little game with the two old men and
with the empty stage, on which an elaborate house, a painting, a living dog
can be created or annihilated at the slave protagonist's word. Played with a
full architectural backing this scene would be both less humorous and less
in keeping with other unusual features of the play. It would be less
humorous, for example, in the business about woodworm damage; for it is
much funnier to complain about a slight defect in an invisible something
which is *entirely* missing than in a real, solid object. It would be less in
keeping with the rest of the play because we have seen already repeatedly

that this comedy and its leading character Tranio boldly manipulate space in ways that suggest little or no house scenery.

Before we leave this play I must explain what I think happened in those two knocking sequences of *Mostellaria* mentioned earlier, at lines 445 and 898–901. One can make an amusing racket by pounding on a real door, of course. This was done – perhaps overdone – elsewhere in Roman comedy (see note 59 above). It is also possible, on the other hand, to make an even more amusing scene by knocking in thin air with a cue to someone else to bang wooden boards, blocks or the like in a prearranged rhythm. Such business would only be right for so playfully anticonventional, so farcical, so *Roman* a piece as the 'Ghost Comedy' of Plautus.

For a brief conclusion to a long paper, let me paraphrase and, I hope in Plautine metaphors, expand upon the notions of the super-slave Pseudolus when he describes what a poet does and what *he* is doing in improvising a plot for the farce named after him. Where there had been 'nothing' (or at most some negligible, entirely too orderly and serious matter, and that with a distracting plot) Plautus fashioned something truly funny and brought it to life; where there had been careful, illusionistic stage business for a theatre with sturdy and permanent architectural set, he cut out all or much of that business and patched on hilarious mimicry; where there had been only venerable, subtle, and humane *Greek comedy*, Plautus, magician-like, chopped it up, waved his Latin hand, and brought forth *Roman farce*.[72]

NOTES

An earlier form of the discussion of *Mostellaria* was presented at the meeting of the Rocky Mountain Modern Language Association in El Paso, Texas, in October 1984.

1 I am indebted most to the following studies of Plautus and later Classical comedy: W. G. Arnott, *Menander, Plautus, Terence* (Oxford University Press, 1975); G. E. Duckworth, *The Nature of Roman Comedy* (Princeton University Press, 1952); A. S. Gratwick, 'Drama' in E. J. Kenney (ed.), *Cambridge History of Classical Literature*, vol. 1: *Latin Literature* (Cambridge University Press, 1982); E. W. Handley, 'Comedy' in P. E. Easterling and B. M. W. Knox (eds.), *Cambridge History of Classical Literature*, vol. 11: *Greek Literature* (Cambridge University Press, 1985); R. L. Hunter, *The New Comedy of Greece and Rome* (Cambridge University Press, 1985); A. Lesky, *A History of Greek Literature*, 2nd edition, trans. J. Willis and C. de Heer (London and New York: Crowell, 1966); F. H. Sandbach, *The Comic Theatre of Greece and Rome* (New York: Norton, 1977); E. Segal, *Roman Laughter: The Comedy of Plautus* (Cambridge, Mass.: Harvard University Press, 1968); N. W. Slater, *Plautus in Performance: The Theatre of the Mind* (Princeton University Press, 1985); and T. B. L. Webster, *An Introduction to Menander* (Manchester and New York: Manchester University Press, 1974) and *Studies in Later Greek Comedy*, 2nd edition (Manchester and New York: Manchester University Press, 1970).

All quotations and other references from/to the works of Plautus follow the text (including the orthography) of W. M. Lindsay (ed.), *T. Macci Plauti Comoediae*, vols. I and II (Oxford University Press, 1904–5).

2 On the origins and history of earlier Attic comedy see F. M. Cornford, *The Origin of Attic Comedy*, ed. T. H. Gaster (Gloucester, Mass.: Peter Smith, 1968), which must be used with some caution, and, less speculative, A. W. Pickard-Cambridge, *Dithyramb, Tragedy, and Comedy*, 2nd edition, ed. T. B. L. Webster (Oxford University Press, 1962), pp. 132–62; as well as Handley, 'Comedy', pp. 355–98, and Lesky, *History*, pp. 233–7 and 417–45.

3 On the means and ends of Aristophanes and Old Comedy see G. Norwood, *Greek Comedy* (1931; repr. New York: Hill and Wang, 1963), pp. 114–201 (other authors) and 202–312 (Aristophanes); K. J. Dover, *Aristophanic Comedy* (Berkeley and Los Angeles: University of California Press, 1972), especially pp. 49–53 and 210–18; Lesky, *History*, pp. 417–45 (the entire section being entitled 'Political Comedy'); and Handley, 'Comedy', especially pp. 444–9 (also on 'Political Comedy', although he treats Old Comedy under other headings as well – fantastic, intellectual, and social). K. McLeish, *The Theatre of Aristophanes* (New York: Taplinger, 1980), pp. 15–17, offers a nice distinction between 'farce' as a separate genre and the undeniably farcical *aspect* of much of the playwright's action.

4 For recent discussions of what is known and what may be reasonably supposed about Middle Comedy see Lesky, *History*, pp. 633–7; Webster, *Studies*, pp. 10–97 (sometimes speculating further than evidence or irresistible argument permits); Handley, 'Comedy', pp. 398–414; and S. Goldberg, *The Making of Menander's Comedy* (Berkeley and Los Angeles: University of California Press, 1980), pp. 1–12.

5 See Webster, *Studies*, pp. 74–82 (*Persa*) and 86–97 (*Amphitruo*), dating both to late within the Middle Comedy period as he defines it. He also proposes (pp. 67–74) a Middle Comedy date for the model of the *Menaechmi*, I think on much less convincing grounds. (Slater, *Plautus in Performance*, p. 46 n. with bibliography, rejects also the early dating of the *Persa* on the controversial historical? fantastic? reference to an expedition of Persians into Arabia, lines 498–507 of the play; while Lesky, *History*, p. 634, casts doubts on all three of Webster's 'Middle Comedy' models.)

6 Certainly modeled – however freely – after Philemon were Plautus' *Mercator* and *Trinummus*, probably also the much better *Mostellaria*; after Diphilus the *Casina* and *Rudens*. Other ingenious ascriptions have been made by various scholars who have not, however, persuaded others; see, for example, Webster, *Studies*, pp. 173–83, arguing less than compellingly that the model for *Miles Gloriosus* was Diphilan.

7 Terence used plays by Menander as models for his *Andria*, *Heautontimorumenos*, *Eunuchus*, and *Adelphoe*. Plautus himself adapted Menandrian originals at least for his *Bacchides*, *Cistellaria*, and *Stichus*, and possibly for one or two more. See Duckworth, *Roman Comedy*, pp. 52–4. Webster, *Studies*, pp. 210–44, maintains that *Pseudolus* (very unlikely, I think) and *Curculio* (much likelier though hardly certain) are also modeled after Menandrian 'originals'; and in *An Introduction to Menander*, pp. 119–122, proceeds on the assumption (which others continue to doubt) that Menander's *Apistos* (= 'The Distrustful Man') lies behind Plautus'

Aulularia. Contrast Arnott, *Menander, Plautus, Terence*, pp. 41 and 59 (n. 52), and Hunter, *New Comedy*, p. 62 and his earlier article 'The *Aulularia* of Plautus and its Greek original', *Proceedings of the Cambridge Philological Society*, NS 27 (1981), 37–49.

On Menander's perhaps uncharacteristic early play *Dyskolus*, see A. W. Gomme and F. H. Sandbach, *Menander: A Commentary* (Oxford University Press, 1973), pp. 126–7, for bibliography; the notable edition is E. W. Handley, *The Dyskolos of Menander* (Cambridge, Mass.: Harvard University Press, 1965).

8 On New Comedy see the two works mentioned by Webster; Lesky, *History*, pp. 642–64; Sandbach, *Comic Theatre*, pp. 55–75; and Handley, 'Comedy', pp. 414–25.

9 It is also worth noting that Apollodorus, a third-century comic poet regarded as a successful disciple of Menander, created especially interesting female characters in the models for Terence's *Hecyra* and *Phormio*.

10 One must compare the famous work of Menander's contemporary Theophrastus on typical, amusing yet humanly understandable 'Characters', which was almost certainly affected by characterization in New Comedy. To what extent, if any, it in turn influenced the playwrights is less certain; see, for example, Lesky, *History*, pp. 644–5 and 660, and Hunter, *New Comedy*, pp. 148–9.

11 *Poetics* 1456a, paraphrasing the tragic poet Agathon.

12 On *tyche* in the Hellenistic age see Lesky, *History*, pp. 659–61; Hunter, *New Comedy*, pp. 141–4; and Gomme and Sandbach, *Menander*, p. 74, with bibliography.

On the *gamos*/wedding as the characteristic ending of Attic comedy see especially Cornford, *Origin of Attic Comedy*, pp. 56–67.

13 Romans and/or other non-Hellenic Italians are *barbari* at several places in his plays; indeed Plautus translated his *Trinummus 'barbarice'*, 'into barbarian', according to line 19 of that play.

For the life and career of Plautus see Duckworth, *Roman Comedy*, pp. 49–51, and, still the most comprehensive treatment, F. Leo, *Plautinische Forschungen*, 2nd edition (1912; repr. Dublin and Zürich: Weidmann, 1973), pp. 63–86.

14 On the early history of Italian theatre see Duckworth, *Roman Comedy*, pp. 3–17; Gratwick, 'Drama', pp. 77–86 and 93–4; and W. Beare, *The Roman Stage*, 3rd edition (London and New York: Methuen, 1964), pp. 10–44.

15 The source is the writer A. Gellius (AD 2nd century) who presumably derived his information from the reliable first century BC scholar Varro; see Leo, *Plautinische Forschungen* pp. 74–7, and Duckworth, *Roman Comedy*, pp. 50–1.

16 On acting companies, whose colloquial name was *greges*, 'flocks', and their development in the Republic period see E. J. Jory, 'Associations of actors in Rome', *Hermes*, 98 (1970), 224–53, and N. M. Horsfall, 'The Collegium Poetarum', *Bulletin of the Institute of Classical Studies*, 23 (1976), 79–95. (I owe these references to Hunter, *New Comedy*, p. 156 n. 44.)

17 Beare, *Roman Stage*, pp. 142 and 151.

On Plautus' perhaps entirely facetious name see A. S. Gratwick, 'Titus Maccius Plautus', *Classical Quarterly*, NS 23 (1973), 78–94.

18 Cf. Sandbach, *Comic Theatre*, pp. 125–6; Hunter, *New Comedy*, pp. 55–57; and above all Gratwick, 'Drama', p. 96, on how Plautus 'subverts' the special features of his New Comedy models.

On the conditions of performance see Duckworth, *Roman Comedy*, pp. 73–94, and Beare, *Roman Stage*, pp. 159–95 and Appendices A, F and G; on the relative unsophistication of the Roman audience, Sandbach, *Comic Theatre*, pp. 118 and 121–6, and B.-A. Taladoire, *Essai sur le comique de Plaute* (Monaco: Editions de l'Impr. Nationale, 1956), pp. 9–34; also see, however, the rather more flattering picture in E. W. Handley, 'Plautus and his Public: Some Thoughts on New Comedy in Latin', *Dioniso*, 46 (1975), 117–32, which perhaps exaggerates the sophistication of the majority of the audience, at least during the first part of Plautus' career when plays were just beginning to be annual events at Rome, but which Slater (*Plautus in Performance*, pp. 7–8) accepts, adducing further the established theatrical traditions of Greek-speaking southern Italy.

19 Although Sandbach (*Comic Theatre*, p. 87) suggests that the *Stichus* may in fact resemble the Menandrian model more closely than has usually been claimed, most others have supposed that in this work 'Plautus all but discards the main action of the *Adelphoi*' (Gratwick, 'Drama', p. 98; cf. Duckworth, *Roman Comedy*, p. 146).

20 Note: Mother Eunomia and Uncle Megadorus at lines 120–76, the first forty lines or so lyrical and probably danced; Euclio in otiose or greatly padded scenes at lines 79–119 (mainly a harangue to a slave), 268–79, 371–97 (with a cook), 415–59 (with the same cook), 460–74 (monologue), 537–79 (with Megadorus on the imminent wedding feast – after Euclio has eavesdropped on M. for over sixty lines), 580–6 (monologue/prayer), 608–15 and 624–7 (monologues), 628–60 (with Lyconides' nosey slave), and 667–76 and 713–26 (monologues).

21 Lines 64–6:

> is . . . hodie in hac comoedia
> in urbem non redibit: Plautus noluit,
> pontem interrupit, qui erat in itinere.

On the prologue of this play *Casina* generally see W. T. MacCary and M. M. Willcock, *Plautus: Casina* (Cambridge University Press, 1976), p. 97, taking a conservative approach to the text and rejecting only lines 5–22 as post-Plautine. E. Paratore, *Plauto: Casina* (Florence: Sansoni, 1959), pp. 7–17, on the other hand, and J. Tatum, *Plautus: The Darker Comedies* (Baltimore and London: Johns Hopkins University Press, 1983), pp. 141–2, reject more of the prologue – and Slater (*Plautus in Performance*, pp. 70–4 and 149) rejects most of it, suggesting that even the whole of it may come from a posthumous revival. Whether Plautus or a later writer is responsible for our information about the playwright's disregard for the integrity of Diphilus' plot, it *is* information. On the mutilation of that plot see Slater, *Plautus in Performance*, p. 72.

22 For the date of the play and of Plautus' death see MacCary and Willcock, *Plautus: Casina*, p. 11, with discussion and bibliography on the playwright's late style.

23 Terence *Andria* 16 and *Heautontimorumenos* 17. For a thorough discussion of '*contaminatio*' see Duckworth, *Roman Comedy*, pp. 202–8, with bibliographic notes, and, more recently, Arnott, *Menander, Plautus, Terence*, pp. 37–8 and 48–50, with later bibliography in his notes.

24 I am aware, however, of the skepticism of Anglo-American scholars about the old theory of separate sources for this play's two sequential plots; see, for example, Duckworth, *Roman Comedy*, p. 206 with bibliography; Webster, *Studies*, p. 174 with further bibliography; Gratwick, 'Drama', p. 98; and M. Hammond, A. Mack and W. Moskalew, *Plautus: Miles Gloriosus*, 2nd edition, revised (Cam-

bridge, Mass.: Harvard University Press, 1970), pp. 25–6. Though the two-model theorists may have exaggerated the proofs of their case, the otiose doubling of fictitious sister and fictitious mother as well as a number of slighter, more technical matters suggest that Leo (*Plautinische Forschungen*, pp. 178–85) and G. Jachmann, *Plautinisches und Attisches* (Berlin: Weidmann, 1931), pp. 162–94, are correct, basically if not in every detail, about Plautus' ingenious yet awkward combination of two distinct plots (with likely extraneous matter, either from a *third* model or of his own invention, for act III, scene ii). See a thorough and unrefuted restatement of the 'contamination' theory by E. Paratore, *Plauto: Miles Gloriosus* (Florence, Sansoni, 1959), pp. 13–43.

25 See Gratwick, 'Drama', p. 113.

26 It is incredible that Leo, '*Plautinische Forschungen*', p. 167, counted *Mostellaria* among those best of Plautus' comedies where the Roman left alone 'deren Form, wie sie dem Geiste des [griechischen] Meisters entstiegen war, und denen er nur in der Ausführung von Spiel und Rede die bunten Züge seines zwischen griechisch und römisch schillernden Stiles aufgeprägt hat'!

That the character Callidamates may be Plautus' invention two things suggest. For one, his *amicus ex machina* appearance at the very end of the play violates the sort of probability we see in the dénouement of the other Philemonian plays *Mercator* and *Trinummus*; and, in fact, Callidamates does not really play the same sort of 'helpful friend' whom Webster, *Studies*, pp. 133–42, sees also in Eutychus and Lysiteles in those others. Secondly, Callidamates' and a speaking flute girl's presence in the carousal scene require a fourth and a fifth actor – which seems unlikely for a Greek model from the third century, whether or not its author was Philemon, as Webster, *Studies*, pp. 133–42, argues and Lesky (*History*, p. 662) and Hunter (*New Comedy*, p. 4 and p. 153 n. 10) allow to be probable.

On the likely limitation of three actors for all roles in Greek comedy in the age of Menander see Lesky, *History*, p. 658; Gomme and Sandbach, *Menander*, pp. 16–19; and Sandbach, *Comic Theatre*, pp. 79–80. As for the latter's concession that 'there are two or three Latin plays, adapted from Diphilus and Apollodorus, in which no simple change suffices [to leave intact the three-actor principle]' (p. 80), two things may be said. The plays modeled after Diphilus (Plautus' *Casina* and *Rudens*) have either *characters* that may be added by the Roman adapter (Ampelisca and Charmides in the latter play) or one or more scenes where Plautus quite surely 'padded' the original with slapstick (e.g., that scene in *Casina* where the two slaves punch each other, a scene so striking that it gave the Greek play its title, *Kleroumenoi*, 'Lot-Casters', yet one where it was hardly necessary that all four participants have speaking parts); while in Apollodorus we have a third-century writer, for whom quite conceivably the three-actor limit may no longer have obtained.

27 On the festival spirit of Plautine comedy see above all Segal, *Roman Laughter*, pp. 8–14.

28 On Plautus' hunt for lusty old men to imitate from New Comedy see MacCary and Willcock, *Plautus: Casina*, pp. 20–1; and on Plautus' violence to the plot and tone of Diphilus' *Kleroumenoi*, pp. 16–17; see also Paratore, *Casina*, pp. 17–47, and Taum, *Plautus*, pp. 86–7.

29 There are New Comedy precedents for this type, of course, in the reasonable,

generous father Kallippides of Menander's *Grouch*; and in Chremes and Micio of,
respectively, Terence's Menandrian adaptations *Heautontimorumenos* and *Adelphoe*; yet these are easy-going, not irresponsible men, do have and maintain
serious moral concerns – and receive in each case a 'comeuppance' that befits
their smugness about liberal attitudes.

30 The former is a play that modern critics like a lot more than the old Romans seem
to have done, for neither its text nor its leading characters are referred to in the
late Republic or Empire nor is there any indication of posthumous revival as, for
example, of the *Casina* in the generation after the playwright's death, of other
plays at unascertainable times, and of the *Pseudolus* in Cicero's day; while the
latter is so unfunny a comedy that Plautus apologizes for it in his prologue at
Capt. 55–62 and in his epilogue at lines 1029–34. (Most readers will, I believe,
find Hunter's statement about the 'comedy and farce which predominate in this
play', *New Comedy*, p. 117, wholly unconvincing.)

31 See above p. 58 and the discussion of how Lyconides' role has been otherwise
greatly reduced in scale and seriousness.

32 I must, of course, concede that the Greeks did the same sort of thing, with
misogyny a common theme in Comedy Old and New alike. Frequently, however,
misogynist characters in the later comedy, at least, were shown to be wrong; see
Hunter, *New Comedy*, pp. 83–95, with bibliographical references, for a careful
discussion.

33 For examples: the slave Sosia on Alcumena at *Amphitruo* 667 and 718–28 and the
parasite Peniculus on the Epidamnian Menaechmus' wife at *Menaechmi* 67–8 and
569.

34 Ampelisca contributes nothing to the plot of the play that Palaestra could not as
easily do and makes an awkward – for Diphilus probably impossible – extra
character on stage in act III, scene iv (where Trachalio, too, is dispensable: a
reasonable reconstruction would limit the scene to Palaestra, Daemones, and
Labrax). Plautus must have added, or if not added developed, Ampelisca for
dialogue with other slaves, that is with her old friend Tranio and with Daemones'
lusty man Sceparnio.

35 See Duckworth, *Roman Comedy*, pp. 258–61, on prostitutes/courtesans in Plautus
and in Terence; and Sandbach, *Comic Theatre*, p. 83, on the diversity of these
characters in Menander.

36 We know most perhaps about cooks and soldiers; see Goldberg, *Menander's
Comedy*, passim, esp. pp. 13–28, on cooks; and on soldiers Webster, *Studies*,
passim, and Sandbach, *Comic Theatre*, pp. 82–3.

37 In fact, it is just possible that Plautus added another otiose character to *Rudens*,
the reprobate old man Charmides, for the sole purpose of expanding the part and
highlighting the nastiness of Labrax. If we again apply the three-actor rule (see
n. 26) we find it awkward or impossible to reconstruct a Diphilan model that
includes him – and he is even less consequential for the plot than Ampelisca,
whom I have above argued to be wholly Plautine.

38 It may also be that older western Greek genres, for example, the social comedy of
Epicharmus and Sophron of Syracuse (early and late fifth century, respectively),
influenced the 'barbarians' of Italy in this respect; see Duckworth, *Roman Comedy*,
pp. 18–20; Pickard-Cambridge, *Dithyramb, Tragedy and Comedy*, pp. 276–88;
Lesky, *History*, pp. 237–40; and Handley, 'Comedy', pp. 367–70.

39 Not only was the dramatic role of Ballio still important in the latest Republic (Cicero's friend Roscius was famous for it) but the name 'Ballio' was proverbial; see Cicero, *Philippics* 2.15, in invective against Mark Antony's friends.

40 See Segal, *Roman Laughter*, pp. 99–169, especially. On Plautus' development of types from farce see especially Gratwick, 'Drama', pp. 104–10.

41 On the contrast between a Plautine 'clever' slave (he uses Palaestrio as an example) and the Menandrian counterpart, see Goldberg, *Menander's Comedy*, pp. 38–41. The one play of Menander that is entitled after a slave, not by name but by function, is *Dis Exapaton*, 'Double Deceiver' – in which, as Arnott has pointed out (*Menander, Plautus, Terence*, p. 38), Plautus has included *three* confidence tricks, and in which the Roman's slave-in-chief Chrysalus disparages unambitious slaves named Parmeno *or* Syrus in other comedies (*Bacchides* 649–50):

> non mihi isti placent Parmenones, Syri,
> qui duas aut tres minas auferunt eris.

In Menander's play 'Syrus' was the deceiving slave's name! (See Slater, *Plautus in Performance*, pp. 102–4), on what he aptly classifies as 'metatheatricality' on at least two levels in this and other passages of the Latin play.)

Of over 350 titles from New Comedy in J. M. Edmonds, *The Fragments of Attic Comedy* IIIB (Leiden: E. J. Brill, 1961), only one (Philemon's *Pyrrhos*, 'Red-Haired') is entitled with a slave's name that could certainly fit an intriguer; while a further two plays (by Philemon and by Menander) had the title *Thyroros*, 'Doorkeeper', which *could* refer to a clever slave (though it rather suggests a dull one like, for example, Sceledrus in Plautus' *Miles Gloriosus*). Another comedy, of unknown period and authorship, is known by a title, *Synexapaton*, 'Associate Deceiver', that probably better describes a free person who abets a young man's and/or a slave's deception than a mastermind-slave himself.

42 On the uniqueness of Pseudolus' 'metatheatrical' role see Slater, *Plautus in Performance*, pp. 118–46 (who verges upon taking the great clown too solemnly in his zealous support of an admirable book's thesis).

43 Earlier in his play Trachalio is consistently quite serious-minded, for example in his first scenes with the unusual chorus of fishermen and with the girl Ampelisca (lines 306–24 and 331–403) as well as in the intervening monologue, in his call for help against the scoundrel Labrax' violence (lines 615–26) and in the ensuing dialogue with the good Daemones (lines 627–60), in the scene with Ampelisca and his master's girlfriend Palaestra (lines 664–704, ending with a pretty prayer to Venus at lines 702–4), in the scene with Daemones and Labrax that follows (lines 706–79, though he does happily threaten Labrax with mayhem at lines 722f and reviles him heatedly, lines 747–51), and in the short exchange with his master Plesidippus before the latter takes on Labrax (lines 839–43).

Surely the funniest scene in *Amphitruo* is that between the mortal slave Sosia and the divine servant Mercury, beginning with asides by the god (lines 176–9 and 185) and, after Sosia's rehearsal of his battle report, proceeding into Sosia's sometimes violent, always confusing confrontation with (so far as he can tell) himself (lines 263–462). On Plautus' likely expansion of this sequence see E. Fraenkel, *Elementi plautini in Plauto* [Italian translation by F. Munari, with addenda, of the 1922 monograph *Plautinisches im Plautus*] (Florence: La Nuova Italia, 1960), pp. 172–5.

44 In fact, certain kinds of verbal and physical humor have long been used as criteria for determining 'the Plautine in Plautus', most notably and authoritatively by Fraenkel in the work cited in the preceding note; other important studies of Plautus' comic language include Duckworth, *Roman Comedy*, pp. 292–5 and 333–60, and recently, summarizing, Arnott, *Menander, Plautus, Terence*, pp. 34–5, and Gratwick, 'Drama', pp. 111–12.

45 There is, to be sure, threat and the beginning of violence in, for example, Menander's *Dyskolos* and the Menandrian *Eunuchus* of Terence; yet there it either characterizes (of Menander's 'grouchy' Knemon and of immature Chaerea and the bluffing soldier Thraso and his ruffian 'troops' in Terence's liveliest play) or contributes to gaiety (where at the end of Menander's play Knemon is forced to join in the general celebration). We also find violence, to a *leno*, in Terence's *Adelphoe*, in the scene that the playwright has 'contaminated' from Diphilus, who, if we may judge from scenes in the two plays of Plautus modeled after him, *Casina* and *Rudens*, was rather readier than Menander to display violent behavior, at least toward slaves and pimps. On the rough stage business – what Webster calls 'thug comedy' – in this author see, besides Webster, *Studies*, pp. 69 and 160, Jachmann, *Plautinisches und Attisches*, p. 121, and Lesky, *History*, p. 663.
   On the Plautine expansion here see Fraenkel, *Elementi plautini*, p. 290.

46 See Duckworth, *Roman Comedy*, p. 325, for a partial list.

47 Note *Miles Gloriosus* 276–585 centering on the stupid slave Sceledrus, esp. 294–8, 310f, 313–18, 341f, 368–74, 396f, 404, 445–6, 471, 475f, 497–513, and 545–8 and *Rudens* 1006–12, 1058f, 1070f, 1089, 1117f, 1125, 1162 perhaps, and 1189f.

48 Note, for examples, besides those from *Rudens* mentioned in the preceding note, Amphitruo's threats to Sosia at *Amphitruo* 556f (to cut out the slave's tongue) and 583f (general torment); at *Casina* good Cleustrata's threats to Olympio at 309 (he may be *baked*) and 337; the Syracusan Menaechmus' to Messenio at *Menaechmi* 249f (mild but ominous; cf. the slave's soliloquy at 970–9); Theopropides' to Tranio at *Mostellaria* 1064–7 (preparations for torture), 1114, 1133, 1167f, and 1174; and Simo's to Pseudolus at *Pseudolus* 447f, 494–503 and 533f (both referring to painful slaving in the *pistrinum*, the dreaded mill), and (Pseudolus' own proposal!) 513.
   On this brutality and the clever slave's remarkable immunity from it see Segal, *Roman Laughter*, pp. 138–62.

49 The curious may see *Pseudolus* 198–201, 212–17, and 228f for non-edification.

50 See, for example, G. L. Brook, *The Language of Shakespeare* (London: André Deutsch, 1976), pp. 172–6 on word-play, or B. I. Evans, *The Language of Shakespeare's Plays*, 3rd edition (London: Methuen, 1964), passim; and H. G. Hall, *Comedy in Context: Essays on Molière* (Jackson: University of Mississippi Press, 1984), pp. 77–100 with further references in his notes.

51 See *Rudens* 101f (Daemones):
> uillam integundam intellego totam mihi,
> nam nunc perlucet ea quam cribrum crebrius.

And *Amphitruo* 556f (Amphitruo):
> ego tibi istam scelestam, scelus, linguam apscidam;

and 546f (Jupiter):
> nunc te, nox, quae me mansisti, mitto ut concedas die,
> ut mortalis inlucescat luce clara et candida.

And *Aulularia* 18f (the Lar Familiaris):

> ille uero minu' minus impendio
> curare minu'que me impertire honoribus.

And, finally, *Rudens* 2 (Arcturus):

> sum ciuis ciuitatis caelitum.

52 *Mostellaria* 427–8:

> ludos ego hodie uiuo praesenti hic seni
> faciam, quod credo mortuo numquam fore.

53 There may even be a fourth reference here, to the fact that the *actor* playing Theopropides can, of course, expect no elaborate funeral games when *he* dies – a common sort of joking in Plautus about the actor's real status. (On actor-jokes and similar playfulness with theatrical convention in Plautus see Duckworth, *Roman Comedy*, pp. 132–6, esp. 135f.)

54 *Miles Gloriosus* 1414–17:

Pyrgopolynices.

> iuro per Iouem et Mauortem me nociturum nemini,
> quod ego hic hodie uapularim, iureque id facturum arbitror;
> et si intestatus non abeo hinc, bene agitur pro noxia.

Periplectomenus. quis si non faxis? *Py.* ut uiuam semper intestabilis.

Cario. uerberetur etiam, postibi admittendum censeo.

Py. di tibi bene faciant semper, quom aduocatus mihi bene's.

Ca. ergo des minam auri nobis. *Py.* quam ob rem? *Ca.* saluis testibus

> ut ted hodie hinc amittamus Venerium nepotulum.

And line 1426:

Pe. si posthac prehendero ego te hic, carebis testibus.

55 See Duckworth, *Roman Comedy*, pp. 345–50.

56 The name means 'Son-of-empty-speech, Son-of-seducer, Son-of-nonsense-speaker, Son-of-silver-from-the-darkness, Son-of-a-speaker-worthy-of-yourself, Son-of-nonsense, Son-of-coaxer, Son-of-what-once-seized, Son-of-never-returned'.

57 Lines 72–76:

> haec urbs Epidamnus est dum haec agitur fabula:
> quando alia agetur aliud fiet oppidum;
> sicut familiae quoque solent mutarier:
> modo hic habitat leno, modo adulescens, modo senex,
> pauper, mendicus, rex, parasitus, hariolus.

58 The text breaks off after line 1034; but from what Lindsay prints as fragments IV and V it is clear that Mercury is on the roof, above the door upon which Amphitruo knocks at line 1020.

59 In addition to the scene from the *Amphitruo* mentioned in the preceding note, see *Stichus* 308–13. A knocking scene that Duckworth singles out (*Roman Comedy*, p. 117), *Bacchides* 578–86, may, however, be another example of miming without a prop – as I must wait to argue elsewhere.

60 The Latin: 'quo modo pultare potui, si non tangerem?'

61 quid istas pultas ubi nemo intus est?

62 See above p. 67 and n. 52.

63 Lines 1000–2:

> *Simo.* uidi ecferri mortuom. *Theopropides.* hem!

Si. nouom unum uidi mortuom ecferri foras.
modo eum uixisse aiebant. *Th.* uae capiti tuo!

64 On the funding of the regular *ludi* see Beare, *Roman Stage*, pp. 162–70.

65 Terence's *Hecyra* (attempted for a second time) and *Adelphoe* were both performed at Scipio's funeral games for L. Aemilius Paulus in 160 BC. Both of these plays have important and natural use of the doors and doorways of *two* on-stage houses in each, though neither of them (or any other play of this author) includes a roof scene. On L. Mummius' scenic construction see Duckworth, *Roman Comedy*, p. 80 and note 20 there.

66 Reclining is mentioned in lines 326, 341, and 343, a dining couch at 327, getting up from one at 376.

67 Line 391: 'uos modo hinc abite intro atque haec hinc propere amolimini'.

68 It is this part of the play, in fact, that caused me my first doubts about its 'normal' staging.

69 Lines 806f:
Si. inspicere te aedis has uelle aiebat mihi.
Th. nisi tibi est incommodum. *Si.* immo commodum. i intro et inspice.

70 Lines 818–20, 824–5:
Tranio. age specta postis, quoiusmodi, quanta firmitate facti et quanta crassitudine.
Th. non uideor uidisse postis pulchriores . . .
Th. hercle qui multum improbiores sunt quam a primo credidi.
Tr. quapropter? *Th.* quia edepol ambo ab infumo tarmes secat.

71 Lines 832–5 and 837f:
Tr. uiden pictum, ubi ludificat una cornix uolturios duos?
Th. non edepol uideo. *Tr.* at ego uideo. nam inter uolturios duos
cornix astat, ea uolturios duo uicissim uellicat.
quaeso huc ad me specta, cornicem ut conspicere possis . . .
Tr. at tu isto ad uos optuere, quoniam cornicem nequis
conspicari, si uolturios forte possis contui.

72 After *Pseudolus* 401–5.

Racine's *Les Plaideurs* – a tragedian's farce*

MAYA SLATER

Les Plaideurs (1668) is Racine's only comedy, a full-length farce popular in his own lifetime,[1] though today it is largely neglected by critics and public alike. At best, the work is accorded a brief comment, and most critics are lukewarm in their appraisals. Nevertheless, the play is of interest. First, it gives a unique insight into the comic powers of a great writer of tragedy.[2] Furthermore, it is the only play we know that incorporates a subject drawn from Aristophanes into a seventeenth-century French context; and Racine's adaptation of a Greek farce illuminates his general approach to his source material.

Does *Les Plaideurs* reflect its author's tragic bent? Racine himself placed it in a separate category, referring to it as 'sketchy',[3] and calling his remarks to the reader an *avis au lecteur* rather than a *préface* (the name he gave to the comments he published with each of his tragedies). In the collected works of 1676 he placed it at the end of the volume, rather than in its proper chronological place (though this may simply be because as a genre farce was considered less worthy than tragedy). He says too that he wrote it reluctantly after coercion by his friends.

And yet, at the time he wrote this play, he was a successful man, well able to select his own topics rather than submitting to pressure from friends. Why did he not choose a tragic subject? he had just scored his first triumph with *Andromaque* the previous year, and could have been expected to try to repeat this success. It has been suggested[4] that he may have wanted to outdo Molière at his own speciality. There was considerable rivalry between Racine's company at the Hôtel de Bourgogne and Molière's troupe at the Palais-Royal (interestingly, Molière is said to have described *Les Plaideurs* as 'worthless').[5] How far, then, is Racine conscious of the properties of tragedy in writing *Les Plaideurs*? To consider this farce as the work of a writer of tragedy, though speculative, can be illuminating. There are in fact a number of common thematic elements in Racine's tragedies

* A draft of this paper was read at the *Themes in Drama* International Conference held at the University of California, Riverside, in February 1986.

and in this farce. Taken together, these throw a somewhat novel light on his predilections as a writer.

The first surprise is perhaps the material itself, before one even starts discussing its treatment: the common elements in Racine's farces and tragedies do not, as one might expect, consist of lighter, more cheerful material. On the contrary, they reflect a dark side of Racine: the three underlying motifs to be considered here are obsession, betrayal and claustrophobia.

Obsession and its embodiment in a character are major elements in seventeenth-century farce. Virtually all Molière's plays tackle this theme, and it is important in farcical writing by other comic playwrights of the seventeenth century such as Corneille or Cyrano de Bergerac.[6] Nevertheless, it is a deeply disturbing subject: the monomania of Racine's Perrin Dandin, the old judge of *Les Plaideurs*, borders on madness. When he tells his son Léandre 'I insist on being ill', Léandre replies 'You are ill, only too ill' (I, iv, 80–1), and there are many other references to his insanity. The same madness is apparent in Molière's comic protagonists, such as Arnolphe in *L'Ecole des Femmes*, who is called 'a complete madman' ('un fou fieffé,' IV, iii, 1091).

Racine in his tragedies reveals a similar preoccupation with the disturbing side of obsession. He consistently examines passions so all-absorbing that those who suffer them are utterly consumed by them. It might seem at first sight frivolous to compare Perrin Dandin to a great tragic heroine like Phèdre; but the obsessions of these two characters are remarkably akin both in strength and in effect. Perrin Dandin neither eats nor sleeps, and is wasting away. His son tells him:

> Take a rest;
> You're nothing but skin and bone
>
> (Donnez-vous du repos;
> Vous n'avez tantôt plus que la peau sur les os). (*Les Plaideurs*, I, iv, 81–2)

while Oenone says to Phèdre:

> Three times the shadows of night have darkened the sky
> Since your eyes have closed in sleep;
> Three times the day has dispelled the darkness of night
> And your body has languished without nourishment.
>
> (Les ombres par trois fois ont obscurci les cieux
> Depuis que le sommeil n'est entré dans vos yeux;
> Et le jour a trois fois chassé la nuit obscure
> Depuis que votre corps languit sans nourriture.) (*Phèdre*, I, iii, 191–4)

Racine, absorbingly interested in this theme of obsession, saw fit to use it as an element in every play he wrote. The treatment he gave it is mostly what one would expect: the obsession enhances the farcical quality of *Les*

Plaideurs and heightens the tragedy of *Phèdre*. But at the end of his farce, Racine subjects the obsession element to more unexpected treatment.

The student of seventeenth-century French comedy, basing his observations on Molière's theatre, has definite expectations: obsession should not be cured at the end of the play. Molière's miser never becomes generous; his hypochondriac never realizes he is healthy. But in Racinian tragedy the opposite must happen. Here the obsession is the fatal flaw, and must lead to ruin; and then, with the fall of the hero, with his recognition of his flaw, the obsession must be dispelled. So before Phèdre dies, she comes to terms with her flaw (in this case her obsession with her stepson).

The question then arises of whether Racine, in *Les Plaideurs*, will choose to follow the Molière tradition, or whether he will rather prefer his own tragic practice. Will he, in short, destroy the obsession at the end of the play, or will he allow it to win?[7]

What actually happens in *Les Plaideurs* is different from both the tragic and the Molière pattern. Clearly, Racine does not want a tragedy; equally clearly, he rejects the triumph of obsession. He defeats the obsession, but in an optimistic way, vanquishing it by means of reason. In a manner that Molière would have found impossible, he allows the most rational character, the sensible son, Léandre, to take complete control of the mad father, Dandin. Léandre channels Dandin's obsession and leaves him happily occupied in a harmless activity of whose unreal nature Dandin is nevertheless fully aware. We last see Dandin satisfying his urge to mete out justice by presiding over an impromptu law-court set up in his own home, with his servants as the lawyers, a dog as the defendant, and some chicken-legs as witnesses. Reason in the shape of the son has triumphed over obsession and righted the wrongs of the situation, since henceforward Dandin will be prevented from harming himself or anyone else. As though in a Racinian tragedy, the catastrophe is firmly set in the context of normality at the end, and life goes on. But as this is not a tragedy, no harm has been done in the process.

This conclusion can seem like the opposite of Molière, whose plays very often end on a paroxysm of unresolved obsession, as when M. Jourdain is left whirling round in a wild dance, believing he has become a Turkish nobleman. The essential difference between Racine and Molière here lies in the protagonist's awareness. M. Jourdain is in a dream-world, and due for a rude awakening after the play has ended: he will have to discover, soon, that the so-called Turkish prince who has married his daughter is none other than the bourgeois Parisian Cléonte. Racine's Dandin, on the other hand, knows perfectly well that he is no longer a real judge. But he accepts the pretence: the mere process of adjudication is satisfaction enough for him.[8] Racine's conclusion is satisfying where Molière's is disturbing. He seems to be producing a farcical version of his own tragic vision; and yet, since the catastrophe is absent, the conclusion here can seem over-tidy and hence dismissive.

The second tragic element to find its farcical counterpart in *Les Plaideurs* is deceit or betrayal. In *Les Plaideurs* both Léandre and Isabelle betray their fathers. In this respect there is a subtle difference between these characters and their Molière counterparts, who are generally reluctant to deceive, although obliged to do so. The young lovers in Molière frequently express their scruples, and seek to justify themselves. Valère in *L'Avare* says: 'My sincerity is rather dented by my behaviour' ('La sincérité souffre un peu du metier que je fais', I, I); Angélique in *Le Malade imaginaire* says 'I think that in tricking my father you're going rather too far', ('Il me semble que vous vous jouez un peu beaucoup de mon père', III, 14), and so on. But Racine's Léandre and Isabelle do not question the rightness of their own duplicity. Léandre, for instance, goes around looking for 'some honest cheat' ('quelque honnête faussaire', I, v, 148) to help him dupe Isabelle's father. In this, Léandre and Isabelle are curiously reminiscent of Racine's tragic heroes, who can be guilty of the same unquestioning dishonesty. To take an extreme example from a Racinian tragedy, Roxane in *Bajazet* adores the eponymous hero to the point of risking death for his sake. Bajazet pretends he loves her while carrying on a clandestine love affair with her confidante. Yet Bajazet never loses his stature as a hero. Oreste, Agamemnon, Mithridate and others are portrayed as equally skilful and practised liars. It seems that for Racine, in tragedy and even in comedy, deceit and dishonesty were morally perfectly acceptable, far more so than for Molière.

The third, and perhaps the most idiosyncratic element in Racine's tragedies to come under scrutiny here, has been endlessly discussed by critics. This is the claustrophobic feeling of incarceration. The characters may be physical prisoners, like Bajazet; or they may feel claustrophobic because they are inexorably enmeshed in their predicament, like Phèdre, who feels certain that there is no refuge for her even in death (IV, vi, 1277–88).[9] In tragedy, the unity of place contributes to make the feeling of enclosed space seem intolerably oppressive.

A similar preoccupation with imprisonment is reflected in *Les Plaideurs*. This emphasis is partly built into the play by the fact that Racine has chosen as his source *The Wasps*, a farce in which the main protagonist is physically incarcerated. In fact, the first part of *Les Plaideurs* merely reproduces Aristophanes' plot, which consists of the foiling of repeated attempts at escape by the imprisoned judge. But, interestingly, Racine has included subplots not found in Aristophanes. In these, three other characters are imprisoned. Isabelle is confined to the house by her suspicious father Chicanneau; Chicanneau in turn, together with his would-be opponent at law the Comtesse de Pimbesche, are imprisoned on a slim pretext by Léandre. Dandin is not the only prisoner in the play. Isabelle, too, is held in thrall by her father, not locked away physically, but consistently prevented from following her own inclinations: this treatment is causing her to wither away (I, v, 145). Three other characters are locked up during the play, and the claustrophobic element is stressed. Dandin screams: 'You're strangling me!' (line 573) and 'Let me breathe!' (line 572); Chicanneau cries: 'They're imprisoning me!' (line 525).

In *Les Plaideurs* in fact Racine takes this theme so far that it becomes an underlying leitmotif. In almost every scene of any substance, there are references to guarding, bondage and imprisonment. These are not just the obvious mentions like the comment in the first scene by Petit-Jean, the servant, that he has to guard the mad old judge closely, day and night (line 41). There are also many more oblique references. For instance, Chicanneau's opening words when he appears for the first time are:

> Let the house be guarded, I'm coming back soon.
> Don't let a soul upstairs.
>
> (Qu'on garde la maison, je reviendrai bientôt.
> Qu'on ne laisse monter aucune âme là-haut.) (I, vi, 165–6)

In I, vii, the Comtesse de Pimbesche explains that the great sorrow of her life is that she has been banned from all litigation by her family, Chicanneau exclaims: 'What! A person of your rank is to have her hands tied!' ('Comment! lier les mains aux gens de votre sorte', line 247). Furthering this leitmotif, the subplot between Chicanneau and the Comtesse depends on a significant misunderstanding: Chicanneau uses the term 'Liez-moi' ('tie me up') as an expletive, just as one might say 'Well, I'll be bound' (line 270). The Comtesse, taking him literally, replies crossly, 'Sir, I've no wish to be tied up' (line 275), and proceeds to make a formal complaint that he has attempted to imprison her. The servant comments: 'They should all be tied up, litigants and judge alike' (I, vii). This remark comes right at the end of the first act (line 298), and so seems like a comment on the whole of this subplot.

To emphasize a subordinate theme that is nevertheless appropriate to the main subject is a common technique of Racine's. It gives coherence to the play and helps to build up the atmosphere. But what seems to me to be of particular interest here is the effect of including in a farce a leitmotif so sinister as to seem more appropriate to the darkest of tragedies. Does one feel in the end that the reiterated references to bondage and incarceration make this farce intolerably claustrophobic? The answer seems to me to be definitely no: the imprisonment of Racine's farcical figures and their repeated attempts at evasion are as untraumatic as the antics of an escapologist. And yet this underlying theme gives perhaps the clearest indication that Racine's farce has serious implications. The bondage element is an enactment of a French idiom, *fou à lier*, 'so mad he should be tied up' (Racine himself uses this idiom in the play, II, ii, 313). The implication may well be that obsessives are imprisoned psychologically by their own flawed personalities, just as they are incarcerated physically by their outraged relatives. Here Racine may be treating a theme in a manner appropriate to farce; but he is also coming close to the underlying awareness and seriousness of a Molière.

When we turn to the characters of Racine's farce, this seriousness disappears. Racine, as one might expect, is at his most different from the Racine who created the tragic heroes. Initially, he tells us, he wrote *Les Plaideurs* with a particular comic troupe in mind, the Italian troupe of Scaramouche.[10] The latter, of course, was to play the mad judge Dandin. This project was abandoned when Scaramouche left Paris, but this comment of Racine's gives one an insight into his whole approach to the characters in his play: they are created to give scope for farcical action.

And yet there are many parallels between the characters in *Les Plaideurs* and Racine's tragic heroes. We are here looking at a formal series of parallels: the characters in Racine's farce do not inspire pity and terror, though their emotions are violent enough. Nevertheless, they exhibit certain patterns of behaviour, certain characteristics that are shared with the tragic heroes. I have already pointed to a parallel between Dandin and Phèdre; let us look more closely at the characteristics shared by these and other characters. The old judge Dandin is undoubtedly a descendant of Aristophanes' Philocleon; but he is also a distant relation of Racine's tragic king Mithridate, a tyrannical, heartless father exploiting his sons to further his own policies as ruler, just as Dandin bullies his son to continue in the family's legal tradition. The difference between these two old men lies in their power or lack of it. Mithridate seems redoubtable: his own sons are terrified of him, as when one says to the other:

> Rarely does his love disarm his rage,
> His own sons have no harsher judge . . .
> Fear for your safety . . .
>
> (Rarement l'amitié désarme sa colère,
> Ses propres fils n'ont point de juge plus sévère, . . .
> Craignons pour vous . . .) (I, v, 347–51)

Dandin on the other hand is weakness itself, and his son has complete control over him. Racine has chosen to exploit in one case the tragic and in the other the farcical potential of the elderly father-figure.

A more fundamental resemblance becomes apparent when we consider the young lovers here and in the tragedies. The précieux literature of seventeenth-century salon society is responsible for many of their traits. They are faithful in their affections. Isabelle in *Les Plaideurs* says: 'Sir, you can rely on Isabelle's constancy' ('Monsieur, assurer-vous qu'Isabelle est constante', II, vi, 495), just as a character like June in *Britannicus* can voice feelings which are very similar, though perhaps more poetic in their expression:

> Your image is always present in my soul.
> Nothing can banish it.

> (Votre image sans cesse est présente à mon âme:
> Rien ne l'en peut bannir.) (*Britannicus*, III, 7–8)

Here some of the seriousness of Racine's tragic portrayal of love seems to have spilled over into farce. Elsewhere Léandre in *Les Plaideurs* adds an unexpectedly moving dimension to the play when he describes love in feeling terms as a madness: 'Alas! I am as mad as my father' ('J'ai ma folie, hélas! aussi bien que mon père', I, v, 123). And he says that his love is killing him: 'I am dying for Isabelle' ('Je meurs pour Isabelle', I, v, 138).[11] Exactly the same things are said by the lovers in the tragedies. Hippolyte in *Phèdre* calls his love mad: 'My youth has embarked on a mad love' ('Dans un fol amour ma jeunesse embarquée'); and, commenting on his love, his confidant says: 'You're dying' ('Vous périssez', *Phèdre*, I, 1).

Incorporating the characters of the young lovers into his farce involved Racine's expanding the skeleton plot he had inherited from Aristophanes. However, seventeenth-century audiences assumed that young lovers would feature in farces; and in Racine's play they enact a standard role. Indeed, the predicament of these young lovers fits perfectly with that traditional comic formula defined by E. J. H. Greene ('The spontaneous loves of the Young, traversed by the Old, are aided and abetted by the Servants');[12] however, the young lover intrigue also has parallels with Racine's tragedies. In almost all of them, a pair of lovers are prevented from marrying by a tyrant, often someone of an older generation. The difference is that in tragedy the lovers lose, while Léandre and Isabelle are victorious.

In the tragedies, the young lovers typically lament their lack of control over the situation. They are paralysed by their powerlessness, frustratedly incapable of action. Monime in *Mithridate* describes herself as a slave, 'esclave infortunée' (II, 6). In *Les Plaideurs* Léandre seems to take over the role of a different character in Racinian tragedy: not the lover, but the man of action. More resourceful than the young lovers of tragedy, Léandre usurps power, takes control of his own father and tricks Isabelle's father into letting her marry him. He is successful both as a man of action and as a lover. No tragic hero achieves this double success in Racine. But Léandre, by solving his problems, loses in stature, for one of the most ennobling qualities of the Racinian hero is that he is involved in a conflict which is insoluble other than by tragedy.

More generally, the overall structure of a Racinian tragedy can show marked similarities to that of *Les Plaideurs*. In Racine's tragedies the audi-

ence learns of the situation in the exposition, is introduced to the protagonists, sees the action set in motion, is thrown off balance by the peripeteia,
and finally witnesses the inexorable progress towards the catastrophe
which forms the conclusion of the play. The structure of *Les Plaideurs* is the
farcical counterpart to this pattern. Petit-Jean the porter gives us an
efficient, though irreverent, exposition at the beginning; the obsession of
Isabelle's father Chicanneau starts off as a separate problem, but alters the
course of the plot like a true peripeteia, for Léandre can use this obsession to
trick Chicanneau into putting his signature to a marriage contract between
Léandre and Isabelle. Naturally, there is no tragic catastrophe to round off
Les Plaideurs (perhaps Chicanneau might not agree); but the structure of the
play rests on a similar framework to that of Racine's tragedies.

When it comes to the details of the composition of his farce, Racine
continually betrays an awareness of tragedy. This is apparent in the
character portrayals and details of structure, plot and theme discussed
above. It is even reflected in the minutest details of the composition. For the
whole play is written in verse, in alexandrines like Racine's tragedies. This
is not the obvious medium for a broad comedy of this kind: all the farces
Molière wrote in the four years preceding *Les Plaideurs* are in prose, and he
had even started to write more serious high comedies like *Dom Juan* and
L'Avare in prose as well. In Racine's play, some of the lines are so elegant
and harmonious that they could easily have been taken from one of his
tragedies. This applies chiefly to the words spoken by the two young lovers.
Léandre laments the fact that his beloved Isabelle is kept indoors by her
mad father in the following words:

> One may not see his daughter; the unfortunate Isabelle,
> Invisible, dejected, is imprisoned in her home.
> She can see her youth melting away in regrets . . .
>
> (On ne voit point sa fille; et la pauvre Isabelle
> Invisible et dolente, est en prison chez elle.
> Elle voit dissiper sa jeunesse en regrets . . .) (I, v)

Throughout the play, Racine shows himself to be conscious of the dignity
of tragic verse. He parodies it frequently, adopting a noble tone to describe
a trivial event. A good example is the speech to the litter of puppies who are
to be orphaned if their father is executed for stealing a capon from the
kitchen:

> Come, O most wretched of families,
> Come, poor infants whom they mean to turn into orphans.
>
> (Venez, famille désolée
> Venez, pauvres enfants qu'on veut rendre orphelins . . .) (III, iii)

Racine even misappropriates lines from Corneille's *Le Cid*, still the most famous tragedy of the period, in ludicrous contexts. For example, in I, v, L'Intimé says of his father

> Ses rides sur son front gravaient tous ses exploits.
> (The furrows on his brow were his noble deeds engraved.)

In *Le Cid* this famous line refers to Chimène's father, the aged hero Don Diègue. The laugh comes when we learn that L'Intimé's father was a disreputable rogue.[13] Racine, writing for an audience familiar with classical French tragedy, is clearly assuming that his audience will know the original. He plays around with his rhyme scheme, again in a way that will appeal to an educated audience, breaking the rules of classical French prosody for comic effect[14] or introducing crudely inappropriate vocabulary or topics which would be unacceptable in tragedy.[15] In short, he consistently demonstrates his awareness of the rules. He clearly feels daring whenever he breaks them.

The liberties Racine takes with prosody here also demonstrate his remarkable expertise as a stylist, not surprising in a playwright noted for his style. But in his tragedies, Racine is famous for his economy of vocabulary, of imagery and of register. In this farce, Racine uses a much wider register, and demonstrates his mastery of every trick of verbal fantasy. His mock-heroic speeches range from the almost acceptable to the wildly extravagant. His characters may ape noble emotions, but they also scratch their heads (line 55), turn the spit in the kitchen (line 100), shout (line 283), slap each other (line 417), and their dogs make puddles on the stage (line 826). Racine parodies not only heroic language but also legal parlance and popular speech (see III, iii and I, i). In this, Racine is taking full advantage of the liberties traditionally allowed him as a comic playwright, and we see a very different process from the paring-down that happens in the tragedies. It is perhaps in this respect that Racine is at his most different from the tragic playwright.

There is another respect in which Racine's treatment of *Les Plaideurs* resembles his approach to tragedy: this is his use of his source material. This element is of such importance that it deserves a rather more lengthy discussion.

Racine made no attempt to invent tragic subjects; as a writer of tragedy, he saw himself as retelling old stories, and apologized or justified himself if he deviated too far from the originals.[16] In writing farce, Racine clearly felt the same need to base his work on a suitable source. He says as much in his comments on *Les Plaideurs* (his aim, he tells us, was to render Aristophanes' witticisms in French). He justifies his play by telling us 'I'm merely translating Aristophanes'. And indeed, this play is often thought of simply as a modern-dress version of Aristophanes' *The Wasps*. However, as R. C. Knight in his book *Racine et la Grèce* rightly reminds us, only about one-third of Racine's comedy is closely derived from Aristophanes.[17] We must now attempt to assess the nature of Racine's debt to his predecessor. Is he respectful of his source material, as he was when adapting material for tragic use, or does he subject Aristophanes to a more cavalier treatment, feeling that he is at liberty to do so since the play is a farce?

In adapting classical source material for his tragedies Racine is careful to preserve the original plots. He often goes to considerable lengths to avoid innovation. With *Iphigénie*, for instance, he studied numerous versions of his chosen myth to find one that fitted in with the line he wished to follow. He tells us this in his preface to the play. The same scrupulous respect for an ancient source is apparent in his borrowing from Aristophanes: the plot of *Les Plaideurs* bears clear traces of *The Wasps*. Both plays are about a litigious old man forcibly prevented by his son from going to court. The mechanics of keeping him imprisoned form the first part of both, with the son and two servants struggling to control the irrepressible old man. The second scene of *The Wasps* and the final act of *Les Plaideurs* show the son's solution to the father's uncontrollable obsession: the father will be allowed to continue his legal career, but in the home.

In portraying this home, Racine betrays a considerable interest in the absurdities of contemporary Paris. Although Racine is here departing from the remoteness he claimed was essential to tragedy[18] and giving us a unique insight into his view of his own times, he is clearly remaining faithful to the contemporary quality of Aristophanes' satire. Both playwrights refer to dress, eating habits, households and so on, as well as discussing the legal system. The latter aspect gives Racine great scope for satirizing his contemporaries. The whole machinery of seventeenth-century French law was much in need of reform: Racine himself had recently fallen foul of it.[19] The law was also a popular subject for satire at the time.[20] No other play gives Racine such scope for undisguised satire (though several critics have expressed the view that Racine's tragedies too contain hidden criticisms of his times.)[21] He attacks with gusto, even, like Aristophanes, aiming at individual targets, for instance in his portrayal of the Comtesse de Pimbesche, who seems to have been modelled on a real figure, the litigious and cantankerous Comtesse de Crissé.[22]

Aristophanes too relies heavily on contemporary satire for his impact. His Philocleon is a juryman in ancient Athens, contributing to the corruption of the state by his self-interested view of justice, where Racine's Perrin Dandin is a fully-fledged seventeenth-century judge. The target of Racine's satire is, however, rather different from that of Aristophanes. The latter is using the juryman to attack the system. Philocleon is backed up by a chorus of jurymen like himself, the Wasps of the title. Racine spreads his net wider, to catch a range of legal 'types', the officers of the court and the litigants, and the frauds who exploit them, as well as the judges, just as in his

tragedies he will study a particular problem through his characters: evil in
Britannicus, passionate love in *Phèdre* and so on. With *Les Plaideurs* Racine's
examination of the central problem is less complete, his satire less concentrated: Dandin is less of a central figure, less consistently under attack,
than Aristophanes' Philocleon. Thus in the central scenes of *Les Plaideurs*
Racine introduces two new litigants, Chicanneau and La Comtesse de
Pimbesche, while Dandin is more or less forgotten. Here, in fact, Racine is
grouping his characters very differently from their tragic counterparts,
avoiding the intense concentration on a nucleus of central figures and
dwelling on a collection of eccentrics whose actions cannot be said to further
the main plot.

Other differences between Racine and his source authors reflect contemporary convention. Comparing him with Aristophanes, we see telling
differences here between the treatment of subordinate characters by the two
playwrights. From the technical point of view, Aristophanes was much
more restricted than Racine. He could use only three speaking actors, all
men, so the numerous male and female parts involved quick changes of
costume and mask, and presumably made it difficult for the actors to enter
into the spirit of each individual part.

Racine's restrictions were more governed by conventions of attitude. In
seventeenth-century French comedy, for example, the young lovers had to
show certain characteristics (modesty, elegance, dignity, high principles)
even if these might seem inappropriate for farce. The result can seem like an
uneasy combination of elegance in the young lovers and gross caricature in
the 'farcical' characters, though this is a criticism that could be levelled at
seventeenth-century comedy as a whole. Again, many of the comic characters were expected to be stock portraits taken from French farce or from
commedia dell'arte.[23] Other parts must have been written for particular actors
in the troupe, as has already been suggested.[24]

Incorporating the young lovers causes repercussions in Racine's plots.
We have already seen that Racine, writing in the seventeenth century,
created plays with a satisfying, rounded storyline, involving some love
interest, whether or not he found the ingredients for this sort of play in his
sources. In this respect, Racine is at his most cavalier in adapting both farce
and tragedy. He has added a new love affair not only to *Les Plaideurs* but also
to such tragedies as *Phèdre* and *Britannicus*.[25] In *Les Plaideurs*, like the
introduction of irrelevant characters, this new emphasis on a subordinate
plot further distracts one from the central theme of the protagonist's
monomania, on which our attention is fixed in *The Wasps*. Incidentally, it is
interesting to note that although the love interest in *Les Plaideurs* is entirely
new, the personality of the young lover (though not his behaviour as a
lover) is modelled on Aristophanes. Both young men are remorseless
bullies, who ill-treat their fathers, and yet show a rough if cynical concern

for their well-being.[26] Of course, the fact that Léandre is in love with Isabelle makes him more endearing as a character than Aristophanes' Bdelycleon, who emerges as a cynical social climber, chiefly anxious to cut a fine figure at a banquet.

We have also seen that Racine, both in tragedy and in farce, ties up loose ends and produces a well-constructed play with a satisfying ending. This is true of *Les Plaideurs*, despite the inclusion of less immediately relevant material. In this he departs from Aristophanes, who does not seem to care about the outcome of *The Wasps*. We last see Philocleon in a drunken frenzy, with numerous angry Athenians out for his blood.[27] Racine's priority is always to produce a well-made play, and in this he often deviates from source works.

Racine's farce is made up of a mixture of scenes from Aristophanes and scenes typical of seventeenth-century comedy. As he finds Aristophanes very funny and wants to share the jokes with the public, he takes over scenes like the trial of the dog and the attempts to imprison the old father.[28] He leavens the mixture by adding a series of seventeenth-century scenes, involving sophisticated verbal comedy without much physical action. An example is the ambivalent conversation between the two young lovers and the girl's father. The lovers are secretly pledging their troth under the father's very nose, but as everything they say is ambiguous, the father remains unaware of what is going on.[29] When Racine takes over the farce, its potential crudeness (the old man is physically ill-treated even in Racine's play) is made acceptable by the addition of elegant scenes like this one. This process has its counterpart in Racinian tragedy – his Hippolyte for example has polite, self-deprecating speeches which have no equivalent in the Euripidean tragedy on which Racine's *Phèdre* is based.

This process of refinement in adapting source material is less apparent when one comes to consider Racine's main protagonists, the obsessive characters. If anything, Racine's monomaniacs, Phèdre, Roxane, Néron, are more extreme than their earlier dramatic or historical counterparts. A similar exaggeration would clearly be impossible in *Les Plaideurs*, since Aristophanes' protagonist is already wildly exaggerated. In adapting *The Wasps*, therefore, Racine has simply kept the character of Aristophanes' Philocleon virtually intact. Hence the protagonists of the two farces have much in common, particularly the frenetic energy of their madness. Racine merely makes minor alterations, adapts or adds little touches to the portrait. For example, Philocleon is so keen to get to the court on time that he complains that his cock is late calling him by crowing, although it is not yet midnight (*The Wasps* 100–3). Racine's Dandin goes even further and 'in a fit of rage, he had his cock decapitated because it woke him later than usual' ('Il fit couper la tête à son coq, de colère, Pour l'avoir éveillé plus tard qu'à l'ordinaire' *Les Plaideurs*, lines 35–6). The two old men also share some peripheral characteristics, which Racine presumably included because they made for a more fully-rounded character. Both have a certain family feeling. Philocleon talks affectionately of his wife and daughter (lines 605–12), while Dandin laments the death of his wife, 'La pauvre Babonette' (line 103). More unexpected, perhaps, is the interest in young women shown by both old men. Philocleon abducts a flute girl, which gives rise to a good deal of bawdy innuendo. Dandin is clearly smitten by the young heroine, Isabelle, who is to marry his own son.[30] This allusion to Dandin's susceptibilities may seem to jar with the rest of the portrait of this unfeeling monomaniac. His amorousness could perhaps be a reminiscence of Aristophanes. But in general the amorous old man is a common character in seventeenth-century comedy – see Molière's *L'Avare*, for instance. And Racine is clearly interested in the elderly lover as a character even outside the context of farce: Mithridate is a serious portrait of such a man.

On the whole, then, Racine is faithful to his irreverent source author, and has dispensed with elements he considers essential in tragedy: remoteness, lack of mundane detail, suppression of trivial topics. But in other respects his adaptation of Aristophanes enables him to include potentially tragic material. In particular, several of the themes I have already singled out as being common to Racine the comic and tragic playwright are present, albeit in rudimentary form, in Aristophanes. The sustained treatment of obsession, for example, finds its equivalent in *The Wasps*. The generation gap is also important in both, though here Racine adheres to the farcical tradition of his time. The prevailing feeling towards the old in seventeenth-century farce is blithely disrespectful, very different from the reverence shown them in seventeenth-century tragedy; it is a watered-down version of the contempt expressed in Aristophanes. On the whole, Racine's treatment of all his borrowings from Aristophanes is more anodyne than the original: doubtless Racine felt he had to be more careful than his unconventional predecessor.

Ironically enough, Racine's only excursion into farce was based on a play that he disliked. Racine laments that he wishes he were adapting Menander or Terence instead. Forced into it by his friends, he ended up adapting a work he viewed with disapproval. But despite his initial diffidence Racine seems to have been pleased with his play once he had finished it. He commented: 'If the aim of my comedy was to make people laugh, never has a comedy achieved its aim more successfully.'[31] In common with the tragedies *Les Plaideurs* also reveals, beneath considerable surface differences, a definite 'Racinian' quality.

NOTES

1 It was initially a failure, but the king saw it and enjoyed it and the public flocked to it thereafter.

2 A typical response would be that of J. Schérer in *La Dramaturgie classique en France* (Paris, Nizet, 1950), who calls the play 'a hastily-written sketch'. For comparisons between *Les Plaideurs* and Racine's tragedies, see Nathan Gross, '*Les Plaideurs* and the Racinian Canon', *Symposium,* 20 (Fall 1966), 226–36. A systematic comparison is made here with *Britannicus*, the next tragedy to appear after *Les Plaideurs.* However, Louise K. Horowitz in 'Justice for Dogs: the Triumph of Illusion in *Les Plaideurs*', *French Review*, 52 (1978), 274–9, argues convincingly that such a sustained comparison with one tragedy is in many ways inappropriate.

3 'Un échantillon d'Aristophane', 'Au lecteur'.

4 R. Picard, *La Carrière de Jean Racine* (Paris: Gallimard, 1961), p. 142.

5 Ibid., p. 144.

6 I am thinking of characters such as Matamore in Corneille's *L'Illusion comique* or Paquier in Cyrano's *Le Pédant joué.*

7 By 1668 Molière had already produced more than half his plays; it must be remembered that Racine was his junior by seventeen years.

8 The suggestion that Racine dispenses with illusion here is not generally accepted; see for example Horowitz, 'Justice for Dogs', p. 278.

9 This claustrophobic element is mentioned by Marcel Gutwirth in *Jean Racine, un itinéraire poétique* (Montreal, 1970), p. 82, and in Gross, '*Les Plaideurs*'.

10 'Au lecteur'.

11 One could add that Molière's lovers make similar comments, but the mood of gentle mockery important in Molière is much less apparent in Racine.

12 E. J. H. Greene, *From Menander to Marivaux* (Edmonton: University of Alberta Press, 1977), p. 2.

13 There are two other parodies of *Le Cid* in lines 368 and 601.

14 The best-known example is the following two lines:
Je veux dire la brigue et l'éloquence. Car,
D'un côté, le crédit du défunt m'épouvante . . . (lines 729–30)
Here the inner rhythm of the first line is cut, and the two lines are run together in a totally unacceptable way.

15 One has only to look at the first speech in the play, with its comments on bribery, expressed in vulgar terms such as 'graisser le marteau', 'graisser la patte' to see good examples of this.

16 A good example is the preface to *Iphigénie* in which Racine cites the many versions of the legends he has amalgamated to build up his version, and excuses himself for not sticking exclusively to Euripides' version.

17 Paris: Nizet, 1974.

18 See his Preface to *Bajazet.*

19 Jean Dubu in 'Racine, les plaideurs et les juges', *Annali Instituto Universitario Orientali di Napoli*, 2: 1 (1969), 5–32, gives a detailed account of litigation involving Racine and his uncle at Uzès, and relates it to the play.

20 Furetière's *Le Roman bourgeois* was published in 1666, two years before the first

performance of *Les Plaideurs*, and is generally acknowledged to have inspired *Les Plaideurs*. Furetière definitely knew Racine personally. Tallemant tells us that the two collaborated on correcting Chapelle's *Le Chapelain décoiffé*. Apart from the shared preoccupation with ligitation, and resemblances between characters like Furetière's Collantine and Racine's Comtesse de Pimbesche, there are many precise parallels between the two works. To name only one, Racine includes a character called Drollichon, who must surely be inspired by Furetière's Vollichon.

21 A striking example is G. Charlier, '*Athalie* et la révolution d'Angleterre' in *De Ronsard à Victor Hugo* (Brussels: Editions de la Revue de l'Université de Bruxelles, 1931).

22 For the first performance, Mme de Pimbesche was dressed up as the Comtesse de Crissé. For further details, see Maurice Rat, 'Une vraie comtesse de Pimbesche', *Cahiers raciniens*, 11 (1962) and 'Avatars de la Comtesse de Pimbesche', ibid. (1963).

23 The play features such stock figures as the resourceful valet, the crusty and gullible old man and the loutish servant. In his 'Au lecteur' Racine claims the play was originally written for performance by the Italian Scaramouche and his troupe. Picard in *La Carrière de Jean Racine* questions this assertion (p. 139).

24 However, many of the details of the original casting are still unknown. See Racine, *Oeuvres* ed. Paul Mesnard, vol II (Paris: Hachette, 1911), p. 132 for informed speculation on this subject.

25 'Love is a quality that lends itself to comedy', Boileau, *Bolaeana*, quoted by R. Picard in 'Racine comique ou tragique?', *De Racine au Parthénon* (Paris: Gallimard, 1977), p. 58.

26 Aristophanes' Bdelycleon says:
> A shawl he shall have, and a rug for his knees,
> And a woman to warm him in bed. (*The Wasps*, lines 736–40)

Racine's Léandre says:
> Put him to bed; shut the doors and windows;
> barricade him in to keep him warm.

> (Couchez-le dans son lit; fermez porte, fenêtre;
> Qu'on barricade tout, afin qu'il ait plus chaud.) (I, iv, 112–13)

27 In actual fact the ending is only partly satisfying – the quarrel between Chicanneau and the Comtesse is not resolved, for example. The 'happy ending' is a superficial impression.

28 *Les Plaideurs* I, iii and iv, III, i–iii.

29 Molière's *L'Ecole des maris* of 1661 contains almost the identical scene.

30 This similarity between the two old men is mentioned by Knight, *Racine et la Grèce*, p. 288.

31 'Au lecteur'.

Nahum Tate's defence of farce

INTRODUCED AND EDITED BY PETER HOLLAND

INTRODUCTION

In 1693 Nahum Tate decided to re-issue the text of his farce *A Duke and No Duke*. The play, first published in 1684, is an adaptation of Sir Aston Cokain's play *Trappolin Suppos'd a Prince* (written c. 1633), itself a version of a *commedia dell'arte* source. Tate included in the new edition a preface defending farce against the contemporary vituperation heaped on the genre. As such it is the first major attempt in English to mount such a defence. Tate, never one to rely on his own wit if he could avoid it, based his preface on a translation of selected passages from an essay by Agesilao Mariscotti, *De Personis et larvis earumq. apud veteres usu, et origine syntagmation*.[1] Mariscotti's book was first published in 1610 and reprinted in 1639. Tate may well have used the reprint of it in volume 2 of Gaudenzio Roberti's *Miscellanea Italica Erudita* (Parma, 1690). It is just possible Tate may have had contact with Johannes Graevius, who later wrote obituaries on both William III and Mary. Graevius reprinted the piece in his *Thesaurus Antiquitatem Romanorum* (volume 9, Lugduni Batavorum, 1699) and may have been the source of Tate's copy. Tate followed Mariscotti for much of the preface, only branching out on his own at the end. Though the farce has been reprinted,[2] the preface has not been. Tate's own source notes are printed here as footnotes; my notes appear at the end of the text. I have not sought sources for all Mariscotti's/Tate's learned authorities, merely given indications for most of them and provided translations of classical quotations.[3] I have modernized long *s* forms throughout.

NOTES

1 Tate's elliptical reference to his source was identified by A. H. Scouten in 'An Italian Source for Nahum Tate's Defence of Farce', *Italica*, 27 (1950), 238–40.
2 In Leo Hughes and A. H. Scouten (eds.), *Ten English Farces* (University of Texas Press: Austin, Texas, 1948).

3 On the contemporary attacks on farce see Leo Hughes 'The Early Career of *Farce* in the Theatrical Vocabulary', *Studies in English* (1940), 82–95 and his 'Attitudes of some Restoration Dramatists towards Farce', *Philological Quarterly*, 19 (1940), 268–87. Tate's preface is discussed in S. A. Golden, 'An Early Defense of Farce' in A. Dayle Wallace and Woodburn O. Ross (eds.), *Studies in Honor of John Wilcox* (Detroit: Wayne State University Press, 1958), pp. 61–70. I am grateful to Richard Beadle for help with a copy of the preface and to Colin Austin for help with some of Tate's Latin and Greek.

NAHUM TATE'S 1693 PREFACE TO *A DUKE AND NO DUKE*

Both *Italy* and *France* have swarm'd with Critiques upon the Business of the Stage, and trac'd it's History up to *Thespis*'s Cart. The *Mimica Satyra Tragoedia Comoedia* have been thoroughly canvass'd. A Man might almost conjure with their *Planipedes, Attalanae, Praetextatae, Tabernariae*, &c. Distinctions, Divisions and Subdivisions, but amongst them All not one word of a   5
Farce. None have taken into Consideration, or condescended to tell us, whether the *Trappolin, Scapin, Harlequin* or *Scaramouch* be Originals; or if *Farce* be a Species of Stage-Poetry unknown to the Ancients. This Subject therefore being yet untouch'd, and the Bookseller having occasion to reprint this short Play, I thought it worth the business of a Preface to speak   10
my Sentiments of the matter, though but to provoke some Learned Person to clear the Doubt, and set the Question in a true Light.

In order to this Enquiry, 'twill be proper first to speak something of those Stage-Properties or Implements called *Personae* and *Larvae*, used by Players of former Times; for *Harlequin* was not the first that acted in a Vizard.   15

Athanaeus in his Twelfth Book mentions one *Aristophanes* of *Byzantium*, with several others, who had written particularly on this Subject. Amongst Latin Writers *Anton. Codr. Urc.* is said to have published an Elegant Epistle concerning this matter. *Caelius Calcagn.* in his Book Entituled, *Personati*, speaks pretty home to the Point; and above all, the Learned *Bullinger, lib. 1.*   20
de Theatro.

But I meet with enough for my purpose in the *Syntagm.* of *Marischott*, who, for the benefit of most Readers, contents himself with citing the *Latin* Version of *Lucian*,* and others, which I have so transcribed on occasion as I there found them. Neither can my Abstract of his Book seem needless,   25
because the Treatise itself having been only Printed in *Italy*, is scarce to be met with in *England.*

'Tis agreed that the Word *Persona* in a restrained Sence signifies only the Vizard or Counterfeit Face worn by the Actor: But in larger and more frequent Acceptation, the whole Habit or Dress of Him that enter'd the   30
Scene; which (under the Reign of Old Comedy) was contrived exactly like the usual wearing Garb of some Person whom they had a mind to represent upon the Stage. An Instance hereof against no less a Person than *Socrates* we find described at large by *Aelian*. The Substance of the Story is this: That *Aristophanes* in his νεφελαι represented both the Figure, Gesture and Habit of   35
Socrates, with which Spectacle the *Athenians* were at first surprized. However, the common sort presently expressed their Applause. *Socrates* himself being then amongst the Audience, not by chance but design, and seated where he might be most exposed to view, encountring with his grave,

---

* *De Personis & Larvis.*

steddy and unconcerned Countenance at once the Mimickry of the Actor,   4(
and Rallery of the Poet.

But whether the Stage-dresses and Masks were made in Imitation of
some particular Person, or contrived by Humour and Fancy, as might be
most agreeable to the Fable, (in which they always observed a *Decorum*.)
'Tis evident, says my Author, that they never enter'd the Scene *nisi Personis*   4
induti.

But who was the first Inventor of them is a matter of no small Dispute.
They appear to be as ancient as the Practice of Plays and Drolls themselves,
which were of as old a date as the Worship of *Bacchus*, or perhaps any other
Gods. That this manner of Celebrating the Rites of *Bacchus* was in use not   5
only among the *Thracians* and *Greeks*, but also very frequent and ancient
among the *Latins*. We have evident Proof from *Virgil's Georgicks, Lib. II.* with
a most Elegant Description of the *Personae* in these Words:

> *—Baccho caper omnibus Aris*
> *Caeditur & veteres ineunt proscenia Ludi:*
> *Praemiaque ingentes pagos & compita circum*
> *Thesidae posuere, atque inter pocula laeti*
> *Mollibus in pratis unctos salire per utres;*
> *Nec non Ausonii Troja gens missa celoni*
> *Versibus incomptis ludunt, risuque soluto*
> *Oraque corticibus sumunt horrenda* cavatis.

Ovid hints almost as much in the *Minores Quinquatrus* celebrated in
Honour of *Minerva*.

> *Et jam Quinquatrus jubeor narrare minores*
> *Huc ades O caeptis flava Minerva meis;*
> *Cur vagus incedat tota tibicen in urbe.*
> *Quid sibi Personae, quid Toga picta velint.*

Suidas affirms *Chaerilus* the *Athenian* to have been the first that erected a
Stage, and used the *Larva*; yet elsewhere (according to *Diomedes* and other
Greek Writers) he makes *Thespis* Inventor of the *Persona*, who at first
discoloured his Face with Vermilion, before he came to use the Juyce of
Purslane; or, according to *Horace*, the Lees of Wine.

> *—Plaustris vexisse Poemata Thespis*
> *Quae canerent agerentur peruncti faecibus ora.*

This Practice, and *Cartshow*'s of *Thespis* were performed about the *56th*
Olympiad. Others give the Honour of this Invention to *Aeschylus*, and
presume that they have likewise *Horace*'s Word for their Opinion.

> *Post hunc Personae pallaeq; repertor honestae*
> *Aeschylus —*

But *Horace* is still confident, if rightly understood; for he does not affirm

Aeschylus to be the absolute Inventor of the *Persona*, but of the *Persona Honesta*, of more graceful Masks and Habits than were contrived by others; for which Reason we may suppose, as *Philostratus* relates, this *Aeschylus* was called the Father of Tragedy. After *Aeschylus* Stage-Habits for Women were also invented by *Phrynicus*. 85

Amongst the *Romans* till *Livius Andronicus* his Time, the *Galeri* and not *Personae* were used upon the Stage; and *Suidas* will have *Roscius Gallus* to be the first that brought the *Personae* into custom with the *Romans*: But *Donatus* tells us, that *Minutius* and *Prothonius* were the first Players that Acted Tragedy, *Personati*: Which Fashion afterwards obtained that Degree, that 90 *Nero Caesar* himself is recorded by *Suetonius* to have appeared in such Dresses upon the open Stage. *Tragaedias cantaverit Personatus; Heroum Deorumque item heroidum & Dearum, Personis effictis.* That pompous and splendid Dresses were proper for Tragedy, both *Pollux* and *Donatus* affirm.

Next to Tragedy came Satyr, which was but a Species of the former, as 95 appears by the *Cyclops* of *Euripides*. This sort of *Dramma* (though less practised as the World grew more civilized) had also it's peculiar *Personae* or χηματισμᾶϱ, made of Goats Skins and Hides, and other Beasts, which are described by *Dyonisius*, *Pollux* and *Causabon*.

The personal Habits used in the Licentious *Comdiaae vetus* were contrived 100 (as we instanced) to represent particular Persons,* which therefore could he no constant or fix'd Garb; For *Suidas* says expresly, ἔθους γάϱ ἦυ τοις ϰομιϰοις, &c— That is, *Moris fuit ut Comici Personas Histrionibus darent eorum similes quos imitarentur.* *Horace* alludes to the same Custom, *Sat 4.L.1* – *Quivis Stomacheter eodem quo personatus Pater.* Their resembling Dresses (says the 105 *Scholiast* upon *Aristoph.*) were so aptly contrived, that the Spectators knew what Person the Actor mimick'd at his first appearance, before he spoke a Word. While *Athens* was a popular State, the Rabble were so much delighted with these Representations of particular Men, that *Isocrates* complains they would run to those Entertainments from their Orators, 110 while they were haranguing upon Matters of greatest Importance to the Publick. 'Tis true, this Practice of exposing Men upon the Stage, was at its beginning more justifiable, while confin'd to those Limits mentioned by *Horace*,

> *Si quis erat dignus describi quod malus aut fur* 115
> *Quod Maechusve foret, aut Sicarius, aut alioqui*
> *Famosus.—*

Nay, it did not a little conduce to the reforming of the State, in deterring Men from Wickedness; upon which *Dionys. Halycarn.* did not stick to† affirm of *Eupolis Cratinus* and *Aristophanes*, that they perform'd the Office of 120

---

* *Poet.Lib.c.4.14.Lib.*xi.*c.*12.1.4.*c.*ix.Morum Charact.*Ch.*6.
† Dionys.

Philosophers and States-men as well as of Poets. But when from represen-
tation of evil Men, the Practice declin'd to the Traducing of the Good and
Vertuous, and even to the Dishonour of Religion, and ridiculing their very
Gods, 'twas high time for the Government to take Cognizance of the
Matter, and enact Laws to restrain their License.

> —*Lex est accepta Chorusq;*
> *Turpiter Obticuit Sublato jure nocendi,*
>
> Horace, Art. Poet.

> —*Jam saevus apertam*
> *In rabiem verti caepit jocus & per honestas,*
> *Ire domos, &c.*

And a little after,

> —*Lex*
> *Poenaq; lata malo quae nollet Carmine quemquam,*
> *Describi.*   Epist. Lib. 3.

Upon this Regulation succeed the *Media* and *Nova Comedia*, in which the
Personae ludicrae & ad risum accommodatae were invented and made familiar to
the Stage. One contriv'd a peculiar Habit, when part of a *Paedagogue* was to
be plaid, another of a Parisite, others of Bawds, Cooks, &c. All which are
recited by * *Donatus*, and more largely by † *Pollux*. That Comedians acted
Personati in *Terence* his time appears by an ancient Copy of that Author
preserved in the *Vatican*, where Figures are drawn of the Actors in the Play,
as they were *Larvati* and *Personati*.

'Tis impossible for us to conceive the Art and Curiosity in the Contrivance and Making of these Shapes, in which these Players acted, or how
much the Player himself was sometimes enamour'd on his *Persona*, or Stage-
dress, attributing his Success and Theatrical Applause to the Semblance in
which he acted. As to this Particular, *Pliny* has given us an Instance of
memorable Event in his Natural History, *Lib. 8. cap.43.* speaking of *M.
Opilius Hilarius.* He tells us, That this Actor having wonderfully pleas'd the
People in performance of a certain Part; He invited his Friends to a Treat
upon his Birthday, and this Shape in which he succeeded so well being
brought into his sight, he pull'd off his banqueting Wreath from his Head to
put it upon the Figure, which he survey'd with such Pleasure, that he lost
his Sense, grew stiff and cold, and unperceived by the Company, expir'd
with Transport.

Hitherto we have discoursed of the *Persona* in the larger Acceptation, as it
signified amongst them, the intire Stage-Habit. But must acknowledge that
it was sometimes taken in a more restrain'd Sense, and used by Actors for
only the *Larva* or Vizard, as the *Larva* again is sometimes mentioned to
express the *Persona* intire.

* *In prolegom. ad. Terent.*   † *Lib.4.c.*19.

Martial uses the Word for a Border or Perriwigg, *Epigr.43. Lib.3.*

> *Mentiris juvenem tinctis Lentine capillis,*
> *Tam subito Corvus, qui modo cignus eras;*
> *Non omnes fallis, scit te Proserpina canum,*
> *Personam capiti detrahet illa tuo.*

But *Seneca* expresly for a Mask or Vizard, *Quid tantopere te supinat? Quid Vultum habitumq; oris praevertit ut malis habere Personam quam faciem.*

The Advantages of using these *Persona* or Disguises on the Stage were, in Comedy, that they might first have Resemblance to the Person imitated, and afterwards adapted for Humour, and to excite Mirth; besides the Consulting the Decency of the Actors, who were in those Days generally too modest to Act barefac'd,* and in usual Habits. In Tragedy the Dress assisted to the Pomp and Show. The Tragedian's Vizard making the Voice to come forth more sonorous, being made with a larger † Mouth that seem *Hiare* as the Actor spoke, which I could almost suppose *Persius* to hint at in that Verse,

> *Fabula seu maesto ponatur hianda Tragedo.*

The Convenience of these Disguises on the other occasions, as in Interludes at Sacred Rites (as they call'd them) is manifest from *Servius* on our forecited place of ‡ *Virgil, Quia necesse erat pro ratione Sacrorum aliqua ludicra & turpia fieri quibus populo possit risus Moveri, qui ea exercebant, propter verecundiam remedium hoc adhibuerunt, ne agnoscerentur.*

Yet were not Disguises Masks and Maskers, employ'd only in the Service of the Theatre and Temples, but promiscuously used by the Ancients on many other occasions, as in Triumphs, Feasts, Marriages, Funerals, &c. the History whereof would be furnish'd with many entertaining Circumstances; but I must remember that I am confin'd to the scanty Limits of a Preface.

The good Uses that have been made of Vizards and Counterfeit-Habits, without the compass of the Theatre would make no small Collection, but the Abuses of them much greater. This would afford more Horror than Diversion. The yearly Harvest of Wickedness, and evil Consequences occasion'd by the Carnival at *Venice*, give too sufficient Proofs of the Mischief. *Larvati* took their Appellation from *Larva*, a Vizard; and *Larva* from the *Lares*, whom the Ancients supposed to possess Men's Minds with Madness. This was ascribed as peculiar to those Powers. Can there be greater Demonstration of Distraction and Frenzy of all sorts, than in the

---

* *Yet* Nero *that Monster having compell'd Noblemen to act Parts in a Play, he Commanded them to pull off their Vizards on the Stage,* Histrionum apparatu eos patefaciens Hominibus apud quos ipsi paulo ante Magistratum gesserant.

† Lucian de Salt *describing the Mimick-Mask, says it was* Larva pulcherrima, Quae non immane hint ut Tragica.

‡ *Upon the –* Baccho caper omnibus aris, &c. *Georg.l.2.*

Impious Practices and Debaucheries at the forementioned Festival? Can all
their Mortifications of the ensuing *Lent* make any tolerable Amends for the
Lewdness then committed? Has the Devil at any time such a Jubilee, where
Vice like an Infernal *Cebele* sees all her black Offspring assembled together?
What are the effects of this Masquerade, but Whoredoms, Adulteries,
Incests, Brawls, Murders, and a general Corruption of Manners. *Pollydor.*
recites it to the Honour of our *English* Ancestors, that they had Law in force
against Masqueradings. *Capitale fuisse si quis personam induisset. De Rev. Invent.
l.5.c.2. Ludovicus vives, lib. de Christiana Faemina,* thinks he did the
Masquerading Ladies no wrong, in affirming, that *detrimentum quod sub
Persona earum accepit verecundia citra personam se proserat & ostendat.* That they
proved after wearing those Disguises just as modest out of their Masques as
they were in them. And honest *Juvenal* civilly puts the Question,

> *Quem praestare potest mulier Larvata pudorem?*

But restoring these Guises to their proper Owners, the Stage-Players, let
us proceed from the Consideration of th *Larva* to our first Enquiry about
Farce, and whether or no the Ancients had any such Species of Stage-Poetry.

In the first place I would ask the Readers Opinion, if he can suppose any
more genuine and natural use of those *Larvae* or Vizards which we have
described, than for Farce-Players, especially if we take in those other
Implements mentioned by *Lucian, de Salt.* thus rendred by *Marisch. Mitto
adscitia pectora & ventres fictitios, adjunctam & arte compositam corporis cras-
situdinem.* One would almost conclude from this Description of their Stage-
Properties, that they could be contrived for nothing but Farce.

I have not yet seen any Definition of Farce, and dare not to be the first
that ventures to define it. I know not by what Fate it happens (in common
Notion) to be the most contemptible sort of the Drama. 'Tis thought to
bring least Reputation to an Author. But if the difficulty of the Task were to
decide the Case, we should soon alter our Opinion. I would desire him who
thinks it an easie thing, to make Tryal of it with all the speed he can, it being
such a Work

> * *As every man may think to write,
> And not without much pains be undeceiv'd,*

The reason of the Difficulty I presume to be this, (and the Undertakers will
find it true) That Comedy properly so called, is an Imitation of Humane
Life, (*quicquid agunt homines*) and subsists upon Nature; so that whoever has
a Genius to coppy her, and will take the Pains, is assured of Success, and all
the World affords him Subject. Whereas the business of Farce extends
beyond Nature and Probability. But then there are so few Improbabilities
that will appear pleasant in the Representation, that it will strain the best

* Ld. *Roscom.* Transl.

Invention to find them out, and require the nicest Judgement to manage them when they are conceived. Extravagant and monstrous Fancies are but sick Dreams, that rather torment than divert the Mind; but when Extravagancy and Improbability happen to please at all, they do it to purpose, because they strike our Thought with greatest Surprise. But to our Question.

I cannot averr, that the Ancients had Entertainments on the Stage entirely resembling the *Harlequin* and *Scaramouch*, but 'tis highly probable that the Satyrical Diversions and Interludes invented to * relieve the Heaviness of Tragedy were of this Nature. For that they were introduced for Mirth and Rallery, and thereby to help off the serious Action, is expresly told us.

> *Carmine qui tragico vilem certavit ob hircum*
> *Mox etiam egrestes Satyros nudavit, & asper*
> *Incolumi gravitate, jocum tentavit: eo quod*
> *Illecebris erat & grata Novitate morandus*
> *Spectator.*

For as Madam *le Fevre* † says, the Stage-Satyr, or Satyrizing Scenes must by no means be confounded with Satyrique Poems written by *Lucilius*, *Horace*, or *Greek* Satyrist. The business of the Satyr-Actors was not to lash out into long Invectives, only now and then a Flurt of such harmless Sarcasm as used to be sometimes thrown out by *Harlequin* or *Scaramouch*, because as *Horace* adds,

> *Ita risores ita commendare dicaces*
> *Conveniet Satyros, &c.*

Which shews they were to keep within Bounds; and what he subjoyns

> —*Ita vertere seria ludo.*

Seems to emply Drollery, Banter, Buffoonry, Vagaries, Whimsies, which are so many Ingredients of Modern Farce. Nay, I have some where read (though I cannot at present recollect my Author) that their Comick Actors used to deliver what they had to say in various and feigned Tones, which was *Harlequin*'s manner.

Nor will this appear unlikely, if we consider particularly the Gesticulations, Tricks, Feats of Activity and wonderful Performances of another sort of Actors whom they called *Mimi* and *Pantomimi*, from their admirable knack at Mimickry; which was not the least of *Harlequin*'s and *Scaramouch*'s Talents. 'Tis unconceivable how expert these Persons were in humorous Actions, as will appear by a few Testimonies very well worth our mentioning.

* *As the* French *now make use of their Farces.*
† *In her admirable Preface to her Version of* Amphitrio.

Their Performance was so extraordinary, that as *Strabo* informs us, *Lib. 14.* their Art was called μαγωδιαν, their Legerdemain Shifts, Slights and Postures, Magical Arts, *Praestigia*: And further asserts, *Eos quam saepissime argumento e Comoediis desumpto varias personas representasse, nunc faeminae, nunc lenonis, nunc Adulteri, nunc temulenti.* To which we may add that old Epigram,

> *Tot Linguae quot membra viro, mirabilis Ars est,*
> *Quae facit Articulos, ore tacente, loqui.*

There was no Fable accommodated to the Stage, which these Mute-Actors could not represent by Gestures and Movements of their Body. For as *Lucian* says, *Personis in Scenam introductis, gestibus per omnia responderent, neque ea quae dicuntur ab introductis optimatibus, aut agricolis, aut mendicis discrepabant sed in unoquoq; illorum proprietas & excellentia demonstrabantur.* In dumb Action and Gestures they could express, and as it were, speak what they pleased. Wherefore * *Tigranes* amongst all the Rarities the World's Imperial City afforded, begged one of these *Pantomimes* to serve him as it were for an Interpreter to all Nations.

Pantomimus (says *Cassiod. Var. 4. Epist. ult) a multifaria imitatione nomen est, idem corpus Herculem designat & venerem, faeminam presentat & marem; Regem facit & Militem; Senem reddit & Juvenem ut in uno videas esse multos.* And *Lucian* seeing a Pantomime prepare to personate five Representations, cries, That the Mimick seem'd to him to have five Souls, who could exhibit so many Personages with one Body. What was all this but Farce to the Degree of *Harlequin* with his Cloak, whisk'd about, and acting a Windmil.

All this, you'll say, was only a Farce of Action, Farce in the Player, nothing on the Poets Part, no Proof that the Ancients had any written Farce.

I will not affirm they had any Stage-Play entirely of *Harlequin* and *Scarramouch*'s Cast; but if *Molier*'s Comedies come under the Denomination of Farce, (as everybody allows) 'tis plain that both the *Greeks* and *Romans* had Farcical Plays. The Comedies of *Aristophanes* and *Plautus* are mostly of this Cut, call them *Palliatae, Togatae,* mixt Comedy, low Comedy, or what you will. Their Old Comedy, generally speaking, had the very Air of Farce. *Aristophanes* his *Socrates* Philosophing in a Basket, &c. is as much Farce as any thing in the Character of Mr *Shadwell*'s *Virtuoso.* The Frog and Swimming-Master, Tame Spider, Bottled Air, &c. are not more Humorous and Farcy. *Aristophanes* his *Frogs* were a very *Rehearsal* of those days: As our *Fletcher*'s *Knight of the Burning Pestle* was a sort of *Quixot* on the Stage. Which teaches us, that Farce is not inconsistent with good Sence, because 'tis capable of Satyr, which is Sence with a Vengeance. The *Amphytrio* and *Menaech* of *Plautus* through the whole Contrivance and Course of Accidents

---

* Vid. Scalig. Poet. *l.*1.

are all Farce. They were the Originals of *Shakespear*'s Comedy of Errours, and the *Italian Trappoline*. I would not be a Heretick in Poetry, but Reason and Experience convince us, that the best Comedies of *Ben. Johnson* are near a-kin to Farce; nay, the most entertaining parts of them are Farce it self. The Alchymist which cannot be read by any sensible Man without Astonishment, is Farce from the opening of the First Scene to the end of the Intreigue. 'Tis Farce, but such Farce as bequeaths that Blessing (pronounced by *Horace*) on him that shall attempt the like.

> —*Sudet multum frustraq; laboret*
> *Ausus idem.*

The whole business is carry'd on with Shuffles, Sham and Banter, to the greatest degree of Pleasantness in the World. For Farce (in the Notion I have of it) may admit of most admirable Plot, as well as subsist sometimes without it. Nay, it has it's several Species or Distinctions as well as Comedy amongst the *Romans Stataria mixta, &c.* but still 'twas Comedy. So Comedy may admit of Humour, which is a great Province of Farce; but then it might be such Humour as comes within compass of Nature and Probability: For where it exceeds these Bounds it becomes Farce. Which Freedom I would allow a Poet, and thank him into the Bargain, provided he has the Judgment so to manage his Excursion, as to heighten my Mirth without too grosly shocking my Senses. I cannot call to mind one Humour in all *Terence*'s Plays, but what he might have taken by Observation, all lies within the Compass of Conversation; but therefore *Caesar* (amidst all his Beauties and Excellencies) says he, wants the *Vis Comica*, which made *Plautus* so diverting. There is so much said for these two Authors by their respective Admirers, that a Man knows not where to give the Preference. All that I would presume to say, is, That I esteem them both admirable in their way; that one chose to write pure Comedy in the strictest Notion, and the other liberty of extending Comedy sometimes into Farce; and each got his Point, *Terence* of being exact, and *Plautus* pleasant. Neat *Terence*, witty *Plautus*, says our greatest * Master of Comedy, who scorn'd not to Copy sometimes from the Ancients; yet for one Hint he has taken from *Terence*, he has borrowed three from *Plautus*. I will instance only that pleasant Passage in his *Alchymist*, where the Confederates banter and play upon *Surly* disguised like a *Spanish Don*, not supposing that he understood them. We find the same Humour in the *Poenulus* of *Plautus*, where the old *Carthaginian* speaks in the *Punick* Language; *Milphio* a *Roman* Servant plays the wagg, and drolls upon him, under pretence of interpreting for him; the Stranger suffers him to run himself out of breath with his Ribaldry, and then surprizes him with thundring out as good Latin as the best of them could speak. *Vulpone*'s

---

* *Ben. Johnson's* Verses on *Shakespear*.

playing the Mountebank in the *Fox* is Farce; and Sir *Politick*'s turning himself into a Tortoise. This Passage however is undiverting, which proves (as I said) the Nicety of Judgment required in managing Improbabilities. Had this been told to the Audience like other Projects which are only recited, it might have made a pleasant Relation.

Now if we enquire into the best of our Modern Comedies, we should find the most diverting parts of them to be Farce, or near akin to it. *Remembrancer John* in the *Cutter*, Sir *Martin* turn'd East-India Gentlemen, the Tryal Scene in the *Spanish Fryar*, where *Gomes* menac'd by the Colonel in dumb shew, runs Counter in his Evidence, says and unsays in a Breath, till he confounds himself and the Court. Such Pleasantry as this is I cannot think below it's great Author, who in the Serious Scenes of the same Play, has shewn us the Refinedness and Perfection of the *English* Style. *Quintilian*, speaking of *Repartees*, after these Words, * *Longe venustiora omnia in respondendo quam in provocando*; That more Wit's required to retort a Jest than to break one, adds this Expression, *Accedit difficultati quod ejus rei nulla exercitatio est, nulli praeceptores.* The same may be said of Farce; there are no Rules to be prescribed for that sort of Wit, no Patterns to Copy, 'tis altogether the Creature of Imagination. And our *English Mecaenas* (to whose Judgment the Muses willingly subscribe) has declared that he approves *Genius* and *Invention* beyond the best Performances of *Imitation*. Such is the Farce-Writers Task. Neither can I assume any thing to my self by the Preference I have given to Farce on account of the *Trapoline*, which I only new modell'd: I pretend but to have Improv'd what I would be proud to have Invented.

* *Lib*.vi.*c*.3. *de Risu*.

NOTES

4 *Planipedes, Attalanae, Praetextatae, Tabernariae*: ballet-dancers, rustic farces, obscene words, low comedies.

6 *Farce: France* 1693.

16 *Athanaeus*: Athenaeus, Greek author of second century AD, best known for his massive work *Deipnosophistae*, 'The Gastronomers'.

18 *Anton. Codr. Urc.;* Antonius Urceus Codrus (1446–1500), Italian humanist philosopher.

19 *Caelius Calcagn.:* Celio Calcagnini (1479–1541), Italian philosopher.

20 *Bullinger:* Heinrich Bullinger (1504–75), Swiss Protestant theologian and reformer.

22 *Syntagm.* of *Marischott: De Personis et larvis earumq. apud veteres usu et origine Syntagmation* (1610) by Agesilao Mariscotti (1577–1618).

24 *Lucian:* Greek satirist (*c*. AD 120–*c*.180).

24n. *De. . .Larvis:* Lucian's piece Πεφὶ Ὀφχήσεως, usually known in Latin as *De Saltatione*.

34 *Aelian:* Claudius Aelianus (*c.* AD 170–235). The reference is to his *Varia Historia* 2.13.

35 νεφελαι: *The Clouds*.

44–5 *nisi. . .induti:* 'unless represented by masks'.

54 *Baccho. . .cavatis:* Virgil, *Georgics* 2.380–7: 'a goat is slain to Bacchus at every altar, and the olden plays enter on the stage; for this the sons of Theseus set up prizes for wit in their villages and at the crossroads and gaily danced in the soft meadows on oiled goat-skins. Even so Ausonia's swains, a race sent from Troy, disport with rude verses and laughter unrestrained, and put on hideous masks of hollow cork' (Loeb).

64–7 *Et. . .velint:* Ovid, *Fasti* 6.651–4: 'And now I am bidden to tell of the lesser Quinquatrus. Now favour my undertaking, thou yellow-haired Minerva. Why does the flute-player march at large through the whole city? what mean the masks? What means the long gown?' (Loeb).

68 *Suidas:* Thought at this stage to be the name of the author of a massive lexicon but actually a corruption of the word for fortress 'suda', describing the encyclopedia.

73–4 *Plaustris. . .ora.:* Horace, *Ars Poetica* 276–7: '[Thespis] carried his pieces in wagons to be sung and acted by players with faces smeared with wine-lees' (Loeb).

78–9 *Post. . .Aeschylus.:* Ibid. 278–9: 'After him Aeschylus, inventor of the mask and comely robe' (Loeb).

86 *Galeri:* caps.

88 *Donatus:* Aelius Donatus (fl.fourth century AD), author of a major commentary on Terence.

92–3 *Tragaedias. . .effictis:* Suetonius, *Life of Nero* 21.3: 'He also put on the mask and sang tragedies representing gods and heroes and even heroines and goddesses having the masks fashioned' (Loeb).

94 *Pollux:* Julius Pollux, Greek rhetorician of second-century AD, author of *Onomasticon*.

99 *Dyonisius:* Dionysius of Halicarnassus, rhetorician of first century BC.

99 *Causabon:* Isaac Casaubon (1559–1614), French (later British) scholar and classical commentator.

100 *Comediaae vetus:* 'Old comedy' (*recte* Comedia).

102 *Suidas: Suidus* 1693.

103–4 *Moris. . .imitarentur:* 'for it was customary for the comic poets to give masks to the actors looking identical to those people whom they imitated'. The Latin translates Suidas's Greek.

104–5 *Quivis. . .Pater:* Horace, *Satires* 4.55–6: 'any father whatever would rage in the same fashion as the father in the play' (Loeb).

115–17 *Si. . .Famosus.:* Ibid. 4.3–5: 'If there was anyone deserving to be drawn as a rogue or a thief, as a rake or cut-throat, or as scandalous in any other way' (Loeb).

126–7 *Lex. . .nocendi:* Horace, *Ars Poetica* 283–4: 'The law was obeyed, and the chorus to its shame became mute, its right to injure being withdrawn' (Loeb).

128–30 *Jam. . .domos:* Horace, *Epistles* 2.1.148–50: 'jest, now growing cruel, turned to open frenzy, and stalked amid the homes of honest folk' (Loeb).

132–4 *Lex. . .Describi: Ibid.*, lines 152–4: 'a law was carried with a penalty, forbidding the portrayal of any in abusive strain'.

135 *Media* and *Nova Comedia:* 'Middle and New Comedy'.

136 *Personae. . .accommodatae:* 'stage masks fitted for laughter'.

162–5 *Mentiris. . .tuo:* Martial, *Epigrams* 3.43: 'You falsely ape youth, Laetinus, with
dyed hair, so suddenly a raven who were but now a swan. You don't deceive all;
Proserpine knows you are hoary; she shall pluck the mask off your head' (Loeb).

166–7 *Quid. . .faciem:* 'What upsets you so much? What is now coming over your
looks and face that you prefer to wear a mask rather than a face?'

172n *Histrionum. . .gesserant:* 'through the costume of actors revealing themselves
to men among whom they themselves had shortly before held office'.

174n *Larva. . .Tragica:* 'a beautiful mask which did not open monstrously as a
tragic one'.

175 *Hiare:* 'to gape'.

177 *Fabula. . .Tragedo:* Persius, *Satires* 5.3: 'whether their theme be a play to be
gaped out by a lugubrious tragedian' (Loeb).

179 *Servius:* Latin grammarian of fourth century AD, best known for his commentary
on Virgil.

180–2 *Quia. . .agnoscerentur:* 'because it was necessary for the purpose of these sacred
rites that certain ridiculous and shameful things should take place by which the
people could be made to laugh, those who put on those shows out of a sense of
shame applied this remedy, not to be recognized'.

203 *Pollydor.:* Polydore Virgil (1470–1555) in *De Inventoribus Rerum* (1499).

205 *Capitale. . .induisset:* 'to have been punishable by death if anyone went out
masked'.

206 *Ludovicus. . .Faemina:* Juan Luis Vives (1492–1540) in *De institutione faeminae
christianae* (1524).

207–8 *detrimentum. . .ostendat:* 'let that harm which modesty received under their
mask display itself and come out in public when they are without their masks'.

211 *Quem. . .pudorem:* Juvenal, *Satires* 6.252: 'What modesty can you expect in a
woman who wears masks?' (Loeb). Juvenal wrote 'galeata', not 'larvata'.

218–20 *Mitto. . .crassitudinem:* from Lucian, *De Saltatione* 27, a Latin translation of his
Πεϕὶ 'Οϕχήσεως: 'to say nothing of the chest-pads and stomach-pads with
which he contrives to give himself an artificial corpulence'.

229n *Ld. . .Transl.:* the translation of Horace's *Ars Poetica* by Wentworth Dillon,
Earl of Roscommon, first published 1684.

233 *quicquid. . .homines:* 'whatever men do'.

250–4 *Carmine. . .Spectator:* Horace, *Ars Poetica* 220–4: 'The poet who in tragic song
first competed for a paltry goat soon also brought on unclad the woodland satyrs,
and with no loss of dignity roughly essayed jesting, for only the lure and charm of
novelty could hold the spectators' (Loeb).

261–2, 264 *Ita. . .ludo*] Ibid., 225–6: 'it will be fitting so to seek favour for your
laughing, bantering satyrs, so to pass from grave to gay' (Loeb).

277 *Strabo:* (64BC–AD21), Greek author of a massive *Geography*.

278 μαγωδιαν: 'rude pantomime'.

279–81 *Eos. . .temulenti:* 'that they most often represented various characters with a plot taken from comedies, now of a woman, now of a pimp, now of an adulterer, now of a drunkard'.

282–3 *Tot. . .loqui:* 'A man has as many tongues as he has limbs. The art is wonderful which makes little limbs speak, even though the mouth is silent.'

286–8 *Personis. . .demonstrabantur:* a version of *De Saltatione* 65: 'When characters are brought on stage, it is through gestures that they act throughout, and the things that are said by the princes, paupers or farmers who are brought on did not differ, but in each one of them their peculiar excellence was shown.'

290n Scalig. Poet: Julius Caesar Scaliger, *Poetices Libri Septem* (1561).

293–5 *Pantomimus. . .multos:* Cassidorus (*c.* AD 490–583), *Variae Epistolae* 4: 'The name pantomime comes from its multifarious imitation. The same body shows Hercules and Venus, presents woman and man, makes king and soldier, offers old man and youth, so that you see many to be in one.'

310 *Virtuoso: The Virtuoso* (1676).

312 *Rehearsal:* Buckingham *et al.*, *The Rehearsal* (1671).

325–6 *Sudet. . .idem:* Horace, *Ars Poetica* 241–2: '[He] may sweat much and toil in vain when attempting the same' (Loeb).

364–5 *Cutter*, Sir *Martin. . .Spanish Fryar:* Cowley, *The Cutter of Coleman Street* (performed 1661, from his *The Guardian*, 1642), Dryden, *Sir Martin Mar-All* (1668), Dryden, *The Spanish Friar* (1681).

372–3 *Accedit. . .praeceptores:* Quintilian 6.3.14: 'We are also confronted by the additional difficulty that there are no specific exercises for the development of humour nor professors to teach it' (Loeb). Tate translates the first piece of Quintilian himself.

His own triumphantly comic self: self and self-consciousness in nineteenth-century English farce*

JIM DAVIS

Farce, on the nineteenth-century British stage, was as popular as melodrama. Like melodrama, it did not presuppose psychological change or development in its protagonists and, as with melodrama again, it was ostensibly concerned with action rather than character. G. H. Lewes seems to acknowledge this when, in describing Charles Mathews the younger's performance as Sir Charles Coldstream in Dion Boucicault's *Used Up* (first performed 1844), he complains that Mathews did not attempt characterization in the second part of the play, but relied on the fun of the situation instead: 'In other words it is farce, not comedy'.[1] Farce also dealt with the same sort of emotions that were depicted in melodrama. According to Westland Marston (1888): 'it deals, in fact, with terror and suffering – with predicaments in a word, which are not the less intense because they have their origin in the absurd'.[2] Invariably, the reaction of the farcical protagonist was contrasted with that of his counterpart in melodrama, in that he was passive and unheroic in the face of adversity. This was certainly true of Robert Keeley, a very popular actor in nineteenth-century farce: 'even in the moments of abject terror (and no one could ever act comic terror better than he did) somehow or other he contrived to make you feel that courage ought not to be expected of him, for cowardice was simply the natural trembling of that human jelly'.[3] Nineteenth-century farce, derived as it was from the afterpieces of the eighteenth century and the decline of the old five-act comedies, often followed melodramatic or more heroic plays in the evening's playbill, providing a comic anti-masque or inversion of what had preceded it. For its audiences it provided an alternative view of how to cope with a threatening incomprehensible world.

Although farce and melodrama both relied on situation and action rather than on character development, they depended strongly on the personalities of the performers to enhance their impact. Indeed, the interaction of personality and performance in nineteenth-century farce sometimes led to the undermining of notions of reality in an almost Pirandellian manner.

---

* A draft of this paper was read at the *Themes in Drama* International Conference held at the University of London, Westfield College, in March 1986.

Despite the technical reliance of farce on trite, conventional situations, on well-worn traditions and plot formulae, it would never have been so successful if it had not made such careful and ingenious use of its actors. Indeed, that farce was a particularly popular genre on the nineteenth-century English stage arose from performance rather than from the form itself: its appeal lay firmly in the acting it inspired. Low comedians such as John Liston, J. B. Buckstone, Keeley and J. L. Toole, light comedians such as William Lewis and Charles Mathews the younger, had developed a stage personality and technique that transcended much of the material in which they appeared. They were not interpretative artists, but self-creating. Joseph Knight puts this rather well in an article on J. L. Toole:

> The fact is that the art of the low comedy actor is seldom purely histrionic, and is sometimes not art at all. Instead of assuming the personality of another man, and fitting his soul as it were and his whole being into another individuality, he obtains ordinarily his most triumphant effects from the obtrusion, through a fictitious character, of his own triumphantly comic self. While the ordinary stage artist is successful in proportion as he hides himself behind the assumed garb, the low comedy actor is successful as he reveals himself.[4]

This was true of many of the major comedians on the nineteenth-century stage. Leigh Hunt commented of John Liston that one wondered 'whether the part he pretends to act is not rather a vehicle for Liston than Liston for the part', since, in many instances, 'the audience are still thinking of Liston and content to give up the character, as it were, for his sake'.[5] Westland Marston accepted the principle that the comedian's personality would often be obtrusive. Of John Pritt Harley he wrote: 'If one never expected Harley to lose himself in his part, one was tolerably content that the part should be lost in Harley.'[6] The same applied to J. B. Buckstone: 'It is true that in almost every part he was Buckstone; it is equally so that the public did not wish him to be anyone else.'[7] What was good for Harley and Buckstone was also good for Keeley: 'to a great extent, he was always Keeley – Keeley with his quiet, effortless art, generally with an expression compounded of obtuseness, perplexity and long-suffering.'[8] Nevertheless, as Lewes pointed out, 'When people foolishly objected that he was "always Keeley", they forgot in the first place that an actor with so peculiar an organisation could not disguise his individuality.'[9] In effect, in order to appreciate nineteenth-century farce, one must know something of the personalities of the actors who played in it – they are the parentheses essential to its reading.

Nineteenth-century comedians were not merely creative in the stage personalities they developed – they were creative, in the broadest possible sense, with much of the material that came their way. At best this could mean a collaborative relationship with the writers who furnished their scripts. James Kenney's first farce, *Raising the Wind* (1803), owed much to

William Lewis's development of the role of Jeremy Diddler, as Kenney's *Advertisement* to the published edition of the play indicates:

> The readers of this Farce will be sensible how much I owe the Performers for the applause with which it has been honoured in the representation. They all evinced a zeal in its behalf, for which I return them my most cordial thanks. To Mr Lewis I am particularly indebted, not only for the very great share he contributed to the performance but also for some friendly suggestions at the rehearsals; which, I have no doubt, proved of considerable advantage.[10]

It was said of Charles Mathews the elder that many of the parts written for him were mere sketches, which he was left to fill in *ad-libitum*.[11] Roles such as Buskin in *Killing No Murder* (1809) were considered to be mere outlines on which Mathews would elaborate. Theodore Hook, the author of this play, pays tribute to Mathews in his preface and also adds that Liston, as Apollo Belvi: 'exceeded my anxious expectations; indeed, all authors must be made by such an actor, because no part as originally written can be equal to his talents'.[12] Equally, in his preface to *Music Mad* (1807), Hook apologizes for publishing 'a mere sketch', which was:

> written last season to show the extraordinary talents of that excellent comedian MATHEWS; now, really, the exertion of these talents, in conjunction with the exquisite acting of the inimitable LISTON, procured so favourable a reception for the piece, that, in common justice to those men, I publish it; that the town, seeing how weak it is in itself, may know what is due to them.[13]

Hook is less sanguine, however, when he describes the experiences of a young playwright, Gilbert Gurney, in his novel of that name. Gurney learns very quickly that he has little power over the form and content of his work: 'it had been hinted to me that it [the play] wanted enlivening; and, moreover, that if Mr Mathews had a song, Mr Liston would expect to have one also; that these were little points of professional etiquette that were as rigidly observed as the rules and ceremonies of other services.'[14] On the first night of the play's performance Gurney is even more chastened: 'I listened to my own words fearfully and tremblingly; not that I heard quite so many of them as I had confidently expected, seeing that most of the low comedians substituted, for what they had not learned, speeches and dialogue, not one word of which I had written.'[15] Despite the expression of such views, it is largely true that the low comedians were the creative force behind many of the farces in which they appeared. J. B. Buckstone, an author as well as a low comedian, was often tempted to rewrite the parts he played in other people's plays. Regardless of the congruity of the piece, interpolations and eccentricities would soon emerge. 'For filling out a meagre sketch, till it appears a very prominent part, Buckstone is your only man', wrote Ben Webster.[16] John Reeve, another improvisatory actor, once appeared with Buckstone in the latter's drama *Isabelle* (1834) and between them the two actors contrived 'to keep the audience in roars of laughter for

1 John Liston as Apollo Belvi in Theodore Hook's *Killing No Murder* (E. F. Lambert, engraved by W. Sheldrick, 1823)

full five and twenty minutes . . . though most of the fun was ad-libitum'.[17] Such a process was later described by John Hollingshead, with reference to J. L. Toole, as 'working up [the] part in good low comedian style'.[18] In effect, whilst the writer of farce might provide the mechanics of situation, the actor retained a strong control over character and even dialogue.[19]

Inevitably, the public began to confuse the characters they saw on stage with the actors who actually played them. Since the stage personality of the actor remained relatively constant and unchanging from play to play, the audience tended to identify the role with the actor. (It is likely, too, that this consistency was at the basis of the reassuring impact of farce – whatever the terrors and tribulations suffered by the actor, his personality remains unscathed and his body physically unblemished, ready for the next comical encounter outside of his control.) That consistency could have far-reaching effects is exemplified by the light comedian, William Lewis. Words like 'bustle' and 'mercurial' were often used of actors like Lewis, Richard Jones, John Harley, Charles Mathews the elder and younger, who embodied the active, energetic principle so essential to farce. Lewis had extraordinary energy, which he evinced in almost every part he played. 'Whether sitting or standing', said James Boaden, 'he was never for a moment at rest.'[20] Leigh Hunt referred to his 'animal spirits' and his 'airy breathless voice'; his energy must have been phenomenal, for 'he jumped over the stage properties as if his leap frog days had just commenced' and 'danced the hay with chairs, tables and sittees'.[21] Hazlitt recorded how Lewis

> never let the stage stand still, and made your heart light and your head giddy with his infinite vivacity, and bustle, and hey-day animal spirits – Nobody could break open a door, or jump over a table, or scale a ladder or twirl a cocked hat, or dangle a cane . . . like him.[22]

One quality of his performance which, said Boaden, 'was an addition to the character, springing from himself', was very striking:

> It might be called the attempt to take advantage of the lingering sparks of gallantry in the aunt or the mother of sixty, or the ancient maiden whom he had to win, to carry the purposes of those for whom he was interested. He seemed to throw the lady by degrees off her guard, until at last his whole artillery of assault was applied to storm the struggling resistance; and the (objects) of his attention sometimes complained of the perpetual motion of his chair, which compelled them to a ludicrous retreat, and kept the spectator in a roar of laughter.

Lewis was a popular Rover (the actor) in O'Keeffe's play *Wild Oats* (1791), as well as the original Jeremy Diddler and the original Goldfinch in Holcroft's *The Road to Ruin* (1792). When Lewis retired, Richard Jones, who quite candidly modelled his acting style on Lewis, took over many of his roles.[23] Like Lewis, Jones 'seldom remained still a moment when engaged in a scene, always bustling about to the distress of his fellow-actors'.[24]

Charles Mathews the elder also developed some of Lewis's bustling
characteristics and became his successor in the role of Goldfinch.
Mathews's son also contributed to the 'bustling' tradition later in the
century, for he was 'eminently vivacious: a nimble spirit of mirth sparkled
in his eye, and gave airiness to every gesture. He was in incessant movement
without ever being obtrusive and fidgety.'[25]

So strong was Lewis's impact that, when actors were subsequently
depicted in plays and novels, they often possessed many of Lewis's stage
characteristics. In Hook's *Killing No Murder*, for instance, Buskin is a
volatile, quick-witted actor, whose dialogue is full of acting metaphors and
mock heroic speeches:

> I dare not – I am – poor – thin, and miserable – he is fat, rich and impudent –
> no, fly I must!
> Fly?
> Yes – (*Exit Buskin the wrong way*) (*Re-enters*) – I have no money.

Mathews, who played Buskin, was well known as an impersonator of his
fellow actors and it would be interesting to surmise that he played the part
in imitation of Lewis's bustling Rover, Diddler or Goldfinch. Lewis's
influence was also apparent in R. B. Peake's play *Amateurs and Actors* (1818),
in which one of the principal characters is called Bustle. Bustle is an actor–
manager whose name, claimed George Daniel, an editor of the play, 'is
sufficiently indicative of his calling and temperament' and whose character
'afforded Mr Harley (who played the part) full scope for his vivacity'.[26] In
The Pickwick Papers Jingle, the actor, possesses a character that closely
approximates to some of the roles that Lewis played: 'an indescribable air of
jaunty impudence and perfect self-possession pervaded the whole man'.[27]
His energy is a legacy from Lewis and Jones, his speech patterns are derived
from Goldfinch and from some of the characters that Mathews the elder
created for his *At Homes*,[28] his Shakespearian allusions follow those of Rover
in *Wild Oats*, and his elopement with Miss Wardle is borrowed from Jeremy
Diddler's attempted elopement in *Raising the Wind*.[29] John Fawcett, another
bustling comedian, had a similar influence on at least one author. One of his
most popular characters, Caleb Quotem (in Colman's *The Review*, 1800), is
referred to in Pierce Egan's *The Life of an Actor* (1825). In the debtor's prison
Proteus, the hero of this novel, is accosted by 'a shabby-genteel dandy
dressed young fellow', named Bob Thimble: 'The volubility displayed by
Mr Thimble was almost as rapid as Caleb Quotem's description of a day's
work . . . he seemed determined to have all the discourse to himself.
Thimble had scarcely taken a breath when he began again.'[30] Since
Thimble is a tailor, it seems that Lewis's and Fawcett's farce characteristics
were not limited to the depiction of actors in drama and fiction. However, at
least neither Dickens nor Egan was as lazy as Hook, who merely charac-

terized the innkeeper, Grojan, in his novel *Doubts and Fears* (1825), by asking the reader to imagine he was watching Mr Liston in one of his parts.[31]

Since the personality of the actor was so pervasive in nineteenth-century farce, it is not surprising that a certain degree of self-consciousness began to creep into some of the plays. An obvious reference to Mathews is slipped into *Amateurs and Actors*, when Harley's character of Bustle tells how, as a younger man, he undertook every department in the theatre:

> Stuck bills, kept box-book, white-washed Pit entrance, counted checks, scower'd gallery stairs, lit lamps, assisted in first music, dressed Prince Edward and the Duke of York, kept places, spoke occasional address, prompted play, then on for Buskin in the Farce – (*Bustle here imitates the best imitator in the world.*)

Self-reference is also apparent at the conclusion of George Colman the younger's *Sylvester Daggerwood* (1808, originally known as *New Hay at the Old Market*), in which Sylvester Daggerwood, an actor, and Fustian, a writer, await an interview with Colman, who was also the manager of the Haymarket Theatre. At the end of the play Fustian (originally played by Richard Suett) and Daggerwood (played by John Bannister junior) are informed by a servant that Colman has gone out:

> *Servant.* He ordered me to tell you, gentlemen, he was particularly sorry, but he was obliged to hurry down to the theatre, to meet Mr Bannister junior and Mr Suett, on particular business.
> *Fustian.* They are! and what the devil, friend, have I to do with Mr Bannister junior! Damn Mr Bannister junior!
> *Daggerwood.* And damn Mr Suett! What the devil have I to do with Mr Suett? Now he has shirted us, I'll lay an even bet he has gone to neither of them.

Although this farce was first performed in 1795 it remained popular on the early nineteenth-century stage and both Mathews the elder and Harley subsequently essayed Bannister's role of Daggerwood (doubtless with appropriate changes made to the lines quoted above). An even more direct acknowledgement of a popular comedian occurred in J. B. Buckstone's *A New Farce; or, A Scene of Confusion* at the Olympic Theatre in 1835, when Liston played Mr Peter Buzzard. Buzzard is insanely jealous and his wife, who is to make her debut as an actress at the Olympic Theatre, fears that he may try to stop her. In the second scene of the farce, in which Buzzard's wife plays in the play within the play, a voice from the side-boxes suddenly stops the action, as Mrs Buzzard is about to disappear into a side-room with her 'stage' husband:

> Stop – Stop – I'll not allow it.

There are cries from the audience (carefully scripted) of 'Turn him out', but the voice, which belongs to Liston as Mr Buzzard, continues. He says that he objects to his wife playing opposite an actor named Mr Salter:

> Get someone else to play the part. I shall be quiet, but I object to *you* – you're
> too handsome – where's Mr Liston – I should not object to Mr Liston – I
> admire Mr Liston – I love him as much as I love myself – *he* may play the part if
> you please, but you shall not.

Madame Vestris, the proprietor of the Olympic Theatre, now appears in
the box opposite Buzzard and insists that Mr Salter plays the role she's
assigned him:

> I want Mr Liston for another piece. Besides, he's not in the house.

Buzzard doesn't believe her:

> He is in the house – Don't tell me, Mrs – Mrs – I don't know her name – he *is* in
> the house – I hear his voice – now – while I'm speaking – there – (*to the audience*)
> ain't that his voice? – to be sure it is – think I don't know Mr Liston's voice.

To which Madame Vestris replies that she's sent to Bow Street to have Mr
Buzzard removed, as he's destroying the performance. In fact, she finally
agrees to let Mr Buzzard take over Salter's role, so that he clambers onto the
stage and reads from a script. Most of the jokes now arise from his
gaucheness on stage, but pandemonium again threatens when Mr Buzzard
resists a stage direction that his assumed character is to be tied down.
Madame Vestris has to appear again to apologize to the audience; she asks
them to be tolerant as the new farce is being produced in 'circumstances
unparalleled on the British stage'. At the end of the farce the curtain falls so
that Mr Buzzard is left alone with the audience. He tells them that it's the
stupidest farce they've seen and that they ought to demand their money
back. He thanks them for their attention and, before going off, invites a
friend whom he recognizes in the audience home for tea.

Self-acknowledgement went even further when an actor actually played
himself. This happened in a short extravaganza, *Harlequin Hoax*, which
Thomas Dibdin wrote for the English Opera House in the summer of
1814.[32] In this play the two leading performers for the season, John Liston
and Fanny Kelly, played themselves. The piece concerns a dramatist,
Patch, who has written a Harlequinade; despite the fact that the Opera
House manager, Mr Raymond, has shown him little encouragement, he
has nevertheless distributed parts to various actors in the company.
Raymond asks him who has been given the part of Harlequin, to which
Patch replies:

> Ah! There I've been at a loss. So, by my friend Bob's advice, here, I gave the
> part to . . .

But he can go no further, for the unmistakable voice of Liston is heard off
stage:

> Oh, but if I do I'll be . . .

It transpires that Liston is in a terrible rage; indeed, he threw the part at the prompter's head as soon as he read it; and his first speech endorses this fact:

> Mr Raymond – I have the highest veneration for my employers, a sincere regard for the welfare of their property, and no man could be more gratefully devoted to the public; but I beg leave to say, with the highest respect to you, Mr Manager, that if I play this part I'll be d....d.

However, in a side-whisper, Liston informs us that he and Miss Kelly have decided to play a hoax on the pretensions of the author, Patch, and that this rage is therefore assumed. The hoax necessitates a rehearsal of the Harlequinade and provides an opportunity for a number of 'in-jokes'. At one point Mr Raymond asks the prompter why he is laughing; the prompter replies that he is laughing at Mr Liston, who has just accidentally struck Raymond:

> *Liston.* Very much obliged to you, (*turning to Raymond he continues*) . . . but my dear sir, I beg ten thousand pardons. I fear I struck you rather forcibly.
> *Raymond.* Never mind, it's a liberty you take with the audience every night.
> *Prompter.* And then who can help laughing.

At another point he is told he will have to black his face or wear a mask: 'Black my face!' exclaims Liston. 'What this face! Zounds, why what will the ladies say?'[33] Like so many of his stage characters Liston makes execrable puns. On learning that one song in the Harlequinade is to be sung in water, Liston says it is 'so we can have a running accompaniment'. The 'hoax' ends when the author is persuaded to substitute the script for the clown in an incineration scene: it catches fire and is destroyed. As Liston departs he says to Patch:

> When you want any more dry jokes, send for me. My dear manager, you can't take too much care of your denouement.

Within the scope of the play there is acknowledgement of Liston's impact upon his audience, his facial appearance, his vanity and his punning. The satire on the Harlequinade, coupled with the seemingly direct presentation of actors as themselves, proved an irresistible combination.

A hoax was at the centre of another farce in which two leading comedians played themselves later in the century. J. B. Buckstone and Robert Keeley had proved a very popular pairing, especially in John Maddison Morton's farce, *Box and Cox* (1847), in which Keeley had taken over Harley's original role of Cox, and their contrasting styles provided great scope for exploitation. According to Westland Marston:

> Keeley and Buckstone were striking contrasts, the latter being the soul of action in humour, enhancing its effects by all that could be done, the former being passivity itself – the *vis inertiae* of comedy, the suffering and often resigned victim of a persecuting fate.[34]

Marston felt that, when Ben Webster and Mark Lemon wrote *Keeley Worried by Buckstone* (1852) for the two comedians, it gave Keeley 'a capital opportunity of contrasting the sedate humour of his own style with the ebullient jocularity of his fellow-comedian'.[35] Walter Goodman, in his memoir of Keeley and his wife, also referred to this; he recalled how Keeley rarely disfigured himself on stage with false noses or eyebrows, for:

> the more Keeley was himself, the funnier he appeared; and much the same may be said of his voice and manner . . . The actor was never more like himself when playing in a little piece called 'Keeley worried by Buckstone' . . . In this dramatic trifle, which I saw half a dozen times at least, Bob Keeley was to be seen very much as he was at his home in Pelham Crescent in the early part of the day, attired in his dressing-gown and slippers, and once, when I witnessed the farce from a stage-box, it was almost like being in his company.[36]

The main purpose of this farce, said Goodman, 'was to bring forward the best known mannerisms and characteristics of the two low-comedians named in the title, and with this in view the authors had represented Keeley as having made up his mind to retire from the stage'.[37] The farce opens with Keeley at home, rejoicing in the fact that he is at last a free man, for he has done with the stage for ever:

> I am no longer an actor compelled to laugh to order. No! I can indulge my natural disposition, which is sentimentally melancholy. Ha! Ha! my laugh is perfectly hollow, and O. Smithish.[38] My face, no longer disfigured with rouge, has assumed an interesting pallor. I can now say what I please, no longer compelled to utter the bosh of authors: I can give the rein to my imagination, and set my eye 'with a fine frenzy rolling'.

Keeley is provided with the low comedian's traditional yearning to play tragedy. As he says, when he had a dispute over his late arrival at the theatre for a rehearsal.

> I looked severe. The latent tragedy which is in me rushed to my face.

He is not, however, left alone for very long, for J. B. Buckstone suddenly walks into the room and, ignoring Keeley, opens a window, throws a flower pot into the street to attract a young lady's attention, blows kisses to her and hugs one of Keeley's bolsters to him. At first Keeley doesn't recognize this eccentric intruder, then he exclaims:

> Bucky!
> Bobby! How's Mrs K?
> Oh! bobbish!
> And the little Ks?
> Bobbish, too!
> Bobby, don't interrupt me. Oh, that I could press thee to my heart. (*Seizes* Keeley *round the neck and drags him to the window.*) Throw yourself from the window.
> Thank you, I'd rather not.

Buckstone decides to go out to the lady and picks up Keeley's hat, which he drives on to his head, crushes against his bosom and generally maltreats as only hats can be maltreated in farce. After trying on Buckstone's hat and finding that it is too small for him, Keeley resolves not to let Buckstone back in, as his presence made him feel too 'stagey':

> I fancied we were Boxing and Coxing again.

Buckstone, however, re-enters by smashing through a window and Keeley decides to send for some tickets to the Adelphi Theatre, so that he can get away from Buckstone. Buckstone, meanwhile, involves himself in pantomimic action, appears in balletic posture to woo an imaginary lady at an imaginary window and, whenever an opportunity occurs, 'sings, fidgets about the stage and disarranges slightly the books, chairs etc'. He stands on a chair at the window, then hops across the room after Keeley on the same chair. He addresses Keeley, pulling a button off Keeley's coat to underline each point he makes, and is so worked up in talking about a moneylender he knows that he seizes Keeley and almost strangles him. When he is served with lunch, he immediately throws two plates and a bottle out of the window, so that Keeley is summoned to the Police Office. Buckstone says:

> It was me! It was me! It is a mania I have in a certain state of excitement; then I throw the house out of windows.

Keeley has managed to remain relatively calm so far, but now he grows more and more angry, especially as Buckstone's next action is to commence rearranging all of his furniture. He is so exasperated that he decides to leave and abandon his house to Buckstone, but he can't hear what Buckstone is saying, for Buckstone is now mouthing all his replies, as if to make Keeley think that he is deaf. Keeley challenges him to a duel, for

> Though I play the fool on stage, I don't here, sir! This house is sacred to respectability, sir!

A messenger arrives from the Haymarket manager, Ben Webster, offering an engagement to Keeley, since Buckstone has apparently left the theatre. Anything for peace and quiet, decides Keeley, thinking he'll be safer at the Haymarket than at home. He is incensed to discover that Buckstone has not left the theatre after all:

> And have I consented to be in the same theatre with you – to be Box'd and Cox'd . . .

The entire scenario has been a stratagem on Buckstone's part to procure Keeley for the Haymarket Theatre. As the curtain falls, it isolates Keeley, who tells the audience he is glad to be rid of Buckstone – but not for long, for Buckstone joins him immediately to take his bow.

'There was, of course,' commented Goodman, 'not much *plot* in this farce, while the fun was of the fast and furious kind.'[39] As in *Harlequin Hoax* the behaviour of a well-known comedian, in this case Buckstone, was accentuated by the fact that he was the instigator of a sustained practical joke. Nevertheless, the blustering, energetic, active comedy for which he was famous was contrasted with the quiet, passive comedy of Keeley, as if to suggest that the private behaviour of both was merely an extension of their stage personalities. The conventional devices and structures of farce were employed, but the emphasis was on the 'personalities' of the two leading comedians. The references to *Box and Cox*, Keeley's terror and Buckstone's bluster and the assumption that, in real life, they enjoyed a relationship similar to that depicted on stage, suggested the identification achieved between the actors and their roles. Like Laurel and Hardy or the Marx Brothers, they remained unchanging, constant within their self-created characters and relationships, whatever the permutations of situation provided by the dramatist.

Consistency of personality in farce after farce was evidently as reassuring as the moral consistency of behaviour displayed by the principal characters of melodrama. In both genres the protagonists were denied the exercise of free will, but were eventually restored to a benevolent and ordered world, whatever upheavals and torments they had experienced. In nautical melodrama T. P. Cooke played one good-hearted, heroic tar after another; at Covent Garden Charles Farley 'the Prince of Bullies and Robbers, and the Hero of black, subterranean dens'[40] was invariably the villain of the piece. Such actors played much the same role in play after play; their characters might as well have been called Cooke or Farley, if the genre had allowed it. Farce, at least, allowed the acknowledgement of this consistency and actors other than Buckstone, Liston and Keeley appeared as themselves. In 1875 the popular J. L. Toole acted in a short farce by Robert Reece entitled *Toole at Sea*. In this play Toole is on a voyage, during which he suffers terribly from sea-sickness. The passengers and crew expect to be regaled by comic anecdotes and jokes and find Toole's illness vastly amusing:

> *Captain.* Ah, what fun we shall have, to be sure, when he's himself again! What songs and imitations! What anecdotes! Delightful anticipation . . . We may persuade him to get up some theatricals. Delicious thought! . . . I can hear his voice already – that voice is full of rollicking fun – so full –
> (Toole *in his berth*)
> *Toole.* Oh Lord! Oh Lord! – Where are we? – What are we doing?
> *Captain.* It is his voice – he's beginning his jokes. Now for a side-splitter . . .

When the Captain says 'Oh, Mr Toole!', Toole merely replies 'Call me "Too-ill"', but he does not receive any sympathy. In fact, he finds himself forced to make love to one of the female passengers on board, so that he can arouse the jealousy of the man she loves and thereby provoke him to propose to the girl. The suffering and the complications that ensue, through no particular fault of Toole, who is merely the victim of circumstances, suggested once more that the comic actor was merely an extension of the characters he normally played.

Another variation in self-presentation occurred in *A Most Un-Warrantable Intrusion Committed by Mr Wright to the annoyance of Mr Paul Bedford*, a farce written for the Adelphi Theatre in 1849 by John Maddison Morton. Michael Booth draws attention to the theatricality of this particular farce in his *Prefaces to Nineteenth-Century English Theatre*, since it contains a very unusual variation on the traditional address to the audience at the end of the play.[41] In many ways this farce anticipated *Keeley Worried by Buckstone*, in that Bedford as Mr Nathaniel Snoozle is contentedly at home in comfortable seclusion, having sent the women-folk off to London and given the servants a day off. His tranquillity is soon interrupted by an intruder (played by Wright), who comes into the house and begins to behave very oddly. He makes very personal remarks about Snoozle's corpulence, fidgets with toasting forks, fish bowls and snuff boxes, then proceeds to move the furniture around, because he doesn't like the way it's arranged. It transpires that the intruder is a man who wants to marry Snoozle's niece and his strange behaviour is a ploy to trap Snoozle into agreeing to the marriage.

Intruder. . . . I wanted to marry your niece – you said I should never have your consent – I said I *would* – and here it is!
  (*Flourishing letter*) I repeat, here it is – Go on Paul!
Paul Bedford. I haven't got any more in my part!
  (*Taking part out of his pocket and showing it.*)
Wright. No more have I!
Bedford. I say, Prompter!
  (*Enter* Prompter)
Prompter. Yes, sir.
Bedford. Hasn't the author sent the tag yet?
Prompter. No sir – here's the manuscript.
Wright. Just like him! You know he didn't send the tag to his last new farce 'til about five minutes before the curtain went up.
Prompter. I heard him say it was no use writing a tag, for Mr Wright always spoke his own.
Wright. That's not the fact. There's no man on the stage takes less liberties with his author than I do. Well, Paul . . . I suggest we must finish the piece as well as we can. The usual thing is to make a pathetic appeal to the audience – so be pathetic, Paul . . .
Bedford. No. You understand that better than I do.
Wright. Then, Ladies and Gentlemen, all I can say is, if we have committed some errors, let us hope that they are trifling ones: at any rate, we'll manage to correct them by tomorrow evening, if you'll oblige us by looking in . . ., and depend upon it, come as often as you like, we shall never consider it an 'UNWARRANTABLE INTRUSION'.

The illusion of performance is suddenly acknowledged in this particular farce, instantaneously transforming characters into actors and providing a strange and rather implosive ending.

Such self-acknowledgement usually served, in the drama of other eras, to fracture the illusion, in order to arouse the audience's judgement or to emphasize their complicity in the action witnessed. Critics such as Ann Barton and Peter Holland have shown that such techniques could achieve great sophistication on the Elizabethan and Restoration stages.[42] In nineteenth-century farce, despite the slightly Pirandellian relationship of the actor to his character and his play, the purpose was far less subtle. Instead of such techniques enforcing a sense of the unreality of what was being witnessed, they served to intensify the identification between character and actor. Wright and Bedford might address each other personally at the end of *An Unwarrantable Intrusion*, but it is likely they retained their stage personalities, whatever name they were called by. The actor remained 'his own triumphantly comic self', as farce after farce celebrated and endorsed his self-created stage personality. However eccentric his behaviour, however extreme his depiction of terror or pathos, he was always reassuringly the same, unscathed physically and undeveloped spiritually. He placed himself firmly at the centre of the genre, in an age when performance arguably counted for more than the play. But, because he, like the protagonists of melodrama, was never changed by his experiences, the exploitation of self-consciousness in nineteenth-century farce was of a somewhat conservative nature. Indeed, the imperviousness of its protagonists to experience and environment transformed it into a protracted celebration of egotism. Paradoxically, nineteenth-century farce sustained its impact through self-awareness and self-consciousness, whilst depicting the least self-aware and self-conscious of individuals. In so doing it reconciled the egotism of the actor with the egotism of the character he depicted and endorsed a consistency of personality that promised a reassuring outcome to the action of the play, however extreme or extraordinary the situations that occurred. It played dangerous to play safe.

NOTES

1 G. H. Lewes, *On Actors and Acting* (London, 1875), p. 68. Lewes is referring to a revival of the play.
2 Westland Marston, *Our Recent Actors* (London, 1888), vol. II, p. 202.
3 Lewes, *On Actors and Acting*, p. 78.
4 *The Theatre*, NS, I (January, 1880), pp. 25–6.
5 *Examiner*, 29 January 1815.
6 *Our Recent Actors*, vol. II, p. 294.
7 Ibid., vol. II, p. 89.
8 Ibid., vol. II, p. 102.

9 *On Actors and Acting*, p. 79.
10 E. Inchbald, *Collection of Farces* (London, 1808), vol. I.
11 A. Mathews, *Memoirs of Charles Mathews, Comedian* (London, 1838–9), vol. I, p. 421.
12 Theodore Hook, *Killing No Murder* (London, 1809).
13 Theodore Hook, *Music Mad* (London, 1808).
14 *Gilbert Gurney* (London, 1836), p. 73.
15 Ibid., p. 80.
16 B. N. Webster, *Acting National Drama* (London, 1837–   ), vol. V, *Memoir of Mr Buckstone*.
17 Ibid.
18 *Gaiety Chronicles* (London, 1898), pp. 124–5.
19 This tendency, of course, was not merely limited to nineteenth-century exponents of farce.
20 Quoted in W. Clark Russell, *Representative Actors* (London and New York, 1888), p. 208.
21 Ibid., p. 209.
22 Quoted in M. R. Booth, *English Plays of the Nineteenth Century* (Oxford University Press, 1973), vol. III, p. 151.
23 W. Robson, *The Old Playgoer* (London, 1846), p. 61.
24 E. Stirling, *Old Drury Lane* (London, 1881), vol. II, p. 105.
25 Lewes, *On Actors and Acting*, p. 62.
26 G. Daniel, Introduction to R. B. Peake, *Amateurs and Actors*, Cumberland's British Theatre (London, 1829), vol. XVI.
27 Charles Dickens, *The Pickwick Papers* (London, 1837), chapter 2.
28 See Earle Davis, *The Flint and the Flame* (London: Gollancz, 1964), pp. 44–6.
29 The similarity between these two characters must have been familiar to Henry Irving, who frequently performed one or other of these roles in tandem with *The Bells* later in the century.
30 (London, 1825), chapter 4. W. Robson also refers to Fawcett's rapidity of speech in this role.
31 Theodore Hook, *Sayings and Doings* (London, 1825), vol. II, p. 64.
32 The term 'extravaganza' raises a basic problem when defining nineteenth-century farce – terms like burletta, extravaganza, comedy, farce are often used very imprecisely. Extravaganzas were normally closer to burlesque, whereas burlettas were often closer to farce, although none of these genres are mutually exclusive.
33 Throughout this period farces contained characters, intended for Liston, who make references to their facial appearance. In Hook's *Catch Him Who Can* (1806) one of the characters tells Liston, as Pedrillos, that the sight of strange faces alarms him. 'I hope, sir', replies Liston's character, 'that you don't see anything *strange* in my *face*.' In George Dance's *Hush Money* (1833) Liston as Jasper Touchwood took part in the following dialogue:

> *Sally.* Ha! Ha! Come that's good again – Lord, how I do like to look at that droll face of yours, when you say them things.
> *Touchwood.* Indeed! Upon my word, I'm obliged to you; but I don't happen to consider my face at all droll.
> *Sally.* Ah! but I do – droll enough to belong to the Funny Club.

34 *Our Recent Actors,* vol. II, p. 99.

35 Ibid., vol. II, p. 105.

36 *The Keeleys on the Stage and at Home* (London, 1895), pp. 149–50.

37 Ibid., p. 150.

38 O. (Obi) Smith was a popular actor in melodrama.

39 *The Keeleys,* p. 150.

40 *Theatrical Observer,* 23 February 1825.

41 (Manchester University Press, 1981), pp. 127–8.

42 *Shakespeare and the Idea of the Play* (London: Greenwood Press, 1962) and *The Ornament of Action* (Cambridge University Press, 1979). Holland draws attention to lines spoken by Monsieur de Paris (probably played by Nokes) in *The Gentleman Dancing Master* (Wycherley) in which reference is made to Nokes and his rival comedians.

Georges Feydeau and the 'serious' farce*

J. PAUL MARCOUX

Aldous Huxley once suggested: 'Tragedy is the farce that involves our sympathies; farce, the tragedy that happens to outsiders.'[1] The comparison seems particularly apt in the case of Georges Leon Jules Marie Feydeau. Born in Paris in 1862, he is remembered as the king of French 'vaudeville' and second only to Molière as a truly great writer of French comedy, but his own life more often bordered on the tragic. Although he seems to have delighted in his early literary attempts, he became increasingly morose and found little satisfaction in the phenomenal success he achieved in his artistic maturity. He considered playwriting a job from which he could not escape and had to force himself to work. In the course of an interview, Feydeau once complained:

> When I start a play, I feel as if I were locking myself up in a cell from which I cannot escape until it is finished. Oh no, I am not among those who give birth with joy. When I plan the silly things that will amuse the public I am not amused; I am very serious; I have the detachment of the pharmacist dispensing medicine. Into my potion I put a dram of complication, a dram of adventurism and a dram of observation. I mix these elements together as best I can. Furthermore, I can almost always tell the effects they will produce.[2]

It is strangely ironic that these plays, which have caused such hilarity throughout the western world for nearly a century, should have been created under these circumstances. But then, a close examination does indeed reveal a strong kinship to tragedy. I shall first examine this kinship in a general way and then with specific reference to three examples of Feydeau's work.

Feydeau, singly or in collaboration, wrote thirty-nine plays, almost all of which are classified as farces. It seems unnecessary to quibble over classification, but it is interesting to note that unlike literary comedy, melodrama, tragedy and other forms of drama, there is little agreement concerning the aesthetics of farce. Furthermore, attempts to define farce are often tinged with philosophical and literary prejudice. Comparing comedy

---

* A draft of this paper was read at the *Themes in Drama* International Conference held at the University of California, Riverside, in February 1986.

and farce, John Dryden said: 'Comedy presents us with the imperfections of human nature. Farce entertains us with what is monstrous and chimerical. The one causes laughter in those who can judge of men and manners, by the lively representation of their folly or corruption. The other produces the same effect in those who can judge of neither, and that only by its extravagances . . .'[3] Whereas Dryden's acerbic comments would seem aimed as much at the audience as at the playwright, there is little doubt about George Bernard Shaw's object of scorn when he argues that conventional farce produces 'base laughter . . . by turning human beings onto the stage as rats are turned into a pit, that they may be worried for the entertainment of the spectators . . . [resulting in] . . . the deliberate indulgence of that horrible, derisive joy in humiliation and suffering which is the beastliest element in human nature.'[4] It is true that farce usually has been regarded as a 'lower' form of comedy, but such harsh criticism does little to help establish standards for judging the aesthetic or social value of a form of writing that has enjoyed almost universal popularity over a very wide spectrum of time and place.

On the other hand, farce does present difficulties which cannot be easily ignored. It is not a gentle form of playwriting. The characters in a farce suffer a great deal; at times the innocent along with the guilty. Physical violence is common; psychological damage often inflicted. We are invited to laugh at what seems to be a monstrous exaggeration of the human condition. Characters in a farce are often out of control and seem headed for inevitable disaster. Since they do not recognize their own self-indulgence, the characters often seem shallow and totally manipulated by circumstances or by their own passions. In addition, since its only purpose seems to be to provoke laughter at any cost, farce often seems to be formless and irrational. Plot seems little more than a mere chain of events, while motives are either non-existent or obviously forced. The dramaturgy of farce is clever but hardly designed to allow for reflection or even for lasting effect. What then is the value of farce, particularly French farce, and why has it endured?

Eric Bentley has suggested:

> Farce in general offers a special opportunity; shielded by delicious darkness and seated in warm security, we enjoy the privilege of being totally passive while on stage our most treasured, unmentionable wishes are fulfilled before our eyes by the most violently active human beings that ever sprang from the human imagination . . . we savor the adventure of adultery . . . without taking the responsibility or suffering the guilt.[5]

It would seem that farce can and probably does serve this function, at least to some extent, but then so does pornography. What is striking about farce, especially French bedroom farce and most especially the work of Feydeau, is that for all of its violence and sexual innuendo it is almost never obscene.

A more compelling explanation of farce is offered by Stuart E. Baker,[6] who suggests that farce fulfills a universal need to make a toy of the world and a game of the activities of its inhabitants. As adults we see too many risks involved to safely view our lives as play. We are far too 'civilized' to think of the human condition as some kind of wonderful joke or at least we are very hesitant to allow ourselves that luxury without the help of an acceptable pseudo-self; so, we keep reinventing the clown. Here is the perfect symbol, the ideal stand-in, the magical everyman. What we cannot or dare not do he can and does. He is not offended by fantasy; he *is* fantasy. Beneath his mask of bufoonery he may have all our terribly human ailments and inadequacies but unlike us, he need never reveal them. He is free to turn the world upside down and never risk feeling anything but the exhilaration of a chaotic slide toward oblivion. The theatrical clown sees his world as a giant plaything. It may be destroyed and rebuilt to his own image, or it may be left intact. We are merely tenants in his world and if we wish to share his wonder at the human condition we must relinquish some and in some cases nearly all of our precious control.

Eugene Ionesco saw interesting implications in this idea of control. Writing in the program for a London revival (1965–6) of *A Flea In Her Ear* by the National Theatre of Great Britain, he compared comedy and drama by suggesting that: 'In drama the progression [of accumulated effects] is slower, with better brakes and steering. In comedy, the movement seems to get out of the author's control. He does not drive the machine, he is driven by it. Perhaps that is the difference between tragedy and a certain kind of comedy.'[7]

Marcel Achard in the preface to the collected works of Feydeau had somewhat the same idea. 'Feydeau's plays have the continuity, the force and the violence of tragedy; and the same inexorable sense of fate. In tragedy, one is choked with horror. In Feydeau, one is suffocated with laughter. We are occasionally given some respite by the heroes of Shakespeare and Racine when they . . . bewail their fate . . . but Feydeau's heroes haven't got the time to complain . . .'[8]

Seen in this light, farce takes on a dimension that would seem to temper Kierkegaard's criticism that farce 'is totally incapable of producing a uniform mood in the more cultured audience'.[9] In fact, it is possible to pursue the image of a 'uniform mood' and come to the opposite conclusion. If farce is a game played by clowns who serve as our understudies, it can be played at a variety of levels, depending on the skill of the players, the degree and type of control employed and the difficulty of the challenges to be overcome. It can be lighthearted without being banal or trivial. It can be chaotic without being totally devastating. And perhaps most importantly, the game, because it refuses to be serious, deprives us of such blinders as moral indignation, fear, anger, prejudice, and the need to prove ourselves.

Stripped of such 'excess baggage', we are better able to use the theatre experience as a means of understanding our world. Since none of the other creatures with whom we share this planet seems to be blessed with the ability to laugh, it may be that we are never more human than when we do laugh. Farce makes it possible for us to laugh at ourselves, thereby permitting a kind of renewal of our relationship with the world in a surprisingly serious way. Aesthetically, this is not far from the classical notion that purgation is the ultimate aim of tragedy.

Henri Gidel in his detailed study of Feydeau's dramaturgy[10] concludes that Feydeau raised the level of the current vaudeville or French popular theatre to a unique art form. He accomplished this not because he was particularly innovative but because he allowed his 'well-oiled machine' to take on a life of its own despite the tight controls inherent in his geometric approach to plotting. In his own words, he did this by 'looking for my characters in living reality, determined to preserve their personalities intact. After a comic exposition, I . . . hurl them into burlesque situations.'[11] By rooting his characters in our world Feydeau allowed us to see them in their own. As exaggerated as they might be, Feydeau's people are utterly believable. If they are fools, are there not fools in the world? And, because they are touchingly human, our reaction to them is ambivalent. We laugh at their folly but we also feel genuine compassion because of their misery. No Feydeau character is easily dismissed. That may well be because we have learned (or are learning) that no human being is easily dismissed.

It is also possible to consider Feydeau an important precursor of the so-called absurdist movement in France. In the same program note quoted earlier, Ionesco suggests that what we see in the well-ordered structure of a Feydeau play is actually a *dis*ordering. Feydeau's 'famous farcical mechanism is one that runs mad, carried away by its own momentum . . . there is a sort of vertiginous acceleration . . . a plunge into madness; I seem to see in it my own obsession with proliferation.'[12] Of course, Ionesco's characters are far more de-humanized than are Feydeau's, but they share a helplessness in the face of ever-increasing and accelerating conflicts and nerve-shattering events. We can see Moulineaux's silly imitation of a dressmaker in *Tailleur pour dames* as an early foretokening of Jean's obsession with metamorphosis in *Rhinoceros*. Surely Samuel Beckett's penchant for clown-like characters places him in Feydeau's company. Is Barillon in *Le Mariage de Barillon* any less pathetic than Estragon in *Waiting For Godot*, or less amusing? They are both touchingly human clowns harshly flung into a world over which they have little or no control. Although both somewhat wearier for their experiences, they both end up exactly where they started. Such comparisons are not to suggest that Feydeau invented absurdism. For one thing, Beckett, Ionesco, Adamov and others write out of a more existential and far less hopeful milieu than that of Feydeau. While Beckett seems to be half-heartedly shaking his fist at God for the cruel joke which is man, Feydeau sits quietly in a café watching the parade of human folly go by. We are not exactly sure what, if anything, is at the end of Ionesco's mysterious tunnel; but, as Feydeau lazily walks the Paris boulevards and stops to chat with the newsman near the Gare St Lazare until dawn, we know that at least here there is tomorrow.

Let us take a closer look at three of Feydeau's lesser-known plays to illustrate his truly remarkable skill as a serious commentator on the human condition. *Tailleur pour dames*, *Le Mariage de Barillon* and *Occupe-toi d'Amélie* are from different periods of Feydeau's life and in some ways representative of particular phases of his career. Once Feydeau had established the pattern of what Clive Barnes has called his 'exquisite instruments for oblivion'[13] he tended to improve but not radically change the basic format. He was a craftsman who knew what the public wanted and he usually gave it to them without becoming overly concerned with innovation. Feydeau's genius lies not in daring dramaturgy but rather in an ability to synthesize and build upon what was already a proven theatrical form. He was able consistently to keep intact what was most appealing in the old French vaudeville, while evoking a genuine sympathy for characters who are disturbingly recognizable.

For all his emphasis on refining a successful pattern of playwriting, Feydeau was clearly influenced by the events in his personal life, by ever-changing fashion and by his own sensibilities. Although most of his plays share a great deal in common, there are marked differences among them which reflect not only artistic development but personal factors as well. During most of his life Feydeau was affected by periods of serious depression. His marriage to the beautiful daughter of the painter Carolus-Duran resulted in three children, was apparently successful at first, but gradually soured. He eventually spent less and less time at home, and over the years established a life style hardly designed to please Madame Feydeau. He was almost constantly in debt, and was particularly crushed when he was forced to liquidate his valuable and much prized art collection. The normal ups and downs of life seemed to have a harsher than normal effect on Feydeau and he often referred to himself as gloomy, taciturn and even unsociable. One has to look beneath the gaiety of a Feydeau farce to see the elegant but sad farceur quietly sipping his mineral water (he never drank spirits) in a Paris café, but he is there.

Feydeau's father, Ernest, was a minor writer of the period who was best known for his friendship with such literary luminaries as Dumas, Gautier and Flaubert. His mother was a strikingly beautiful Polish woman who was reported to have had affairs with several prominent men. Although the family was not particularly stable, young Feydeau was obviously

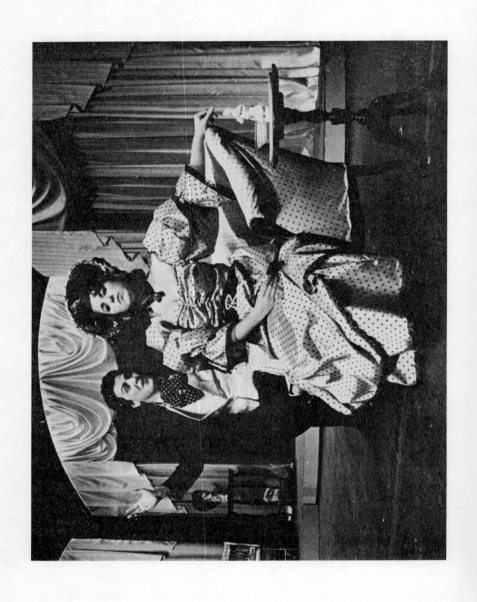

2 and 3 Feydeau's *Tailleur pour dames*, Boston College production

pampered. He seems to have been indifferent to his studies, and his one passion was the theatre, which he discovered at an early age. After his father's death and his mother's subsequent marriage to a well-known drama critic, Feydeau lived away from home. Following his military service, he worked as a secretary for the Renaissance Theatre in Paris where his first full-length play, *Tailleur pour dames*, was presented in 1886. Despite the fact that it had taken Feydeau three years to see the play produced, it enjoyed immediate and lasting success. Although *Tailleur* is not as complex as the later plays, it has most of the ingredients of the better-known *Puce à l'oreille* and *L'Hôtel du Libre-Echange*. The characters are presented as reasonably normal; the situation well within the realm of possibility. The 'machine' starts off in low gear. In fact, the opening scene is almost pedestrian. However, the pace soon quickens and the fuel is the 'white lie'. As soon as Moulineaux, a successful physician, tries to lie his way out of the first of a series of embarrassing situations (his night out), the consequences become more and more intolerable. One lie leads to a bigger lie and the audience anxiously waits for the liar to be discovered.

Unlike the characters in some of the later plays, the women here are above reproach and very bourgeois, perhaps reflecting the playwright's premarital idealism. The shadowy demi-monde of Feydeau's later plays is not explored or even referred to. Yvonne, the wife, is innocent, in fact, naive; Suzanne, the intended mistress, is faithful to Aubin, her own husband, for all her flirting; Rosa, who represents the past, is eventually reunited with her husband Bassinet, despite her protestations and her affair with Aubin. Even the men's intentions are stronger than their deeds. Moulineaux never goes beyond the wishing stage; Bassinet innocently and rather frantically searches for his wife; Aubin really does love Suzanne despite his bragadoccio, which in fact seems more fantasy than reality.

It is this moral ambivalence which seems to give *Tailleur* its controlling force. Although Feydeau will deal with less innocent people he will stand fast with the belief that we cannot laugh at evil. He will place his characters in situations where they yield to temptation; but they do so for the sheer fun of it and rarely out of defiance. Is Moulineaux 'wiser' for his close call with disaster? Probably not. The play represents a circumscribed mental system. Things are what they are and if we (and they) were not laughing so hard we'd be crying at that very fact. The play begins and ends with a lie but what comes in between is really rather moving as well as hilariously funny.

Le Mariage de Barillon premièred in 1890, and was co-authored by Feydeau's good friend, Maurice Desvallieres. It belongs among those plays which represent an attempt to duplicate the enormous success of *Tailleur pour dames*. The collaboration with Desvallieres was part of this attempt. It is now impossible to tell how much of the play is Feydeau's but it is interesting to note that later he was to enjoy equal success with the plays he authored alone as with those for which he used a collaborator. Unfortunately, this particular play was received with only lukewarm notices and shortly afterwards Feydeau began a self-imposed two-year exile during which he was determined to perfect his craft by intensively studying the techniques of the leading playwrights of the day.

When he did return to the Paris theatre scene in 1892 he enjoyed enormous popularity with one hit after another. However, this early period evidently haunted him throughout his life and may well have contributed to the emotional condition which eventually forced him to retreat to a private sanitarium.

The characters in *Barillon* are more complex than those in *Tailleur*; they are also a bit darker. Although Madame Jambart, an attractive if overly aggressive lady, never actually breaks her marriage vows, Feydeau does present her (and us) with an intriguing possibility: two husbands! In fact, the whole idea of 'female bigamy', despite the fact that a simple clerical error is at the bottom of it, raises far more complex problems than a mere extra-marital affair. The characters remain innocent but sometimes more accidentally than deliberately. Ursule, the maid; Brigot, the uncle; and Planturel, the mayor; who represent the larger society, are offended, even shocked at the idea of this peculiar menage. It is clear that they would look the other way if it were simply a matter of an amorous liaison or two. This kind of hypocrisy surfaces in several of Feydeau's plays and seems to be a reflection of his own attitude. Or, perhaps it is simply that Paris society was too jaded to be intrigued by a simple affair but could still squirm a bit in the face of polygamy. In either case, the supporting characters are excellent foils, especially Planturel. His Honor the Mayor is brilliantly drawn and an actor's delight. Pompous and crafty, he deserves the abuse heaped upon him and yet we feel a twinge of sympathy for him because nothing that happens is really his fault. In a sense, he is as much a victim as Barillon, although Barillon is more likeable.

Jambert, although stereotyped as a slightly less than civilized seaman, is also an essentially sympathetic character. His two-year absence is never adequately explained, but his return is accepted almost immediately. Feydeau cleverly plays with the audience by not asking them to choose between Barillon and Jambart but rather to accept both – a totally absurd alternative. This has the effect of keeping the audience off balance and the outcome is not as predictable as it is in *Tailleur*. The ambivalence is further strengthened when Jambart is about to go back to the island where he was shipwrecked and leave Madame Jambart to her new husband. The audience is already torn between the two husbands and Jambart gets a good deal of sympathy despite the silliness of the ritual leave taking.

As in *Tailleur*, at the end of the play nothing is really changed. Barillon is still a bachelor; the Jambarts are reunited; the young lovers are still in love; Planturel's honor is intact; Brigot is still confused. This circular dramaturgy marks most of Feydeau's work. It is a pattern that allowed him to sandwich unadulterated madness between a seemingly normal beginning and a reasonably restful conclusion. It gave him the opportunity of reassuring the audience that as crazy as things might get, all would eventually get back to normal. It also provided a kind of safety valve for upholding the mores of the time. One could safely laugh at marital infidelity knowing that absolute fidelity was there at the beginning and would be there at the end. What might come in between was then forgivable and amusing. In *Barillon* the audience is more shaken at the prospect of polygamy than it might have been witnessing a simple affair but even so, the all's-well-that-ends-well dramaturgy takes over and all the fears are put to rest. The audience is not morally outraged because the moral issues have been scrupulously circumvented. Although his own marriage was foundering, Feydeau reaffirms the normality of monogomy for the sake of his audience. This was not necessarily hypocrisy but simply a sign of the times. Outward appearances would gradually become less important as 'la belle époque' came to a conclusion during the first decade of the twentieth century. As painful as his relationship with his wife would become, he remained married, perhaps for the sake of his family. On the other hand, there is little doubt that Feydeau's view of women became increasingly cynical. This is reflected in his characterization of the wives in his plays ranging from the too sweetly innocent Yvonne in *Tailleur* to the nagging, thoroughly obnoxious Julie in *On purge bébé*, a late one-act play. The women in *Barillon* are certainly less naive than those in *Tailleur*, but they are not as unpleasant as those who will appear in later plays. At this point in his development Feydeau was perhaps more concerned with achieving commercial success than philosophizing about women and marriage. Audiences could comfortably leave a performance of *Barillon* reaffirming their faith in God and la belle France.

Occupe-ti d'Amélie was one of Feydeau's last full-length plays and is representative of several attempts on his part to move away from the standard formula which had brought him so much success during most of his career. For one thing, the play is less symmetrical and somewhat more loosely constructed than most of his work. Although it carries a situation to the point of near madness as nearly all of his plays do, Amélie remains one of Feydeau's most charming and sophisticated heroines. She seems less frantic, not as breathless as are characters in other plays in which deception is the keystone among Feydeau's building blocks. It also departs from tradition by having the 'cocotte' as the central figure. Amélie presides over the madness with almost benign detachment. It is not necessary for her to move anywhere; everyone and everything seems to come to her. She rarely initiates an action but is invariably and deeply involved in whatever is going on. She enjoys herself hugely and, because of her position in the French demi-monde, can do so without a hint of self-consciousness.

By 1908, the year *Amélie* was first seen by the French public, 'la belle époque' had died a natural death. What had been seen as decadent, esoteric, even ersatz and strictly reserved for the upper class, was moving much closer to the middle class. The once clear lines which existed between what was acceptable in polite society and what was relegated to the demi-monde were beginning to fade. Certainly kept women were still not invited to the best homes, but many of them found their way into the best beds and with probably much less fussing from 'Madame' than would have been the case in the days of *Tailleur*. It was still important to keep up appearances, but it was generally accepted that just beneath the polished surface lay the persistent itch for self-gratification. After all, Paris was once again the cultural center of Europe (if not the world!); scientific breakthroughs were announced with amazing regularity; the cafés were crowded with every brand of philosopher imaginable and beneath it all, scandal and corruption, even murder and anarchy threatened to topple the heady world of Toulouse-Lautrec, Sarah Bernhardt, and Sigmund Freud.

One senses this ambivalence in *Amélie*. Whereas the situations are neither forced nor shocking, the characters remain guarded. Of course, because they are so wary we laugh even harder when they are hoisted by their own petards. For instance, Marcel's absolute determination not to marry, even to get his inheritance, literally backfires and he ends up married; but what is even worse, he is married to a cocotte! To a turn-of-the-century Parisian male there could be no worse fate. The ambivalence is also present in the attitude of Pochet, Amélie's father, who is not at all concerned with her occupation and in fact goes to great lengths to protect her 'reputation'. What makes the play work so well is indeed the ease with which *almost* anything goes. Feydeau knew his audiences well, and would not have shocked them, but he was clearly not above titillating them, and by this time in his career, not at all adverse to a bit of self-indulgence, which he seems to throw in for good measure. His own marriage had become intolerable and within a year he would leave his wife, Leocardie, to live in a fashionable hotel on one of his beloved boulevards. In *Amélie* there is a sense of the futility of marriage, but later plays would be far more bitter. Here there is still a puckish quality which belies the suffering he must have been experiencing in his personal life.

Feydeau had a deadly fear of boredom, a fact which is reflected in the characters he carefully assembled from reality. They plunge themselves into situation after situation with nearly tragic abandon. They want desperately to escape the tedium of daily living and of course most of them choose sex as their means of escape. Feydeau sees tragedy behind the farce of bed-hopping but his characters do not, although many of them do eventually face up to their own folly. It is particularly ironic that Feydeau's mental stability was seriously impaired in the last years of his life by a syphilis infection he probably contracted as a result of his own promiscuity. He died in a mental hospital outside Paris in 1921.

NOTES

1 Aldous Huxley, *Ape and Essence* (London: Chatto and Windus, 1951), p. 43.
2 Jacques Lorcy, *George Feydeau* (Paris: La Table Ronde, 1972), p. 193.
3 John Dryden, 'An Evening's Love', *The Poems of John Dryden*, ed. James Kinsley (Oxford: Clarendon Press, 1958).
4 George Bernard Shaw, *Our Theatres In the Nineties* (London: Constable, 1932), p. 106.
5 Eric Bentley, *The Life of the Drama* (New York: Atheneum, 1967), p. 34.
6 Stuart E. Baker, *Georges Feydeau and the Aesthetics of Farce* (Ann Arbor: UMI Research Press, 1981).
7 Billy Rose Theater Collection, New York Public Library (Lincoln Center) File, *Feydeau*.
8 Marcel Achard, *Georges Feydeau, Theatre Complet* (Paris: Le Belier, 1956), vol. I, p. 12.
9 Søren Kierkegaard, 'Farce Is Far More Serious', *Yale French Studies*, 14 (New Haven: Yale University Press, 1955), p. 4.
10 Henri Gidel, *Le Théâtre de Georges Feydeau* (Paris: Editions Klincksieck, 1979).
11 Lorcy, *Feydeau*, p. 198.
12 See note 7, above.
13 Clive Barnes, 'The Theater: "Hair", a Love-Rock Musical Inaugurates Shakespeare Festival's Anspacher Playhouse', *New York Times*, 30 October 1967, p. 55.

SELECT BIBLIOGRAPHY

Anon. 'Forms of Shock Treatment for a World Out of Plumb'. *New York Times Literary Supplement*, 18 June 1971, pp. 89–90
Baker, Stuart E. *Georges Feydeau and the Aesthetics of Farce*. Ann Arbor: UMI Research Press, 1981
Barnes, Peter. *Frontiers of Farce*. London: Heinemann, 1977
Bentley, Eric. *The Life of the Drama*. New York: Atheneum, 1967
  Introduction, 'The Psychology of Farce', *Let's Get a Divorce! and Other Plays*. New York: Hill and Wang, 1958
Corrigan, Robert W. Comedy: *Meaning and Form*. San Francisco: Chandler, 1965
Davies, Frederick. *Three French Farces*. Baltimore: Penguin, 1973
Esteban, Manuel A. *Georges Feydeau*: Boston: Twayne, 1983
Frye, Northrup. *Anatomy of Criticism: Four Essays*. Princeton: Princeton University Press, 1957
Gidel, Henry. *Le Théâtre De Georges Feydeau*. Paris: Editions Klincksieck, 1979

Glenville, Peter. 'Feydeau: Father of Pure Farce'. *Theatre Arts* 66 (1957), 86–7
Kerr, Walter. *The Silent Clowns*. New York: Knopf, 1975
Kierkegaard, Søren. 'Farce is Far More Serious'. *Yale French Studies*, 14. New Haven: Yale University Press, 1955
Lorcey, Jacques. *Georges Feydeau*. Paris: La Table Ronde, 1972
Marcoux, J. Paul. *Georges Feydeau: Three Farces*. Lanham, MD: University Press of America, 1986
Pronko, Leonard C. *Eugène LaBiche and Georges Feydeau*. New York: Grove, 1982
Shapiro, Norman Richard. *Feydeau, First to Last: Eight One-Act Comedies*. Ithaca: Cornell University Press, 1982
   Four Farces by Georges Feydeau. Chicago: University of Chicago Press 1970
   'Suffering and Punishment in the Theatre of Georges Feydeau'. *Tulane Drama Review*, 5 (1960), 117–26
Shenkan, Arlette. *Georges Feydeau*. Paris: Editions Seghers, 1972
Stephenson, Robert C. 'Farce As Method'. *Tulane Drama Review*, 5 (1960), 85–93
Taylor, John Russell. *The Rise and Fall of the Well Made Play*. New York: Hill and Wang, 1969
Van Druten, John. 'A Gem from the French Crown'. *Theatre Arts*, 67 (1958), 19–21
Wimsatt, W. K. *The Idea of Comedy*. Englewood Cliffs, N.J.: Prentice-Hall, 1969

Feydeau and the farcical imperative*

MICHAEL R. BOOTH

Farce is a theatrical form in which Molière happily rubs shoulders with Ray Cooney, Pinero with Ben Travers, *Box and Cox* with a scenario from *commedia*, and Gros-Guillaume of the Hôtel de Bourgogne Company with Brian Rix of the Whitehall Theatre. The appeal of farce is universal, yet it is curiously narrowminded and almost monomaniac in its exploitation of man's fears and weaknesses. As a form which has entertained audiences for centuries, it has obviously changed and evolved in technique as well as social content. Yet despite its evolutionary history it has been – unlike comedy and tragedy – remarkably consistent in its objectives and methods, and it has never ceased, even when apparently at its most trivial, to speak powerfully and truthfully about the human condition.

When one examines the comic methods of farce, one always finds that its technique is not merely structural and mechanistic, but is also a way of expressing a view of the human predicament. Evidence of this can be advanced from an appropriate selection of plays and dramatists, but for my purpose here the entire matter can be contained in the nutshell of the second act of Georges Feydeau's *A Flea in Her Ear (La Puce à l'oreille)*,[1] and an explication of this act, with relevant references to other farces, should prove the point.

As background, it is necessary to engage briefly in plot summary. Act II of *A Flea in Her Ear* brings all the characters to the unsavoury Coq d'Or, a hotel notorious for lovers' assignations. Chandebise's wife, Raymonde is there, for believing him unfaithful she has had her friend Lucienne write him a letter, as from an unknown female admirer, making an assignation at the Coq d'Or; Raymonde goes to keep it herself in order to find out the truth. Not exactly a man about town, Chandebise believes that the letter must be intended for his bachelor friend Tournel, who unknown to him lusts after Raymonde. So Tournel arrives at the Coq d'Or in Chandebise's place. Chandebise's nephew Camille is there for a bit of fun with the maid, Antoinette, who is married to Chandebise's servant, Etienne, who also

* A draft of this paper was read at the *Themes in Drama* International Conference held at the University of California, Riverside, in February 1986.

turns up at the Coq d'Or trying to prevent a disaster: the fiery, passionately jealous Spaniard, Carlos Homenides de Histangua, believes (mistakenly) that his wife Lucienne is that evening taking a lover at the Coq d'Or, for he has seen the note to Chandebise which is in her handwriting. Etienne must warn Tournel. Eventually a worried Chandebise also arrives at the Coq d'Or with the same purpose, almost immediately followed by Homenides himself, who has come to the conclusion that Tournel *is* Lucienne's lover. To recapitulate: three wives, three husbands, and two would-be lovers are milling in and out of the Coq d'Or's bedrooms and public areas (the set puts all this on stage), all desperately trying to avoid or pursue each other. Completing the cast for act II is the staff of the Coq d'Or: the manager, Feraillon; the proprietress, Olympe; the chambermaid, Eugénie; the drunken porter, Poche; and decrepit old Baptistin. Poche has the great plot advantage of looking *exactly* like Chandebise, and Baptistin is paid by Feraillon to lie in bed in order to deceive jealous husbands who may break down the doors of bedrooms in which they believe their wives are besmirching the family name. Finally there is Schwarz, a guest at the hotel, who is on his own, though very much hoping that a willing female will come his way in such an establishment.

The first indication of the disasters to come in act II actually occurs at the end of act I, when Camille is trying his best to stop Tournel from going to the Coq d'Or. Tournel cannot understand a word he is saying because Camille has a cleft palate and is entirely incomprehensible unless he puts in his mouth a new silver roof, which is at present soaking in boracic acid on the mantelpiece. By the time Camille reaches it and can speak clearly, Tournel is gone. At moments of dreadful crisis in farce, characters are frequently unable to communicate with each other, either by a device of this kind – another such occurs in Feydeau's and Desvalliers's *L'Hôtel du Libre-Echange* when Martin, with absolutely crucial information to impart to the police, succumbs to his old malady of stuttering incoherently at the sound of thunder – or by a rapid series of exits and entrances in which they just miss each other, or simply by the opposite, an obsessive desire to prevent communication at all costs. The function of Schwarz in act II of *A Flea in Her Ear*, at the centre of a malestrom of confusion and frantic stage action, speaking only German which nobody understands and himself understanding nobody, is another expression of this theme and at the same time a clever variant of a basic farcical technique. Much modern drama – Beckett and Pinter, for example – deals with this theme of the inability or unwillingness to communicate, of the attempts of individuals to hide in their own insecurities. This is a theme of weight and seriousness in both drama and fiction. Farce has extensively treated the same theme, no less serious because it is developed on a comic level.

Some minutes into act II of *A Flea in Her Ear* Tournel and Raymonde, much to their mutual surprise, find themselves together in one of the Coq d'Or's bedrooms, a rather special room, since the bed set into the wall is built, in moments of difficulty and embarrassment for its occupants, to revolve, along with the wall, and disappear into the next room, bringing on in its place another bed containing old Baptistin complaining of his rheumatism. This mechanism has already been demonstrated by Feraillon, who has pushed a button in the wall to activate it. Flustered by Tournel's vigorous attempts at seduction, Raymonde presses the button, thinking it a bell that will summon help. Tournel has turned away to tear off his coat; turning back he leaps on the bed only to find himself embracing a querulous Baptistin with Raymonde nowhere in sight.

Not only is this moment a splendid example of one of a dramatist's, and especially a farceur's, most powerful weapons, the denial of expectation for a character and its simultaneous fulfilment for the audience, but it is also a demonstration of one of the most absurdist of dramatic techniques, the frustration of man by machine. The harlequinade of the Regency pantomime is full of unexpected terrors for Clown and Pantaloon when apparently harmless objects suddenly transform themselves into dangerous devices capable of inflicting serious physical harm. No one who has seen it will forget the sight of Charlie Chaplin in *Modern Times*, the victim of a food-serving machine that is supposed, by being attached to the assembly line worker and feeding him automatically as he works, to eliminate the necessity of a lunch break. It goes hopelessly wrong, of course, slopping food all over the helpless and immobilized Chaplin. Towards the climax of the second act of *A Flea in Her Ear*, Homenides bursts into the bedroom and exhibits his deadly marksmanship before a panic-stricken Camille by shooting at and hitting the same button, which causes a serious malfunction in the revolving bed mechanism. Until the end of the act both beds, containing a shrieking Camille and a shrieking Baptistin, continue to revolve rapidly before the audience. Here is an excellent demonstration of the Bergsonian view that as man begins to resemble a machine so he becomes less human and increasingly an object of laughter. In this case, and in complete harmony with the extremism of farce, man no longer commands the machine; it commands him – indeed, Camille and Baptistin have become a part of it, subsumed into the machinery as it spins heedlessly out of control. This is a truly farcical position, and it is surely also a philosophical one.

The acceleration of the revolving bed occurs at the end of act II, when the stage is the scene of the rigidly disciplined chaos so characteristic of Feydeau's dramatic climaxes. Well before this characters have started to run, a certain sign in farce of increasing pace and increasing pressure upon the individual. The hotel's proprietress, Olympe, is successively pushed, pulled, and knocked about by seven characters who rapidly enter and exit, each finding her in the way. Olympe does not have the slightest idea of what is going on or why they are acting this way; such characters are essential in Feydeau and other farceurs, a point worth returning to in a moment. After this incident the pace grows even faster: distraught men and women, most of them pursued by a raging Homenides with a gun, rush in and out of bedrooms and up and down the staircase. Shots are fired; other male guests and their half-clad lady friends join the mêlée, all shouting and screaming at once as the bed revolves wildly and the curtain comes down. The whole impression is that life is out of control, unmanageable, ungovernable, beyond the power of the individual to determine it or even influence it. The farce author's technique of compressing a great number of exits and entrances into a very short time and directing his actors to run, shout, scream, faint, and fire pistols is thoroughly indicative of this view of the human condition.

In act II of a late Victorian farce by Sydney Grundy, *The Snowball*, the harassed hero, seeking frantically to escape domestic complications of his own making, is pursued several times across the stage by five different people, all trying to deliver notes to him, none of which he wishes to receive. Of course they are all running. The speeding up of stage action is an old and familiar technique in farce, and it is also used in comedy, as in the famous inn scene in *The Servant of Two Masters* where Truffaldino successfully serves meals to two masters simultaneously without his deception being discovered by either of them. The meals are eaten offstage right and left; the stage itself is the scene of frenzied activity as Goldoni steadily increases the pressure on Truffaldino to take the dishes from a stream of waiters, convey the right dish to the right table, clear away the empties, and so forth. Truffaldino, however, remains in control and emerges triumphant; the speeding up of farce is there but not its pessimism. Much more farcically characteristic is the use of the same technique in Joe Orton's *What the Butler Saw*, which towards the end of the play contains the following stage direction and dialogue. (It is necessary to explain that police sergeant Match is wearing a woman's dress and Nick only underpants.)

> Mrs Prentice *fires*. Dr Prentice *ducks and runs quickly from the room into the garden.* Mrs Prentice *follows and fires again.* Sergeant Match *runs out of the dispensary, terrified. Seeing him* Mrs Prentice screams. Sergeant Match *gives a bellow of fright and runs into the hall.* Nick *runs from behind the desk into the hall.* Mrs Prentice *squeals with surprise.* Geraldine, *wearing the top half of* Nick's *uniform and no trousers, runs into the dispensary.* Mrs Prentice *runs to the ward door. As she reaches it a shot is heard and* Nick *re-enters, moaning and clutching his shoulder. Screaming with terror* Mrs Prentice *fires wildly at* Nick *who gives a yelp of pain and runs into the garden.* Dr Rance *enters from the ward holding a smoking gun.* Mrs Prentice *flings herself upon him.*
>
> Mrs Prentice. Doctor, doctor! The world is full of naked men running in all directions![2]

There is much more of this sort of thing in the next few minutes of *What the*

Butler Saw, performed necessarily at a tremendous pace. As she lies trussed up in a straitjacket, the weeping and uncomprehending Geraldine, who has done absolutely nothing wrong but has been subjected to a long series of physical and mental indignities, asks Dr Rance, 'What have I done to deserve this? I've always led such a respectable life.' He replies, 'Your mind has given way. You'll find the experience invaluable in your efforts to come to terms with twentieth-century living.'

Geraldine's innocence and respectability have the real dramatic function of being a touchstone by which to judge the increasing insanity of a world of which she is the helpless victim. Such a character is essential to farce and is often the hero. The more innocent and socially respectable he is the further he has to fall and the deeper the abyss of farcical degradation and exposure yawning beneath his feet. Pinero's Mr Posket in *The Magistrate* is a man of impeccable propriety, a magistrate and minor figure of the establishment, extremely conscious of the dignity of his position. He is of course fearfully humiliated, by having to escape in compromising circumstances from a restaurant of doubtful reputation with the police in hot pursuit; a mental and physical wreck the next morning – he has had no chance to get home – he is required to administer justice in his courtroom. The stage action is most effective but would not be so funny if Posket were not a respectable magistrate. Similarly, the gentle Dr Jedd, Dean of St Marvell's in Pinero's *Dandy Dick*, descends into farcical calamity through his attempt to save the church steeple by betting a large sum of money on a horse. Like Posket, a pillar of the law, Jedd, a pillar of the church, emerges besmirched and tattered from his dark odyssey.

It is interesting to observe that since farce functions by profaning approved moral, sexual, social, and familial codes it flourishes only in periods of stability when such codes are the received dogma of the audience. Not surprisingly, then, the golden age of farce has been the mid and late Victorian period in England and the France of the Second Empire and Third Republic, when one of the dominating obsessions of the elite was the fear of social exposure and the consequent loss of reputation, and when professed public adherence to agreed codes of conduct was very strong. Molière's popularity in the reign of Louis XIV and the rise to fame of Joe Orton in the relatively stable and prosperous England of the 1960s are lesser examples of the same phenomenon. It is difficult to succeed with farce today because there are so few ironclad moral and social taboos to which the majority of an audience subscribes, and because we live in a period of great political instability.

In *A Flea in Her Ear* Chandebise, the worthy bourgeois householder and managing director of an insurance company, guiltless of any marital wrongdoing or even intention to engage in it, makes a shocking transition from the calm, ordered household of the opening of the play to the wild anarchy of the Hotel Coq d'Or in act II, and does it with catastrophic effect upon his physical person, his nervous system, and his very identity.

The consequences of the extreme pressures of farce upon the individual are profound. These pressures exert themselves through a skilful combination of comic techniques, but once again it is much more than a matter of technique: the actual sanity and existence of the individual are at stake in a world of accumulating disorder and disaster, a world that goes so far as to refuse to recognize him as a person and denies his identity. A whole series of English farces of the first half of the nineteenth century reiterates this point. For instance, the central character of Thomas Dibdin's *What Next?*, Colonel Touchwood, is impersonated by a nephew who looks very like him. The Colonel's lawyer declares that he was called to see him; a dentist arrives, unasked, to pull his teeth; post-horses are brought that he has not ordered; and he is arrested for fighting a duel he knows nothing about. Grimshaw of John Maddison Morton's *Grimshaw, Bagshaw, and Bradshaw* is mistaken for both Bagshaw and Bradshaw. The plot drives him to answer the question, who am I? with the answer, 'Whatever you like . . . The fact is that I'm in such a state of confusion that I neither know nor care who I am.' Tom Cobb, the eponymous hero of W. S. Gilbert's farce, is driven virtually mad – like every character in *What the Butler Saw* – by the unbearable hostility of events, and cries, 'I've no idea who I am, or where I am, or what I am saying or doing.' The weary Pontagnac in Feydeau's *Le Dindon* addresses a speech to the married woman he is vainly trying to seduce which is thoroughly typical of the farce character *in extremis:*

> For love of you, I'm in the most appalling mess. Two cases of adultery, which I didn't commit. Caught by a husband I don't know, with a wife I don't know. Caught by my own wife, with the same woman I don't know. My own divorce pending. Another divorce of the woman I don't know and the man I don't know, with me as co-respondent. A quarrel with my wife. The woman I don't know arrives this morning and tells me in a German accent I owe her reparation, complicated by the man I don't know taking the law into his own hands. Worries, lawsuits, scandals, the lot. All to throw you into the arms of another man![3]

In another Feydeau farce, *Champignol malgré lui*, the unfortunate St Florimond is mistaken for somebody else and given military punishment as an army deserter, thus suffering aggravated identity problems.

Long before Feydeau and the nineteenth-century English farceurs, the doubling of identity had been used with great comic effect by Shakespeare. The plot complications of this doubling in *The Comedy of Errors* drive Antipholus of Ephesus nearly to madness; indeed, his family and friends think he *is* mad and lock him up. Antipholus is the first modern farce hero. In *The Comedy of Errors* individuals seem fissiparous. The reproductive process of binary fission is actually achieved before the eyes of Gorgibus in

Molière's *Le Médecin volant* when to save his scheme from discovery Sganarelle pretends to be a doctor as well as the doctor's brother. The pace of the scene naturally increases, for this is a farce, and at its climax Sganarelle, by embracing a cloak and hat as he stands at the window, appears in front of Gorgibus as both men simultaneously.

In act II of *A Flea in Her Ear* the problem of identity and fission is encountered, typically of Feydeau, in an extreme form. It will be remembered that Poche of the staff of the Coq d'Or is Chandebise's double. Whereas Shakespeare in *The Comedy of Errors* splits identities between twins of equal rank – two masters and two servants – Feydeau creates an identical pair of opposite social rank: Chandebise the managing director, Poche the drunken hall porter. Chandebise is the head of a prosperous household, catered to by respectful family members and servants; Poche, the lowliest of servants, is regularly beaten by the hotel manager. Feydeau does it this way, of course, to make the experience even more traumatic for Chandebise, to make him feel that his class status, his elevated place in the world as well as his whole personality and identity is slipping away from him in the inexplicable breakdown of hierarchy and the brutality of events. He also does it further to desecrate, as Eric Bentley puts it, household and family gods; Feydeau was aggressively and relentlessly anti-familial at a time when the bourgeois family was the official cornerstone of French society.

The specific techniques of writing in act II all express these goals. When in the bedroom with Raymonde Tournel presses the button to get rid of Baptistin, the bed revolves to bring on Poche clutching a bottle. Believing that he is Chandebise, Raymonde's husband, Tournel and Raymonde collapse before him, begging understanding and forgiveness, protesting their innocence. All this is incomprehensible to Poche, and his reaction is equally unintelligible to the distressed couple. He leaves, much to their mystification, to deliver his bottle of vermouth to another room, and comes across Camille and Antoinette about to enjoy their little affair; they of course flee from him as Chandebise. Etienne, Chandebise's servant, next meets Poche, who is by that time carrying a basket of logs – Feydeau always emphasizes Poche's menial characteristics when he is taken for Chandebise – and then it is Chandebise's turn: he runs up against Feraillon, the hotel manager, who assumes he is Poche, insults him, kicks him unmercifully, pulls his hat and jacket from him, forces him into the porter's cap and uniform, and sends him about his duties. (Poche immediately enters and, not finding his uniform, puts on Chandebise's hat and coat, which leads to further complications of identity in act III when he arrives at Chandebise's house.) Dressed as the porter, Chandebise confronts his wife and Tournel for the first time. They tell him, not unnaturally, that they explained everything to him before. Feraillon re-enters and kicks him off the stage. In contrast to Chandebise, Poche remains calm and stolidly uncomprehending of the bit of bother around him, while the former, by now thoroughly humiliated and terrified, is virtually demented. The techniques of farce have seemingly destroyed him and the world he thought he lived in. It is important that the only people amused and entertained by this spectacle are the audience; nobody in *A Flea in Her Ear*, or in *What the Butler Saw* and many other farces, has the slightest sense of humour. What is uproariously funny to the audience is a dreadful nightmare to the characters.

That most perceptive of critics of farce, Eric Bentley, has linked farce with melodrama as 'arts of escape, and what they are running away from is not only social problems but all other forms of moral responsibility'.[4] Bentley says many good things about farce and melodrama, but this is not one of them. It seems to me, in conclusion, that farce is anything but an escapist art. Rather, the best farce, like Feydeau's and Orton's, takes man into the heart of a malicious, cruel, and absurdist universe which everywhere conspires against him and which he is utterly powerless to direct. In the hands of the masters farce is the bleakest of all dramatic genres, since it offers neither the redemptive power of tragedy nor the love and human sympathy of comedy. Nobody ever sympathized with an Orton character or a Feydeau character. As to the question of moral responsibility it is simply irrelevant, as irrelevant as it is in the plays of Beckett and Pinter. Farce is of course a remarkable paradox. The darkness of its world, the emptiness it sees at the heart of the human condition, are conveyed to its audience by marvelous comic techniques which are not only superbly entertaining and laughter-producing but are also entirely expressive of the nature of that condition and the content and viewpoint of farce itself.

NOTES

1 The text used for this discussion is John Mortimer's translation (London: Samuel French, 1968).

2 *Joe Orton: The Complete Plays* (London: Eyre Methuen, 1976), pp. 436–7.

3 *Sauce for the Goose* in *Georges Feydeau: Three Farces*, trans. Peter Meyer (London: British Broadcasting Corporation, 1974), pp. 105–6.

4 *The Life of the Drama* (New York: Atheneum Press, 1964; repr. 1983), p. 255.

From Arlequin to Ubu: farce as anti-theatre*

W. D. HOWARTH

Alfred Jarry's *Ubu roi* has a habit of being all things to all men. Venerated as a revolutionary thinker by members of the Collège de Pataphysique and other luminaries of the Absurdist movement, Jarry has regularly been identified as the precursor of the Dadaists, of the surrealist theatre of Vitrac and others, and of the kind of iconoclastic and subversive satire which has in our own day found expression in *The Goon Show*, *Monty Python's Flying Circus* and *Spitting Image*; the importance of his example is acknowledged both by those who approve wholeheartedly of avant-garde experiment in the arts, and by those who think the twentieth-century theatre has suffered from a surfeit of self-indulgent experimentation. My intention in this paper, however, is to look backwards rather than forwards, to try to identify some of Jarry's predecessors, and in particular to examine certain affinities that suggest themselves between *Ubu roi* and the eighteenth-century *parade*, which Jacques Scherer has characterized as the 'anti-theatre' of its day.[1]

At the time of the first performance of Jarry's play, it did not take long for commentators to detect affinities between *Ubu roi* and the tradition of Punch and Judy, *le guignol*;[2] even – striking a more exotic note – between *Ubu roi* and the *karagoez*, or Turkish shadow-play. Catulle Mendès wrote of Père Ubu that he was 'compounded of Pulcinella and Polichinelle, of Punch and Karagoez, Mayeux and M. Joseph Prud'homme, Robert Macaire and M. Thiers ... an enormous and unsavoury parody of Macbeth, of Napoleon and of a pimp turned king ...'[3] – in other words, offering a caricature of nineteenth-century bourgeois 'ventripotence' similar to those created by the clowns, mimes and caricaturists of previous generations. In borrowing the idiom of the non-literary theatre, no less than in the rudimentary parody of *Macbeth* which provides the outline of such plot as the play possesses, the author was seen to be reacting in a devastatingly hostile way against the conventions of the well-made play. Both of these factors point in the direction of an anti-theatre, a reductive critique whose aim was to replace the literary drama as it had evolved in western Europe

* A draft of this paper was read at the *Themes in Drama* International Conference held at the University of London, Westfield College, in March 1986.

since the Renaissance with something much cruder, more elemental, and more vigorous. Many contemporaries must have looked ahead with apprehension, as did Yeats, at the destructive power unleashed by the 'savage god'; and critical comment since 1896 has also largely concentrated on the iconoclastic trail blazed by Jarry and his successors, without considering the extent to which *Ubu roi* may itself have been related to traditions well established in the French theatre. An exception is Apollinaire, who on Jarry's death commented on his notorious play as follows:

> *Ubu roi* is one of the great comic masterpieces of the French theatre. It has all the powerful simplicity of the works of classical antiquity, the aggressive commonsense of Rabelais and his contemporaries, the clarity and the vigour of Molière's dialogue, the fantasy, the lyricism and the comic verve of Shakespeare; but it has, over and above all this, something that makes it unique . . .[4]

It will be noted, though, that Apollinaire chooses to refer exclusively to Jarry's *literary* antecedents, and makes no mention of more popular theatrical forms. Whatever affinities may, or may not, exist between *Ubu roi* and Rabelais, Molière or Shakespeare, it seems to be worth considering possible links with the equally time-honoured extra-literary[5] traditions of popular farce: that art form which, to quote Morton Gurevitch, 'rightly disrupts civilized dignity, responsibility, and guilt';[6] and which can be seen in one of its most vigorous manifestations in the eighteenth-century *parade*.

The popular genre of the *parade* developed, it is generally agreed, from the simple dramatic sketches which were used by fairground quacks in the seventeenth century to attract customers; though the term itself appears not to have been current until the early years of the eighteenth century.[7] By this time, the farces associated with the 'charlatans' or *opérateurs* of the fairs were becoming established as a form of entertainment in their own right, and acquired their distinctive style principally by borrowing a more or less fixed cast list of character types from the Comédie-Italienne: the lovers Léandre and Isabelle, Cassandre (usually the girl's father), Arlequin and Gilles (the servants of Léandre and Cassandre). Characters and plot remained more or less constant, and the attraction of each new play was to be found in the colourful, racy dialogue in which puns and other forms of word-play proliferated, and colloquial obscenities were to be found side by side with the burlesque and the mock-heroic.[8]

Established in this way as a vigorous form of popular farce, the *parade* appealed not only to its traditional audiences, but also to those wealthy, and even aristocratic, spectators who as early as the 1720s were beginning to find the literary repertory of the official theatres (whether the Comédie-Française or the Comédie-Italienne) increasingly insipid, and to seek the spice of a more plebeian kind of entertainment. Once it had attracted these more sophisticated patrons, the *parade* was ready for the next, and most important, stage in its evolution. This seems to have taken place about 1730, when the upper-class *aficionados* started to indulge their taste for low-class comedy by building their own theatres and commissioning a steady supply of texts. The *parade* was to remain a favourite dramatic form in the private theatres of the gentry from the 1730s up to the Revolution. Its vogue was kept going by minor men of letters such as Gueullette, Fagan and Collé; Voltaire is known to have written at least one example in his youth;[9] and it was in the genre of the *parade* that no less a comic dramatist than Beaumarchais made his debut as a writer for the theatre, catering for the enthusiasm of Le Normand d'Etiolles, ex-husband of Madame de Pompadour. At Etiolles in the 1760s, with the help of professional actors from Paris like Préville and Dugazon, Beaumarchais entertained a sophisticated audience with what, as Jacques Scherer has said, had by then become a 'genre pseudo-populaire'.[10]

As illustrative examples of these stylized eighteenth-century farces, I propose to consider the early *Arlequin roi de Sérendib* by Lesage;[11] Gueullette's *Léandre fiacre* and *Isabelle grosse par vertu*;[12] and from Beaumarchais's pen, *Les Bottes de sept lieues, Léandre marchand d'agnus*, and in particular the play which specialists of the comic theatre in this period would almost certainly identify as the outstanding surviving *parade, Jean-Bête à la foire*.[13] Reference will also be made where possible to contemporary prefaces, reviews and critical essays. While it would be quite impossible, I am sure, to demonstrate any certain influence of these or similar texts on Jarry as a playwright, I think it can be established that the dramatic composition, the relationship between visual spectacle and text, and above all the linguistic and stylistic devices used by the eighteenth-century writers show striking similarities to those of their nineteenth-century counterpart; and that Jarry was working along longstanding traditional lines. Perhaps we ought rather to say Jarry and his collaborators, his fellow pupils at the Lycée de Rennes; for it is important to remember, not only that *Ubu roi* started life as a school entertainment, a sort of end-of-term revue lampooning the unfortunate physics master le père Hébert, but that the original authorship was a collective affair. One can only guess at the means by which the popular (or pseudo-popular) farcical style of the previous century may have been kept alive for the *collégiens* of the 1880s – for there is little trace of its vulgarity and its vigour on the professional stages of nineteenth-century France – but kept alive it does seem to have been.

As the first, and most obvious, example of the uninhibited obscenity that is common to Jarry and his eighteenth-century predecessors, let us consider the case of Père Ubu's notorious opening word 'Merdre!' The thirty-three occurrences of this vulgarism, in Jarry's piquant variation of its normal form (rendered in English translations of *Ubu roi* as 'Shittle!', 'Pschitt!' or 'Shittr!') have inspired a wealth of commentaries, some of them more than a little pretentious (as might be imagined from works with titles like *Les Langages de Jarry: essai de sémiotique littéraire*).[14] The substitution of *merdre* for the homely *merde* has been variously interpreted, as a case of prudent bowdlerism:

> It should not be forgotten that we were still children; our parents would naturally not have wanted us to use the word in its normal form, so we had the idea of interpolating the 'r': that's all there was to it![15]

or as an example of insolent provocation:

> This opening word of the play, which had certainly never before been pronounced on stage, and which, as it is thrown in the face of the spectators, seems to attack them personally, crystallises all Jarry's condemnation of bourgeois cowardice and mediocrity. That was the play's intolerable provocation, its unforgivable offence.[16]

Merdre appears most often as an oath or interjection; it appears in various composite forms: *croc à merdre, sabre à merdre, sac à merdre, ciseau à merdre* ('shit-hook', 'shit-sword', 'shit-bag', 'shit-scissors'); and there is one passage that is much more explicit in its literalness, when Ubu's lieutenant is asked what he has had for his dinner:

> *Ubu.* Eh bien! capitaine, avez-vous bien dîné?
> *Bordure.* Fort bien, monsieur, sauf la merdre.
> *Ubu.* Eh! la merdre n'était pas mauvaise. (Act I, scene 4)
>
> (Well, captain, have you had a good dinner? – Good enough, sir, except for the pschitt. – Oh come now, the pschitt wasn't all that bad.)

Now it may be true that the schoolboy neologism 'merdre' had indeed never been heard on a public stage by the playgoers of 1896; but in its unbowdlerised form, the word *merde* is omnipresent in the eighteenth-century *parades*. And not only as an interjection: Jessica Milner Davis chooses as typical of what she calls 'humiliation-farces' an anonymous piece from this period, *Le Marchand de merde*, in which the simple-minded Gilles attempts to make a living by selling his own excrement, and finishes with the barrel containing his wares emptied over his head.[17] Among the more colourful oaths in the extant texts, we find 'Sainte merde!' ('Holy shit!') (*Léandre fiacre*, scene 9) and 'Merde à votre nez!' ('Shit in your face!') (*Isabelle grosse par vertu*, scene 5); while Beaumarchais's unfortunate Gilles expresses the prospect of remaining penniless in the following picturesque phrase: 'sans hériter tant seulement d'un misérable tonneau de merde ni de la peau d'un chien mort' ('without inheriting so much as a wretched barrel of shit or the skin of a dead dog') (*Les Bottes de sept lieues*, scene 9).

What were evidently traditional vulgarities can be seen to have been inherited by Beaumarchais from the earlier practitioners in the genre; and if there seems to be nothing quite so provocative to good taste as the 'balai innommable', the lavatory-brush which Ubu throws on to the dinner table in act I, scene 3 of *Ubu roi*, it is surely only a difference of degree between that and the following *lazzo* in which Gueullette's Gilles offers Cassandre a rather special form of hot poultice for his injured nose:

> *Gilles.* Attendez: ne vous êtes-vous pas fait mal au nez?
> *Cassandre.* Oui, coquin, je me suis fait mal au nez.
> *Gilles.* Il faut le tenir le plus chaudement que vous pourrez. Approchez, approchez. (*Il lui montre le cul.*) (*Isabelle grosse par vertu*, scene 2)

> (Wait a minute: haven't you injured your nose? – Yes, you villain, I've injured my nose. – Well, then, you must keep it as warm as you can. Come here. (*He shows him his bare backside.*)

The same sequence is found almost word for word both in Beaumarchais's *Léandre marchand d'agnus* (scene 2) and in his *Jean-Bête à la foire* – in the latter case with the embellishment that when Gilles shows his bare backside to his master, he comments:

> Vous qui aimez les porcelaines: c'est ça qui serait z'un beau morceau, s'il n'était pas de deux pièces!

> (You're a connoisseur of fine china, aren't you? Wouldn't this be a splendid piece, if it weren't split in two!)

and Cassandre responds by repeatedly holding his nose at the offensive smell (scene 2).

In the *parades*, this kind of scatological vulgarity is regularly accompanied by sexual licence, both in the form of innuendo and as frank bawdy. The heroine, Isabelle, is usually sought after in marriage by Léandre (or by Beaumarchais's Jean-Bête) only after several lapses from the straight and narrow path. In *Isabelle grosse par vertu*, where she pretends to be pregnant in order to discourage her elderly suitor Le Docteur, the servant Gilles makes it clear that her 'vertu' is only relative:

> L'an passé que vous l'étiez, vous avez bien fait comme si vous ne l'étiez pas; vous pouvez bien faire à présent comme si vous l'étiez. (scene I)

> (Last year when you were pregnant, you pretended not to be; so now, you might at least act as if you were.)

When Jean-Bête – who 'depuis deux ans que j'en suis t'aimé comme un lion' ('for the last two years, during which she's loved me like a lion') has had 'trois petits Jean-bêtes' by his Isabelle – says of Gilles: 'Ce drôle-là z'en veut sûrement à la virginité de ma chère Zirzabelle' ('That crook has his eye on my little Isabelle's virginity'), Arlequin replies:

> Ça pourrait être en vérité; car c'est zun enfonceux de portes ouvertes. (*Jean-Bête*, scene I)

> (It could well be: he's always one for pushing at open doors.)

And when, at the denouement of this play, Beaumarchais's hero steps out of his disguise as a doctor, he reveals:

> vous rencontrez en moi, z'outre un médecin très-éclatant, le beau Léandre qui a déjà t'eu l'avantage d'administrer à Mamaselle le sacrement d'fornication, z'en attendant mieux. (scene 9)

> (You see in me not only a brilliant doctor, but also the handsome Léandre who has already taken the opportunity of administering the sacrament of fornication to your daughter, until something better should turn up.)

The following passage is quoted in an early study of the *parade* in order to give, as the authors claim, 'an idea of Gueullette's flair for ribald invention':

> *Le Maître*. Où diantre te fourres-tu donc?
> *Gilles*. Parbleu, maître, je ne peux pas être partout. J'étais allé à la cave tirer un petit coup de vinaigre avec Jacqueline.
> *Le Maître*. Je crains bien plutôt que tu n'y sois descendu pour boire mon vin.
> *Gilles*. Au contraire, maître, la dernière fois qu'un de vos tonneaux était en vidange et que vous accusiez Jacqueline de l'avoir bu . . .
> *Le Maître*. Il est vrai que je me suis bien aperçu deux ou trois fois qu'elle avait l'haleine vineuse . . .
> *Gilles*. Eh bien! maître, cela a piqué au vif cette pauvre fille; elle m'a montré le trou par où votre vin avait passé et je travaillais actuellement à le boucher quand vous m'avez appelé.
> *Le Maître*. Le Ciel soit loué! Il ne s'enfuira donc plus par là.
> *Gilles*. Oh! maître, je ne vous en réponds pas, mais quand Jacqueline me le montrera, je serai toujours prêt à le boucher.[18]

> (Where the devil have you been? – For heaven's sake, master, I can't be everywhere at once. I was down in the cellar drawing off some vinegar with Jacqueline. – I fancy you were more likely down there drinking my wine. – Not at all, master; and the last time one of your barrels was broached, and you accused Jacqueline of drinking it . . . – It's true, I've thought more than once that her breath smelled of drink . . . – Well, master, it really upset the poor girl. She showed me the hole your wine had poured out from, and I was just on the point of stopping it up for her when you called me. – Thank heavens for that! There'll be no more going out that way, then. – Oh, master, I wouldn't promise that; but whenever Jacqueline shows me that hole again, I'll always be ready to put a stopper in it.)

If this reminds us of the uncomplicated bawdiness of Rabelais (for instance the episode of Hans Carvel's ring, *Tiers Livre*, chapter 28), it is surely a pointer to one of the principal sources of inspiration common to the *collégiens* of the 1880s and the eighteenth-century *farceurs*.

However, it must be admitted that sexual references are much less prominent in *Ubu roi* than in the *parades*. To take a simple example: Gilles is describing the 'horse-play' that Léandre, disguised as a cab-driver, and Isabelle are engaged in:

> Le fiacre va bien, mais les chevaux ne marchent point . . . Par le masque de

mon derrière, je crois qu'ils faisaient le manège dans le carrosse . . . Le manège se fait sans éperons, et les écuyers n'ont besoin que d'une baguette de six ou sept pouces de long. (*Léandre fiacre*, scene 7)

(The cab's going along well enough, but the horses aren't budging . . . By the mask of my backside, I think they're having riding lessons inside the cab – a sort of horsemanship without spurs, in which all the rider needs is a stick six or seven inches long.)

In *Ubu roi* by contrast, the 'bâton à physique' and the 'petit bout de bois' ('physic-stick', 'little bit of wood') which form part of père Ubu's idiosyncratic weaponry, instead of being the vehicles for a simple and obvious sexual allusion, seem rather to belong to a secret mythology of the Lycée de Rennes, for which a sexual interpretation is by no means self-evident. Although Michel Arrivé, arguing from the later incorporation of a large part of the text of *Ubu roi* into Jarry's *César Antéchrist*, where the 'bâton' is 'explicitly presented as a phallic symbol', assigns to both of these accessories a sexual connotation,[19] it might be prudent here to pay attention to the remarks of Charles Chassé (who was admittedly bent on challenging Jarry's authorship of the original *Ubu* text, and establishing the claim of the brothers Morin):

In my opinion, the proof that Jarry was not the author of *Ubu roi* is to be seen in the fact that there is absolutely no sexual reference in this text; whereas overt sexuality is everywhere present in Jarry's authentic works, for he was obsessed with such matters from his childhood. *Ubu roi* on the contrary is merely scatological. As Morin said to me: 'It's the most chaste play in the world. Its language is dirty, without being sexually suggestive.'[20]

In spite of Chassé's *a priori* bias, it does seem that he is in this respect nearer the truth: the 'sexuality' of *Ubu roi* remains, on Arrivé's own admission, on the level of 'connotation' rather than of 'dénotation',[21] and is perhaps unlikely to catch the attention of a spectator or reader less single-minded in his pursuit of such features.

On the other hand, as regards the imaginative quality both of the neologisms and of other kinds of word-play, there is a real family likeness between the eighteenth-century *parades* and *Ubu roi* – or, indeed, the whole group of *Ubu* texts. Thus the interjection 'Par les mamelles de mon cul!' ('By the tits of my backside!'), which is from the pen of Gueullette (*Léandre fiacre*, scene 2), could just as well have come from Beaumarchais – or from Jarry a century later. If the following list of *dramatis personae* from Grandval's parodic *parade Sirop-au-cul, ou l'Heureuse Délivrance, tragédie héroï-merdifique* ('Arse-juice, or the Fortunate Delivery, heroical-shittical tragedy') of 1754:

Sirop-au-cul, roi de Merdenchine
Etronie, amante de Sirop-au-cul, fille d'Etronius, roi détrôné par Saligot et
    réfugié à la cour de Sirop-au-cul

Curidé, confidente d'Etronie
Dégoûtant, capitaine des gardes de Sirop-en-cul (*sic*)
Morvenbouche, confident de Sirop-en-cul
Merdencour, ambassadeur du roi Saligot
Pécorus, Sçavantinet, Barbarisme, Artichaut, médecins et grands du royaume
Couleuvre, apothicaire
Chiant-lit, Cubreneux, Galenmain, Né-pourri, gardes[22]

(Arse-juice, King of Shittin-china; Turdula, in love with Arse-juice, daughter
of King Turdus, dethroned by Bastard, in exile at the court of King Arse-juice;
Wrinkle-arse, confidant of Turdula; Disgusting, captain of the guard; Snot-
nose, confidant of Arse-juice; Courtlycrap, ambassador from King Bastard;
Imbecile, Pedant, Barbarian, Yokel, doctors and notabilities; Grasssnake,
apothecary; Crapinbed, Shittyarse, Scurvy, Putrid, guards)

seems to be far richer in this respect than its counterpart in *Ubu roi*, we
should note that the names Pissedoux and Pissembock (Piss-sweet, Piss-
bitter) in *Ubu enchaîné* and Merdanpo (Crapincan) in *Ubu cocu* exhibit a very
similar linguistic invention.

The homely wisdom of the popular proverb is to be found throughout the
eighteenth-century *parades*:

– Oui, souhaités dans une main et crachez dans l'autre: vous verrez dans
laquelle il en restera plus. (*Jean-Bête*, scene 3)
– Autant vaut son écuelle vuide que rien dedans. (ibid.)
– A gorge coupée et à fille dépucelée, il n'y a point de remède. (*La Chaste Isabelle*,
scene 1).

(That's right: wish in one hand and spit in the other; you'll soon see where
there's something left to look at! – Nothing much to choose between an empty
bowl and one with nothing in it! – There are two things you can't do anything
about: a throat that's been cut and a girl who's lost her maidenhead!)

Sometimes, the popular locutions are subjected to comic deformation by
the simple Gilles:

– Ah, vous allez voir de queu bois je me mouche. (*Jean-Bête*, scene 2)
– Vous avés raison Monsieur chat z'échaudé crains l'eau froide. (*Les Bottes de
sept lieues*, scene 6)

([Literally:] You'll soon see what sort of wood I blow my nose with. –
You're quite right, sir: a scalded cat is afraid of cold water.)

Arlequin and his master, on the other hand, handle language with greater
panache, even when they are deforming it. 'Vous auriez dû me dire ça
pluton qu'plutarque', cries the servant (*Jean-Bête*, scene 1) and 'Vlà qu'est
horrible, ça crie vendange' (ibid.) (literally – the puns and word-play are
untranslatable: 'You should have said that sooner rather than later. –
That's awful, that calls for vengeance.'); and he stands up to his master's
imprecations with a spirited riposte:

Pardi, Monsieur, faut que vous soyez devenu tout d'un coup sourd, aveugle et muet de naissance . . . (ibid.)

(Good Heavens, sir, you must suddenly have become blind, deaf and dumb from birth.)

The following exchange shows the linguistic play at its most characteristic, with tautology, incongruity and logical contradiction providing the impetus for the dialogue:

Jean-Bête. Ah mon cher Arlequin, tu me vois t'abimé dans un débordement de douleur.
Arlequin. Vous me percez le coeur de Parque en Parque, est-ce qu'on vous a flanqué en prison?
Jean-Bête. Cq me serait, je t'assure, ben inférieur!
Arlequin. Est-ce qu'on vous aurait passé par les verges?
Jean-Bête. Pus pire encore, pus méprisable!
Arlequin. Fouetté z'et marqué par le boureau?
Jean-Bête. Je prendrais ça de la part d'où ça me vient.
Arlequin. Fouré z'une basse fosse dans le cul, peut-être?
Jean-Bête. V'la z'une belle fichaise auprès de mon état . . .
Arlequin. Quoi donc? pendu? z'étranglé? z'aux galères? z'est puis t'exilé hors du royaume?
Jean-Bête, d'un ton théâtral. Tout cela peut-il z'approcher de l'éclatant z'inconvénient qui vient de me couler sur la teste?
Arlequin. Z'a moins d'être sorcier ou lieutenant de police, on ne devine point.
Jean-Bête. Tu connais la charmante Zirzabelle? . . . (ibid.)

(My dear Arlequin, you see me in the depths of melancholy. – Your sufferings are a mortal blow to me: have they thrown you into prison? – That would be much less serious. – Have they beaten you? – Much, much worse. – Whipped and branded by the hangman? – I should take all that in my stride. – Thrown into a deep, dark dungeon? – That would be a mere trifle compared with my present situation. – What then? Hanged? Strangled? Sentenced to the galleys? And then sent into exile? – (*theatrically*) None of all that could begin to approach the calamity that's just beset me. – There's no way of guessing, unless one were a magician or a police captain. – You know the lovely Isabelle?)

And later in the same scene, Jean-Bête expresses his despair at the prospect of losing his Isabelle in the following fanciful terms:

Non. Z'il vaut mieux que je vienne massacrer le père, la fille, Gilles, enfin tous mes ri-de-vaux, z'et que je m'empoisonne après d'un grand coup de plat d'épée z'au travers de l'âme.

(No: I'd be better off slaughtering the father, the daughter, Gilles, and all my rivals, and then poisoning myself afterwards by piercing my soul with the flat of my sword.)

The naming of names is of particular importance in Beaumarchais's *parades*. In one of the most linguistically inventive passages in *Jean-Bête*, the playwright makes his hero recite a veritable litany of his ancestry – 'past, present and future':

> *Jean-Bête.* . . . pour vous le couper court, Mosieur, je ne suis pas t'un véritable beau Liandre comme vous le croyés. Je m'appelle Jean-Bête, auteur de parades, fils de Jean-Broche, petit-fils de Jean Fonce, arrière-petit-fils de Jean Logne, issu de Jean Farine, qui sortait de Jeandesvignes, lequel descendait en droite ligne de Jean Sans Terre, et de Jean Sans Aveu, qui sont z'une famille aussi z'illustre que les bonshommes Cassandre; vous saurez t'en outre qu'un de mes grands-pères . . .
> *Cassandre.* Du côté des hommes ou des femmes?
> *Jean-Bête.* De tous les côtés, Monsieur, de tous les côtés. (scene 9)

(To cut things short, sir, I'm not the handsome Léandre you take me for. I am Jean-Bête, composer of parades, son of Jean-Broche, grandson of Jean-Fonce, great-grandson of Jean Logne, of the family of Jean Farine, who was descended from Jean des Vignes, who was of the direct lineage of Jean Sans Terre and of Jean Sans Aveu, whose family is just as illustrious as that of the Cassandres. You must know in addition that one of my grandfathers . . . – On the male or the female side? – On every side, sir, on every side . . .)

After a slanging match with Gilles, it is the deformation of his name that provokes Arlequin to violence:

> *Gilles.* Comment dis-tu ça, mannequin?
> *Arlequin.* Je ne m'appelle pas mannequin. Z'on me nomme Arlequin, fils de Vilbrequin, issu de Maroquin, surnommé chasse-coquin. (*Il les rosse avec sa batte, les pousse, ils tombent l'un sur l'autre* . . .)
> *Giles.* Ah! Monsieur Charlequin Vilbrequin! Maroquin! z'au guet! z'au guet!
> *Arlequin.* Je vous apprendrai à estropier mon nom, faquin! (scene 6)

(Say that again, scarecrow. – That's not my name. I'm called Arlequin, son of Vilbrequin, descended from Maroquin, nicknamed Chasse-coquin. (*He beats them with his slapstick and pushes them; they fall over each other*). – Ah! Charlequin Vilbrequin! Maroquin! Help! police! – I'll teach you to treat my name like that, you scoundrel!)

Perhaps the most characteristic sequences in all of these *parades*, from Gueullette through to Beaumarchais's *Jean-Bête* – and a feature which offers an immediate affinity with *Ubu roi* – are those (especially between Gilles and Cassandre) in which verbal abuse is followed by a beating; the following passage from *Jean-Bête* is very closely modelled on similar texts in *Isabelle grosse par vertu* (scene 2) and *Léandre marchand d'agnus* (scene 2):

> *Gilles.* . . . vous avez la figure d'un singe, vous êtes fait comme un scorpion, lourd comme un boeuf, bête comme un carpe, sale comme un porc, puant comme un cul-de-sac. Votre fille Zirzabelle la pucelle vous mène par le nez comme un sot et vous a dindonné de trois marmots dont que vot' famille s'est z'accrue z'en deux ans et sans mon Jérôme qui vous a tricotté z'un beau Léandre ce matin, il allait z'en fricasser peut–être un quatrième.
> *Cassandre, le battant.* Tiens, maraud, v'là pour t'apprendre à dire des mots à double entendre. (scene 2)

(You've a face like a monkey, and you look like a scorpion. You're as clumsy as an ox, as stupid as a fish, as dirty as a pig, and you smell like a back alley. Your daughter, the virginal Isabelle, is leading you a fine dance: she's fooled you with the three nippers your family has increased by in the last two years; and but for my Jerome, who sent that handsome Léandre packing this morning, you might well have been landed with a fourth one. – (*Beating him*) There you are, you scoundrel: that'll teach you to indulge in suggestive word-play.)

For examples of similar sequences in the *Ubu* plays depending primarily on verbal invention, with a similar thwarting of our logical expectations, we can turn to act IV, scene 5 of *Ubu roi*, where Père Ubu boasts of his courageous exploits in battle:

Pile. Hon! Monsieuye Ubu, êtes-vous remis de votre terreur et de votre fuite?
Ubu. Oui! Je n'ai plus peur, mais j'ai encore la fuite.
Cotice, à part. Quel pourceau!
Ubu. Eh! Sire Cotice, votre oneille, comment va-t-elle?
Cotice. Aussi bien, Monsieuye, qu'elle peut aller tout en allant très mal. Par conséquent de quoye, le plomb la penche vers la terre et je n'ai pu extraire la balle.
Ubu. Tiens, c'est bien fait! Toi, aussi, tu voulais toujours taper les autres. Moi, j'ai déployé la plus grande valeur, et sans m'exposer j'ai massacré quatre ennemis de ma propre main, sans compter tous ceux qui étaient déjà morts et que nous avons achevés.

(Sire Ubu, have you recovered from your scare? Do you still want to run away? – I'm no longer afraid, but I'm still on the run. – What a hog! – How's your ear doing, Cotice? – It's as good as you could expect, Sir, as long as it's so bad. As a result, the lead is pulling it downwards and I haven't been able to get the bullet out. – Well, it serves you right! You were always one for wanting to get into a fight. As for me, I have shown extraordinary courage, and without exposing myself to any danger I killed four enemies with my own hands, not counting those who were already dead that I finished off.)

On receiving news of the death of 'le petit Rensky', he laments:

Ainsi que le coquelicot et le pissenlit à la fleur de leur age sont fauchés par l'impitoyable faux de l'impitoyable faucheur qui fauche impitoyablement leur pitoyable binette, ainsi le petit Rensky a fait le coquelicot . . . (*Ubu roi*, act IV, scene 5).

(Just as the poppy and the dandelion are scythed down in the flower of their youth by the pitiless scythe of the pitiless reaper who pitilessly scythes their pitiful heads off, so poor little Rensky has played the poppy's role.)

And the whole of the episode of the bear in scene 6, in which Père Ubu behaves like Rabelais's Panurge, at a prudent distance from any danger, shows a relationship between dialogue and action, or between verbal and visual effect, very like that of the *parades*:

Cotice. A moi, Pile, à moi! au secours Monsieuye Ubu!
Ubu. Bernique! Débrouille-toi, mon ami; pour le moment, nous faisons notre Pater Noster. Chacun son tour d'être mangé.

Pile. Je l'ai, je le tiens.

Cotice. Ferme, ami, il commence à me lâcher.

Ubu. Sanctificetur nomen tuum.

Cotice. Lâche bougre!

Pile. Ah! il me mord! O Seigneur, sauvez-nous, je suis mort.

Ubu. Fiat voluntas tua!

Cotice. Ah! j'ai réussi à le blesser.

Pile. Hurrah! il perd son sang.

Cotice. Tiens-le ferme, que j'attrape mon coup-de-poing explosif.

Ubu. Panem nostrum quotidianum da nobis hodie.

Pile. L'as-tu enfin? je n'en peux plus.

Ubu. Sicut et nos dimittimus debitoribus nostris.

Cotice. Ah! je l'ai. (*Une explosion retentit et l'ours tombe mort*).

Pile et Cotice. Victoire!

Ubu. Sed libera nos a malo. Amen. Enfin, est-il bien mort? Puis-je descendre de mon rocher?

Pile, avec mépris. Tant que vous voudrez.

Ubu, descendant. Vous pouvez vous flatter que si vous êtes encore vivants et si vous foulez encore la neige de la Lithuanie, vous le devez à la vertu magnamine du Maître des Finances, qui s'est évertué, échiné et égosillé à débiter des patenôtres pour votre salut, et qui a manié avec autant de courage le glaive spirituel de la prière que vous avez manié avec adresse le temporel de l'ici présent Palotin Cotice coup-de-poing explosif. Nous avons même poussé plus loin notre dévouement, car nous n'avons pas hésité à monter sur un rocher plus fort pour que nos prières aient moins loin à arriver au ciel.

(Help, Pile! Help, Monsieur Ubu! – Not likely! You'll have to help yourself, my frield: we are saying our prayers, and it's not our turn to be eaten yet. – I've got him! – Hold on, friend, he's beginning to let go of me. – Hallowed be Thy name. – Cowardly sod! – Ah! He's biting me! O Lord, help us, I'm dying. – Thy will be done. – There, I've managed to wound him. – Good! He's losing blood. – Hold him, while I unleash my explosive punch. – Give us this day our daily bread. – Have you got him yet? I can't hold on any longer. – As we forgive those that trespass against us. – Got him! (*There is an explosion, and the bear falls dead.*) – Victory! – But deliver us from evil. Amen. Well, is he dead yet? Can I come down from my rock? – (*Scornfully*) Whenever you want. – You may congratulate yourselves that if you are still alive, and treading the snows of Lithuania, you owe it to the generous spirit of your Master of Finance, who exerted himself, strained himself, and shouted himself hoarse offering up paternosters for your safety, and who wielded the spiritual sword of prayer with just as much courage as you showed skill in wielding the explosive punch of our friend Palotin Cotice here. Our own self-sacrifice was even greater, for we did not hesitate to climb up on a big rock so that our prayers wouldn't have so far to go to reach Heaven.)

Although the gratuitous violence of the *Ubu* plays goes well beyond anything that is characteristic of the *parades*, this is often accompanied by a litany of insults very reminiscent of the verbal felicity of the eighteenth-century authors:

Bougrelas, le frappant. Tiens, lâche, gueux, sacripant, musulman!

Ubu, ripostant. Tiens! Polognard! soûlard, bâtard, hussard, tartare, calard, cafard, mouchard, savoyard, communard!
Mère Ubu, le battant aussi. Tiens, capon, cochon, félon, histrion, fripon, souillon, polochon! (*Ubu roi*, act v, scene 2)

(*Beating him*) Take that! coward, tramp, bully, infidel! – (*Replying in kind*) Take that, Polsky! drunkard, bastard, hussar, Tartar, humbug, stoolpigeon, chimney-sweep, communist! – (*Beating him in her turn*) Take that, coward, pig, gaolbird, actor, scoundrel, sloven, windbag!)

Finally, as an example of comic effect deriving from burlesque deformation of a technical language, the following passage from the scene where Père Ubu and his companions are escaping by sea matches some of the malapropisms quoted from the *parades*:

Le Commandant. N'arrivez pas, serrez près et plein!
Ubu. Si! Si! Arrivez. Je suis pressé, moi! Arrivez, entendez-vous! C'est ta faute, brute de capitaine, si nous n'arrivons pas. Nous devrions être arrivés. Oh, oh, mais je vais commander, moi, alors! Pare à virer! A dieu vat! Mouillez, virez vent devant, virez vent arrière. Hissez les voiles, serrez les voiles, la barre dessus, la barre dessous, la barre à côté. Vous voyez, ça va très bien. Venez en travers à la lame et alors ce sera parfait.
Le Commandant. Amenez le grand foc, prenez un ris aux huniers!
Ubu. Ceci n'est pas mal, c'est même bon! Entendez-vous, monsieur l'Equipage? Amenez le grand coq et allez faire un tour dans les pruniers (act v, scene 4)

(Don't bear away! Hug the wind! – No, let's get away. I'm in a hurry, I am! Let's away, do you hear? It's your fault, you oaf of a captain, if we haven't got away. We ought to have been well away by now. It's time I took command. Ready to tack! About ship! Cast anchor, go about, wear ship! Set more sail, take in sail, helm up, helm down, helm sideways on! You see, it's all going splendidly. Broadside on to the sea, now, and it will be perfect. – Haul down the main jib, take in a reef in the topsail! – That's not bad, it's even quite good! Do you hear, sir Crew? Fetch the cockerel and go for a walk in the orchard!)

In spite of the obvious differences in subject matter and tonality, the affinities between Jarry's *Ubu* plays and the eighteenth-century *parades* will, I hope, be regarded as established. The essential similarity lies, I think, in the challenge both present to the conventional canons of literary drama – whether in tragedy or in comedy – by virtue of what may be called their inconsequentiality. By this I mean the arbitrariness of action and plot – the scant regard paid to the logic of cause and effect – as well as the lack of verbal and logical coherence in the dialogue. While both of these features tend perhaps to be more readily recognized in the case of Jarry, cocking a snook at the tradition of the well-made play, it is not difficult to distinguish something analogous in the *parades*, the anti-theatre of their time. In the *Lettre à Madame* [xxx] *sur les parades* which appeared at the head of volume II of *Le Théâtre des boulevards ou Recueil des parades* of 1756, Gueullette emphasizes the continuity of the farce tradition from the Middle Ages onwards, as something independent of the literary theatre and, indeed, subject on occasion to the anathema of the civil authorities on account of its anarchic qualities:

> This kind of farcical prologue was banned from the Parisian stage, and rightly so; but the fairground actors kept it going under another guise: in order to attract audiences to their booths, they appeared on a long, narrow platform, and there performed their farces on the basis of *scenari* they had inherited, or which they composed themselves. That, Milady, is what we call the *parade*; but this sort of spectacle has now disappeared from the Paris theatres, and survives only in the imagination of authors who, capable of exploiting the ridiculous wherever it can be found, have been able to seize on the careless and slipshod language, the mispronunciations, and above all the affected delivery character-istic of such plays, and to recreate the conditions in which those unfortunate actors were able to utter, with confidence and in complete security, sentiments and expressions devoid of all verisimilitude.

On the other hand, it would be misleading to suggest that the *parades* existed in a state of complete independence of the conventional literary drama of their day, any more than did the *Ubu* plays. A significant part of the appeal *Ubu roi* makes to its audiences must lie in its parody of *Macbeth*, its reduction of Shakespeare's tragedy to the dimensions of the strip-cartoon; by the same token, literary parody makes an important contribution to the *parades*, and more particularly, perhaps, to the fairground theatre from which the *parades de société* derived: there are plenty of examples of the popular theatre of the eighteenth century employing similar reductive techniques and appealing to its audiences by the burlesque treatment of the mythological subject matter of tragedy.

It will be apparent that what we are considering here – the popular, or pseudo-popular, comic forms of the pre-Revolutionary theatre in France – highlights a significant difference between English farce and *la farce française*. As Jessica Milner Davis's study makes clear, what we normally understand by the term 'farce' at any rate in modern English usage – the plays of Ben Travers, the Whitehall farces of Brian Rix, the lightweight television sit-coms – have as their French counterpart (and origin) the *vaudeville* of Scribe and countless other nineteenth-century practitioners, which was to be raised to its highest artistic level by Labiche and Feydeau. Far from providing a positive influence for Jarry, nineteenth-century *vaudeville* was of course part of the conventional theatrical establishment against which *Ubu roi* was a gesture of revolt; and it is a fact of theatrical history that the cruder form of sub- or extra-literary *farce* of the seventeenth and eighteenth centuries, with its greater potential for anarchy and subversion, seems to have gone underground from the moment of the French Revolution onwards until, perhaps providing part of the inspiration for Jarry and his young collaborators at the Lycée de Rennes, it surfaced again publicly at the Théâtre de l'Oeuvre in 1896.

There seems to have been no recorded use of the term 'anti-théâtre' in the eighteenth century; though G. von Proschwitz quotes the preface to a play by Beaunoir in which the author, creating the neologism 'anti-drame', equates this with the *parade*:

> This word 'anti-drame' should not surprise the reader. Since my play is not a comedy, still less a *drame*, I ought simply to have called it a *parade*.[23]

In adopting the label 'anti-theatre', I am borrowing the term used by Jacques Scherer, and amplifying and extending the argument developed by Scherer in his Oxford inaugural lecture of 1975: *Théâtre et anti-théâtre au xviiie siècle*. Scherer's thesis is that in both the novel and the theatre, the eighteenth century offers analogues to our own day in the form of a self-conscious critical enquiry into the nature of the chosen genre itself; that Ionesco's 'anti-pièce', and the 'anti-romans' of the *nouveaux romanciers*, have their counterparts in the literature of the *ancien régime*. In the case of the anti-novel, the paternity of Diderot's *Jacques le fataliste* (or perhaps the joint parenthood of Sterne and Diderot) has long been recognized; but, says Scherer, when we turn to the theatre we have to look below the surface at the 'underground current it is fed by': the more conventional and conservative a medium the official theatre had become, the more necessary that it should 'secrete as an antibody its own critical conscience, in the form of that fertile source of provocative texts that we propose to call anti-theatre'. What Scherer calls 'the dominance of the visual . . . an attack on the very notion of a dramatic text'[24] may well have been a major attraction of the parodic, subversive fairground theatre for the blasé patrons of the official theatres; but it is significant that the custard-pie routine that he quotes occurs in an early text, *Arlequin roi de Sérendib* of 1713. When we come to the 'pseudo-popular' *parades* of Gueullette – and *a fortiori* to those of Beaumarchais – the relationship between text and spectacle, and the status of the text itself, are surely rather different; and I would argue that this is equally true of *Ubu roi*.

The custard pie, or its equivalent, does play a part, in both cases, in the onslaught on the text; but paradoxically, the main thrust of this onslaught is delivered by means of the text itself. This is always bound to be so. Even Pixérécourt, who wrote his popular melodramas around 1800, according to his own assertion, 'for the benefit of the illiterate' – and who did, as I have suggested elsewhere, in large measure reduce the playwright's craft to the dramaturgy of the strip-cartoon – even Pixérécourt was happy to rely on a text which possessed its own crude rhetorical and sentimental effects. Neither Gueullette and Beaumarchais, nor Jarry and his friends, were writing for an uncultured public: far from it; and the 'dominance of the visual' is much less to be taken for granted in their plays than in Pixérécourt's melodramas. However, the language used for their subversive purposes was in neither case the polished literary language that these cultured playgoers were used to. It is in both cases a jargon, based on the colloquial patterns of ordinary demotic speech, but shaped into a stylized literary idiom by the selection and accumulation of certain special features.

The most striking linguistic feature in the *parades* is without a doubt the use of 'cuirs': the misplaced liaisons which turn Isabelle into 'Zirzabelle' ('la charmante z'Irzabelle et son cher z'amant')[25] and produce sequences like the following:

> Non. Zil vaut mieux que je mette l'épée t'a la main zet que je vienne tuer le pere la fille tous mes ridevaux, et que je m'empoisonne enxuite d'un grand coup z'au travers du corps. Après j'iray rejoindre le regiment pour eviter les poursuites qu'on pouroit faire contre zune action zaussy barbare. (*Léandre marchand d'agnus*, scene 1)

Add to this feature the continual stream of malapropisms and pleonastic repetitions, the puns and other devices we have already illustrated, and it can be seen that this is a manner cultivated with a comic writer's skill, something which leaves far behind the popular diction that may have served as its source. 'It is the speech of the fish-markets, cleaned up a bit', said Fréron;[26] but he was displaying prejudice rather than objective judgement. For if this kind of dialogue does owe its origin to 'le langage des Halles', it has been transformed out of all recognition. To quote Pierre Larthomas on the style of Beaumarchais's *parades*:

> The characters of the *parades* are, of course, low-life characters with no education, but the way they deform language leaves reality far behind. The exaggerated use of liaisons . . . even frequently gives the impression that these people are using some strange dialect. In this context, Beaumarchais goes much further than Vadé or Gueullette, for he is guided less by any question of realism than by the wish to give all his plays a certain uniformity of tone, a distinct linguistic colouration.[27]

Elsewhere, the same critic writes:

> It is quite obvious that popular speech in the eighteenth century was never like this. And in one sense, no plays have ever been so carefully *written* as these; no one has ever made use of such artificial stylistic devices.[28]

Robert Garapon concludes his book on *La Fantaisie verbale et le comique dans le théâtre français* with the observation that 'word-play is on the point of dying out at the beginning of the eighteenth century';[29] but however true this may be of the official offerings at the Comédie-Française, a more vigorous popular drama was to keep verbal invention alive throughout the *ancien régime*, and to provide the continuity with the *parades* we have been considering. 'We are dealing here with a form of word-play, or verbal fantasy, which has its own rules, or rather its own tricks of the trade', writes Larthomas:[30] it has long been a commonplace to seek the origins of the stylistic 'recettes' that are typical of *Le Barbier de Séville* and *Le Mariage de Figaro* in the verbal exuberance of Rabelais and his contemporaries, and in that filiation the *parades* of Gueullette, Collé and Beaumarchais himself provide an essential link.

A not dissimilar process lies behind the linguistic idiosyncrasies of *Ubu roi*. Just as the cultured patrons of the 'parades de société' were presented with a stylized version of 'le langage des Halles', so the audience at the Théâtre de l'Oeuvre were offered a dialogue based on the schoolboy *argot* of the Lycée de Rennes, which had been subjected to similar procedures of selection, exaggeration and repetition. A good deal of scholarly attention has been devoted to this aspect of Jarry's work – much more than to the language of the *parades*; and this provides useful confirmation of Jarry's systematic application of 'recettes' similar to those of Gueullette and Beaumarchais, as a means of creating his unique form of verbal comedy.

There is perhaps a greater differentiation between the speech styles of the various characters here than was commonly the case in the *parades*. It takes the form of a more distinctive language in the mouths of the two principals: 'It is above all the idiolect of Père Ubu himself, and to a scarcely lesser degree that of his wife,' writes Arrivé, 'which mark a departure from standard speech';[31] and it is in the language of these two characters that Jarry shows the greatest stylization of the basic material provided by his schoolboy *argot*. The most obvious feature of the special jargon of the *Ubu* plays is the sort of 'déformation lexicale' of which the celebrated *merdre* is a typical example. Others are *oneille* (for *oreille*), the verb *tuder* (for *tuer*), and *Monsieuye* (for *Monsieur*): the spelling of the latter, like that of the phrase *par conséiquent de quoye*, indicates a genuine phonetic idiosyncrasy, whereas *phynances* for *finances* is a purely orthographic variant. The neologism *rastron* is explicitly identified by Chassé as having formed part of the *argot* of the Lycée de Rennes; and other inventions such as *salopin*, *bouffre* (with feminine form *bouffresque*), and the 'lexico-stylistic microsystem'[32] *boudouille – bouzine – giborgne – gidouille* (with its derivatives *cornegidouille – corne de ma gidouille* etc.) bear all the likely marks of a similar origin. In addition, allowance must be made for the importance of terms which no doubt carried a special connotation for the initiates, and therefore whose repeated occurrence in our text possessed a significance we can only guess at today: *caban, capeline, finances/phynances, mirliton, parapluie*. It is of such elements that the richness and vigour of Jarry's dialogue is composed: as in the text of the *parades*, what may at first sight seem to be aimless vulgarity is rather to be seen as the product of deliberate stylization.

As has been said, there is no evidence to show that Jarry was familiar with the eighteenth-century antecedents I have been examining – though he was writing at a time when the *parades* were beginning to come to the attention of both academics and men of the theatre.[33] Of the works of eighteenth-century literature to which he makes passing reference (in connection with other texts of his), Lesage's *Gil Blas* and Florian's theatre are a far remove from the *parades*; and although he makes positive acknowledgement of his debt to an earlier writer who also strongly influenced Beaumarchais – namely Rabelais[34] – there can be no proof of his acquaintance with the popular (or pseudo-popular) farce which was responsible for keeping a Rabelaisian spirit alive in the theatre up to the Revolution. Bernard Shaw, who looked down on farce, nevertheless showed a shrewd appreciation of its essential nature when he wrote of 'that fantastic atmosphere of moral irresponsibility in which alone the hero of farcical comedy, like Pierrot or Harlequin, can realize himself fully'.[35] I hope to have shown that Père Ubu was just as much at home as Arlequin in that atmosphere of irresponsible fantasy; and perhaps this may have been due in some small part to those eighteenth-century predecessors who created such an atmosphere and kept it alive.

However, moral irresponsibility – the assertion of the autonomy of the popular entertainer, his independence of society's conventions – carries with it a subversive implication. *Ubu roi* has been called, in a recent work, 'another skirmish in the long war between artist and bourgeois'.[36] Both of these terms, with their modern connotations, belong essentially to the nineteenth century, the materialist society of post-Revolutionary France and the revolt against its values which brought together writers, cartoonists and clowns. It is no doubt easier, therefore, to recognize the subversive, anti-theatre aspect of farce in Jarry's play; but the eighteenth-century Arlequin, like the nineteenth-century Pierrot, was also an anti-establishment figure, and it surely does not call for too great an imaginative effort to recognize in him a remoter ancestor of Père Ubu.

NOTES

1 See in particular *Théâtre et anti-théâtre au xviiie siècle* (Oxford University Press, 1975).

2 'Adopt the style of *guignol* as much as you can' (Rachilde, quoted in K. Beaumont, *Alfred Jarry: A Critical and Biographical Study*, Leicester University Press, 1984, p. 97): it should be noted that Jarry's own directions to Lugné also stressed the connection with *guignol* (ibid., p. 92).

3 Catulle Mendès, quoted in C. Schumacher, *Alfred Jarry and Guillaume Apollinaire* (London: Macmillan, 1984), p. 78.

4 *Ubu roi, Ubu enchaîné*, préface de René Massat (Lausanne, 1948), p. 11.

5 'The discipline of farce is certainly extra-literary', Jessica Milner Davis, *Farce* (London: Methuen, 1978), p. 17.

6 *Comedy: The Irrational Vision* (Ithaca, NY: Cornell University Press, 1975), p. 234.

7 Beaumarchais, *Parades*, ed. P. Larthomas (Paris: Société d'Edition d'Enseignement Supérieur, 1977), p. 16.

8 For an account of the evolution of the *parade*, see G. von Proschwitz, *Introduction à l'étude du vocabulaire de Beaumarchais* (Stockholm, 1956), pp. 23ff.; and Larthomas, Introduction to Beaumarchais, *Parades*, pp. 7ff.

9 Cf Scherer, *Théâtre et anti-théâtre*, p. 12.

10 Ibid., p. 19.

11 *Théâtre du xviiie siècle*, ed. J. Truchet, vol. I (Paris: Gallimard, 1972), pp. 165–90.

12 Ibid., pp. 1309–16, 1327–35.

13 Cf. the critical edition in *Parades*, ed. Larthomas, pp. 185–324.

14 By M. Arrivé (Paris: Klincksieck, 1972).

15 C. Chassé, 'Le Vocabulaire de Jarry dans *Ubu roi*', *CAIEF.*, XI (1959), p. 365. While on the subject of bowdlerization, it is worth noting that when the University of Bristol Drama Department presented the first full-length production of *Ubu roi* and *Ubu enchaîné* in this country in 1962, one of the conditions on which the Lord Chamberlain's office granted a licence was that the rendering of 'merdre' adopted in Trevor Vibert's translation ('shittle') should be further travestied as 'shickle'. See Schumacher, *Jarry and Apollinaire*, p. 185.

16 J. H. Levesque, quoted in Arrivé, *Langages de Jarry*, p. 220.

17 *Farce*, pp. 31–2. *Le Marchand de merde* is by Piron, according to Collé: see H. d'Alméras and P. d'Estrée, *Les Théâtres libertins au xviiie siècle* (Paris, 1905), p. 39.

18 D'Alméras and d'Estrée, *Théâtres libertins*, p. 29.

19 *Langages de Jarry*, p. 174.

20 Chassé, 'Vocabulaire de Jarry', p. 365.

21 *Langages de Jarry*, p. 174.

22 D'Alméras and d'Estrée, *Théâtres libertins*, p. 48.

23 *Avertissement* to *La Philosophie* (1775); cf Proschwitz, *Introduction*, p. 6.

24 *Théâtre et anti-théâtre*, pp. 7, 11, 10.

25 Proschwitz, *Introduction*, p. 25.

26 Quoted by Proschwitz, *Introduction*, p. 26.

27 *Parades*, ed. Larthomas, pp. 27–8.

28 P. Larthomas, *Le Langage dramatique* (Paris: Armand Colin, 1972), p. 245.

29 (Paris (Paris: Armand Colin, 1957), 1957), p. 368.

30 *Parades*, p. 28.

31 Arrivé, *Langages de Jarry*, p. 291.

32 Ibid., p. 201. The same author points out (p. 211) that *bouzine* has its source in Rabelais, and suggests that *gidouille* may have a similar origin.

33 J. Truchet in *Théâtre du xviiie siècle*, vol. I, p. 1479.

34 A comic opera *Pantagruel* remained unfinished at his death; see Beaumont, *Jarry*, p. 263.

35 *Our Theatres in the Nineties* (London: Constable, 1932), vol. II, p. 121.

36 See Schumacher, *Jarry and Apollinaire*, ch. 3 and Beaumont, *Jarry*, ch. 4.

Grotesque farce in the Weimar Republic*

CHRISTOPHER BALME

'In the aftermath of a disastrous war comedies must be written' proclaimed Hugo von Hofmannsthal in 1921.[1] Indeed in the extraordinarily productive theatre of the Weimar Republic comedy is undoubtedly the dominant dramatic form, and amongst the rich palette of comedy forms farce occupies a prominent yet largely ignored position. The authors under discussion here – Bertolt Brecht, Robert Musil and Ödön von Horváth – took a decidedly jaundiced view of post-World War I German society and looked to farce as one means of depicting this disharmonious world. In 1919, the pre-epic theatre Brecht wrote five one-act plays, of which one, the farce *Lux in Tenebris*, will be examined in detail. Robert Musil, an Austrian, is known chiefly for his monumental novel *Man Without Qualities*, without doubt one of the most important contributions to the modern European novel. During the early 1920s Musil also devoted considerable energy to the theatre, worked as a theatre critic and wrote two plays. Of interest here is the second of these, a farce entitled *Vinzenz and the Girlfriend of Important Men*,[2] which was completed in 1923 and successfully premièred in December of that year. In contrast, the farce *Round About the Congress* of 1927 by the Austro-Hungarian dramatist Ödön von Horváth remained unperformed in the author's lifetime. Horváth is best known for his folk play *Tales from the Vienna Woods*. Horváth, although less well known internationally, is after Brecht the most influential German dramatist on contemporary German playwrights. His use of dramatic dialogue anticipates by thirty years modern drama of non-communication. Horváth's comedies document the incomplete linguistic transition of the petty bourgeoisie from autochthonous dialect to the High German of the educated middle classes. His characters are depicted entangled in an inauthentic language which provides for comedy of the darkest hue.

These works will be examined within the following framework. Firstly, why should farce be adopted by serious dramatists? This question is particularly intriguing in the context of the German theatre which has

---

* A draft of this paper was read at the *Themes in Drama* International Conference held at the University of London, Westfield College, in March 1986.

always been polarized between 'serious' and 'trivial' drama to a degree
unknown in most European cultures. Until the 1920s farce had been almost
exclusively the preserve of the commercialized 'boulevard' theatres.
Secondly, it is important to analyse how all three authors blend farce with
the grotesque to create fresh dimensions for the genre. Thirdly, each work
will be briefly examined in terms of its genre expectation and how each
author manipulates this expectation for a critical purpose.

To begin with the third question, the generic classification of the plays.
Brecht does not provide his early one-act pieces with any kind of generic
designation. The meagre amount of criticism available has tended to label
them variously as *Schwank*, *Posse* or *Farce*, all of which approximate to the
English term 'farce' in its broadest sense of an uncomplicated, comic
genre.[3] Whatever problems of formal classification they might present,
these pieces are united by the common denominator of comic intention,
brevity and unmistakable allusions to genres of the popular theatre. Musil's
Vinzenz and the Girlfriend of Important Men and Horváth's *Round About the
Congress* both bear the subtitle 'Posse'. The term *Farce*, while existing in
German literature, is restricted primarily to a form of literary parody much
favoured by eighteenth-century dramatists of the Storm and Stress period,
including Goethe. Its present-day meaning is linked almost exclusively to
the nineteenth-century French farce. The German equivalent to the farce is
the *Posse*. It has similar origins to its French counterpart[4] but reveals an
independent development. It evolved into the most important dramatic
form of the Viennese Popular Comedy in the late eighteenth and early
nineteenth century. This Viennese genre, known as the magic *Posse*
(*Zauberposse*), specialized in the interaction of fantastic, fairy-tale worlds
inhabited by spirits and fairies with local settings and characters. Another
variety, the local *Posse*, was derived from the immensely popular French
vaudevilles. This form spread throughout Germany during the last century
and engendered variations in local dialect.[5] A sophisticated synthesis of the
magic and local *Posse* was achieved by the Viennese actor-dramatist
Nestroy who rescued the genre from the realm of spirits and goblins. He
retained the musical element and deliberate theatricality in acting and
staging but at the same time infused the genre with a new critical
dimension. This is most apparent in his subtle use of dramatic dialogue
where language itself becomes a thematic concern which opens in some
cases a tragic-comic perspective. Nestroy has been rescued from oblivion
for the English-speaking theatre by Tom Stoppard's *On the Razzle*, a hectic
adaptation of *Einen Jux will er sich machen*. On a formal level, Stoppard's
version owes more to the mechanistic French farce of Feydeau than to
Nestroy's more leisurely original. Although Nestroy had been rehabilitated
as a serious author by the 1920s and had paved the way for the acceptance
of farce in the serious theatres, the genre expectation associated with the

Posse remained that of uncomplicated, frequently rustic humour with a fair spicing of the burlesque performed in a local dialect. It is only once the German farce begins to incorporate elements of the grotesque that the genre begins to command greater recognition and offer scope for serious dramatists.

The grotesque is a frequently recurring motif in German art and literature. A renaissance of this phenomenon in German drama can be detected around 1900, particularly in the work of Frank Wedekind and Arthur Schnitzler. The reasons for the resurgence of the grotesque and its merging with the farce in the 1920s must be seen in the wider social and artistic context of the Weimar Republic. The end of the second German Empire in 1918 and the transition to a new political and social order marked a radical break with traditions, forcing a re-evaluation of all spheres of life. Even before the outbreak of war, Expressionist painting had given voice to a violent urge to portray the inner life of the artist. Expressionist drama forged an image of a disorientated and tormented 'new man' as the focal point of a revolution on the German stage with abstract, utopian visions. At the same time, Dadaism, beginning in Zürich in 1916 and transferring to Berlin and Paris at the end of the war, espoused a form of artistic expression bereft of links with traditional formal, conceptual and thematic conventions. With the end of a war once welcomed by the patriotic German middle classes, an artistic war was declared on the German bourgeoisie by the younger generation. The rejection of bourgeois ideology implied also a rejection of its art forms. The bewildering demands for innovation which made Berlin an artistic capital and focal point of the European avant-garde during the 1920s is on one level a reflection of this problem. On another it is the result of a generation gap. With the loss of practically an entire generation, the young survivors were able to start afresh in a situation of productive discontinuity.

The proliferation of the grotesque in art and literature in this period is in many ways a logical expression of this discontinuity. The grotesque is a powerful means of portraying a world of gaping contradictions since its effect is generated by the oscillation between the contradictory elements of horror and the ridiculous.[6] An early example of a grotesque, satirical farce is Ivan Goll's *Methusalem or the Eternal Burgher*, written in 1922, which Martin Esslin considers to be a precursor of the Theatre of the Absurd.[7] It uses masks, film projection and other modern technological gimmicks for grotesque effects. In his foreword to the play, Goll calls for the use of the grotesque and surrealism in drama in order to sharpen the satirical thrust and advocates the use of masks: 'coarse, grotesque like the feelings they express'.[8] Goll's satire was directed against the German *Spiessbürger* or philistine whom he describes as the typical bloated, bald, gouty and avaricious citizen. The link between the grotesque in the visual and theatrical arts is evident by the fact that George Grosz designed the masks for the 1924 production and illustrated the published text (See plates 4–7).

However, as early as 1919 the young Brecht had been experimenting with short farce forms which abound in both satirical and grotesque elements. Of the five one-act plays[9] completed, we will focus on *Lux in Tenebris* which reveals striking thematic parallels with the farces of Musil and Horváth. Although *Lux in Tenebris* was never performed in the Weimar Republic it is worthy of note, manifesting as it does the interrelated elements of prostitution, the commercialization of life, and the adaptation of a trivial genre which mark the more complex works of Musil and Horváth. The theme of prostitution was recurrent in German art of the early 1920s, the most famous exponents being George Grosz and Otto Dix whose crude, grotesque caricaturistic style could be seen as a visual equivalent of the unsubtle farce in drama. Prostitution in Brecht's early works is not depicted as a sociological phenomenon or as a potential for a tragic treatment familiar in naturalism. It is rather a metaphor for the basis of all relationships in society, a metaphor for the second of the three elements: *the commercialization of all spheres of life*. While this standpoint is clearly based on a critique of capitalism, an explicitly Marxist commitment is not evident in any of the farces to be examined. *Lux in Tenebris* is also an early example of the third element: the subversion of a 'harmless' genre, a form of mass entertainment, for a social critical purpose. Brecht termed this strategy 'Umfunktionierung' in his notes to *The Threepenny Opera* where he re-adapts the tired, outworn conventions of the opera into a new form of musical theatre. Recourse to forms of the popular theatre such as the operetta, folk comedy or farce can be construed as a strategy of audience enticement aimed primarily at the petty bourgeoisie.

In nine brief scenes Brecht portrays the conversion of the central character Paduk from a fanatical opponent of prostitution to a partner in a brothel. At the start of the play Paduk has erected in a red-light district a successful sex educational booth giving illustrated lectures on the horrors of venereal disease. Needless to say, the adjoining brothels are starting to feel the pinch. It soon transpires that Paduk's undertaking is not motivated by any profound moral mission but as revenge against a particular brothel which threw him out for maltreating the girls. On the one hand he presents himself to the press as an idealist, working for 'purely moral reasons' and motivated by a 'revelation'. On the other, he is seen to ruthlessly exploit his assistant. The conflict attains a mock comic resolution through the persuasive arguments of the brothel madam Frau Hogge. She demonstrates to Paduk that his campaign will ultimately lead to the extinction of prostitution and hence to a fall-off in attendance of his lectures. She points out that people only attend his show once, whereas her establishment has a high customer-return rate and a far better prospect of long-term financial stability. Paduk bows to her business acumen (helped by the offer of a partnership and free access to the girls) and closes his booth. Brecht's farce follows a line between social reality and grotesque exaggeration. His brand of black humour is illustrated in scene 3 when the Chaplain of the Christian Catholic Young Workers' Association haggles with Paduk for a group reduction. Although such scenes and exchanges seem to resemble a Monty Python sketch, a number of Brecht's later major themes are already prefigured here. The piece was allegedly inspired by the spate of sex education films which flooded German cinemas at the end of 1918 in the wake of the abolition of censorship.[10] These films demonstrated in a spectacular fashion the potential of cinema for commercial exploitation by capitalism. This trend was confirmed by the mid 1920s when German cinema was controlled by American finance and the remarkable creative impulses of German Expressionist cinema had been effectively stifled.[11] On an abstract level Brecht cynically demonstrates the ability of commercial interests to reduce anything to a marketable product – even the unappetizing subject of venereal disease, provided it is presented in an appropriate wrapper, here under the slogan of education and enlightenment.

The figure of Paduk also bears closer examination. He is characterized as the prototypical *Kleinbürger* or petty bourgeois. He admits to having had no secondary education, being a product of modern circumstances: his father was a 'small shopkeeper, ruined by drink. My mother was always ailing. My early years were marked by poverty, deprivation and humiliation'.[12] His campaign against prostitution is described by the journalist as being motivated by 'fanatical hatred'. He also reveals himself to be an effective demagogue: the Chaplain considers him 'divinely inspired' while Paduk believes himself to be 'filled by the Holy Ghost'.[13] As indicated above, Paduk's elaborate mission is in fact motivated by a petty personal vendetta based on sexual frustration. On a psychological level, he corresponds in all facets of his characterization to the psychogramm of the petty bourgeois personality with strong leanings towards fascism as elaborated by Wilhelm Reich in *Mass Psychology of Fascism*.[14] *The Wedding*, the longest and dramatically most mature of these one-act farces, was retitled *The Petty Bourgeois Wedding* in the later 1930s by a politically more aware Brecht who no doubt wished to stress the political implications of a work which depicts the social class most responsible for Hitler's rise to power. Here Brecht mixes traditional peasant farce motifs – the bride is pregnant, the humour often crude slapstick – with an insightful psychological portrayal of the thought and linguistic structures of the lower-middle class. The action takes place during the wedding-breakfast. The festive meal – a catalyst of all lower human instincts – recurs in Brecht's later works, most notably in *The Threepenny Opera* and in the film *Kuhle Wampe*. Brecht continued to experiment with the grotesque farce in the comedy *Man Equals Man* (1925), and particularly in the two so-called 'elephant farces', each conceived as a play within a play, making extensive use of clowning, circus, and cabaret elements.

The early works of Brecht were also one of the more important influences on Robert Musil's *Vinzenz and the Girlfriend of Important Men*, as Musil notes in a diary entry of 1924. Most critics saw in his intellectual farce a parody of Expressionist drama. Musil counters that the antecedents can be found in the writings of Christian Morgenstern, Joachim Ringelnatz, Dada and 'in one sense in the scally-wagging of Brecht and Bronnen'.[15] This paternity indicates that Musil saw his farce in the context of the iconoclastic avant-garde rather than as part of an established comedy tradition. The central character Alpha, a femme fatale, has gathered about her a circle of influential 'friends' who represent different aspects of political, business and cultural life. These functionaries of public life think, feel, speak as a group and remain nameless which imbues the 'arrangement' with a decidedly grotesque aura. Vinzenz, Alpha's teenage beau, is a con-man who plans to convince Alpha's gentlemen admirers to invest in his bogus mathematical system which can supposedly break the bank at Monte Carlo and all other casinos. Indeed, all the characters are fraudulent in some way. Even Alpha herself, the brilliant conversationalist and in the forefront of fashion, turns out to be the artificial product of her homosexual ex-husband who claims to be her 'creator'. The appearance of Vinzenz, however, disturbs the delicate equilibrium of pretence and artifice. The Important Friends therefore resolve that Alpha should remarry her ex-husband as he poses no challenge to any of them. At the last minute Alpha decides to marry a certain very rich Baron Ur Von Usedom whom she describes as a 'chimpanzee with a rash on his head'. Vinzenz must also compromise his ambitions somewhat: he resolves to become a manservant.

Musil describes the work as 'a practical joke, an attempt to stretch the stupidity of the theatre so far that it tears holes through which then some more serious perspectives become apparent'.[16] And shortly after the première he wrote to the theatre critic Alfred Kerr: 'The mood in which I wrote this joke was that of not taking things seriously; not the world, much less the theatre. It was meant to show the idiocy, the lack of motivation, the dadaization of a *Posse*. With insights and an ichy dialogue skin.'[17] For all its artifice, the complex characterization of Vinzenz and Alpha pushes the play beyond the bounds of 'drawing-room comedy' or light farce. The elements of travesty and literary parody which provide for much of the intellectual humour also allude to the thematic core of Musil's play. On closer examination it becomes apparent that it is less the over-earnest Expressionist drama which is the object of satire. Rather, Musil is reflecting on contemporary trivial literature and the commercial theatre with its attendant trivialization of the consciousness of the consumer. For example,

Alpha derides Bärli, the successful business man, for his lack of literary education which reduces his emotional responses to the level of a 'Mills & Boon novel' as she puts it (in a free translation). Feelings are thus determined by a form of mass-produced literature subject solely to commercial considerations. Vinzenz, the cynical world-weary con-man believes that money ultimately dictates all facets of human activity: 'With our money we can elevate ourselves to anything we wish in all aspects of life, in politics, art, morality, and destroy what we dislike.'[18] Money is then the final arbiter of taste and values.

The contrived artificiality of Musil's farce reveals its weaknesses, but at the same time contributes to its claim to literary merit. Even those characters portrayed in some complexity such as Vinzenz and Alpha have a haze of unreality about them which is not unusual in farce. Musil employs, however, this constituent element of the genre for a critical purpose. The reality of his characters is a theatrical reality: their lives are derived from literary and theatrical traditions. They are forever 'staging' scenes and concocting plots and schemes which have a legitimacy only in the world of second-rate novels or plays. This results in the situation whereby all statements are relativized, for all the characters lack substance or credibility. It is also impossible to detect a clear authorial stance or perspective on moral questions although these are constantly the subject of conversation. At the end of the play, Vinzenz sums up his lack of a firm identity and justifies his decision to become a manservant: 'If one cannot find one's own life, one must follow behind someone else's. And then it is best to do so, not out of enthusiasm but straight away for money.'[19] This is of course an oblique allusion to the theme of prostitution which metaphorically at least determines the interrelationships in the play. Alpha admits to Vinzenz that she has never asked her admirers directly for money, receives instead advice on how to play the stockmarket. That the values of these respectable gentlemen are also in a state of disarray is indicated by the fact that they are shocked to discover that Vinzenz has been staying in Alpha's apartment, considering that to be improper.

The modernity of the work lies precisely in its lack of an ethical centre. The moral laws which supposedly govern human relationships are suspended while the only unequivocal moral standpoints are derived vicariously from the theatre or from serialized novels. Musil's standpoint is essentially a cynical one. He shows the farce to be anachronistic by dusting off and manipulating its generic elements. Thematically and with regard to the milieu it depicts, Musil's farce juggles with the generic expectations of the nineteenth-century French farce and the well-made play. In these plays, in spite of all attempts by errant husbands to break out of the social and moral confines of middle-class values, it is precisely the values of money, marriage and bourgeois respectability that are affirmed in the end.

The end of Musil's play depicts this stasis in a far bleaker light: Alpha abandons one situation of financial dependence for another, while Vinzenz, his get-rich schemes having failed, gives up his freedom to become a servant. His progress is in fact retrograde and demonstrates a reversal of the traditional comedy ending. He slips from a bourgeois life-style, albeit a shady one, into a social position which in the 1920s was essentially anachronistic.

While prostitution might only be practised in a figurative sense in *Vinzenz and the Girlfriend of Important Men*, in Ödön von Horváth's grotesque *Posse Round About the Congress* it is the central theme. The initial impetus for Horváth's farce is mentioned in an article in the *Filmkurier* of October 1929: 'He calls his new play a *Posse* because it deals with the farce of the commission of the League of Nations which was meant to investigate the White Slave Trade but did nothing more than ask the traders about their methods.'[20] The play, which depicts a group of characters involved in prostitution, takes place while 'The International Congress for the International Struggle against International Prostitution' is holding a convention. Alfred, a pimp, has hired out a young woman to the Congress for questioning as to her motivations for becoming a prostitute, although she is about to be shipped off to South America. She tells of poverty, a broken family, maltreatment and finally of romantic disillusionment. She has been abandoned by her husband who, as chance would have it in farce, is Ferdinand, Alfred's brother. Her reasons are greeted with derisory scorn by the members of congress. The White Slave Trader, Alfred, is welcomed, paid for his trouble and asked to fill out a questionnaire. Meanwhile Ferdinand, who had become a partner in his brother's business transactions, decides to withdraw his capital when he realizes he is selling his ex-wife into prostitution. He offers to mend his ways, remarry the Fräulein and set up a modest little tobacco shop. The Congress, however, is opposed to this turn of events and finally the Fräulein rejects Ferdinand's offer to return to petty bourgeois respectability. The stalemate is broken with the appearance of a member of the audience on stage protesting against this 'fraud' as he terms it. He had bought a ticket because it said on the poster that a farce in five scenes was showing and not a tragedy. He demands his farce or his money back and suggests that the Fräulein marry Ferdinand and that they live happily ever after. In accordance with his wishes the play closes to the strains of a wedding march.

The term *Posse* which Horváth gives his play can be interpreted on three levels. In a figurative sense it is, as already mentioned, an allusion to the 'farce' of an enquiry conducted by the League of Nations. Secondly, the subtitle is intended to upset the genre expectations of the audience because it bears no resemblance to either the *Lokalposse* or the magic *Posse*. On a third level, the combination of grotesque satire and social criticism suggests a rejuvenation and remodelling of the *Posse*. By drawing together notions of black humour, elements of the grotesque and absurd situations, a new farce form is created which prefigures in many ways the modern Theatre of the Absurd.

Of the three farces examined, *Round About the Congress* manifests the most intensive use of the grotesque. Horváth employs a process of gradual intensification. While evident in subtle ways in the first two scenes, in the third scene the grotesque elements reach the balance between the horrific and the ridiculous that is requisite for its full effect. The Secretary General threatens a Marxist journalist named Schminke (make-up) with execution by firing squad if he does not desist from criticizing the Congress, yet it is Schminke himself who brings about the catastrophe by defiantly counting to ten. Suddenly soldiers appear in gas-masks, the captain in command alternates between an Austrian and a Prussian accent while Schminke continues his demands to be executed. Afterwards Schminke remains standing and lives on as an idea. He calls the Captain of the firing squad 'the Roman Centurion' who in the Bible recognized Christ's divinity. He compares his own immortality as an idea (the Marxist utopia) with the Christian faith so that the whole scene becomes a grotesque travesty of the Crucifixion.

The grotesque reaches a peak in the final scene at the banquet where the Congress is shown 'at work'. The bizarre and cruel contrasts are signalled in the stage directions. The stage directions are always an essential part of a Horváth text. They determine the exact placement of musical cues, gestures and pauses which, particularly for farce, occupy an equally important place in the play's structure as the dialogue. The first reads: 'discreet dinner music by Mozart' accompanies 'feeding and boozing' (III, 119). The Congress is depicted as a body and not as a collection of individuals: 'The Congress jerks, rises, becomes rigid' etc. (III, 119f). The depersonalization is further underlined by the fact that the delegates lack names and respond to stimuli by mouthing an assortment of clichés and prejudices. They strongly resemble the marionettes and automata that Wolfgang Kayser lists among the recurrent motifs and devices found in the literature and art of the grotesque.[21] This image of collectivized human degeneracy and brutality has a visual correlation in the work of George Grosz as mentioned earlier in connection with Ivan Goll. Grosz's caricatures of a decadent German bourgeoisie during the 1920s not only earned him a reputation as a leading exponent of the grotesque satire but also prosecution for pornography. His fusing of animalistic with human features places his work in an almost 'classical' grotesque tradition.[22] It is not difficult to ascertain similarities between the avaricious and drunken members of the Congress and the bloated, distorted shapes of Grosz's well-dressed citizens who are often portrayed frequenting prostitutes. There is even an illustration in *Ecce Homo* (1923), one of Grosz's more notorious collections, entitled 'The White Slave Trader'. Many of the illustrations indicate parallels with the members of the Congress as Grosz concentrates on important representative groups, the so-called ruling class, of the Weimer Republic.

Just as Grosz's titles contrast so vividly with the actual portrayal, the Congress's activities are depicted as a gaping contrast between ideal and reality. It is grotesque that the Congress is not only resigned to accept prostitution and the White Slave Trade but actually encourages Alfred in his work. This is both ridiculous (because the situation seems so absurd) and horrific (owing to the seriousness of the problem). The final grotesque incongruity is the forced happy ending because it is only by recourse to the hackneyed devices of second-rate comedy that the fate of the Fräulein can be resolved in a positive manner. The argument that this is a fictional world totally divorced from the reality of the audience is contradicted by the play's many references to social and political events in Weimar Germany. Thus, her fate is a direct result of the audience's own society and its unwillingness to help her.

Horváth's satire culminates in the final scene when Schminke unmasks himself as a closet capitalist by reading the stockmarket results: 'Schmink dich ab' ('Take off your make-up'), Alfred says to him. The image of removing make-up points to an interpretation of the piece as a satire on the relationship between commerce and theatre. Schminke's recitation from the share market blends with the strains of the wedding music, the phony happy ending that commercial theatre demands. Thus even a dedicated Marxist is defeated by the ubiquitous, all-pervading commercialization of all spheres of life. By having a member of the audience demand a happy ending, a comedy marriage, even when the action of the plays forbids it, Horváth highlights the audience expectation of the traditional farce and its link with the commercial theatre, i.e. the theatre should provide escapist fantasies which ignore the realities of the outside world.

In hindsight, it is difficult to ascertain accurately the influence that this movement in German drama has had on the later development of comedy and farce in particular. Apart from the fact that the pieces by Brecht and Horváth have enjoyed only a limited stage life, the whole question of influence and impact is impossible to answer in a satisfactory way. The three works examined were chosen because they are thematically inter-related and representative of a trend which can be viewed as a revival and rehabilitation of the farce form in serious German drama. Its influence can definitely be seen in the comedies of Friedrich Dürrenmatt and Max Frisch, the two Swiss dramatists who dominated post-war German drama, and who have strong affinities with the Theatre of the Absurd. Dürrenmatt's famous comment that tragedy is impossible in an age where the Antigone case would be dealt with by Creon's secretary is followed by the claim that the grotesque comedy is the only possible dramatic form in an absurd world dominated by bureaucratic procedures. The German farce of the Weimar Republic lacks the metaphysical orientation of the Theatre of the Absurd. Instead it is a reaction to the breakdown and calamity of a particular society and thus retains an element of social and political commitment that the modern metaphysical farce has forfeited.

NOTES

This paper was completed during the author's tenure as Alexander von Humboldt Research Fellow at the Institut für Theaterwissenschaft, University of Munich.

1 Hugo von Hofmannsthal, 'Die Ironie der Dinge', *Prosa* IV, ed. Herbert Steiner (Frankfurt: Fischer, 1955), p. 40. Hofmannsthal's own attempts at the genre *Der Schwierige* (1918) and *Der Unbestechliche* (1922) are concerned with the demise of the Viennese aristocracy and question the very foundation of human communication within the framework of the well-made play. Unless otherwise indicated, all translations from the German are my own.

2 The German original is entitled *Vinzenz und die Freundin bedeutender Männer*. The other play, a serious drama, *Die Schwärmer* (1921) was not produced until the late 1920s and considered a flop.

3 'Schwank' refers to the crudest of the German comic genres. They are mainly simple peasant romps, involving cuckolding and devoid of any attempt at realistic motivation. For a discussion of the generic classification of these one-act plays see Hans-Peter Bayerdörfers article: 'Die Einakter – Gehversuche auf schwankhaftem Boden' in *Brechts Dramen Neue Interpretationen*, ed. Walter Hinderer (Stuttgart: Reclam, 1984).

4 The earliest 'Possen' date back to the sixteenth century and are short, partly improvised interludes characterized by crude, sexual humour.

5 It has been suggested that the local *Posse* assumed the function of dealing with social and political problems in a local context, a responsibility which the serious German theatre of the mid-nineteenth century had abnegated; cf. Volker Klotz, *Bürgerliches Lachtheater: Komödie, Posse, Schwank, Operette* (Munich: Deutscher Taschenbuch Verlag, 1980).

6 This definition is derived from Wolfgang Kayser's seminal study, *The Grotesque in Art and Literature*, translated by Ulrich Weisstein (New York: McGraw Hill, 1966), p. 187. The etymology of *Posse* indicates an affinity with the grotesque. In the late Middle Ages *possen* were grotesque–comic decorations on public buildings.

7 Martin Esslin, *The Theatre of the Absurd* (Harmondsworth: Penguin, 1968), p. 360.

8 Ivan Goll, *Methusalem oder Der ewige Bürger: Ein satirisches Drama* (1922), in *Schrei und Bekenntnis Expressionistisches Theater*, ed. Karl Otten (Darmstadt: Luchterhand, 1959), pp. 426f.

9 These one-act pieces are available in English translation in the volume Bertolt Brecht, *A Respectable Wedding and Other One-act Plays* (London: Methuen, 1970).

10 The reference is to Richard Oswald's film *Es werde Licht* first released in 1917 and

rereleased in 1919 under the title *Prostitution*. In 1919 Brecht noted in a theatre review the cynical, exploitative potential of such films: 'Sex education has been filmed. The product wasn't new because it had to be profitable. Up until now the police, which was not exactly a friend of the brothels, had always banned this type of education. But now it was earning heaps of money and everybody could be enlightened about the fact that the fate of the fallen women was certainly pitious but all the more spectacular.' Bertolt Brecht, *Gesammelte Werke*, vol. 15 (Frankfurt/M: Suhrkamp, 1967), p. 6.

11 This is the argument forwarded by Siegfried Kracauer in *From Caligari to Hitler: A psychological study of the German film* (Princeton, NJ: Princeton University Press, 1947), pp. 139f.

12 Bertolt Brecht, *The Respectable Wedding*, pp. 61f.

13 Ibid., pp. 62, 70.

14 Wilhelm Reich, *Mass Psychology of Fascism*, trans. Vincent Carfagno (Harmondsworth: Penguin, 1970). A revised version of Reich's *Massenpsychologie des Faschismus* (Copenhagen, 1933).

15 Robert Musil, *Tagebücher, Aphorismen, Essays und Reden*, ed. Adolf Frisé (Reinbek: Rowohlt, 1955), p. 290). The reference here is to Arnolt Bronnen's grotesque and controversial comedy *Exzesse* (1922).

16 Letter to Arne Laurin, 18 Jan. 1924, cited in Helmut Arntzen, *Musil-Kommentar* (Munich: Winkler, 1980), p. 123.

17 Robert Musil, *Briefe 1901–1942*, ed. Adolf Frisé (Reinbek: Rowohlt, 1981), p. 325f.

18 Musil, *Gesammelte Werke*, vol. vi (Reinbek: Rowohlt, 1978), p. 431.

19 Ibid., p. 452.

20 Cited in Ödön von Horváth, *Gesammelte Werke*, vol. iv (Frankfurt/M: Suhrkamp, 1972), p. 649. All quotations from the play will be given in the text.

21 Ibid., Kayser, *The Grotesque in Art and Literature*, p. 183f.

22 See ibid., pp. 19f. The ornamental paintings discovered in Italy in the fifteenth century depicted strange combinations of human, plant and animal forms which gave rise to the adjective 'grotesque' from the Italian *grotta* meaning cave.

Yvan Goll: profane and sacred farce*

JOHN SWAN

Aristophanes, Plautus, Molière, were lucky. They achieved their strongest effects with the simplest means in the world: slapstick. Such naïveté has been lost to us. The circus clown and Chaplin in the films still deal in this sort of knockabout. But these are the moments when the audience laughs least. A lack of primitive naïveté. Or is perhaps our refined ethos responsible? . . . the modern adult more often carries a gun than a club. A shot has a less comic effect than a crack on the head, however.[1]

The Preface to *Methusalem* begins thus with a yearning for a more physical theatre, a theatre of movement and direct action. The call is familiar, and so, now is its author's proposed solution to the modern theatrical malaise in the tenets of *Überrealismus*, surrealism, and *Alogik*, the absurd:

The task of the theater of the absurd is to ridicule all our everyday speech and to destroy the fundamental lies of mathematical logic and even dialectics themselves. Simultaneously the absurd will serve to illuminate the tenfold brilliance of the human brain, which thinks one thing and then speaks another and then leaps and wriggles from thought to thought without the slightest sign of logical connection.

Words used to destroy the old, traditional power of words, the stranglehold of law and logic. This too is familiar, especially when these emancipated words are accompanied by dramatic action similarly unencumbered by the connectives of plot and realism:

The action of the drama? Events by themselves are so strong that they are their own action.

But if the arguments are familiar, it is because of the flowering of the absurd and the surreal in the theatre that, for the most part, followed these statements by a good many years. They were set down around 1920 by one of the most fascinating, and these days most under-recognized, literary figures of modern Europe, a man whose small fame is based on his poetry, but whose contributions to the theatre merit a great deal more study than they have received. In particular, his unique way – or ways – with farce

* A draft of this paper was read at the *Themes in Drama* International Conference held at the University of California, Riverside, in February 1986.

demand attention, especially as embodied in a grotesque comedy of revolution and in a fantastic, dream-like 'film play' about a transfigured Charlie Chaplin. In these nearly contemporaneous works he demonstrated that the images, the associations, and the physicality of farce can serve as the essential impulse for utterly different dramatic statements.

Yvan Goll (1891–1950) is best known for his cycle of poems *Jean Sans Terre*, and his birth, his life, even his death are heavy with the theme of the man without land, without a country. He was born Isaac Lang ('Ivan Goll' was his favorite of several pseudonyms) in the Vosges region of France, the offspring of a father from Alsace, a mother from Lorraine. In an early autobiographical note he described himself as 'Jewish by destiny, born in France by chance, described as a German by a piece of stamped paper.'[2] French was spoken at home, German by most of his teachers. In 1912, when he received a doctorate from Strasbourg, he also published an ode to the brotherhood of man, an idea that would persist in his poetry and his politics. When the war began he went into Swiss exile to avoid German conscription, and there he joined the circle of pacifists and *avant-gardistes* that included Romain Rolland, Franz Werfel, Stefan Zweig, and Jean Arp. He met Claire Studer, also a writer, who became his wife. In Zürich he founded a small and adventurous publishing house, Rhein Verlag, which eventually published the first German version of *Ulysses*, by another friend made during these years of war exile.

After the war, in 1919, the Golls left Switzerland for Paris, where Yvan Goll continued to work with Joyce on the German *Ulysses*, and where he soon enlarged his circle of modernist friends to include Breton and Eluard, Chagall and Picasso. It was in this period that the poet turned to the theatre, perhaps inspired by the strong interest in the drama, the circus, movies, indeed in everything vividly theatrical and visual, evinced by his friends of Dadaist, Expressionist, Surrealist, and other revolutionary persuasions. Whatever his inspiration, he poured some of his most intense social and political vision into these works, and in the most striking instances he anticipated some signal devices and insights of modernist theatre and gave his clearest theoretical and polemical expression to the ideas behind the dramatic innovation.

His two *Überdramen*, 'superdramas', jointly called *The Immortals (Die Unsterblichen)* and individually *Der Unsterbliche* and *Der Ungestorbene (The Immortal* and *The Not Dead)*, were published in 1920 in Berlin. *Die Chaplinade* was published in 1920 in Dresden with illustrations by another significant friend, Férnand Leger; *Die Melusine* was written around 1922; and *Methusalem* was created between 1919 and 1922, when it was published in Berlin. The surreal and the absurd are more or less vividly present in all these works. More insistent is the urge to revolution in and through the theatre. The language of Goll's preface to *The Immortals* makes clear his commitment to an aesthetic of upheaval, not only in defying logic and realism, but also by overturning visual decorum by way of the mask and the grotesque:

> We have forgotten entirely that the stage is nothing other than a magnifying glass . . . We have forgotten that the first symbol of the theatre is the mask. The mask is inflexible, solitary and penetrating. It is unalterable, inescapable, fate. Every man wears his mask, which the Ancients called his guilt. Children are afraid of it and they scream. Man, the complacent, the sensible, should learn to scream again. That is what the stage is for . . . Art is not for making the fat *Bürger* comfortable . . . Art should make man into a child again. The simplest means is the grotesque, but without charming him to laughter. The monotony and stupidity of men is so enormous that they can only be reached with enormities. The true drama must be an enormity.[3]

Goll's 'theatre of enormity', comfortably in advance of the Surrealist Manifestoes, is one of the most eloquent early entries on the modernist agenda – as theory more than as stage practice – but it has obvious precedents. They connect to Goll most directly through a shared fascination wih the power of the farce, not the farce of Feydeau, which for all its scathing wit does 'charm' man 'to laughter', but a farce with more unsettling ambitions. To choose one such predecessor with a quite similar belief in the rejuvenating power of farce, there is Meyerhold, who had been preaching and practicing his version of the grotesque for fifteen years. In 1905, before their epochal collaboration *Balaganchik*, or the *Fairground Booth*, the *commedia* that thrust Meyerhold into the forefront of the modernist theatrical revolution in Russia, Alexander Blok wrote to him that '*Any* farce . . . strives to be a *battering ram*, to break through the lifeless . . . In the embraces of a fool and a farce the old world will wax beautiful and grow young . . .'[4]

In 1913 Meyerhold visited Paris and briefly entered the circle of the leading Parisian modernists and formed a friendship with Apollinaire. The great aesthetic revolutionary died the year that Goll went to Paris, but the spirit of Apollinaire was still strong among Goll's friends there. The great event of Parisian modernist farce had occurred two years before, the 1917 première of the Cocteau–Satie–Picasso–Diaghilev *Parade*. This had provided Apollinaire with the occasion, in his program notes for that scandalous opening, for his coinage of the very term 'surrealism'. *Parade* also stands among the precedents for Goll's theatre, and Goll himself has been credited for carrying the word 'surrealism' into German through the essayÜberrealismus, which is the preface to *Methusalem*.

Methusalem, or The Eternal Bourgeois is Yvan Goll's best-known play, the only one to have enjoyed a few revivals. It was published with three illustrative water-colors by George Grosz, the 'Dada Field Marshal', who also produced two sets of stage designs for it, although only his costume sketches managed to find their way, modified, into the first productions of the play in Berlin and Paris in 1924.[5] Grosz's ideas for the play were influential nevertheless, because the designs were widely circulated in avant-garde circles. They are important to the understanding of Goll's theatre because the designs, especially the second, more radical set, were produced after much discussion with Goll himself. Grosz's designs were Constructivist, involving angular, mechanical shapes around which the actors moved. As for the figures, 'The vision was the total disguising of the actor's face and body, a transformation which would involve the modification of all conventional acting technique.[6] Grosz's costumes, surely descended from Picasso's Cubist costumes for the *Parade* 'Managers', were large cutouts that the actors were to carry about like shields. This total concealment of the human form was never realized, but the notion is embedded in Goll's instructions for the play, especially in his grotesque and surreal vision of Methusalem's son Felix: 'He is the modern regimented man. Instead of a mouth he has a copper megaphone; instead of a nose, a telephone earpiece; instead of eyes, two five-mark pieces; instead of a forehead and hat, he has a typewriter; and above it, antennae which spark when he speaks.[7]

This is clearly the sort of thing that Goll had in mind when he asserted the necessity for reinventing the mask in modern guise in his preface to *The Immortals:*

> The new drama must have recourse to all the technological props which are contemporary equivalents of the ancient mask. Such props are, for instance, the phonograph which masks the voice, the denatured masks, and other accoutrements which proclaim the character in a crudely typifying manner: oversized ears, white eyes, stilts. These psychological exaggerations which we, shapers of the new drama, do not consider exaggerations, have their equivalents in the inner hyperboles of the plot . . . We seek the most fantastic truth.[8]

The two plays comprising *The Immortals* do not, in fact, carry out this radical vision; they are full of surrealist tricks – grotesque masks, film projections, dancing advertising slogans, characters dying and coming to life (hence the titles) and even a young man throwing his brain on the floor and then retrieving it – but both plays remain so faithful to conventional lines of assault on the commercialization of modern man that the modernist devices, at least on paper, seem to be little more than interesting embroidery, for all their anticipation of the Theatre of the Absurd.

Esslin considers *Methusalem* to be guilty of similar failings – 'witty and charming' though it is, it 'proves to be little more than the conventional satire against the *Spiessburger* with his shoe factory and his greedy, business-like son'.[9] There is truth to this, but it does not take into account the full potential visual impact of the play, especially as a collaboration of Goll and

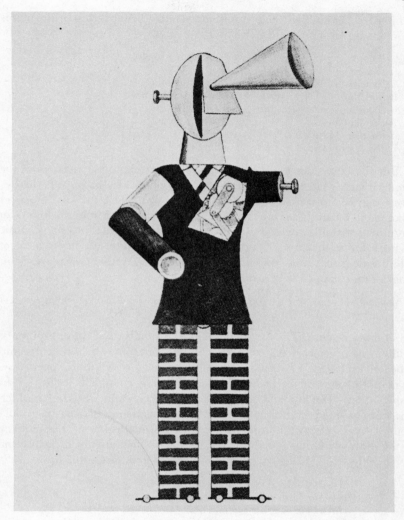

4 'Felix' by George Grosz

Grosz. It also does not grant enough credit to Goll for his success in integrating his surrealist bag of tricks into the play to heighten both its farcical and satirical force.

The opening image of Methusalem, 'the archbourgeois' sitting in a plush armchair, 'smoking a fat cigar', with his gouty leg wrapped in flannel, his beet-red face, tiny eyes, and massive watch chain, promises a satiric farce in the tradition of Alfred Jarry. Much of the dialogue, from the opening, anticipates the studied banality of Ionesco and other absurdist critics of this same bourgeois materialism:

> *Methusalem.* Nothing new. The world is getting so old.
> *Amelia, his wife.* Life is hard.
> *Methusalem.* Six of one and half a dozen of the other.
> *Amelia.* Nothing? Not even a teensy murder in the news?
> *Methusalem.* Seven marks fifty.
> *Amelia.* Noodles?
> *Methusalem.* Margarine.
> *Amelia.* If only there were plastic umbrellas.

But the play does more than echo and pre-echo other masters of the modern farce. The mix of domestic satire, political message, and surreal, even playful fantasy is very much Goll's own. The dream sequences manage to be all these things at once. In one of them Methusalem has an argument with his alter ego, who has just stepped out of the mirror in the living room in the guise of 'a rather fat man in a white suit' in order to get Methusalem to 'Know thyself' and change his ways. The response is an angry tirade capped with a smashed mirror:

> You son of Freud, you agent of psychiatric clinics, you'd like to turn me into a hypochondriac, wouldn't you? . . . Get the hell out of here! Idiotic conscience.

In another dream, 'The Revolution of the Animals', the various animals, stuffed and otherwise, that adorn the living room come alive and enter into a heated exchange. The bear – erstwhile bear rug – growls for the overthrow of man, 'the archenemy', while the dog, naturally enough, is for the established order. 'The human being is the crown of creation,' says he, to which the stag (having been promoted from being a head mounted over the door) replies, 'As you know, the apple never falls far from the horse.' The monkey is the most vociferous revolutionary, calling on the animals to cleanse the earth of 'human garbage' who 'foul our rivers' and 'fart at the heavens'.

> Has any animal ever had to blush?
> Has any bird ever sung a false note?
> Did a deer ever have gonorrhea?
> Did a tiger ever have to read Nietzsche to be Dionysian?
> Man is the disgrace of this earth!

But these ringing phrases are somewhat undercut by the monkey's demands, which include 'the right to copulate in the middle of boulevards . . . without fear of scolding spinsters' and 'the right to piss on all monuments, mailboxes, and fountains'. When Methusalem awakens, the animals return to their lifeless positions, but in the course of time there is a revolution. It is led by the Student, who is represented by three identically clothed and masked figures, each wearing a hat bearing letters that indicate that each is a different aspect of the Student's personality: the 'I', the

5 'The Student' by George Grosz

'Thou', and the 'He'. Together they constitute a young man who is by turns a romantic, an uncertain idealist, and a crass manipulator who manipulates the daughter of Methusalem into a pregnancy. At times he speaks with the voice of Goll:

> The stupidity of man is so vast,
> That just to recognize it makes one a genius.

6 'Methusalem' by George Grosz

But overall he is about as ambiguously palatable a revolutionary as the aforementioned monkey. Indeed, the revolution itself does not come off well, even in success, as we see the Student and Ida, the daughter of the overthrown Methusalem, sitting on a park bench in the final scene. They are poverty-stricken and have a child ('It started pissing on my dress again'):

7 'Ida' by George Grosz

Student. Oh God, life is boring.
Ida. When will the revolution be over?
Student. When the others no longer have their villas.
Ida. And when we have one?
Student. That's when the next revolution begins.

Yvan Goll the pacifist, the social and aesthetic revolutionary, certainly believed in revolution, but as the proponent of a new order of reality he was not about to deny himself or his audience the profanation of either side in the old war of the haves against the have-nots – even if it meant denying the concrete realization of his own ideals. *Methusalem* demanded something of an aesthetic revolution to be realized at all on stage, but beyond its masks, constructions, and film projections, it is the 'satiric drama' that its subtitle claims it to be. Its undeniable freshness rests not so much on its innovative theatrical radicalism as on the cleverness of its farce and the penetration of its satire. Goll succeeds in balancing the lines of assault, sometimes raucous and cheerfully vulgar, with a larger, more human perspective, and for all the literal and figurative cardboard in the characters, there is real humanity in the amalgam.

But if *Methusalem* fails, despite its strengths, to be a truly original modernist farce, Goll did create a piece for theatre – if it is for theatre – in this same period of intense theatrical activity that is genuinely *sui generis*. *Die Chaplinade* is sub-titled 'Eine Filmdichtung', a 'film poem'; the original edition also bore the subtitle, 'Kleines Kino der Menschlichkeit', 'Little Film of Human Nature'. It has never been filmed or staged, and in 1920 it would certainly have taxed the imagination of a film or stage director well beyond any known limits. Goll's great gifts as a poet are for the most part under severe restraint in his other, more vigorously satiric plays, but they are given full scope in *Chaplinade*. The work is a poem, but it is insistently theatrical, not only in its format, which is indeed that of a play or a film script, but in its intrinsically dramatic nature and in its reliance upon, and celebration of, the farce. It is farce with roots in Goll's surrealism and Expressionism, to be sure, and it flirts heavily with philosophy. But it is not heavy; for all its spiritual ambition, it conveys a light, sad magic worthy of its subject.

Of all the clowns of the circus, vaudeville and the film, Charlie Chaplin was the most universal object of love, fascination, imitation, adaptation, and exploitation in the decades around *Chaplinade*. For Charlie the Tramp, Charlot, the Little Tramp, laughter was obviously an essential, and very public, part of the image and the attraction, as it was for all the major film comedians. But the forces of identification and attraction that drew people to him were, at bottom, more inward in nature; the comedy that was the overt, shared ingredient of the fascination was rooted in the pathos, the private vulnerability of the individual. For all Chaplin's kinship with the swaggering, mischievous Harlequin of *commedia dell'arte*, it is the solitary and lovelorn Pierrot in him that pulls longest and deepest at the heart. The power of *Die Chaplinade* lies in its penetration to this level of Chaplin's comedy, its exploration of his role as bearer of the heart's burdens. In short, Goll centers his little drama on the Chaplin most recognizable to us at the end of *City Lights* (still over a decade off), rather than in countless pratfalls and sight gags.

Die Chaplinade opens with a poster Chaplin, one of thousands of posters of

8 Charlie Chaplin as the Vagabond

the Tramp depicted as the King of Hearts that are mounted about the city, coming to life. This Chaplin steps down from his pillar and pitches his crown, orb and scepter into a trash bin. 'I want to be myself', he declares, 'to be able to cry when I suffer', rather than 'grinning into the eternal moment!' ('zu grinsen in den ewigen Augenblick!'). This irritates the poster hanger ('Back on the poster, fool! Work, smile, that's your job!'), and there is a heated exchange. Chaplin bemoans the eternal lot of the performer:

> Tragedy of fools, who must mime stupidity,
> Of acrobats, who die for a smile:
> They are the loneliest in the world!
> And woe to them if they are recognized!
> The crowd does not forgive the lonely
> For their loneliness![10]

At this, the poster hanger grabs him by the collar and presses him back onto the pillar. Chaplin suddenly takes on the appearance of Christ with a crown of thorns, and passers-by greet him with smiles. A wretched hunchback comes by, and Chaplin, at first dismayed, finally does his duty and smiles, laughs and clowns until the hunchback laughs. Eventually children come springing up excitedly, laughing, and Chaplin (who in true tears-of-the-clown tradition had just wiped away a secret tear) becomes happy. Goll's extensive, expressive instructions here read, 'Chaplin is just the mirror of the world.' A film subtitle is supposed to appear: 'Let the little children come unto me.'

A riotous chase scene occurs when Chaplin jumps off the pillar again and is pursued through the town by a crowd of people grasping for escaping happiness. But suddenly all the Chaplin posters in the town come to life, with multiple Chaplins in all manner of costumes (cook's boy, soldier, king, violin virtuoso . . .), and soon the crowd of the pursued is larger than that of the pursuers, who are hopelessly confused as they grab Chaplins who promptly slip to the ground as posters again. Soon everyone is laughing and embracing one another, a scene accompanied by another philosophical aside: 'Symbolic victory of the good creative spirit [*des guten Genies*] over the poor in spirit.'[11]

Charlie escapes and is pursued again, confronting again and again the yearnings of his devoted millions.

> Ave Charlot!
> Hail to the deliverer from the century of labor!
> Lead us back to ourselves!

Goll sustains a strangely mixed chord of tones: social agitation, spiritual salvation, satire, farce. The same elements are there in *Methusalem*, but there the effect is more earthy, more obviously directed at mankind's pretensions. In *Chaplinade* we are shown, by way of sudden film panoramas and absurdly swift changes of scene, a whole world of labor, struggle, turmoil, people helping one another, people oppressing one another. There is still absurdity and illusion clearly visible in all the work and strife, as we see Charlie flee to Cairo, Hong Kong, Marseilles. As the playwright asserted in the preface to *The Immortals*, art is not for making one comfortable, and here Chaplin has been transformed from being a source of escape and comfort to being the repository of all the world's yearnings. As the leader of a great mass of supplicants puts it,

> Pour heaven into our eyes again.
> We can no longer think!
> We can no longer recognize ourselves!
> Save us from work! Bring us the communism of the soul!

The suffering is real, the urge for a new and better world is real – but so are the illusions spun out of the yearning. Chaplin takes the leader to one side and says, 'Can I tell you something on the side? You're always spitting on me!' He refers to the leader's sloppy speech habits, but he is also reminding us that he is no savior; he is just Charlie, a figure of farce whose genius is to bring forth the humanity that lies beneath the farce.

He escapes again, and in the course of his flight through a wood he picks up a companion, a deer who, after a good many more encounters with the world of longing and alienation, changes into a young woman. But there is no fairytale end to her devotion: fed up with Charlie's endless search for peace, nature, love, she snaps at him.

> Enough of mimed sentimentality!
> From yearning one only gets tuberculosis.

The disappointed Chaplin has his own illusions. He can only respond,

> I believed in dreams:
> But even the nymphs have become bourgeois!

The deer/woman has had enough of this romantic nonsense:

> Can one be satisfied with the stars?
> Can one be respected just for loving mankind?
> The whole world just laughs at you.
> You are a poor hypochondriac
> And no fun at all [*keine glückliche Partie*]!
> I love you no more! I love you no more!

She runs off, but being the figure of practical action, she sees a wild boar pursued by a hunter, and she attacks the pursuer. Meanwhile, Charlie, shattered, goes through a series of routines that make his kinship with Pierrot explicit. This is a series of 'Komische Intermezzi' that are straight out of the most traditional Pierrot *commedia*: The attempted-suicide skits. Charlie attempts to hang himself, but in the last moment a squirrel eats through the cord; then he tries to drown himself, but the water is too cold. Meanwhile the deer/woman flees from the enraged hunter, and she is shot down. Chaplin hurries to help her, but in vain.

In the end, Charlie is 'poorer than on the first day' and 'lonelier than everyone'.

> Europe laughs, New York and all the villages laugh,
> And they don't believe my deep suffering.

We believe in his suffering – and we don't. Goll keeps him before us both as the burdened genius of laughter and as the dreamy little farceur. In the final moments of the play he finds himself gradually surrounded by a host of Chaplin poster boards. The poster hanger seizes him and puts him back in place.

It is very probable that *Die Chaplinade* will never be other than a poem, and a strange, obscure one at that. Now that we do have the means to realize it on the stage or in film, it would be very difficult to get anyone to bankroll such a time-locked fantasy. But Yvan Goll's obscurely haunting little would-be film is worth a close look because it does manage to weave together the cinema farce, the *commedia*, the emotionalism and the fantastic atmosphere of the Expressionists, and the visionary absurdity of the Surrealists. But beyond all these ingredients, however successful the mixing thereof, there are more compelling reasons for finding the work interesting. Yvan Goll the *avant-gardiste* and seeker after a new society clearly proved elsewhere his commitment to the social and aesthetic potential of satire, especially in *Methusalem*. But in *Die Chaplinade* Yvan Goll the poet also asserts himself in a searching examination of the other side of farce, specifically the farce of Chaplin and Pierrot. Beneath the chases and the absurdities of this farce lie the less funny elements of vulnerability, isolation, loneliness, even fear. This is inevitably akin to sad-clown sentimentality, but it is deeper than that – 'Enough of mimed sentimentality!' says the deer/woman – because Chaplin's power to bring laughter and to reawaken the burdened spirit has brought to the surface the longings, the consciousness of the human condition, in his far-flung audience as well as himself. Farce has become the engine for uneasy, unappeasable tension between what we are and what we should be.

Die Chaplinade is unique among Goll's works, as it is among works of theatre and film in general, but his Chaplin does stand behind his most famous poetic creation, Landless John. Both are unaccommodated, wandering figures, Chaplin fleeing his burdens, his crucifixion upon a pillar of fame and collective longing; Landless John fleeing – and seeking – death, love, meaning. Like Chaplin, Landless John is the King of Hearts:

> I am the Unique and the Double Being
> The King of Hearts upright and reversed
> Losing winning passed passer-by in death out
> I am the Self . . .
> Gambler on both sides: I must win –death!
> ('Jean Sans Terre the Double Man')[12]

Like their cousin Pierrot, Landless John has an uneasy relationship with his shadow:

> You follow me all the faster
> The faster I try to flee you
> You cover the globe by evening
> And I am forced to see you
> ('Jean Sans Terre and his Shadow')[13]

Like Pierrot, he also has a special relationship with the moon:

Often late at night
John Landless drinks
The beer of moonlight
That foams in silence
     ('Jean Sans Terre Weds the Moon')[14]

And he has Pierrot's fate – and his face:

My white-faced solitude
Faithful in spite of all
Whose clipped wings lie folded
Under a worn shawl
     ('Jean Sans Terre at the Edge of the Road')[15]

In his Chaplin and his Jean, Goll evoked the bleakness of the human condition, but he also sang of the dreams and desires and the laughter that make that condition palatable. As he lay dying of leukemia in a Paris hospital in 1950 – kept alive, in a final symbol of his own landlessness, by blood donated by fellow artists from five countries – Yvan Goll wrote *Traumkraut, Dream Plant*, his poetic testament. Among the poems of this astonishing little collection is one final glance at the world of masks, of Pierrot, of laughter:

Over night the snow
Has made my death mask

White was the laughter of the snow
And it dressed my shadow
In carnival clothes . . .
     ('Schnee-Masken' or 'Snow Masks')[16]

Perhaps the richness of Goll's poetry and of his *Chaplinade* lies in this ability to create a laughter strong enough to embrace death as well as life.

NOTES

1 Yvan Goll, *Methusalem, or The Eternal Bourgeois* in *Plays for a New Theater*, Playbook Two, trans. Arthur S. Wensinger and Clinton J. Atkinson (New York: New Directions, 1966), p. 58. All subsequent references to the play and its Preface are from this translation.
2 Quoted in Martin Esslin, *The Theatre of the Absurd* (New York: Anchor, 1961), p. 267.
3 Yvan Goll, *Die Unsterblichen*, Vorwort in *Dichtungen: Lyrik, Prosa, Drama*, ed. Claire Goll (Darmstadt: Hermann Luchterhand, 1960), p. 65. My translation.
4 Quoted in Konstantin Rudnitsky, *Meyerhold the Director*, trans. George Petrov (Ann Arbor: Ardis, 1981), p. 105.
5 Andrew DeShong, *The Theatrical Designs of George Grosz* (Ann Arbor: UMI Research Press, 1982), p. 36.

6 Ibid., p. 36.

7 Goll, *Methusalem*, p. 73.

8 Quoted in DeShong, *Theatrical Designs*, pp. 40–41.

9 Esslin, *Theatre of the Absurd*, p. 270.

10 Yvan Goll, *Die Chaplinade* in *Dichtungen*, p. 54. My translation.

11 Ibid., p. 55.

12 Yvan Goll, 'Jean Sans Terre the Double Man', trans. John Gould Fletcher, in *Jean Sans Terre*, Preface by W. H. Auden (New York: Thomas Yoseloff, 1958), p. 29.

13 Yvan Goll, 'Jean Sans Terre and his Shadow', trans. Robert Wernick, in *Jean Sans Terre*, p. 33.

14 Yvan Goll, 'Jean Sans Terre Weds the Moon', trans. Eric Sellin, in *Jean Sans Terre*, p. 96.

15 Yvan Goll, 'Jean Sans Terre at the Edge of the Road', trans. Clark Mills, in *Jean Sans Terre*, p. 80.

16 Yvan Goll, 'Schnee-Masken', in *Dichtungen*, p. 455. My translation.

Farce after Existentialism: Pirandello's *It Is So! (If You Think So)**

RICHARD L. HOMAN

Mutation of form is now generally accepted as a fact of twentieth-century drama. Introductory textbooks routinely explain that we have tragi-comedy, for the same reasons as we have impressionism in painting, existentialism in philosophy, relativism in science, and so forth. If the emergence of a new sensibility at the end of the last century was so comprehensive, we should expect that farce, too, has been revised.

Ionesco's plays are this century's most obvious alternative to classical farce. The dialogue in *The Bald Soprano* which begins with Mr and Mrs Martin getting acquainted and ends with their discovery that they are already married seems a perfectly modern answer to centuries of adulterous couples in bedroom farces. These mutations of dramatic form and sensibility do not happen overnight. If, after Beckett and Pinter, we have come to look anew at Chekhov and the later work of Ibsen, and see in them an emerging tragicomic sensibility, we might also look earlier in the century for an emerging impulse toward farce in the modern sense.

Pirandello's *It Is So! (If You Think So)* seems like a kind of farce.[1] It seeks to unravel convoluted circumstances, and goes at it with a madcap air. We have tricksters trying to keep their dubious arrangements concealed from society which is composed of self-righteous, pompous fools. Yet, at the end of the play we are left with ambiguities and may be unsatisfied. *It Is So!* doesn't leave us in love with life, the way farce usually does. If this play points the way for farce in this century, we may wonder if this age-old genre is hereafter irrelevant, given the relativity of modern life.

Yet, in *It Is So*, Pirandello has incorporated the usual elements of farce, and has altered the sensibility of these elements by a single, bold device – the sort of device which makes his *Six Characters in Search of an Author* so extraordinary. In considering how and why this play feels different from a classical farce, we might start with John Dennis Hurrell's description of the usual experience of farce: 'The world is a well-ordered place, thanks to our hard-won sense of morality, and we have allowed ourselves temporarily to

* A draft of this paper was read at the *Themes in Drama* International Conference held at the University of California, Riverside, in February 1986.

forget this.'[2] Farce is the form in which we 'temporarily forget' what makes the world a well-ordered place. In *It Is So!*, Pirandello takes on a social aspect of morality which is necessary if the world is to be a well-ordered place: that is, the notion that we can understand and hence judge the actions of others. *It Is So!* takes us on a holiday from that normal perception just as surely as the bedroom farce takes us on a holiday from conventional sexual morality; whether the holiday is temporary, remains to be seen.

Signor Ponza and Signora Frola fit the traditional mold of farce heroes, as Hurrell describes it; they 'contrive escape or concealment' and exhibit 'the tendency to solve problems not by contemplation of their moral significance but by ingenuity and action' (pp. 125–6). Ponza's antics reach a climax at the end of act II when he is lured back to Agazzi's apartment. Agazzi's wife has invited Signora Frola over as part of a plot to make the two of them face one another with their contradictory stories. In front of the Agazzis and their neighbors, Ponza throws a fit when he hears Signora Frola playing her daughter Lena's favorite song and speaking of her in the present tense. He demands that she admit that her daughter, his first wife, is dead and that he presently lives with his second wife, Julia. Signora Frola admits this, but she winks at the Agazzis and their neighbors as she does so, suggesting that she is only agreeing with him to humor his madness. Signor Ponza proceeds to rage uncontrollably and falls to his knees, sobbing, as Signora Frola leaves the room. The matter seems to be decided – her story must be correct since he is obviously unbalanced – until Ponza stands and says, 'I beg pardon for the sad spectacle I've had to present before all you ladies and gentlemen . . .' (p. 114). When asked if his carrying on was only pretended, he says it was, 'It's the only way to keep up the illusion for her, don't you see?'

In Pirandello's puzzle, a husband and mother-in-law disagree about the identity of the wife; each believes the other is emotionally unbalanced, and each believes he or she has the complicity of the wife in pretending the other is right. The same material might have made a delightful farce in the old style. In fact, Pirandello includes what should be the hilarious climax in which we see Signora Ponza, the wife, juggling her ambiguous, mutually contradictory agreements with Ponza and Signora Frola. At her entrance, Frola rushes forward and embraces her as 'Oh, Lena, Lena, Lena, Lena!', the daughter's name, and Ponza steps forward, angrily shouting 'No! Julia, Julia Julia!' (p. 137). the lady in question says simply to Ponza, 'Don't be afraid! Just take her away! Go!' Signora Ponza appears to be siding with her husband, that is, agreeing that the old woman is mad; but the old woman joins in the supposed humoring of Ponza with, 'Yes, yes, you poor boy, come with me, come with me!' They leave together, each thinking he, or she, has the agreement of Signora Ponza. With very few words and some simply pantomime, Pirandello accomplishes the sort of ingenious forestalling of the discovery of circumstances, which typically happens in farce.

Yet, in neither of these instances do we exalt – 'Hooray, the trickster got away with it!' This is not because the subject of the play is too serious to be made fun of. Although the motivations here are not the usual fare of farce – food, sex and money – the potential insanity of the trio at the center of the play does not place them beyond the genre. Hunger, sexual inadequacy and poverty are serious problems in real life, yet we accept them as material for farce. So too, 'going crazy', and 'the loony bin' have been treated in farce. Nor is Pirandello's treatment of the characters especially sensitive. Ponza in particular is described almost as caricature with his 'distinctly unprepos-sessing appearance'; and, 'When he speaks his eyes are invariably hard, fixed sinister' (p. 84). The characterizations in the play are in the tradition of the Sicilian Theatre of the Grotesque which produced 'highly fanciful parodies of the old bourgeois sentimental theatre' in a style harkening back to the *commedia dell 'arte*.[3]

Rather, their contrivances do not delight us because they take place off stage. The audience at a farce expects to identify with the hero in his predicament and to be privy to his ingenuity at escaping from society's all-too-predictable censures. In *It Is So*, we are not so privileged and cannot feel superior to the stereotyped responses of society, because we are limited to society's viewpoint. The play has a peculiar flavor because, as in the instance of Signora Frola's first-act visit, we learn that she is explaining her way out of something only afterward. We too have been fooled by the tricksters! Through this simple device – as palpable as that which, in his masterpiece, brings six characters onto a stage where actors rehearse, searching for an author – Pirandello gives us a play which has the feel of farce, covers the same territory, yet changes its sensibility in a distinctly modern way.

Around these brief appearances by the tricksters, and constantly on stage, Pirandello builds a second story. It is also a farce. It is as if Pirandello is saying, implicitly, by the structure of the play, 'Yes, this is the kind of thing that happens in a farce, but don't worry about those little people trying to pull a fast one on society, look instead at the fix society itself is in.' Instead of following the tricksters, we follow the efforts of society to discover the tricksters. It is a story usually left to be assumed: of course, when they find out, they'll be enraged and punish the fellow. The Agazzis, Sirellis and others are as self-righteous and as broadly played as the usual cuckolded husband, cheated wife, and town authorities in farce. Yet, halfway through the first act, it is a bit less fun to see them as the butt of the joke, because Pirandello has made us as curious as they are to know these people's business.

By the end of act I, we and they have had enough to cure us of insensitive meddling. What started out as a farce of offended social conventions, and suspicions that a man might not be housing his wife and mother-in-law properly, has changed. Society has discovered the great misfortune of these people and is quite willing to learn compassion, if only we knew with whom to sympathize – Ponza or Frola. Madness has struck and the town would even be willing to join in the pretense in order to keep one or the other sane. It is the pretending in order to keep *both* sane which we and the people in the play cannot stand. We and society are in a pickle, as absurd as any besetting the usual trickster-heroes of farce.

In the second and third acts, society, and, by implication, the audience, go through ever more elaborate manipulations to try to get out of this fix. Their efforts are hindered by yet another trickster, Laudisi. From the start, the audience enjoys Laudisi. He cries out for compassion when Amalia and Dina talk of snubbed social conventions. He seems a proper scourge of their offended propriety. When the Sirellis and Signora Cini enter, he ties them up with seeming paradoxes:

> . . . do not tell your husband, nor my sister, nor my niece, nor Signora Cini what you think of me; because if you were to do that, they would all tell you that you are completely wrong. But, you see, you are really right; because I am really what you take me to be; though, my dear madam, that does not prevent me from also being really what your husband, my sister, my niece and Signora Cini take me to be – because they also are absolutely right! (p. 70)

From which, Signora Sirelli concludes, 'All you are saying is that we can never find out the truth! A dreadful idea!' (p. 71).

Since the issue in *It Is So!* is only one of offended social proprieties, Signora Cini sounds humorously petty, exclaiming about a 'dreadful idea'. However the same dreadful idea pertains, for instance, in the case, reported by the *New York Times* on 30 March 1985, in which Cathleen Crowell said she had falsely accused Gary Dotson of raping her when she was sixteen years old. Dotson had already been in prison for six years when Crowell said that religious reasons compelled her to come forward with the truth: that she had made up the rape story out of fear that she might be turned out of her foster home if she became pregnant after her first sexual encounter with her teenage boyfriend.[4] The 'dreadful idea' is that, since she has contradicted herself, we know she was lying one of the two times. She gives a plausible motivation for lying the first time, yet the implications of reversing a court conviction decision are unsettling. Even if we could be absolutely certain she is now telling the truth, we would not dare pass sentence in the future, having admitted the fallibility of our system. So, however, petty the situation in *It Is So!* may be, we feel instinctively that, as in all farces, the issue is one of ultimate importance to society. We must not allow institutions or even ideas which make the world a well-ordered place to become 'a farce'.

Normally, we rejoice, in farce, with the character who, like Algernon in *The Importance of Being Earnest*, confuses our usual explanations of things, speaks in riddles and paradoxes and so edges us along toward a better understanding of things than normal logic can provide. Yet, with Laudisi, it is as if the typical bedroom farce had a character saying 'What does it matter if he's discovered keeping a mistress? Isn't bourgeois marriage just institutionalized prostitution in which a woman accepts her husband's money in return for care? Isn't marriage itself just a financial arrangement?' We would say to such a character, and would hope the play would bear us out, 'Marriage is more than that, or should not be reduced to that.' Similarly, we want to say to Laudisi, 'No, reality is not whatever you decide to make of it!'

Of course, Signora Sirelli is not precisely correct in her assessment of what Laudisi is telling us. On the contrary, he is constantly telling us that we all always know the truth, even when our respective truths do not agree. We would protest, as the characters in the play do, that this is not what we mean by 'truth'. This is where Pirandello, in effect, subjects farce, with its dependence on discovering circumstantial truth, to the test of twentieth-century perceptions. Pirandello asks whether farce can survive the relativity of modern life; whether farce still works, if we see life from an existentialist perspective. If the modern perception of truth and reality have taken us on a permanent holiday from a well-ordered world, then moral judgements and hence morality are impossible. If in fact the world is no longer a well-ordered place, then we have no further use for farce heroes taking us on temporary holidays from a well-ordered world.

I suggest that Pirandello's *It Is So!* proves, to the contrary, that farce remains useful and relevant. It also shows that farce will feel slightly different in this century, rather the way tragicomedy comprehends the sensibilities of tragedy and comedy without denying either. The new sensibility of farce becomes apparent at the play's conclusion, when Signora Ponza, the wife, appears, as previously described. After sending away Ponza and Signora Frola, she asks, 'What else do you want of me, after this, ladies and gentlemen? There is a misfortune here, as you see, which must stay hidden: otherwise the remedy which our compassion has found cannot avail' (p. 137). And when asked her identity, she says 'for myself I am nothing'. The ending is problematic because we are horrified by the idea that she is on a holiday from identity from which she can never return. Her last utterance may mean that she absolutely has no identity, that she has forgotten her identity, or that she lives by denying it. The reader conjectures that when the old lady dies, she will no doubt say to her husband and everyone else, 'Now the pretending is over'; but we will never know whether the opposite is true, that is, whether she has now only the pretending left.

In an existentialist age, these questions are pseudo-questions, and although she does not say whether she is Frola's daughter or Ponza's second

wife, her appearance is not anticlimactic, as some critics have held.[5] The
solution to the problem is here. First, she admits there is a truth when she
says it 'must stay hidden'. It is not as if there is no reality. To say so is a gross
exaggeration of Pirandello's point. Pirandello does not ask us to agree that
she does not know who she is; only that she has chosen to be, for herself,
nothing, and that whatever she tells us, we would never know.

Second, she says 'compassion' has found the remedy. The remedy is then
provisional; it is not immutable truth, but rather is true if we choose to make
it so, as the title tells us. In fact, Pirandello's conclusion here that, though
we all believe in morality and justice, we also are willing to 'temporarily
forget' these fine things, out of compassion, is a very old theme and one well-
suited to farce and comedy. To say that Laudisi, and, by implication
Pirandello, takes us on a holiday from reality from which we can never
return is to misinterpret the play. As Laudisi says, 'I've been doing my best
to bring these people to common sense' (p. 126). He means, of course, the
common sense of this century. At the end of *It Is So!* we do return to a well-
ordered world, as long as we remember how this century defines order.

John Dennis Hurrell, says, in 'A Note on Farce', 'the writer of farce
knows that morality is what we turn to when all else fails, but he is a man
who has not been made cynical by this knowledge' (p. 126). Many readers
come away from *It Is So!* feeling that the ending is anti-climactic, that the
whole thing has been a practical joke on them, and that Pirandello and his
character Laudisi are cynics. If so, Pirandello's writing marks the end of
farce and the loss of a sensibility, rather than its mutation for the twentieth
century. Yet the play differs from the usual material of farce only in
changing the audience's point of view from that of the trickster to that of
society. By doing so, Pirandello achieves a view truer to that of the modern
age in which truth and reality are relative. Pirandello is not a cynic because
a relative truth is a truth all the same and is a basis for a morality, if only we
are willing to forget, temporarily, our need to make absolute judgements.

NOTES

1 *It Is So! (If You Think So)*, trans. Arthur Livingston in *Naked Masks: Five Plays by
   Luigi Pirandello*, ed. Eric Bentley (New York: Dutton, 1950), pp. 61–138. All
   references are to this edition and are included parenthetically in the text.
2 John Dennis Hurrell, 'A Note on Farce', *Quarterly Journal of Speech*, 45: 4 (1959),
   426–30.
3 Renate Matthei, *Luigi Pirandello*, trans. Simon and Erika Young (New York:
   Ungar, 1973), pp. 18–26.
4 *New York Times*, 30 March 1985, 1, 6:1.
5 *The Reader's Encyclopedia of World Drama*, ed. John Gassner and Edward Quinn
   (New York: Thomas J. Crowell, 1969), p. 712.

The fool and the clown: the ironic vision of George S. Kaufman*

JEFFREY D. MASON

Theatre suggests two coextensive worlds. An actor is both himself and the character he plays; a stage is both a platform and an illusion. While all art engages in the creative interpretation of the human condition, theatre actually re-enacts life, introducing the constant, tantalizing risk that the distance and the distinction between art and life will diminish to the vanishing point.

The farceur revels in reducing that distance to an excruciating minimum, forcing the audience to accept a double vision that will never quite come into focus. All theatre employs artifice, contrivance and convention, but while comedy and tragedy might ask their audiences to suspend disbelief, farce embraces the separation between object and representation. Farce challenges the spectator, vacillating between an apparent depiction and a travesty – between what *seems* to be and what lurks, leering gleefully, just beneath the surface. The farceur acts on the knowledge that probability necessarily implies an improbability which carries a license for wild nonsense.

Both the form and the content of George S. Kaufman's farces derive from his recognition of the incongruous distance between actuality and imagination, his narratives incarnating the unlikely as he embraces farce's liberation from the merely apparent reality of the ordinary world. He deals in opposites – he mingles the frank theatricality of farce with the realistic production style that prevailed on the commercial Broadway stage during his career, and his attitude towards humanity alternates between sentiment and cynicism. The form and content of his work are interdependent, for while Kaufman's farce expresses his ironic vision of life, the vision itself is farcical because it makes light of the limitations of the ordinary world.

Kaufman conveyed his double vision most clearly in two kinds of farce that he wrote from 1921 to 1930, depicting his American Everyman alternately as a fool and as a clown. The most characteristic examples of the fool farce are *Merton of the Movies* (1922, with Marc Connelly), the tale of a

* A draft of this paper was read at the *Themes in Drama* International Conference held at the University of California, Riverside, in February 1986.

dreamer who travels to Hollywood to become a silent-screen star; *The Butter and Egg Man* (1925), the story of a gullible young man who believes that investing in a Broadway show is a sure thing; and *Once in a Lifetime* (1930, with Moss Hart), the history of a charmingly inept vaudevillean's rise to the top of a film studio. The clown farces include the scripts that Kaufman, with Morrie Ryskind, wrote to display the caricatures that Groucho, Chico and Harpo Marx had developed during fifteen years in vaudeville – the original Broadway versions of *The Cocoanuts* (1925) and *Animal Crackers* (1928), and the screenplay for *A Night at the Opera* (1935). Since *The Butter and Egg Man* is the only play Kaufman wrote without a collaborator and *The Cocoanuts* was his first vehicle for the Marx Brothers, each play may serve as the model for its kind.

OF FOOLS AND DREAMS

The story of *The Butter and Egg Man* is a variation of the archetypal tale of a young man who travels to the big city to win fame and fortune. Peter Jones arrives in New York with an inheritance that is not quite large enough to help him fulfill his dream of buying and managing a hotel back home in Chillicothe, Ohio. He has heard that investing in Broadway theatre will make him rich in record time, so he introduces himself to Mac and Lehman, a pair of ex-vaudevilleans who seek backing for a script they control. He tries to treat the partners' extravagant promises with what he considers to be shrewd skepticism, but his resistance crumbles when he meets Jane, their sweet young secretary, and he gives the sharpers nearly all of his money in exchange for a forty-nine per cent share of the production. The plays opens out of town and it is clear to everyone but Peter that the script is a disaster. During the post-mortem conference, Lehman insults Jane, and Peter's sense of gallantry moves him to take an option on the entire production. He opens the play on Broadway, where it is, astoundingly, a smash hit, but he discovers that he is the object of an airtight plagiarism suit – the script turns out to be a shameless theft from a published short story. With the help of Fanny Lehman, the producer's wife, he sells the entire production back to his former partners, reaps a gigantic profit, and returns to Chillicothe with Jane to buy his hotel and live happily ever after.

Peter is an exemplary Kaufmanic fool, a natural hick whose ingenuousness first leaves him vulnerable to the city slickers and then enables him to defeat them. He is truly innocent, as pure and untouched as on the day he was born. Neither education nor experience have marred him, so he remains naïve and artless, eternally childlike, and forever honest and trusting.

Virtue is Peter's keystone. He believes that morality and ethics are simple and absolute, applying with equal strength and validity to all men in all situations; it never occurs to him that values might be complex, relative or situational. He believes that all men achieve success – as he hopes to do – through righteousness, dedication and hard work. He assumes that everyone else shares his faith in the power of good, and he takes for granted that others' motives towards him are benevolent and unselfish. His innocence makes him highly gullible, and it is difficult for him to imagine skulduggery or malice. He trusts Mac and Lehman because he *wants* to trust them, because skepticism and suspicion are completely alien to him. That his partners might find him ridiculous, that they might not respect him, that they would lie and cheat without qualm, that they befriend him only as a last resort to raise money – none of this occurs to him.

The catalytic episode in any Kaufmanic fool's life occurs when he stumbles upon a dream, finds that he cannot realize it at home, and decides to undertake a journey to a strange land, an Oz, a world that seems all fantasy and delight. Peter finishes act I alone in the producers' office, taking in the exotically unfamiliar atmosphere, admiring the photographs on the wall, and finally settling into the swivel chair and propping his feet up on the desk. He looks at a business that is marked by its anxiety and uncertainty, and he sees only the romance and the glamour, believing that to produce a show is to have a hit, for a flop is inconceivable to him.

Every fool learns that in order to realize his dream he must become part of the institution that dominates the new world, but the established members of the institution treat his overtures with suspicion or contempt. Peter discovers that the theatre demands certain rites of passage before it is willing to accept him; the director and the leading lady consider Peter to be a rank outsider, beneath their notice, until he becomes the only owner of the property. After his fool's lucks turns a disaster into a smash, only a combination of farcical coincidence and foolish inspiration allows Peter to escape from the plagiarism suit with his prize intact. He wins *because* he is ignorant and innocent; those he befuddles are accustomed to the onslaughts of their own kind and they are vulnerable to the fool's ingenuousness. His triumph is the defeat of craft and sophistication by intuition, innocence, and faith.

There are two important women in the fool's life. The first is the ingenue, Kaufman's wholesome girl next door. Jane matches Peter in virtue, but she has learned a little from experience and she unobtrusively guides him when his intuition goes awry. When her talents aren't equal to the demands of the situation, in walks a character we might call the 'sophisticated lady'. Clever, experience and perceptive, Fanny Lehman is a survivor who expects the worst of everyone, so the fool's well-meaning helplessness startles her protective instincts into action. She passes out of Peter's life when the quest is finished, but Jane marries him and becomes the typical life of Kaufman's cynical version of the American dream.

The fool's quest and his beliefs combine to lead him into adopting certain endearing attitudes towards himself. First, he cannot imagine his own failure; he believes that to attempt is to succeed. Second, he never questions the source or the validity of his dream, even if he finds it in rumor, the contrived fiction of the movie screen, or the seductive advertisements in the back pages of a cheap magazine. Third, he is absolutely unable to perceive his own comic potential, making him a susceptible target for the laughter of others.

Even without the contrasting presence of the clown, the fool displays Kaufman's irony. The fool succeeds not because he is exceptionally brilliant or talented, nor because he is skilled or trained in any special way. He succeeds because he is himself; sheer existence is sufficient cause for reward. His career celebrates the common man and affirms the American dream of the simple backwoods boy who makes good, a myth which includes a contradiction, because while it applauds individual effort it also denies the uniqueness of the hero. It supports the belief that all men *are* created equal, that no one is better than anyone else, and that the best sort of citizen is the 'regular guy' who does not stand out from the crowd. The myth demands a hero without remarkable qualities – something for nothing. The fool's career resolves the contradiction because his very commonness makes him uncommon. His achievement also vindicates the American belief that a man can be free without violating the system, and that any little boy from humble origins can become President if he perseveres and doesn't upset the status quo.

Yet even while Kaufman neatly resolves these contradictions, the structure of the farce awakens the uneasy suspicion that the playwright mocks the American dream. The disciple and paragon of the dream is a fool – it may be that *only* a fool can place his faith in the dream and succeed according to its principles. While the tragic hero faces destruction because he is exceptional, the farcical fool enjoys success because he is ordinary; instead of tragic catharsis, Kaufman gives us a farcical slap in the face. The fool is an unsettling mirror held up to the complacently smiling gaze of Kaufman's audience – each spectator suddenly wonders whether or not he is seeing a reflection of himself. Kaufman may be offering a disquieting choice: to remain un-foolish and settle for less than a dream, or to become a fool and win.

OF CLOWNS AND NIGHTMARES

The clown is the fool's opposite: experienced where he is innocent, crafty where he is artless, cynical where he is trusting, committed to shattering the rules rather than living by them, a sly devil who would rather cheat than work. While the fool works within the system and ingenuously charms his way to the top, the clown takes control, creating the world anew at every moment, shattering the status quo and completely confusing the other characters. While the fool inspires our affection with his endearing smile, the clown is a frightening juggernaut. The fool makes us feel superior, for he is a man who lacks even average gifts, a rustic without even minimal polish and worldly wisdom, delightful because he is so clumsy and so inept; but the clown moves too fast, startling and bewildering us with his unexpected and inexplicable choices. Either fool or clown may be mad, but the fool's madness has more to do with happy, innocent idiocy than with manic terror. The fool is a collage of quite natural flaws, while the clown is artificial because he is too perfect a machine.

The clown is an emblem of disorder, or at least of an order that is separate and estranged from our own familiar order. He is free from restraint, a spirit of revelry and license. He scoffs at absolute values and questions everything, showing no willingness to adhere to any set principle or law. He is a vice figure in an amoral time, not a spirit of evil but a nihilist who espouses nothing but the mischief and chaos he so joyfully creates. Kaufman's clown is a grotesque travesty of mankind, a character who, like the farce itself, presents the appearance of reality without becoming that reality.

Each of the clown farces employs a tight structure, building from a simple situation that provides a foundation for character and story. *The Cocoanuts* is set in an hotel in the midst of a land boom in Florida, offering a location public enough and a situation open enough to allow the authors to move characters in and out with a maximum of flexibility and a minimum of justification. The phenomenon of the hotel leads the characters into certain associated formal behavior patterns, products of etiquette and custom that are almost rituals, offering a predictability that the clowns can shatter.

The cast includes a set of conventional characters – a gullible dowager, a couple of villains, a clumsy detective, and a pair of lovers – whose simplicity and artificiality leave them vulnerable to the clowns' tricks and susceptible to the playwrights' manipulation. The dowager is Mrs Potter, who seeks to maintain her status in society by arranging an acceptable match for Polly, her daughter. She chooses Harvey Yates, not knowing that he and Penelope, his secret paramour, are fortune hunters – the villains of the play – who covet the Potter millions. Groucho is on the scene as the manager of the hotel (named 'The Cocoanuts'), and he hopes to persuade Mrs Potter to invest in some chancy real estate. Chico and Harpo arrive to try to make a killing in land speculation, with a detective named Hennessey hot on their trail, an unwitting symbol of authority who offers an easy target for farcical assault on order. Finally, there are the lovers, Polly and a charmingly ambitious young architect named Bob Adams, whom Mrs Potter scorns because he is temporarily employed as a clerk. They are an innocent, attractive, sentimental pair who recall the fool and his ingenue in their search for domestic tranquility.

Kaufman begins each of his clown farces by using the dowager as the catalyst as she attracts attention from the lovers, who need her approval or recognition; the villains, who covet her money or resent her social prominence; and from Groucho, who pretends to aid her social aspirations while actually making a fool of her. The action of *The Cocoanuts* follows a pattern of countervailing intrigues between the villains, the lovers, and the clowns. Harvey and Penelope steal Mrs Potter's necklace and hide it in a stump at Cocoanut Manor, Groucho's land development. Harpo finds the jewels during the land auction, and Hennessy arrests Bob for the theft because the young man has just bought the lot containing the stump. The clowns trick Mrs Potter in order to get the money for Bob's bail, and Harpo gives him a scrawled map of Cocoanut Manor that shows the location of the stump and the jewels. Polly tricks Harvey into drawing a similar map, and the lovers discover that the handwriting is the same on both. At the dinner celebrating Polly's engagement to Harvey, Bob produces the matching maps to prove that Harvey was the thief. The play ends happily as the villains quit the scene, the lovers plan to marry, and Groucho learns that a millionaire intends to make him a handsome offer for Cocoanut Manor.

Situation, character, and story are all subordinate to the buffoonery or *lazzi* of the clowns. Through verbal and physical mayhem, the clowns offer zany, alternative behavior patterns that assault the polite formality of the conventional characters. The *lazzi* range from Groucho's witticisms to Chico's *non sequiturs* to Harpo's taxi horn. Some offer slight development of character or story, while others digress wildly from the action, as when the Brothers turn Hennessey's investigation into a minstrel show, complete with music and 'Mr Bones', when the hapless detective gives them the traditional opening line, 'Ladies and gentlemen, be seated!' Still others have no relationship at all to the plot, as when Groucho interrupts the show to perform a brief vaudeville sketch. The ultimate form of *lazzi* shatters not only the conventional characters' expectations but also the audience's belief in the stage illusion, as in *Animal Crackers*, when Groucho protests, 'Why, you can't arrest them. That's the hero and the heroine.'[1]

BEYOND LANGUAGE

Through the Marx Brothers, Kaufman turns language into a madly comic weapon against the conventional characters, who are trapped in cliché, formula and banality. Kaufman creates a parody of a love scene so Groucho can make fun of Mrs Potter's desirability and femininity, of himself as a lover, of Bob and Polly as the genuine lovers, of the audience's expectations concerning love interests on stage, and of love scenes in general.

> *Groucho.* Well say that you'll be truly mine, or truly yours, or yours truly, and
> that tonight when the moon is sneaking around the clouds, I'll be sneaking

around you. I'll meet you tonight by the bungalow, under the moon. You
and the moon. I hope I can tell you apart. You wear a red necktie so I'll know
you. I'll meet you tonight by the bungalow under the moon.
Mrs Potter. But suppose the moon is not out.
Groucho. Then I'll meet you under the bungalow.[2]

The clowns also use pun mercilessly, pushing it to the limit when Groucho
goes beyond mere words to reassemble sounds according to his whim.

Guatemala every night or you can't Mala at all. Of course, that takes a lot of
Honduras. (*Animal Crackers*, I, 2, 41)

The clowns raise the stakes by moving beneath language, working on the
meaning it is intended to convey, and fracturing the logic of thought. Early
in *The Cocoanuts*, Groucho addresses a crowd of underpaid bellboys:

I want you to be free. Strike off your chains. Strike up the band. Strike three,
you're out. Remember, there's nothing like liberty. That is there's nothing like
it in this country. Be free. Now and forever, one and indivisible, one for all, and
all for me and me for you, and tea for two. Remember, I have only my best
interests at heart, and I promise you, that it's only a question of a few years
before some woman will swing [sic] the English Channel. I thank you. (p. 209)

Kaufman uses word associations and the rhythms of phrases to turn
Groucho's oration into a parody of political rhetoric, destroying the
relationship of word to idea and permitting him to gull the bellboys into
cheering the man who refuses to raise their wages.

Once meaning and language are divorced, Kaufman can twist them in
different directions, forming a convolution or perversion of their original
relationship. In this next passage, Chico and Harpo arrive at the front desk:

Chico. Hello. We sent you a telegram. We make reservache.
Groucho. Oh. Welcome to Cocoanut Manor. What do you boys want? Garage
   and bath?
Chico. We go together him.
Groucho. You go together him?
Chico. Sure me.
Groucho. Would you mind coming in again and starting all over? (*The Cocoanuts*,
   p. 213)

The clowns use their lingo to maintain their control over the situation, and
the conventional characters are completely unable to follow them. The key
quality is indirection – while most people value language that communi-
cates simply, clearly and directly, the clowns prefer to say one thing while
meaning another.

While the clowns impose their meta-language on the world they invade,
the fool discovers that the world of his dreams demands that he learn a
jargon, or target language, in order to succeed. At the beginning of *The
Butter and Egg Man*, Mac and Lehman demonstrate their control of the
situation by displaying their linguistic facility.

Lehman. Anybody comes in on this trick'll clean up! I can do it for fifteen
   thousand. I'd take twelve.
Mac. You'd take one.
Lehman. You don't say? Let me tell you this, sweetheart, there ain't going to be
   no bargains, not if I have to throw it in the ash-can! This show's a pipe, and
   any bird that comes in is going to make plenty.[3]

This jargon depends heavily on slang, and it is boldly colloquial, idiosyncratic and crudely expressive. Peter discovers that his accustomed speech
patterns brand him as a greenhorn, so he must master at least the style of
the jargon, if not its content, in order to remove it as a barrier to his success.
At first the new slang bewilders him – when Lehman informs him that 'I'm
doing a wow,' Peter has to ask for a translation. Later in the play, he has
retained enough fragments from several overheard conversations to be able
to assemble a speech that will fool the uninitiated, even though he's not
quite sure of what he's saying.

> Everything happens to this girl – she marries a fellow, only she's going to have
> more sympathy . . . It's going to make millions of dollars – thousands. It's
> going to be the biggest thing that ever was in the theatre . . . and it's going to
> have Hongkong [sic] in it! A great big scene instead of where it's a trial! It's
> wonderful – it's a hop joint and he turns out to be her father and she comes back
> at him with the strong talk and so-and-so and so-and-so and so-and-so. (p. 166)

Peter captures just enough vocabulary and rhythm to produce the effect he
seeks. Meaning is absent or fractured, so the jargon becomes a hastily-
constructed mask that changes who he *seems* to be, not who he *is*.

CRAFTSMAN AT WORK

Although Kaufman's expertise shines most clearly through his re-creation
of various lower forms of spoken American English, he is equally adept at
creating farcical situation. He uses realism as the basis, creating a world
that mimics – but does not become – the ordinary world. He begins with an
apparently solid foundation of familiar materiality – walls, doors, everyday
paraphernalia and recognizable people – in order to encourage his
audience's conventional expectations and to lull them into a false sense of
security. Then he distorts his creation, veering towards the improbable and
introducing a logic that only resembles that of the ordinary world. If
Kaufman departs from reality completely, he robs the audience of their
point of reference and forfeits his ability to seduce their belief, while if he
sustains a perfect or even apparent identity with the ordinary world, he
must follow ordinary rules and sacrifice his control. To maintain that
control is to be free from the predictable and the plausible, so the impossible
is rife – rascally clowns escape the clutches of the law, and a fool finds the
money he needs in the nick of time.

To its inhabitants, the farce-world appears to be as capricious and as unreliable as Alice's Looking-Glass World; not only does it refuse to follow the laws of the ordinary world, it declines to be consistent within its own context. It is inimical one moment and friendly the next, becoming an ineffable or hostile mechanism to the characters who are trapped within its closed system. It is the product of the tension between its realistic basis and the farcical artifice that dominates the action.

Kaufman mocks traditional farcical devices even while he uses them, again conveying two points of view. Harpo finds Mrs Potter's missing jewels with none of the suspense and anxiety that characterize Sardou's use of the trick in *A Scrap of Paper*. When the clown leads the matron to the tree stump, he points out not only the necklace but also the ease of the discovery and the folly of playwrights who build entire plots around such gimmicks. If one of Feydeau's dupes is caught in the hall without his trousers, reaching for the door just as it swings shut and locks, then he is simply an unwilling victim of the farceur's machinery. But in Kaufman's door-slamming scene, when the three clowns rotate positions between the hallway and the two adjoining rooms, befuddling the hotel guests and joyfully slamming doors as they dive in and out of their hiding-places under the beds, they are the farceur's accomplices, and they act with full awareness of their theatrical mischief. Lady Teazle may hide behind the screen merely to escape detection, but Kaufman's clown hides under the bed both to annoy the conventional characters and to create a parody of concealment, coincidence, and the rapid, mechanical pace that is farce's hallmark.

With relation to character, the classic farcical device is mask. For many of his creations, Kaufman offers two masks – the one the individual sees and the one that others see – making each role an exercise in dissonance and incongruity. The inept character has little self-awareness and he insists on the self-image he cherishes even when circumstances deny its validity. A mask acts as a disguise only when the wearer recognizes the distance between appearance and actuality; when the wearer's incomprehension turns that distance into a chasm, it becomes a trap. *Pour le Bain*, a sketch that Kaufman wrote with Howard Dietz in 1931, describes a society woman's discomfort when shopping for bathroom fixtures. Her mask of gentility so confines her that she cannot even bring herself to ask for a toilet by name; the mask stands between her and her needs. In the case of the clowns, character *is* mask. Groucho's character has little or no personality beneath the garish mustache, eyebrows and glasses; he is as fixed in his zaniness as the mask is in its features. The fool, on the other hand, creates and dons a mask in order to deceive others into believing he is someone he is not. His conscious masquerade raises him above simplicity and artlessness towards the realm of roguery. As long as Peter Jones *knows* he wears a mask, he is safe from its inherent trap, but when he loses sight of the distinction between his true self and his appearance, he begins to lose both Jane and the fortune he seeks. Kaufman uses the mask to explore the folly of those who wear them in the ordinary world.

THE VEILED COMMENTARY

With the mask, the playwright holds folly up to inspection but not to punishment. Does Kaufman embrace the cynical view of man as essentially foolish and given to error, or does he accept the sentimental vision of man as essentially weak but progressing inevitably towards goodness and perfection? He vacillates between the two, sometimes using one to undercut the other. In this moment, he attacks man's folly, using his acid wisecracks to ridicule and deride certain characters. In the next, he presents a warm picture of man striving for self-improvement and placing his trust in the generosity and benevolence of others. In a single play, he may offer an unashamedly sentimental couple whose romance holds the play together, while providing a contrast with a decidedly unsentimental couple whose unsurprised, experienced attitude dilutes the sweetness of the hero and heroine. The clown is the sharp instrument of cynicism, but the fool is the apotheosis of the sentimental dream.

Kaufman may present man as a weak, inept, and sentimental fool, but he approaches his folly with humorous tolerance. Kaufman never loses sight of man's absurdity – that is his cynicism. He prefers to use the fool as a focal point of laughter, and although the audience may laugh at the fool's mistakes, they also laugh with his victories. Kaufman tempers his cynicism with sentiment in that his fools survive their missteps and win the prizes they seek. The fool may be a boob, but he's improving just the same.

Kaufman's combination of cynicism with sentiment leaves little room for the spirit of saturnalia and revelry that farce often offers. Cynicism declines to believe in celebration, while sentiment crushes it with prudery. Another playwright might find in sexuality a chance to explore the themes of birth and the renewal of the world, or an opportunity to present a wild, joyous, physical release at the end of the play. In Kaufman's work, sexuality loses the capacity for abandon. Beautiful women become untouchable, comfortless sex symbols, while others turn away from sensuality and formalize it into their social roles as wives and helpmates, defining themselves in terms of their men's success and taking a firm but discreet hand in the course of events. Sentimental, middle-class values insist on the wife helping the husband along the road of self-improvement, so there is little time for the wild affirmation of life that is Bacchanalia.

In the end, Kaufman is a pessimist. His farces end happily, but they neither affirm life nor offer genuine answers to real-world problems. There is no sense that the fool's victory carries any implication or message for those of us in the ordinary world. His fools solve or avoid the dilemmas confronting them, but their solutions work only within the controlled environment of the farce. He sees too clearly the absurdity in the world, and if one accepts absurdity, then one relinquishes the right to expect the consistency of cause-and-effect that social cures require. Kaufman does not believe in solutions, and his work seldom seriously questions the system or its values.

Joseph Wood Krutch criticized Kaufman for failing to adopt a single, coherent point of view, but Kaufman's ironic vision – the very vision that makes his work possible – prevents him from doing so.[4] Kaufman sees man as fool *and* hero, clown *and* dupe, so he cannot for more than a passing moment commit himself to one or another model of human nature. At one point Kaufman sees the world as a rationalist mechanism that submits to man's tinkering, a device that rewards craft and sophistication. At another point he sees the world as an organism that remains ineffable to the scientist but which encourages the trusting wanderings of that strange Romantic hero, the Kaufmanic fool. He cannot commit himself to a single interpretation because he looks at the world and sees its farcical reflection beside it, an image that reproduces the original with startling accuracy but without achieving or desiring genuine identity.

NOTES

1 George S. Kaufman and Morrie Ryskind, *Animal Crackers*, ts, Sam H. Harris Collection, William Seymour Theatre Collection, Princeton University Library, II, 1, 36.

2 George S. Kaufman, *The Cocoanuts* in Donald Oliver, ed., *By George* (New York: St Martin's Press, 1979), p. 219.

3 George S. Kaufman, *The Butter and Egg Man* (New York: Boni and Liveright, 264)

4 Joseph Wood Krutch, 'The Random Satire of George S. Kaufman', *The Nation*, 137 (1933), 157; and review of *First Lady*, *The Nation*, 141 (1935), 694.

The cruciform farce in Latin America: two plays*

ANDREA G. LABINGER

Nearly everyone who has ever written about farce acknowledges the brutality that lurks just beneath its festive surface. For Bermel, it is an 'objective brutality' in which the audience is emotionally distanced by a constant awareness that the blows delivered are unreal.[1] Eric Bentley defends the violence in farce as a healthy outlet for our wildest repressed desires.[2] Still another element – humiliation – is signalled by Jessica Davis[3] as fundamental to the farcical dialectic of hostility and festivity. We laugh at the unfortunate recipient of the pie-in-the-face, scarcely aware of the innocent sadism that provokes our laughter.

Latin American theatre, like the troubled societies it represents, is no stranger to brutality, violence and humiliation, either in its unadulterated form – tragedy or melodrama – or in more ebullient guise. Indeed, humor tends to be the most frequent vehicle for social assault on the Latin American stage, perhaps because for Latino playwrights the theatre must often be a clandestine activity, or simply because, as William Oliver has observed: 'Direct assault is not the way of Spanish American drama'.[4] While admittedly most Latin American playwrights rely on black humor, heavy-handed satire and the grotesque to communicate their dissatisfaction with social and political realities, the occasional farceur does surface now and then to relieve the bleakness and to throw pies, rather than bombs, in the face of the oppressor. Most of these lighthearted works, however, do contain the requisite modicum of violence, humiliation and brutality, and most of them, predictably, concern themselves with the class struggle and the plea for human dignity.

An interesting manifestation of the class-struggle *buffo* in Latin America might be called the cruciform farce. This X-shaped configuration is ideally suited to the needs of the Spanish American playwright because it depicts very graphically the rise of the humble and the well-deserved decline of the mighty. Humiliation and ridicule become the primary operating principles in these works, as those characters invested with status and power attempt

* A draft of this paper was read at the *Themes in Drama* International Conference held at the University of California, Riverside, in February 1986.

to mock the lowly and powerless by initiating a 'joke' or 'game' in which temporary role reversal takes place. Central to the cruciform structure is the mask or disguise, one of the most basic elements of farce. The disguise becomes the fulcrum upon which the entire cruciform structure is hinged. Underlying this structure is the assumption that external trappings are the only determinants of social status. Role reversal, or the transfer of these trappings from one character to another, can topple the entire social order, while at the same time eliciting our laughter. The two plays to be discussed here, one from Chile and the other from the earliest body of Chicano theatre, illustrate the mechanism and implications of the cruciform farce.

In 1965 a young Chicano dramatist named Luis Valdez revolutionized both agribusiness and the theatre by introducing a series of improvisational farces or *actos* to a group of striking farmworkers in Delano, California. Valdez's purpose was more political than theatrical: he hoped to alert the as yet unorganized farmworkers to the seriousness of their plight through laughter and collective creativity. His goal, like that of his colleague César Chávez, was unionization of the workers. The earliest, simplest and most blatantly farcical work produced by Valdez's group, El Teatro Campesino (or Farmworkers' Theatre), was an exquisitely brief cruciform piece called *Las dos caras del patroncito*, or *The Two Faces of the Boss*.[5]

The situation of *Two Faces* is easily summarized: an undocumented worker, generically labelled El Esquirol (or Scab), has just arrived in California, 'the land of sun and money . . . more sun than money' (p. 9), to prune grape vines for an unnamed grower or Patrón. The Patrón enters immediately after the Farmworker. In the best farcical tradition, both characters are readily identifiable by visual clues: the Farmworker wields a pair of pruning shears, while the Patrón sports a pig mask. Jorge Huerta, in his comprehensive study, *Chicano Theater: Themes and Forms*, has observed the two-fold importance of the mask in this play. According to Huerta, not only does the pig mask provide instant recognition of the character for a relatively unsophisticated audience, but it also serves as 'a form of protection for the wearer [the original actors were themselves farmworkers], separating him or her from the character assumed'.[6] Once recognized by the audience and by each other, the two characters engage in a rapid-fire exchange in which they define their roles in life: the Farmworker's is to serve, the Patrón's to command. When the Patrón facetiously suggests that the responsibilities of his station have become too burdensome and that he would prefer the freedom and uncomplicated existence of the Farmworker, both men know that the Patrón is speaking in jest. Yet when the Patrón persists and compels the Farmworker to exchange roles with him by accepting his cigar and whip and donning his cape and mask, the joke attains more serious dimensions. The Farmworker, understandably, enjoys flaunting the newly-acquired power conferred upon him by the disguise, and at first he refuses to relinquish it. A noisy argument follows, attracting the attention of the Patrón's ape-like henchman, Charlie, who, unable to recognize his former master without the mask, drags the protesting Patrón off stage. The real Farmworker then agreeably removes the mask and confides to the audience:

> Bueno, so much for the patrón. I got his house, his land, his car – only I'm not going to keep 'em. He can have them. But I'm taking the cigar. Ay [*sic*] los watcho [See you around]. (p. 19)

Although the audience never learns what has become of the Patrón, order is ultimately restored when the Farmworker voluntarily despoils himself of the trappings of power. This, then, is a 'classic cruciform', one in which it is demonstrated, or at least strongly suggested, that the two antagonists will resume their normal positions in the world. While it is clear that this is farce with political punch, the restoration of harmony at the conclusion saves *Two Faces* from abandoning the farcical *genre* in favor of more mordant satire. Jessica Davis observes that farce 'invites laughter by the violation of social taboos, whether those of adult propriety or those of hierarchy. It nevertheless avoids giving offence (which would diminish the laughter), usually by adhering to a balanced structure in which the characters and values are ultimately restored to their conventional positions.'[7] This is not to suggest that Valdez is in any way a proponent of the status quo; on the contrary, in all of Chicano literature he is one of the most outspoken advocates of change. By renouncing the luxury car, the house and the Patrón's blonde wife in her 'mink bikini', the Farmworker ennobles himself. He does not embrace materialism as a way to achieve glory. His dignity and status radiate from within, aided perhaps by the faint glow of the Patrón's cigar.

About the same time Luis Valdez loosed his Teatro Campesino upon the unsuspecting farmworkers in central California, a Chilean playwright named Sergio Vodanovic produced a trilogy entitled *Viña: Three Beach Plays*.[8] Viña is, of course, Viña del Mar, the ocean resort where many Chilean aristocrats and *nouveaux riches* spend their vacations. The beach at Viña is the setting for *El delantal blanco (The White Uniform)*, a 'borderline farce', as Davis might call it, which, like *Two Faces*, presents a patently cruciform design. Like the Chicano play, this piece is brief and unsubtle, and provides a humorous treatment of the inversion of the master–servant relationship. In this case, however, the protagonists are both female.

A wealthy young matron, accompanied by her young son and her maid, has come to the beach to spend still another indolent afternoon of a rather lonely, boring summer. The child, Alvaro, is never seen; he is assumed to be playing in the surf, somewhere just beyond the footlights, and is simply alluded to, chided or gently reprimanded by one or other of the women. The

Señora and the Maid are the two foci of this work; their interdependence
and eventual exchange of roles give the play its shape. Just as in *Two Faces*,
here too the social positions of the two principals are indicated by visual
signs; the Maid wears a white uniform, while the Señora is attired in a
beach robe and swimsuit, and possesses all the 'right' accoutrements,
including sunglasses and suntan lotion.

Again, as in the Valdez work, it is the employer who first proposes the
exchange as an amusing way to relieve the tedium of the afternoon: 'Give
me your uniform,' demands the Señora imperiously. 'I want to see the
beach from behind a white uniform' (p. 265). She compels the reluctant
Maid to enter a nearby *cabaña* and remove her uniform. When the Maid
emerges, dressed in her mistress's beach attire, her entire demeanor
changes. She struts onto the beach, stretches out languorously on the
Señora's beach towel, and begins to apply suntan oil to her legs. When
Alvarito needs to be summoned back from the threatening waves, the Maid
simply directs a haughty glance to her former superior, who hurries to do
her bidding. Only after a few moments does the Señora stop in her tracks
and do the usual farcical double-take when she suddenly realizes she is
acting out of character.

Just as the 'game' gets out of hand for the Patrón in *Two Faces*, so too does
the pretense wear thin for the Señora in *The White Uniform*. 'That's it!'
screams the Señora. 'The game is over! . . . It's finished!' (p. 268). The
Maid, naturally, refuses to yield, and a physical struggle ensues for
possession of the sunglasses, beach robe and suntan oil. The Maid appeals
to some passers-by for help (Vodanovic's equivalent of Charlie in the
Valdez play). The wildly protesting Señora is dragged kicking and screaming from the scene, as the Maid nonchalantly 'stretches out on the sand as
though nothing had happened' (p. 269).

Vodanovic ends his beach play on a somewhat ironic note, however, as
the return to the norm is never achieved. The Maid, unlike Valdez's
Farmworker, is more than slightly corruptible. Enamored of her new
persona, she plays the role of Señora to perfection. As the house lights dim,
the Maid calls out maternally to Alvarito: 'Be careful, you might get a
scratch. Yes, that's better, run on the sand. That's right, Alfie, that's right,
my son . . .' (p. 270). The transformation is complete.

A final irony is provided by an Elderly Gentleman, one of the passers-by,
who casually remarks that this social unrest and dissatisfaction among the
working classes is attributable to the insidious effects of communism. 'But
we don't need to worry,' he reassures the Maid-*cum*-Señora. 'Everything is
back to normal again. Order is always re-established in the end' (p. 270).
Vodanovic's sympathies are unmistakably with the Maids; for him, order
has been restored, but it is a new order entirely.

Surely this play is cruciform, one might argue, but is it farce? In *The White*

Uniform, the original structure is never reinstated, and this topsy-turvy state of affairs becomes the new status quo. If, as Davis insists, farce is obliged to use jokes for their own sake and not 'primarily as dramatic vehicles for satirical comment upon the way of the world',[9] then *The White Uniform* falls slightly outside the boundaries of this *genre*. Yet, it seems unfair to exclude from the domain of farce a piece which so obviously contains many other farcical characteristics. The repetitious actions and parallelisms in the two women's posturing and speech are fairly commonplace farcical features. While admittedly there is a minimum of physical action and pratfall, farce can and does exist on a purely verbal level, as Stephenson has pointed out.[10] Interestingly, there is the intervention of another element – the intoxication factor – in both of these plays. Often, as Bermel suggests, a farcical character may be liberated from quotidien social constraints through inebriation, trances, spells, demonic possession or other similar devices.[11] In *The White Uniform*, Vodanovic utilizes sun intoxication as a possible precipitating factor for the Señora's eccentric behavior. The play opens with the Señora's complaint: 'Sunshine! Sunshine! Three months of sun-bathing. I'm drunk with sunshine' (p. 260). The intensity of the California sun is similarly emphasized in *Two Faces*, when the Farmworker, picking furiously in the midday heat, remarks that there is 'more sun than money' to be had in his miserable job. Yet Valdez never really exploits the sun-inebriation motif, for the brevity and simplicity of his play preclude too much dalliance in exploring motivation.

One of the funniest and paradoxically cruelest aspects of these two pieces is the authors' reliance upon mechanization and dehumanization of the underling. This dehumanization is accomplished through both verbal and non-verbal signs. Valdez, a master of both kinds of language, telegraphs his message most efficiently when the Patrón is unable to recognize his Worker as a human being, much less recall the man's name. When, for example, he prods the Worker into denouncing César Chávez and his union associates as a 'bunch of lazy, no-good Reds' (p. 11, translation mine), the Patrón commends the Worker in terms more suitable for a house pet than for a fellow human: 'That's right, son. Sic 'em. Sic 'em, boy! . . . Good boy' (p. 11). The stage instructions indicate that 'the Farmworker falls to his knees, hands in front of his chest like a docile dog; his tongue hangs out', while the 'Patroncito pats him on the head' (p. 11). The degradation is culminated by the Patrón's bending over to enable the grateful Worker to kiss his derriere. Obviously, one dog is indistinguishable from another, so it is no surprise that the Patrón cannot remember the Farmworker's name: he and all his kind are simply 'Pancho'. Less significant than a nameless dog, the Farmworker becomes a picking machine, as earlier in the play he responds to the Patrón's command to 'work harder' by miming the grape-picking activity at an increasingly frenetic pace. As Jorge Huerta observes, 'the worker is no more than a machine to this pig-faced grower, who can turn him on, set his pace and stop him at will' (p. 21). Yet one mustn't forget that it is the Worker who stops himself, as the 'machine' finally breaks down and sighs in protest, 'Ay, that's too hard, patrón!' (p. 9).

The White Uniform presents a similar approach to the dehumanization process, although again, most of the humor here is verbal rather than visual. The Señora compares the Maid to her luxury car, and appears to value both equally, as illustrated by the following exchange:

> *Señora.* . . . You know, I like coming to the beach with you.
> *Maid.* Why?
> *Señora.* Oh, I don't know. I suppose for the same reason that I like coming in the car even though the house is only a couple of blocks away (*She chuckles*). I like them to see the car. It never fails. Every day someone stops to look at it. Of course you wouldn't notice a thing like that. I suppose you're used to it . . . in a way. (p. 261)

Unaware of her casual cruelty, the Señora persists in destroying all remaining vestiges of her maid's dignity as she laughingly recalls the tattered swimsuits that the poor women rent at the public beach at Cartagena. This is, in fact, the only kind of swimsuit that the Maid, by her confession, has ever worn before. The Señora's description of the rented suits is at once ludicrous and painful:

> We had to stop once at Cartagena for gas, so we got out to look at the beach. It was really funny! And those rented swimming suits, some of them were so big they hung like bags all over! Other were so tight, the women's breasts were nearly popping out! What kind did you rent? A loose one or a tight one? (p. 264)

The tone of the foregoing monologue hovers precariously between farce and melodrama, depending on the skill and interpretation of the actress delivering it. By using exaggerated movements to illustrate the absurd fit of the rented swimsuits, the actress can incite laughter. A more serious delivery would downplay the visual image evoked by the description in order to emphasize the deliberate degradation of the Maid by the Señora. Jessica Davis insists that the farcical character is totally unselfconscious and lacks insight into his own motivation. 'Farce', writes Davis, 'risks its immunity when its jokes become shame-faced about their aggressions' (p. 91). When the audience is allowed to empathize with the victim, Davis continues, the result is softened farce, or farce 'en rose', while excessive cruelty, terror or black humor can result in what she calls farce 'en noir' (p. 93). *The White Uniform* leads the audience to the frontier of both these areas, as the Maid occasionally excites our empathy and the dialogue at times invades the tautological regions of the Absurd. The farcical tone all but disappears when the Señora and the Maid engage in the following Pinteresque conversation:

Señora. We're playing a game.
Maid. When?
Señora. Now.
Maid. And before?
Señora. Before?
Maid. Yes. When I was dressed in the uniform.
Señora. That's no game. That's reality.
Maid. Why.
Señora. Because it is.
Maid. It's just a game . . . a longer game . . . like cops and robbers. Some have
   to be cops, and some have to be robbers. (p. 267)

Here one of the characters, the Señora, remains blissfully oblivious to the more profound implications of the dialogue, while the Maid demonstrates a keen understanding of the meaning of the 'game'. Had Vodanovic chosen to pursue this philosophical bent, the play would have sacrificed its farcical moments to become something else entirely. Not everyone, in fact, views *The White Uniform* as a farce. For Marjorie Agosin, the play is '[una] excelente comedia',[12] while William Oliver avoids altogether any classification of the play, preferring to focus on its 'believability' and its thematic 'relationship to the early work of Tennessee Williams' in its concern for 'the dissolution of the old class system' (p. 259).

The inversion of the master–servant relationship as a device for exploding social and economic myths is obviously not a Latin American invention, nor is it always comic, as witnessed by Genet's *The Maids*, in which the horrific and ritualistic aspects of the role-playing are of primary importance. There is also a tendency in this type of reversal play to feed upon the audience's maudlin identification with the underdog, thus catapulting the play into the realm of melodrama. An example is Lina Wertmuller's 1975 film, *Swept Away*, which despite some manifestly silly moments (the elegant blonde Signora, stranded on a deserted island with her manservant, trips and tumbles most unelegantly down a hill with the servant in lustful pursuit), evolves, alas, into melodrama, for the characters commit the unpardonable crime of falling in love. In the farce, adversaries must not succumb to any kind of emotional bond – neither love nor hatred – in the end. The best one can hope for is an insouciant shrug of the shoulders, as if to say man is no more than a puppet, subject to caprices both human and cosmic. The Maid-*cum*-Señora in the Vodanovic play luxuriates in the Chilean sun, neither relishing her triumph nor wasting time in self-recrimination. She simply exists. The Farmworker, newly liberated from the oppression of the Patrón, puffs contentedly on his cigar, as he delivers his priceless farcical farewell in classic *caló*: 'Ay los watcho' (See you around).

NOTES

1 A. Bermel, *Farce* (New York: Simon and Schuster, 1982), p. 22.

2 Eric Bentley, 'Farce' in *Comedy: Meaning and Form*, ed. Robert W. Corrigan (New York: Chandler Publishing Co., 1965), p. 279.

3 Jessica Milner Davis, *Farce* (London: Methuen, 1978), p. 24.

4 *Voices of Change in the Spanish American Theatre*, ed. and trans. William I. Oliver (Austin: University of Texas Press), p. xviii.

5 Published in *Actos* (Fresno: Cucaracha Press, 1971).

6 Jorge Huerta, *Chicano Theatre: Themes and Forms* (Ypsilanti, Mich.: Bilingual Press, 1982), p. 19.

7 Davis, *Farce*, p. 85.

8 Published in Oliver, *Voices of Change*.

9 Davis, *Farce*, p. 35.

10 'Farce as Method' in Corrigan, *Comedy*, pp. 322–3.

11 Bermel, *Farce*, p. 39.

12 Marjorie Agosin, 'Interview with Sergio Vodanovic', *Latin American Theatre Review* (Spring 1984), p. 66.

Joe Orton's Jacobean assimilations in
*What the Butler Saw**

WILLIAM HUTCHINGS

> There is a grotesque horror about [life's] comedies, and its tragedies seem to culminate in farce. (Oscar Wilde)

With the possible exception of Tom Stoppard, no contemporary English playwright has written with more conscious awareness of the literary tradition within which he works than the late Joe Orton – and nowhere is this consciousness more evident than in *What the Butler Saw*, the controversial playwright's last and most controversial play. Denounced by some critics as nearly incoherent, it is acclaimed by many others as his masterpiece – a wild and outrageously bawdy farce which combines brilliantly polished epigrammatic wit and an elaborately contrived, maniacally fast-moving plot. Set in a contemporary psychiatric office, the play's action involves multiple mistaken identities, numerous disguises, repeated allegations of madness, and a surprisingly violent conclusion in which the text calls for copious bloodshed that is often omitted or downplayed in production. When the play opened in London in 1969, nineteen months after the author's untimely death at the age of thirty-four, audiences and critics alike were shocked by the outrageousness of its characters and by their blithe but clinical frankness in discussing a panoply of sexual practices and preferences: cross-dressing (both male and female), nymphomania, necrophilia, exhibitionism, voyeurism, sado-masochism, hermaphrodism, lesbianism, various fetishes, bondage, double incest, and rape. Even when the theatre was becoming increasingly daring and uninhibited with such plays as *Hair* and *Oh! Calcutta!*, Orton's play seemed unprecedented in its flaunted outrageousness and its violation of conventional taboos. Yet, as the play's admirers have pointed out, *What the Butler Saw* is in many ways comparable to the works of many of the greatest comic writers of all time; thus, the brief chapter on the play in Maurice Charney's study of Orton's works, for example, cites precedents and parallels from Aristophanes, Plautus, Shakespeare, Molière, Congreve, Feydeau, Wilde, Lewis Carroll,

* A draft of this paper was read at the *Themes in Drama* International Conference held at the University of California, Riverside, in February 1986.

Stoppard, Pinter, Ionesco, Beckett, and Brecht.[1] Even though all of these comparisons are quite valid and such precedents are now known to have been familiar to Orton when he wrote the play (as John Lahr's biography of him, *Prick Up Your Ears*, reveals)[2], the conventions of one particular literary period supersede all other sources and analogues: *What the Butler Saw* is a virtual compendium of the most outrageous excesses of Jacobean drama transposed into a modern context – an assimilation of such standard motifs as the changeling, inadvertent incest, madness, and tragicomic violence into a twentieth-century setting. Orton's interest in parodying such conventions and excesses is clear even in his first play, *The Ruffian on the Stair* (1966); in that play, as Lahr indicates, 'Mike's revenger's "aria" was meant as a parody of Jacobean tragedy.'[3] In *What the Butler Saw*, the prevalence of such Jacobean motifs not only helps to explain the unity and cohesion of the text in a way that other analyses of the work have not done, but it also provides ample precedent for both the outrageousness of the characters' actions and the violence of the play's ending.

Orton's most obvious acknowledgment of the Jacobean tradition is found in the play's epigraph from Cyril Tourneur's *The Revenger's Tragedy* (1607): 'Surely we're all mad people, and they / Whom we think are, are not' (III, v, 79–80). The inherent theatricality of madness, with its potential for bombast and startling action, had long been exploited by Elizabethan dramatists, beginning with Hieronymo's madness in Kyd's *The Spanish Tragedy* (1586), but feigned or *misapprehended* madness was a more prevalent Jacobean theme – following the first production of *Hamlet* in 1602, the year before James I assumed the throne. The assertion embodied in Tourneur's line, however – that both sanity *and* madness are misapprehended – inverts the usual 'normal' order and invites a riotous moral and sexual anarchy that is especially conducive to farce. In Orton's play, such misapprehensions not only prevail but also compound each other; the more a character attempts to represent reason and authority or to take control of a chaotic situation, the less able he or she is to recognize madness *or* sanity when he or she sees it. Accordingly, the play's representative of the highest authority of the state – an inspector of psychiatric hospitals – identifies himself as 'represent[ing] Her Majesty's government[,] your immediate superiors in madness';[4] even his name, Dr Rance, contains an obvious pun on 'rants' – that most frequent of all symptoms of theatrical madness in the Renaissance. To such 'superiors in madness' who represent the prevailing social order, the most innocent will naturally appear to be the most guilty, and the most sane appear the most mad – even (or *especially*) to the psychiatrists, whose clinical training itself dismisses or precludes usual concepts of 'normality'. Thus, as the play's central character, Dr Prentice, assures his prospective secretary as he attempts to seduce her at the beginning of the play, 'What I see upon the couch isn't a lovely and desirable young girl', though that is precisely what she is; instead, he insists, 'It's a sick mind in need of psychiatric treatment' (p. 366). As in Jonson's plague-infested London in *The Alchemist* (1610), the prevailing 'sickness' that is thus presumed to be pandemic allows rogues and charlatans of every sort – but especially 'mad' psychiatrists – to flourish. Like Celia in *Volpone* (1605) or the title character of Middleton's *A Chaste Maid in Cheapside* (1611), the prospective secretary in Orton's play, Geraldine Barclay, finds her virtue almost immediately assailed in a world where lechery, cunning, and deceit prevail. When she protests to Prentice's superior that she is not a mental patient but a job-seeker from the Friendly Faces Employment Bureau, she is immediately assumed to be suffering delusions, and committal papers are hastily signed.

In many ways, the psychiatrist's office in which Orton's play takes place is the modern counterpart of the Jacobean stage's Italianate court. Each is a place where – amid elaborate intrigues, disguises, and self-serving duplicities – all sorts of passions and lusts, however forbidden or illicit, flourish outside any norms of moral judgment, unrestrained by social taboos and regarded with clinical detachment by both the perpetrators and the authorities in charge. The play's intricate plot begins as Dr Prentice's attempted seduction of his new secretary is interrupted by the arrival of his wife, from whom he tries to conceal his liaison; she too, however, has had an illicit relationship with the page-boy of a local hotel, who demands money and a job before turning over incriminating photographs taken by the hotel manager. Within the opening minutes of the first act, therefore, a number of favorite Jacobean conventions have been brought into play: seduction and concealment, cuckoldry, a secretly observed assignation, and the threat of disclosure of incriminating evidence. The photographs in question are the modern technological counterpart of the 'ocular proof' of assignations on which so many Jacobean intrigues depend; like the child's horoscope intercepted in *The Duchess of Malfi* (1613), the photographs are directly incriminating – and far less subject to misinterpretation than Desdemona's lost handkerchief, for example. As Orton's intricate plot advances, both the prospective secretary and the hotel page disguise themselves in clothing belonging to other characters. Like Euphrasia in Beaumont and Fletcher's *Philaster* (1610), who also disguises herself as a *page* (called Bellario), Geraldine Barclay presents herself as a male, having donned the uniform of Nicholas Beckett, the hotel employee whom Mrs Prentice wants her husband to employ: Beckett, in turn, puts on the clothing that Miss Barclay has shed. This use of disguise, like the comic concealment (and confusion) of sexual identities, is among the foremost conventions that Orton has adapted from the Renaissance stage.

After many complications and mistaken assumptions, this portion of the plot of *What the Butler Saw*, like that of Jonson's *Epicoene*, is resolved when the character mistaken for a young woman is revealed to be a man (Nicholas Beckett in a disguise); then, as in *Philaster, Twelfth Night*, and numerous other plays, the person thought by many of the characters to be male is found to be female. However, in the final moments of the play, Orton adds further contrivances which compound the coincidence – and the out-rageousness – of their situation, exceeding and parodying the excesses of the most melodramatic Jacobean plots. Because they bear the two halves of a unique charm given them by their unknown mother at birth, the two are revealed to be the long-separated twin children of Dr and Mrs Prentice, begotten in the linen closet of the Station Hotel where, years later, Mrs Prentice and her unknown son were intimately – and incestuously – reunited. Similarly, Geraldine Barclay, whom Rance has long assumed (without reason) to have been the victim of an incestuous attack in her childhood, is in fact revealed to have been the object of such an attempt by her then-unknown father when the play began. Orton's double-incest plot (father–daughter, mother–son) embodies the ultimate taboos of repressed desire in a way that is particularly appropriate for a play set in a psychiatric clinic, but it exceeds even the various forms of incest that provided a recurrent motif in Jacobean theatre – occurring, for example, between brother and sister in John Ford's *'Tis Pity She's a Whore* (1627) and in Beaumont and Fletcher's *A King and No King* (1611), as well as between uncle and niece in Middleton's *Women, Beware Women* (1623). Yet whereas in Ford's play, for example, the incest of Giovanni and Annabella brings bitter remorse to her and leads to madness for him, Orton's characters face the situation with the sort of modern aplomb of their counterparts in Ivy Compton-Burnett's *Darkness and Day* who, confronting an Oedipal situation within their own upper-middle-class family, contend that their ancient counterpart did tend to react rather excessively – blinding himself, talking about it in public, wandering from town to town repeating the story, and becoming a burden on the daughters who must provide his care. 'Perhaps we are [more] fortunate' than those who lived in earlier, less civilized times, as one of Compton-Burnett's characters remarks, 'Or perhaps fashions have changed.'[5] Rather than being based on changes of fashion, however, the aplomb of Orton's characters is a product of their recognition that their relationships are merely the fulfillment of impulses which are, in psychiatric terms, presumed to be universally human (and therefore nothing to be particularly ashamed of). Appropriately, in the final line of the play, Rance encourages all to 'put our clothes on and face the world' (p. 448) in much the same way that Compton-Burnett's intend to do. Never-theless, this reconciliatory aspect of the plot also has direct Jacobean affinities; as Orton himself wrote in 1967, 'the ending works as "all is forgiven" – just as in the later Shakespeare plays'.[6]

As the complex plot of *What the Butler Saw* becomes increasingly manic in the second act, several startling incidents in the final minutes of the play contribute to a seemingly radical shift in tone. Amid frantically rapid entrances and exits of characters in assorted disguises and various states of undress, the action is punctuated with gunshots – certainly a standard device in comic alarums of various kinds. However, the shots in Orton's play hit their targets with potentially fatal accuracy. Sergeant Match, the policeman investigating a number of rapes that young Beckett allegedly committed in a girls' school, enters with 'blood *pouring* down his leg' after the first shot is fired by Mrs Prentice (p. 436; emphasis mine). Shortly thereafter, Beckett too enters 'moaning and clutching his shoulder' (p. 437), 'anguished [and] fainting' (p. 440) with 'his wound streaming blood, his face white and ill' (p. 441). Suddenly, unexpectedly, the madcap antics and wild confusions of the play's characters become far more serious and sinister; theirs is clearly not the usually 'painless' violence of most farce, whose characters typically display a certain Punch-and-Judy resiliency if not an apparent imperviousness to pain. Amid the characters' illusions of madness and Orton's witty legerdemain with the plot, the pain and bloodshed are intended to remind the audience abruptly of what is 'real': 'If the pain is real, I must be real,' Nick insists, though Rance replies that he would 'rather not get involved in [such] metaphysical speculation' (p. 443). Neither, apparently, would many directors of the play – or at least not at the climax of a frantically active farce; for this reason, as a reviewer of Lindsay Anderson's 1975 successful 'unexpurgated' revival of the play remarked, the final ten minutes of *What the Butler Saw* are 'arguably the trickiest in modern drama'.[7] The omission of the bloodshed from many productions of the play, as if the shots have simply missed their targets, enables the director to avoid many of these problems – and particularly the radical shift in tone. Unlike the punishments meted out at the end of *Volpone*, which cause a similarly problematical shift in tone, the gunshot wounds in *What the Butler Saw* are unrelated to any righting of a 'moral balance' or any reestablishment of justice (whether civil or poetic); neither are they 'necessary' for any apparent thematic intent, since equally 'guilty' character do not suffer alike. Such seemingly gratuitous violence, with such blatantly gory effects, will surely only discomfit the audience as the enjoyably madcap antics of Orton's outrageous but likeable and witty characters suddenly become potentially lethal for no *apparent* reason.

Yet, however effective – or even *necessary* – directors may find the omission of the bloodshed to be in wholly pragmatic *theatrical* terms, such an alteration seriously distorts the playwright's *literary* conception of the play. Though it has been given scant attention by most critics, Orton's insistence on blood is neither capricious nor extraneous to an understanding of the work; it is clearly a central and carefully considered aspect of the plot. Repeatedly, the stage directions specify that copious amounts of blood are to be shed, with it 'pouring down [Match's] leg' (p. 436) and 'oozing between [Nick's] fingers' (p. 440) until both are 'streaming with blood' (pp. 441, 446) in the final minutes of the play. Such bloodshed, without which no Jacobean tragedy would be complete, is in fact an *essential* part of the action of any play set in the modern counterpart of the Jacobean theatre's Italianate court. There, tragi*comic* actions as well as tragic ones frequently result in characters' loss of blood – as in Beaumont and Fletcher's *Philaster*, the subtitle of which is *Love Lies A'Bleeding*. The fact that Orton's stage directions repeatedly insist on the presence of blood at the end of his farce demonstrates the depth of his commitment to the assimilation of Jacobean motifs, no matter how radically the bloodshed seems to alter the modern audience's mood or violate the director's conception of the production's tone.

When the play's events reach their most anarchic point, as the characters grapple to confine each other in straitjackets in their various drunken, drugged, wounded, half-dressed states, Dr Rance sets off the clinic's security alarm, causing sirens to wail and metal grilles to fall over the doors. Prentice's clinic, like the asylum run by Alibius and Lollio in Rowley and Middleton's *The Changeling* (1622), is ultimately and literally a cage, a profit-based prison in which the keepers can hardly be distinguished from the kept and the sane are mistakenly perceived to be insane; indeed, as Nicholas Brooke has remarked in his study of Jacobean theatre entitled *Horrid Laughter*, 'the only distinction between the inhabitants of Alibius's asylum is that the Fools are harmless and the Madmen are dangerous'.[8] There, like Isabella in *The Changeling*, Mrs Prentice finds that she needs not leave home in order to 'stray from virtue'; repeatedly, as the play nears its climax, she encounters (and shoots at) panic-stricken, half-clad, partially disguised men whom she believes to be pursuing her. In the darkness of the power-failure caused by an overloaded circuit when the alarm is tripped, 'the room is lit only by the glare of a blood sunset shining through the trees in the garden' (p. 442); when the characters can no longer flee each other, the plot's multiple misunderstandings are quickly resolved and the play's 'darkest' secret – its double incest motif – is brought to light, confirmed by the matching pieces of the long-lost siblings' lucky elephant charm. Then, in what Orton referred to in his diaries as the play's '"Golden Bough" subtext . . . [including] the descent of the god at the end' for a 'Euripidean ending',[9] Sergeant Match enters through the room's skylight; clad in a leopard-skin gown originally worn by Mrs Prentice, he leads them 'weary, bleeding, drugged and drunk, [up] the rope ladder into the blazing light' (p. 448) as the play ends.

The play's *other* final classical obeisance – a decidedly 'Aristophanean' moment at the end of the play – was edited out by Sir Ralph Richardson before the first production of the play in 1969.[10] A search for the 'missing part' of an exploded statue of Winston Churchill culminates in the discovery of the 'part' in a gift-wrapped box that Geraldine Barclay brought on stage at the beginning of the play. In Orton's original script (though not in the original printed edition of it, nor in any production until Lindsay Anderson's 'unexpurgated' one in 1975), the missing part – a 'larger-than-life-size bronze' phallus – is pulled from the box, held aloft before the audience, and hailed as 'an example to us all of the spirit that won the Battle of Britain' (p. 447). In the altered version, the contents of the opened box remain unseen by the audience, and Dr Rance and Geraldine Barclay give predictably different characterizations of what the 'missing part' really is. Though Orton's original ending makes a wholly appropriate obeisance towards the origins of all farce in phallic fertility rites and Aristophanean Old Comedy, and though most critics have approved its 'restoration' as the clearest indication of Orton's intent, the posthumously altered version may well sustain the overall tone of the play more effectively than the one the author intended. For all its Fraserian subtext and 'Euripidean ending', the prevailing tone, theme, and structure of *What the Butler Saw* are most directly Jacobean rather than Attic in their origins; the farce observes the (neo-) classical unities with a scrupulousness worthy of Ben Jonson, and its tone is equally carefully sustained, dealing with even its most scandalous and scabrous subjects in language that is often clinical but contains no 'obscene', 'vulgar', or 'four-letter' words (in contrast to David Storey's farce *Mother's Day*, for example, or Caryl Churchill's *Cloud Nine*). Arguably, the defect that Orton himself cited in changing the ending of *Entertaining Mr Sloane* is equally apparent in the phallus-flaunting one that he intended for *What the Butler Saw*:

> The original ending [of *Sloane*] was quite different and much more complex, and it was wrong. Many writers I think compromise themselves with over-subtle endings – Tennessee Williams is an obvious example. The new ending . . . is very simple, but a natural outcome[,] . . . letting the characters take over.[11]

Though there is certainly nothing subtle about the *action* of brandishing an enormous bronze phallus on stage, its *use* as the culmination of a Fraserian subtext and an oblique homage to the origins of all farce may well constitute an 'over-subtle ending' that does not fit in with the rest of the work. Even by Orton's own standard, the altered ending is the more 'simple' and 'natural'; unlike its predecessor, it continues the vital ambiguity of perception on which the entire play depends while 'letting the characters take over'. In the altered ending, the 'actual facts' remain unknowable, while the audience is presented with multiple possibilities and divergent interpretations; each of Orton's characters, however 'mad' or however naive, sees what he or she is *predisposed* to see, *whatever* the reality may actually be. Predictably, Rance sees only a phallus (though his perceptions have been thoroughly discredited throughout the play); Geraldine – with her equally untrustworthy 'illusions of youth' still remarkably intact (p. 488) – sees only a cigar. The audience, seeing neither, must imagine the contents of the box for itself and must decide, in effect, which character is right. Yet in the play's altered ending, as in Pirandello's *Right You Are, If You Think You Are* and Stoppard's *After Magritte*, all such perceptions are shown to be wholly subjective; accordingly, they are just as unreliable as any of the characters' judgments of sanity and insanity, as Orton's epigraph (and the play itself) makes clear.

Even though *What the Butler Saw* features many of the familiar characteristics of traditional farce (e.g., mistaken identities, uninhibited lechery, manic action, hastily assumed disguises, mutual misunderstandings, and frantic but precisely timed exits and entrances), its carefully polished, epigrammatic script demands of its actors a rigorous control at all times and permits them none of the raucous excess or improvisational 'free play' that more traditional, broadly physical farce allows. Accordingly, any productions that treat the play *merely* as farce invariably fail; neither the physicality that is appropriate for *Gammer Gurton's Needle* (or *Lysistrata* or even *No Sex, Please, We're British*) nor the polished delivery required for *The Importance of Being Earnest* will suffice alone, since Orton's work demands, uniquely, a synthesis of both. In creating such a synthesis, and in accommodating within it the outrageousness of the Jacobean aesthetic as well, *What the Butler Saw* extends – and therefore, to an extent, redefines – the capabilities of farce as both a literary genre and as a theatrical form.

Whereas Tom Stoppard's assimilations of *Hamlet* in *Rosencrantz and Guildenstern are Dead* and of *'Tis Pity She's a Whore* in *The Real Thing* are openly acknowledged within the plays themselves, Joe Orton's Jacobean affinities in *What the Butler Saw* tend to be cunningly concealed in surprisingly congruent twentieth-century counterparts. In the excesses of the Jacobean stage aesthetic, Orton found a particularly appropriate precedent for his own satirical vision – in much the same way that Thomas Pynchon had done in *The Crying of Lot 49*, published in 1966.[12] The extensive presence of such motifs in *What the Butler Saw* not only unifies the play in ways that were not apparent to its earliest reviewers but also justifies the seemingly inapposite bloodshed that continues to be omitted from productions even today. Furthermore, it confirms Orton's status as a master farceur who, transforming specific literary traditions through his unique and inimitable talent, willingly dared to defy audience expectations and to outrage conventional proprieties – and did both with evident and unparalleled delight.

NOTES

1 Maurice Charney, *Joe Orton* (New York: Grove Press, 1981), pp. 97–110.
2 John Lahr, *Prick Up Your Ears: The Biography of Joe Orton* (New York: Alfred A. Knopf, 1978), *passim.*
3 Ibid., p. 136.
4 Joe Orton, *What the Butler Saw*, in *Orton: The Complete Plays* (London: Methuen, 1976), p. 376. All subsequent references cite this edition and have been inserted parenthetically into the text.
5 Ivy Compton-Burnett, *Darkness and Day* (New York: Alfred A. Knopf, 1951), p. 136.
6 *The Orton Diaries*. ed. John Lahr (New York: Harper and Row, 1987), p.242.
7 Frank Marcus, 'Butler Observed', *The London Sunday Telegraph*, 20 July 1975.
8 Nicholas Brooke, *Horrid Laughter in Jacobean Tragedy* (New York: Barnes and Noble, 1979), p. 81. 'Before Marlowe and Kyd,' Brooke contends, '*English* tragedy . . . was largely violent moral farce. It emerged from late medieval morality plays where sardonic humourists mocked and derided the solemn morals with strikingly ambivalent results . . . Any pretensions of humanity to secular glory . . . were seen as farcically evil . . . The [figure of] Vice . . . [offers] witty-destructive commentary [which] makes everybody, good and bad alike, absurd' (p. 7). The description of such 'violent moral farce' is equally applicable to Orton's plays and may even suggest a common 'ancestor' for his works and those of the Jacobeans.
9 *Orton Diaries*, p. 237.
10 Lahr, *Biography*, p. 237.
11 'The Biter Bit: Joe Orton Introduces *Entertaining Mr Sloane* in conversation with simon Trussler', *Plays and Players*, August 1964, p. 16.
12 Thomas Pynchon, *The Crying of Lot 49* (New York: Bantam Books, 1967). In the latter half of third chapter of the novel (pp. 44–53 in the Bantam edition), Pynchon summarizes the bizarre and intricate plot of *The Courier's Tragedy* by Thomas Wharfinger, which begins a number years after 'Angelo, [the] evil duke of Squamuglia, . . . murdered the good Duke of adjoining Faggio, by poisoning the feet on an image of Saint Narcissus, Bishop of Jerusalem, in the court chapel, which feet the Duke was in the habit of kissing every Sunday at Mass' (p. 45). After myriad complications that are rife with intrigue and incest as well as murder and mutilation in the best (i.e., most excessive) Jacobean style, the resolution of *The Courier's Tragedy* – like that of *What the Butler Saw* – depends (in part) on the discovery of what Pynchon characterizes as '*the usual* amulet placed round [the character's] neck as a child' (p. 51, emphasis mine), acknowledging the extent of this particular plot device in plays of the time.

The stereotype betrayed:
Tom Stoppard's farce*

GABRIELLE ROBINSON

'What I like to do,' Stoppard once said, 'is to take a stereotype and betray it.'[1] The interplay between stereotype and betrayal can be used to define Stoppard's plays. It explains their parodic structure, which in itself is a super-stereotype and a betrayal, as well as the optical illusions underlying so many of his plots and it determines his characters' existence as doubles, secondaries and stand-ins.

Stereotype and betrayal create constant reversals of perspective, a proliferation of interpretations, 'multiplying madly'. Although this freeplay, characteristic of post-modernist works, determines much of Stoppard's farce, the very term betrayal indicates aversion to a world view where multiplicity replaces meaning and certainty. Stoppard cannot tolerate a random, chaotic world and his plays do not present uncertainty, but rather man's victimization, his betrayal, by uncertainty. Similarly his tendency to collapse the parodic complexity of his plays into parodic simplicity indicates – in addition to his acrobatic gamesmanship – his desire to limit the limitlessness of freeplay. As he implies in his much-quoted statement about infinite leapfrog, this exhausting exercise is forced on him because 'there is never any point . . . at which I feel *that* is the speech to stop it on, *that* is the last word'.[2] Infinite leapfrog therefore not only is a game, but also a desperate and hectic quest for the last word which is bound to be a betrayal, creating permanent mortification as the only possible permanence. The characters' persistent yearning for a stereotypic beginning, middle and end is met by an equally persistent lack of consummation which plagues them in all reaches of their existence. Thus Moon of the early novel *Lord Malquist and Mr Moon* (1966), unable to find a beginning for his historical work and obsessed by an unconsummated marriage, is caught in an endless leapfrog, 'refuting myself and rebutting the refutation towards a truth that must be a compound of two opposite half-truths. And you never reach it because there is always something more to say.'[3]

Stoppard has found his place in contemporary literature by acrobatically

* A draft of this paper was read at the *Themes in Drama* International Conference held at the University of California, Riverside, in February 1986.

balancing between post-modernist techniques of parody and play and a simpler, more conservative position which affirms not only the value of his acrobatic artistry, but the truth of naive generalizations and their 'utterly simple shape'.[4]

Stoppard admits that he admires stereotypes and naive generalizations because of their inherent truth. 'Many Frenchmen _are_ like Maurice Chevalier.' He believes that there is 'a correspondence between easy stereotypes and truth',[5] that in fact the real thing is a stereotype. This is one reason why in Stoppard's work the extraordinary tends to turn into the mundane. Stoppard's characters, the professors, butlers, lords, detectives, artists and journalists, to say nothing of Hamlet, Gwendolyn or Joyce, are stereotypes. They are poor imitations, secondaries like Rosencrantz and Guildenstern, doubles like a philosopher called Moore, but not _the_ Moore, substitutes like the second-string critic Moon, or epigones like a latter-day Boswell: all of them versions of the average thinking man.

Critics, who deplore Stoppard's lack of depth, fail to acknowledge that he sees man and his predicament as stereotypic so that there is nothing but stereotypes in his vision of the world. Focusing on the revelation of the stereotypic nature of existence, Stoppard's plays present the farce of limitations. The stereotype therefore reveals a truth which in itself is a betrayal. Testifying to man's fundamental obsessiveness and lack of freedom, stereotype can be seen as a betrayal of personality. Its savage simplification is a way of being precise about our world as well as a betrayal of our aspirations.

Such view corresponds to the rejection of depth, whether metaphysical or psychological, which is adopted by many contemporary dramatists. Thus Ionesco finds truth 'in the profoundly simplified form of caricature',[6] and Dürrenmatt says in his second note to _Romulus_ that 'today is a time when unfortunately there are nothing but trivial truths [_Binsenwahrheiten_]. Profundity has become a luxury.'[7]

Yet the stereotype can be only a half-truth, which Stoppard feels compelled to compound with another one, so that paradoxically his second reason for liking stereotypes is that he can betray them and shock us into seeing the falseness of accepted notions. In his own favourite term, Stoppard likes to create an 'ambush'. His plays are a series of surprise attacks on both audience and characters. Malquist's coachman in _Lord Malquist and Mr Moon_ at first acts and talks like a predictable Irish stereotype, reassuringly called O'Hara. But when next Moon meets him he has turned into a Jew and then into a black. These betrayals of the stereotype unsettle Moon, making him feel 'trapped in a complex of shifts . . . being edged towards panic' (p. 46). Ultimately both Moon and O'Hara are betrayed when they are exploded in Malquist's coach in mistake for the stereotypic lord.

Stoppard's hero is the stereotypic ordinary man, who is betrayed by being always 'out of his depth', or 'in over his head'. He struggles to establish a rational as well as a moral world, which he envisages in totally stereotypic terms. George Moore of *Jumpers* invariably traduces 'a complex, logical thesis to a mysticism of staggering banality',[8] or the playwright in *The Real Thing* suggests that 'loving and being loved is unliterary. It's happiness expressed in banality and lust.'[9] They are betrayed by simplicity as much as by complexity; in fact the two often are indistinguishable. When a strange vision of pink lips and green eyes resolves itself into his wife's made-up face, Moon concludes that 'Once more the commonplace had duped him into seeing absurdity, just as absurdity kept tricking him into accepting it as commonplace.'[10] Always in a mad rush to reach a conclusion and preserve his dignity, Stoppard's betrayed stereotype succeeds only in aggravating the situation. Constantly mortified, he yet carries on bravely until he pays for his naive defiance with his very life. His desire for a firm structure with a beginning, middle and end is exploded in the many collapses of Stoppard's plays: Malquist's coach, the bridge in *Albert's Bridge*, the pyramid of acrobats in *Jumpers*, the repeatedly collapsing wall in *Dogg's Hamlet*, even to the house of cards in *The Real Thing*. Nevertheless his need for value and certainty is affirmed – despite its 'staggering banality' – as an at least emotionally indispensable half-truth.

These examples already indicate that both the stereotype and the betrayal are parodic. Parody, in fact, can be called a super-stereotype, a poor copy, creating a double betrayal. It is the form of the epigone, defining the afterness of our time by its poor imitation. With its reduction and trivialization parody becomes a significant way of dealing with the proliferation of stereotypes which is the inevitable consequence of a world without centre. Functioning on several levels simultaneously, parody is a game which creates a succession of appearances and interpretations, all of which betray man's aspirations, because they reduce everything to the hackneyed or the absurd, and because their sudden confrontation causes further dislocations, a 'collision of styles',[11] and of mutually exclusive propositions.

Optical illusion, always paramount in Stoppard's work, is a form of parody and it is also, of course, the perfect betrayal, resulting in an infinite series of interpretations. As Keir Elam has shown in Stoppard's borrowing from Wittgenstein's 'it could be this, too' – game, optical illusions explain the infinite multiplicity of forms and the difficulty of distinguishing one game from another.[12] The different appearances in an optical illusion are equally valid yet mutually exclusive. Therefore in a Stoppard play characters and audience are forever caught between equally true and false versions, fixed in flux, at a moment of transition between incompatible points of view. An optical illusion never allows one 'the luxury of a continuous seeing'.[13] There is no point of rest in Stoppard's world, only 'ubiquitous obliquity'[14] at a hectic pace. Being unable to perceive the images of an optical illusion simultaneously or see any of them exclusively causes permanent frustration. George Moore of *Jumpers*, opening the bedroom door and finding Sir Archibald Jumper kneeling before his wife and kissing her hand, may see them playing a charade; or he may see Archie serving in his capacity as either Dottie's doctor, psychiatrist or legal adviser since she is suffering from a nervous breakdown. George never knows – nor do we – whether Dottie, who refuses to make love with him, is having an affair or whether it only looks as if she did. The Stoppard hero thus becomes a 'victim of perspective' (p. 35). Fraser in *Albert's Bridge* illustrates this point with his very life. Overwhelmed by 'the enormity' of the world's disorder, he climbs to the top of the railroad bridge for a suicidal jump down. But each time he reaches the top, he has his confidence restored by 'perspective', which he loses again as soon as he descends and so goes 'up and down like a yo-yo'.[15]

Several plays, such as *After Magritte* and *Artist Descending a Staircase*, consist entirely of optical illusions. *After Magritte* occurs after a Magritte showing at the Tate and is itself 'after Magritte', modelled on his surreal style. Ironically the characters charge Magritte with being unrealistic, but fail to see that their own lives are at least as surreal. At the opening they have barricaded themselves in their apartment where the mother – the middle-aged couple cannot agree whose mother she is – is lying on an ironing board, covered by a towel, while Thelma is sniffing the ground in a ballgown, and her barechested husband Harris, clad in thigh-length fishing waders, is balancing on a chair. The plot centres on a suspicious figure which the couple has glimpsed on their return from the exhibition and which Inspector Foot of the Yard is trying to track down. Thelma insists that this was a one-legged footballer with shaving cream on his face, carrying a football, while Harris has seen an old man, dressed in pyjamas, with a tortoise under his arm. But neither is right and there was no crime, although the inspector does not realize this even at the end. Not only did he invent or deduce a crime, but he himself was the suspicious figure doing something trivial in an outlandish, surreal way. The inspector had rushed into the street, both legs caught in one pyjama leg and clutching his wife's purse, in desperate haste to avoid getting a parking ticket. Parodic complexity slips into parodic simplicity and it is appropriate that the culprit turns out to be the inspector himself since the crime is his invention.

Artist Descending – the title itself is a multiple parody – is another detective story without a crime, in contrast to *Jumpers* where there is a crime in the first scene which is never solved and of which the hero remains unaware. Using three artists as his heroes, Stoppard connects the optical illusions of the detective story with those of art. All art creates optical illusions. Thus one of the three, Martello, plans to do a sculpture of a cripple as a 'wooden man with a real leg where the real leg is made of wood' (p. 32), since 'the greater the success the more false the result' (p. 39). His friend Beauchamp is engaged in making tapes of random noises which he likes to interpret as the 'detritus of audible existence', but Donner, the third artist in the group, hears not an artistic 'tonal debris', but simply rubbish (p. 19). For Donner rejects experimental art, advocating a return to the representational. Trying to justify a work of art to a man with an empty belly, Donner has hit on the solution of edible art. 'Imagine my next exhibition, thrown open to the hungry' (p. 26).

As with George Moore, optical illusions dominate the characters' intimate lives as well. Donner loved a blind girl who was in love with the painter of a snow scene, thought to be Beauchamp's 'Border Fence in the Snow'. After a brief affair, Beauchamp abandoned the girl who fell, or jumped, out of a window and was killed. Donner has mourned her all his live. Yet it might have been Donner she loved who had painted the inverse picture of a white fence on a dark background, so that he lost his love to an optical illusion.

When Beauchamp and Martello find Donner dead at the bottom of the stairs, Stoppard adds an auditory illusion to the optical ones. One of Beauchamp's tapes recorded the event. Listening to the combination of stealthy footsteps and Donner's exclamation 'Ah, there you are', followed by a thump, makes the two friends suspect each other of murder. After a proliferation of accusations and counter-accusations, which serves to develop their lives in flashback, Beauchamp accidentally explains the mystery by reproducing the exact sequence of the tape when he creeps up to swat a fly. The old man simply fell downstairs while trying to kill a fly.

Stoppard's most poignant and persistent plot pattern, involving parody and optical illusion, concerns the betrayed double, the stereotypic minor character or substitute and, generally, the epigonish figure whose utter smallness is contrasted by an elaborate political, philosophical and artistic superstructure. Most often parodic innocence meets labyrinthine confusion and becomes 'trapped and betrayed'. Rosencrantz, Guildenstern and the critic Moon are caught up in elaborate parodies of plays which will lead to their deaths. Similarly Henry Carr of *Travesties*, like George Moore, is exposed to moral, political and artistic convolutions which confuse and humiliate him. In *Dogg's Hamlet, Cahoot's Macbeth*, a character stereotypically called Easy enters a bizarre world where familiar words have new meanings and becomes involved in two more Shakespearian parodies. As soon as he has learnt this new language, however, people switch back to ordinary English, leaving him to speak apparent gibberish. This confrontation of simplicity and complexity is expressed in the 'double acts'[16] of contrasting characters, where the protagonist, who does not understand the world, is juxtaposed to a cynically experienced antagonist, a man apparently in the know and in control, who seems to befriend but ends up victimizing the hero. The two, such as Moon and Malquist, Guildenstern and the Player, George and Archie, form the stereotypic opposite ends of an optical illusion. This is Stoppard's version of the perennial duo of farce which, as Feydeau remarked, consists of 'the one who delivers the kicks to the backside and the one who receives them'.[17] Although Stoppard maintains an acrobatic balance between these double acts, he does appear to lean towards the betrayed stereotypes and their staggering banalities.

In *Jumpers* the double acts are represented by George Moore and Sir Archibald Jumper, Chancellor of the university and leader of the radical-liberal revolution. For the philosopher George Moore every attempt to establish meaning and certainty dissolves into confusion and betrayal: his wife's possible adultery, Archie's political and academic power plays, such as making the agnostic spokesman for agriculture Archbishop of Canterbury, passing George over for a chair in philosophy, which goes instead to Crouch, the janitor, and transforming the university chapel into a gymnasium for his philosophical jumpers. George, who refuses to participate in their physical and mental acrobatics, is merely tolerated as the 'tame believer' amidst these logical positivists and yellow radical-liberals. The world gives proof of nothing but betrayed stereotypes. A television report of the moon landing by astronauts Scott and Oates depicts the contemporary version of the famous arctic explorers. Instead of dying heroically to save his companions, Oates is abandoned by Scott on the moon, where he remains 'a tiny receding figure waving forlornly from the featureless wastes of the lunar landscape' (p. 22). The popular stereotype of English history has been betrayed by Stoppard's parody which in itself is a stereotype and a betrayal.

Struggling to prove the existence of absolute values in a world which denies them, George cannot find a beginning for his lecture about the existence of God, which turns into a series of parodies, poor copies which betray both his search for meaning and his ambition. At one point George ambushes himself by 'beginning at the beginning' with 'secondly!' (p. 24). This poor copy of a philosopher cannot control even the most palpable facts, and instead of ordering his world only compounds the chaos and betrayals. While he is seeking a beginning for his argument, his colleague McFee is shot at George's own party, blown out of a human pyramid of philosophical jumpers. Although the corpse remains hanging on a door or stuffed into a closet, George is as unaware of its existence as he is of his wife's pleas to help her dispose of it. George succeeds in nothing, except to add to the confusions and betrayals himself by accidentally killing the hare and the tortoise with which he was to prove Zeno wrong. Zeno's parodoxes incidentally are also a betrayal of logic and perception; moreover they all have to do with the inability to get started or ever reaching a destination.

The hare's poignant end is the result of an auditory illusion. Dottie's cry of 'Fire!' makes George fire an arrow and, in retrieving the impaled animal, he crushes the tortoise. Nevertheless the play affirms at least the emotional power of George's stereotypic half-truths, the 'staggering banalities', which express man's perhaps childish need for value and purpose in a world lost in yellow relativism and brute force.

The Real Inspector Hound offers an extreme example of the betrayed double. Although the play rightly is judged unsuccessful, it is essential Stoppard, combining the portrayal of theatrical, critical and human stereotypes.

Second-string Moon, a substitute for the chief critic Higgs, is the stand-in, the epigone par excellence. He is obsessed with the grandiose but stereotypic ambition of seeing his words emblazoned in neon lights and produces the most hackneyed of reviews. Moon ends up ultimately betrayed when he is pulled into the action of the second-rate and absurdly imitative detective play he is to review and murdered on stage by the third-string Puckeridge.

Naive Moon is forever out of his depth, the victim of one optical illusion after another. He is bewildered by the commonplace switching of partners at stereotypic Muldoon Manor, 'cut off from the world' (p. 15) by fog and swamp, just as he is by his colleague Birdboot's equally hackneyed involvements with the actresses they are watching and by the parody or the betrayed stereotype of an inspector who does not discover the corpse under the couch until nearly the end when he declares: 'One of us ordinary mortals, thrown together by fate and cut off by the elements, is the murderer!' (p. 34). The inspector never finds the guilty man, but instead takes the critic's place in the audience, judging that the play 'lacks pace. A complete ragbag . . .' (p. 44).

Moon responds to this parody of a detective play with a parody of a review. He begins by asking 'does this play know where it is going?' but then concludes that it 'aligns itself uncompromisingly on the side of life', from where he meanders on to wonder 'where is God?' (p. 28) and ends his leapfrogging with a reference to the 'ubiquitous obliquity' of the human condition (p. 36). These critical nonsequiturs mock and betray both the critic and the play, turning everything 'into a complete farce' (p. 43). Yet they also contain a truth about Stoppard's intentions and his world view in that they deplore the loss of absolutes and affirm simple vitality.

We are implicated in these betrayals, for Stoppard begins his play with an optical illusion for the audience: 'the first thing is that the audience appear to be confronted by their own reflection' (p. 9). It is from this fake audience that Moon and Birdboot originally watch the play and later, answering a phone call on stage, become involved in the action, like Rosencrantz and Guildenstern forced to perform in an unfamiliar play which constantly slips into different versions. For example, at the beginning we, including the two critics, watch a trite jealousy scene in which Simon Gascoyne, having jilted Felicity for the wealthy Cynthia, faces Felicity's anger. Their stagey-sounding repartee is replayed later, but now Birdboot is speaking Simon's lines. Since Birdboot also has switched his preference from the actress playing Felicity to the actress playing Cynthia, the repeated lines take on a new meaning and instead of laughing at dramatic convention we laugh at emotional cliché. This parody generates another one – 'I'll kill you for this, Simon Gascoyne' (p. 37) – which causes Birdboot's death which in turn leads to Moon's death.

Like second-string Moon, the protagonists of *Rosencrantz and Guildenstern* are stereotypes whose perception of the world likewise is stereotypic and thus both a betrayal and a half-truth. They are secondaries thrown into a parody of a play 'without possibility of reprieve or hope of explanation',[18] lines which also appear in *Malquist and Moon*. From the moment the unknown messenger knocks at their doors, Rosencrantz and Guildenstern are precipitated from parody to parody, meeting betrayal everywhere, in the ordinary as well as the absurd: Hamlet's acting 'stark raving sane' (p. 68), the ambush of Shakespeare's poetry into their everyday modern prose, the Player's death which turns out to be another performance, the crowds of the *Hamlet* play sweeping around them, mistaking Rosencrantz for Guildenstern and vice versa, until they themselves do not know who they are. This succession of betrayals leaves them obsessed to 'glean' some meaning which is not a parody but, to use the title of a later play, 'the real thing'. Their frantic obsession with significance, however, leads only to their increasing mortification.

While Rosencrantz and Guildenstern are forced to play minor parts in an unfamiliar play, the Player takes a major one in a work of his choosing. Instead of being the victim of optical illusions, he creates them, extracting a significance from his melodrama 'which it does not in fact contain' (p. 83). The Player may appear immune to betrayal because he believes only in make-believe, but he, too, suffers a betrayal when no one watches his performance and he must act out his optical illusion in a void. A confrontation with death, however, reveals the differences between players and secondaries, those who knowingly perpetrate stereotypes and those who are betrayed by them. The actors show that they 'can die heroically, comically, ironically, slowly, suddenly, disgustingly, charmingly, or from a great height' (p. 83). But Guildenstern is certain that he can tell the difference between their fake deaths and the real thing which is simply 'a man failing to reappear, that's all – now you see him, now you don't' (p. 84). The Player, however, proves him wrong by dying from a dagger wound Guildenstern has inflicted on him. He ambushes the horrified Guildenstern by showing the betrayer betrayed, hoist by his own petard – just as he is in the *Hamlet* play – since the dagger turns out to be an actor's trick weapon and the death a performance. Yet Guildenstern's clichéd and pathetic version is a half-truth, too, when 'now you see me, now you –' (p. 126) becomes a last word after all. This last word, however, can only literally be his last word, which is particularly appropriate in that it refers to an optical illusion. As with Moon, his readiness to keep adapting his games and fall in with those of others, no matter what the cost, turns the play into a complete farce which not only mocks and hurts him, but which sustains his vitality even to the end. They are indeed 'dead lucky' (p. 119).

   The early novel *Lord Malquist and Mr Moon* (1966) is the paradigm of the Stoppard plot, focusing on betrayal, uncertainty and lack of consummation, which begins with the very title of the first chapter 'Dramatis Personae and Other Coincidences'. Malquist and Moon are the prototypes of Stoppard's farcical couple, parodic experience and parodic innocence, the one who kicks and the one who gets kicked. Malquist, the aristocrat and stylist, is one of Stoppard's artist and power figures who prides himself on 'withdrawing with style from the chaos' (p. 16). Moon is the victim of proliferating optical illusions, always caught between absurdity and the commonplace and 'betrayed at every turn' (p. 55). As virginal husband he finds his wife invariably in deceptive situations such as with a cowboy who rubs cold cream into her buttocks. As Boswell Inc. he is the model epigone and second-string, vainly 'snatching at the tail-ends of recollection, trusting the echo in his skull to reproduce a meaning that had not touched him' (p. 3) and finally being killed in mistake for his subject; as historian, he is unable even to begin his personal history.

   Although Moon lives in the seemingly ordinary geography of twentieth-century London, he is everywhere ambushed by extravagant complexity: a lion in Hyde Park, two cowboys, named Jasper Jones and Slaughter, having a shoot-out in front of his house, a figure calling himself the Risen Christ swaying in on his donkey amidst the masses of people who make the familiar London streets unrecognizable as they gather for the state funeral of a national hero; and last but not least lilac-gloved Lord Malquist, distributing epigrams incomprehensible to Moon as easily as the chocolate coins with which he tricks the eager crowd. But the commonplace presents no less treacherous optical illusions so that his fears are about 'something as real as a coffee-pot' (p. 18). Moon's most poignant betrayals, however, occur even closer to home. His marriage to Jane remains unconsummated while she flirts with both cowboys and shares embraces of 'Laocoon complexity' (p. 96) and a bubble bath with Lord Malquist. Lack of consummation becomes symptomatic of Moon's career as well. He aspires to be a historian and begins modestly enough by wanting to write his personal history. He cannot, however, even begin this work because he is always thrown back further in a 'cause and effect chain reaction that appalled him at its endlessness'. Even his simplest, most trivial gesture, like straightening a tie becomes 'the culminating act of a sequence that fled back into pre-history and began with the shift of a glacier' (p. 63). As Lord Malquist's biographer Boswellian Moon is caught in a similarly parodic predicament. Trying to capture the 'cosmic accuracy' of Malquist's position he can only scribble 'with a kindergarten fist' 'comic inaccuracy' (p. 3) which is a betrayal of significance as well as a half-truth, if not an astute perception. Like all Stoppard heroes he is committed to moral values, but can establish only stereotype and parody. Thus he will not dismiss suffering humanity in an epigram as does Malquist. But in contrast to Malquist's well-turned phrases, Moon can only stammer: 'I mean it's all *people*, isn't it? That's what the world *is*' (p. 176). Although Moon's cliché is parodied, it is also, one is convinced, one of those naive generalizations that Stoppard sees as truth.

Moon's betrayals culminate in the parody of his bomb attack which ironically pre-empts his own death. From the beginning of the novel Moon has cherished a bomb, a gift from an eccentric and supposedly anarchistic uncle, with which he hopes to make an impact should all else fail him. When all else does, the bomb goes off appropriately enough in a crowd in Trafalgar Square to the tune of the national anthem. But instead of shocking people 'into a moment of recognition' (p. 108) as he intended, it blossoms into a translucent pink balloon with a two-word message, 'familiar, unequivocal, obscene' (p. 154). He has been doubly betrayed, by his commonplace desire of shocking the bourgeois and by having his ambition once again mortified and turned into a parody. But the ultimate betrayal is yet to come when shortly thereafter Moon is blown up by the real bomb of an anarchist in mistake for Malquist. Thus he is a substitute even in death. The anarchist, however, himself is parodic; he is merely an outraged husband avenging his wife's death. She has been run over by Malquist's coach as she was attempting to hand him a petition.

Moon's accidental death constitutes only the final stage of a martyrdom which has haunted him throughout the novel. He has fallen victim to painful and painfully mundane accidents, betrayed likewise by the trivial and the absurd. Slipping in the bathroom, cutting his hand, stepping on a broken bottle, Moon finally is so beset by injuries that, his shoes filled with blood and his body distorted by pain, he barely can drag himself along. Having searched in vain for any sign of stigmata on the Risen Christ, he himself now bears the marks of suffering on his own hands and feet, a parody of a Christ figure and therefore doubly betrayed.

Henry Carr of *Travesties* is Moon grown old. He embodies the betrayed stereotype of an old man, forgetful and self-aggrandising, senility making his mind go off its tracks and his life into a string of travesties. But he also represents the ordinary man, adrift in an absurd world. Like all Stoppard heroes, he is a 'small cup', as Wilde puts it in *De Profundis*, surrounded by extraordinary men and incomprehensible events. And, of course, Carr who played 'not Ernest, the other one', is another of Stoppard's doubles, as *Travesties* turns into a travesty of the confusion over doubles in *The Importance of Being Earnest*.

Like other Stoppard protagonists, Carr tries to cling to stereotypic moral and aesthetic absolutes with a mind caught in leapfrog; it leaves him, as Stoppard says of himself, only 'the courage of my lack of convictions',[19] which is a parody of a stereotype. Duty, patriotism, freedom are as meaningful to Carr as seeing the war in terms of a spoiled wardrobe, while poetry, Tzara tells him, is words pulled out of a hat or the 'reshuffling of a pack of picture cards'.[20] Like Moon, Carr can set against Tzara's radical relativism only a vague consciousness of human suffering. Moon's 'it's all *people*, isn't it?' corresponds to Carr's remembrance of the blood and fear of trench warfare which makes him criticize those who have stayed in the cosiness of peaceful Switzerland. But Carr remains another victim of perspective. Since most Stoppard characters like to formulate epitaphs – last words – for themselves and others, Carr's 'I was uncertain' (p. 81) can serve as epitaph for them all. But even that is an illusion since he uses it to explain why he had not 'stopped the whole Bolshevik thing in its tracks' (p. 81). This is like Guildenstern saying: 'There must have been a moment . . . where we could have said – no. But somehow we missed it' (p. 125).

Again like Moon whose attempt at a personal history loses itself in the history of the world, Carr imagines his as being entangled with the political and artistic revolutions of his day as represented by Lenin, Tzara, Joyce; but that illusory proximity does not give him any insight other than 'I was here. They were here. They went on. I went on. We all went on', to which his wife adds: 'No, we didn't. We stayed' (p. 98). It is the parody of the man whose desire for significance has turned into a complete cliché and a literary parody of old Carr sounding like a Beckett character, both of which are betrayed by his wife's contradiction. Even the revolutionaries as reflected in Carr's mind are caught in parodic dislocations: Lenin disguised as a Swedish deaf-mute, his manuscript exchanged for that of Joyce's *Ulysses*; Marx as victim of historical perspective; the confusion of Rumania, Bulgaria and Belgium; Hans Arp and Jean Arp; Tzara's double identity as Ernest and Algernon, like that of Carr himself who never remembers which of the two he was in *The Importance of Being Earnest*, and who confuses himself with his butler; and finally Joyce – Augusta, Deirdre, Phyllis – stepping into the role of Lady Bracknell and, in the most obvious display of an optical illusion, pulling a rabbit from his hat.

But Joyce is indeed the artist-magician and as such does achieve a lasting triumph. Carr dreams that during the trial over a pair of trousers he suddenly confronts Joyce: '"And what did you do in the Great War?" "I wrote *Ulysses*," he said. "What did you do?" Bloody nerve' (p. 65). The artist is a magician who conjures form out of shambles. With *Ulysses* Joyce claims to have doubled the immortality of the *Odyssey*, a process which Stoppard continues with *The Importance of Being Earnest* and *Travesties*. Although art, too, depends on stereotypes, on doubles and dislocations, it doubles and redoubles immortality. It is the clearest indication of Stoppard's farce not only as betrayal and quintessential optical illusion but as triumph. Out of the endless ambushes and collapses, art creates a firm structure with a beginning, middle and end.

With stereotype and betrayal as the fundamental characteristics of Stoppard's farce, it can be said that it represents, as Dürrenmatt says of his own, 'the worst possible turn a story can take'.[21] It exposes 'the trembling raw meat which, at heart, is all, of us';[22] the very phrasing indicates the gyrating spiral of a cliché which is a parody which is a truth which is a cliché, where parodic betrayal avoids the sentimentality inherent in a perception of men as victims. For Stoppard's farce manifests not only man's pathetic struggle but the gamesmanship of infinite leapfrog. It amounts to a celebration, a celebration, however, not of life but of art where alone events play themselves out to their 'aesthetic, moral and logical conclusion'[23] according to the Player, another of his artist figures in authority. No matter what the consequences of an infinite series of stereotypes and betrayals, acrobatic artistry can express and finally control the rational madness of leapfrogging between stereotypes, parodies and betrayals. Stoppard's 'pan-parodic'[24] creation doubles and redoubles immortality. As Joyce says in *Travesties*: 'If there is any meaning in any of it, it is what survives as art . . . yes, even in the celebration of nonentities' (p. 62).

There are indications particularly in his later work that Stoppard is abandoning parodic betrayals. Inherent in infinite leapfrog, the search for the last word and even the emphasis on ambush is the desire for a leap of faith, a last word and an epiphany. This indeed may help to explain the direction of some of Stoppard's more recent plays, such as *Professional Foul*, *EGBDF*, *Day and Night* and *Cahoot's Macbeth*, which tends to express a commitment to political freedom and human rights that goes beyond a fatalistic acceptance of betrayal. Donner's edible art therefore is not entirely a joke. Stoppard himself speaks of art as 'the moral matrix from which we draw our values'.[25] And he says in *The Real Thing* that words 'can build bridges across incomprehension and chaos' (p. 55). In other plays, such as *Dogg's Hamlet* and *On the Razzle*, he moves towards simple slapstick. Perhaps Stoppard is trying to set his own infinitely leapfrogging mind at rest or come to terms with what Jim Hunter identifies as a split between thinking and caring. 'It is a pattern which goes deep in Stoppard's temperament as revealed in his writing: on the one hand the attractions of sheer brainwork, deduction, calculation, order; on the other, the fundamental moral imperatives "beyond utterance", of diminishing human suffering, responding to human need, and pursuing the good.'[26] As early as *Lord Malquist and Mr Moon* Stoppard has portrayed similar self-divisions. There Moon says about himself that 'my emotional bias towards the reactionary and my intellectual bias towards the radical do not survive each other, and are interred by my aesthetic revulsion of their respective adherents . . .' (p. 74). Concentrating on the aesthetic for its own sake causes moral malaise and Stoppard's work reflects his uneasiness about the artist's lack of commitment. As Carr says 'to be an artist *at all* is like living in Switzerland during a world war' (p. 38). In turning to either slapstick or to a new commitment, Stoppard may be trying to achieve the 'utterly simple shape' (p. 39) with which, like his painter Martello in *Artist Descending*, he could ambush us without betraying the stereotype.

This raises the question whether Stoppard's betrayed stereotype, his seeing everything as parody and optical illusion, is just a flamboyant way of handling material or whether it is more meaningful and substantial. It is a question which does not concern any single author or even just modern literature, but which characterizes most contemporary discourse and has shaped post-modernism. It is implicit in the Derridean erasure and deconstruction which in fact can be seen as a way of defining parody. The 'crossing out' borrowed from Heidegger which indicates the difference between the word and its meaning functions much like a parody. 'Under its strokes the presence of a transcendental signified is effaced while still remaining legible . . . is destroyed while making visible the very idea of the sign.'[27] And the problem is current in other fields as well: it is implicit in the notion of a double bind, in discussions of schizophrenia and the idea of a para-world which suddenly can impinge on us. Perhaps Stoppard himself is unsure whether he has chosen this mode for substance or for effect when he wonders: 'I never quite know whether I want to be a serious artist or a siren.'[28] Or perhaps he has made his choice when he admits: 'I like showbiz, and that's what I'm true to.'[29]

NOTES

1 Kenneth Tynan, 'Profiles', *The New Yorker*, 19 December 1977, p. 51.
2 Tom Stoppard, 'Ambushes for the Audience: Towards a High Comedy of Ideas', *Theatre Quarterly*, May–June 1974, p. 7.
3 Tom Stoppard, *Lord Malquist and Mr Moon* (London: Faber and Faber, 1966), p. 53.
4 Tom Stoppard, *Artist Descending a Staircase* (London: Faber and Faber, 1973), p. 39.
5 Ronald Hayman, *Tom Stoppard* (London: Heinemann, 1979), pp. 140–1.
6 Ronald Hayman, *Theatre and Anti-theatre* (Oxford University Press, 1979), p. 49.
7 Friedrich Dürrenmatt, *Theater-Schriften* (Zürich: Verlag der Arche, 1969), vol. II, p. 178.

8 Tom Stoppard, *Jumpers* (London: Faber and Faber, 1972), p. 72.
9 Tom Stoppard, *The Real Thing* (London: Faber and Faber, 1982), p. 41.
10 Stoppard, *Lord Malquist*, p. 30.
11 Andrew K. Kennedy, *Dramatic Dialogue* (Cambridge University Press, 1983), p. 233.
12 Keir Elam, 'After Magritte, Afer Carroll, After Wittgenstein: What Tom Stoppard's Tortoise Taught Us', *Modern Drama*, December 1984, p. 481.
13 Ibid., p. 482.
14 Tom Stoppard, *The Real Inspector Hound* (London: Faber and Faber, 1968), p. 36.
15 Tom Stoppard, *Albert's Bridge* (London: Faber and Faber, 1969), p. 36.
16 N. S. Hardin, 'An Interview with Tom Stoppard', *Contemporary Literature*, 22:2 (1981), 158.
17 Eric Bentley, *Let's Get a Divorce and Other Plays* (New York: Hill and Wang, 1958), p. 356.
18 Tom Stoppard, *Rosencrantz and Guildenstern Are Dead* (New York: Grove Press, 1967), p. 121.
19 Hayman, *Tom Stoppard*, p. 2.
20 Tom Stoppard, *Travesties* (New York: Grove Press, 1975), p. 53.
21 *Theater-Schriften*, vol. II, p. 176.
22 *The Real Inspector Hound*, p. 19.
23 *Rosencrantz*, p. 79.
24 Andrew K. Kennedy, 'Tom Stoppard's Dissident Comedies', *Modern Drama*, December 1982, p. 469.
25 Tynan, 'Profiles', p. 82.
26 Jim Hunter, *Tom Stoppard's Plays* (London: Faber and Faber, 1982), p. 169.
27 Jacques Derrida, *Of Grammatology*, trans. G. C. Spivak (Baltimore, MD: Johns Hopkins University Press, 1976), p. 23.
28 Hayman, *Tom Stoppard*, p. 139.
29 Ibid., p. 8.

On stage, off stage, and backstage with Alan Ayckbourn

ALBERT E. KALSON

In his preface to his best-known work, *The Norman Conquests*, Alan Ayckbourn describes the Yorkshire coastal resort where he serves as Artistic Director of the theatre where all his plays are tested: 'Scarborough is a holiday town, which means that a large proportion of the potential audience changes every week of the summer. On Saturdays, the roads in and out of the town are scenes of mile-long queues as visitors leave and arrive.'[1] Britain's most prolific dramatist is indeed intrigued by traffic jams. One of his first plays, *Standing Room Only*, produced in Scarborough in 1961, is a comic nightmare set in the future in a London traffic jam lasting twenty-five years during which time a family struggles to maintain a normal existence while stranded on a bus in Shaftesbury Avenue. Since then, much of Ayckbourn's work, ingenious and entertaining farces to begin with, more serious but still comical explorations of marital and mental breakdowns later on, depends on the dramatist's deliberate manipulation to avoid traffic jams by carefully maneuvering his actors through the intricacies and obstacles of both onstage and offstage theatrical space.

Farce frequently depends on an enclosed space to which access is provided by various doors. The joke of such a Feydeau play as *Occupe-toi d'Amélie* (1908) is that a character within a theatrical setting, expecting a second character with whom he is hoping to form an alliance, is suddenly confronted with a third character who poses a threat to the new relationship. A man expecting his mistress, for example, is startled by the appearance of his wife. But there is always another door proffering escape. Within a fixed setting, the relationships remain in flux as doors swing wildly open only to be slammed shut. The audience's delight, however, is determined not so much by the agility of the performers, which may be noted in direct proportion to the speed with which they enter and exit, but by the cleverness of the situation, the plot in which performers lose their identities as actors and transform themselves into characters. In the Feydeau farce, it is the characters with whom an audience becomes involved.

This is true too of Ayckbourn's early play, *Relatively Speaking*, written in

1965, in which he spins out a case of mistaken identity with a skill equal to that of Feydeau or even Oscar Wilde whose *The Importance of Being Earnest* may have served as its model. Four years later, by the time he came to write *How the Other Half Loves* (1969), however, the dramatist had discovered an idiosyncratic means of adding to a farcical concoction what might be termed the Ayckbourn effect, an effect in part related yet finally diametricaly opposed to Bertolt Brecht's alienation effect which prevents an audience's identification with the characters. *Verfremdungseffekt* distances an audience with its emphasis on theatre as theatre. The audience knows the actor is an actor, commenting on the situation of the character he is representing in order to lead the spectator to think about that situation, even to consider alternatives to it. Brecht's plays may entertain incidentally, but they are didactic in intention; Ayckbourn's distancing effect, by contrast, enhances an audience's pleasure.

In *How the Other Half Loves* Ayckbourn begins to play the role for which he is best known today – the documentor of the maddening rituals of suburban life, the social chronicler. Yet the play, while foreshadowing the more serious tribulations of daily life which take center stage in such works as *Absent Friends* (1974) and *Just Between Ourselves* (1976), is primarily lighthearted entertainment. Bob Phillips is involved in an affair with his employer's wife, Fiona Foster. Inventing a marital break-up for the socially backward Featherstones as an excuse for coming home in the middle of the night, he unwittingly sets off a chain of misunderstandings which nearly wreck three already unstable relationships. Before mate is reunited with proper mate, Teresa Phillips and Frank Foster learn the truth and forgive their wayward spouses, but hapless, innocent Mary and William Featherstone are not quite reconciled to what they now perceive to be a sterile relationship.

What sets *How the Other Half Loves* apart from other mindless West End farces about marital mix-ups is a telling contrast of social and economic status made evident by the play's complicated but ingenious setting which makes the Ayckbourn effect possible. It is Ayckbourn's masterstroke to place the living–dining area of both the tasteful Foster home and the cluttered, uncared-for Phillips home on stage together, not side by side as one might expect from a conventional playwright presenting two locales, but actually superimposed. The expensive Foster period furniture shares a one-room stage with the modern, trendy Phillips pieces. (In the West End production the sofa was even sectioned into Foster cushions and Phillips cushions.) Yet, by means of clashing styles and colors, the audience has no difficulty in discerning who lives where, once the actors establish their roles.

As if such invention were not enough, Ayckbourn adds still another. In the play's most remarkable innovation, which leads to one of the most hilarious scenes in modern comedy, a single enclosed theatrical space, already accepted by the audience as two distinct locales, is viewed as existing in two distinct moments of time – Thursday night at the Fosters and Friday night at the Phillipses. Two dinner parties take place simultaneously at one extended dining table where the Featherstones are at once the guests for an elegant and properly served meal with linen napkins and crystal, and a slopped-together supper with paper napkins and tumblers. The scene ends with poor William Featherstone wringing wet – hit with the soup which an enraged, drunken Teresa throws at Bob on Friday in the very spot where the Fosters' upstairs loo suddenly leaks through the ceiling on Thursday.

The space, ingeniously and imaginatively employed, provides the play with yet another dimension, one beyond the visual. The audience is not kept in a state of apprehension as in a Feydeau farce wondering which character will next be revealed as doors open and close. The suspense in *How the Other Half Loves* transcends plot in involving the audience's appreciation of the characters as actors negotiating the onstage traffic to which they must appear oblivious. Actors portraying characters supposedly miles apart occupy the same space as they circle one another, seemingly on a collision course, then veer to relative safety to the audible sighs of relief from an audience savoring the illusion, willing it to be maintained. *How the Other Half Loves* depends as a consequence more on perfect timing than on plot or language. Added delight comes from the realization that Ayckbourn's special form of distancing requires that that dimension be supplied by the actors themselves. Through his management of space, Ayckbourn has manipulated his audience to identify not merely with his characters, but also with his performers.

A decade later, in *Taking Steps* (1979), a farce set in a symbolically decaying Tudor house which a drunken bucket manufacturer is considering for purchase, Ayckbourn attempted a similar manipulation of space that once again thrust his actors into the limelight as actors. The title wittily refers to more than theme, describing in fact the staging on which much of the action depends. Having written the work originally for the single-level stage of Scarborough's theatre-in-the-round, Ayckbourn makes frequent use of flights of stairs to accommodate slapstick pratfalls, somersaults, and general frenzy. But in *Taking Steps* the stairs are flattened, merely indicated, so that three levels supposedly exist on a single stage floor, which means that actors rushing about the attic or the first floor actually move in close proximity to, are in danger of colliding with, other actors on the ground floor. Reminiscent of the superimposition of two households in *How the Other Half Loves*, the device makes perfect sense in the theatre for which it was designed. On a proscenium stage which can accommodate various levels, however, it reduces to pure gimmickry, assuring laughter without providing the telling social counterpoint of the earlier play.

More indicative of Ayckbourn's developing mastery of the use of theatrical space are two plays written between *How the Other Half Loves* and
Taking Steps, *Absurd Person Singular* (1972) and *The Norman Conquests* (1973) in
which the dramatist addresses the dramatic possibilities of offstage action.
In the preface to *Absurd Person Singular* he writes,

> Very early on in my career as a dramatist I discovered that . . . an audience's
> imagination can do far better work than any number of playwright's words.
> The offstage character hinted at but never seen can be dramatically as
> significant and telling as his onstage counterparts. Offstage action is more
> difficult. Unless care is taken, if the dramatist chooses to describe rather than
> show his action, the audience can rapidly come to the conclusion that they're in
> the wrong auditorium.[2]

Shortly after beginning to write the play, which originally took place at
three parties on three successive Christmas Eves in the sitting rooms of
three different households, Ayckbourn came to the conclusion that he was
in the wrong room: 'Dick and Lottie were indeed monstrously overwhelm-
ing . . . and far better heard occasionally but not seen. By a simple switch of
setting to the kitchen, the problem was all but solved, adding incidentally
far greater comic possibilities than the sitting room ever held. For in the
particular case, the obvious offstage action was far more relevant than its
onstage counterpart' (p. 7). In the subsequent reversal of offstage and
onstage action, the guests in act I seek sanctuary in the kitchen to avoid the
awful jokes of the hearty, unseen Potters; in act II they are held hostage by
George, a large unseen pet dog who has just bitten the still unseen Mr
Potter in the adjoining room; and in act III the Brewster-Wrights and the
Jacksons hide unsuccessfully from the uninvited Hopcrofts. What matters
in *Absurd Person Singular* happens in the kitchen, but what adds bite to this
black farce about sexual incompatibility and class warfare is that the
characters in each act are trapped on stage by the off stage characters, some
of whom never appear, with whom the audience grows more and more
familiar as the play progresses.

In *The Norman Conquests*, a trilogy comprising *Table Manners*, *Living
Together*, and *Round and Round the Garden*, first performed in Scarborough in
1973, Ayckbourn exploits the ultimate possibilities of offstage action
through a single set of characters in a house and its surroundings where
Annie awaits her brother Reg and his wife Sarah. They are to relieve her of
caring for their bed-ridden and unseen mother so that Annie may take a
well-deserved holiday. Unknown to the others, who suspect she may be
going off with her neighbor Tom, the local vet, Annie is in fact about to
leave for a 'dirty weekend' with Norman, who is married to her sister Ruth.
Bewildered by the multiplying complications which ensue, dull-witted
Tom suspects that all the women have designs on his person. Through it all,
exasperating, inept Norman remains the surprisingly irresistible shaggy

dog whom all the women actually wish to cuddle. And all of them do – in a corner of the dining room in one play, on a rug in the sitting room in the second play, or in the bushes of the garden in the third. Ultimately, the entire household is frustrated as they are trapped in the rituals of a summer weekend – eating, drinking, storytelling, game-playing, wooing. The male–female relationship with its dream of blissful happiness is reduced in *The Norman Conquests* to the comedy of furtive coupling and interrupted groping.

The three parts of *The Norman Conquests* combine cleverly to enable the audience to know what every member of the household is up to at any given moment in any part of the house. When Sarah sends Reg from the dining room in *Table Manners* to fetch something from the sitting room in order to spy on Annie and Norman and he returns foolishly carrying a waste-paper basket, the audience is amused. In *Living Together* when Reg interrupts Annie and Norman in the sitting room and grabs the basket in embarrassed confusion, that part of the audience which has already seen *Table Manners* is implicated in an expanding joke.

According to Ayckbourn, *The Norman Conquests* 'to all intents and purposes was the end of my exploration of offstage action. Three plays, two of which were happening off stage simultaneously with the one on stage, were quite enough.'[3] What the dramatist still had left to explore was the possibility of turning an audience's attention not so much to some fictional offstage action, but to place in focus once more the actor as actor, to invite an audience to follow imaginatively the actor moving from onstage theatrical space to the theatre's unseen backstage area. Both Ayckbourn, and, to some extent, Michael Frayn, employing the Ayckbourn effect in *Noises Off* (1982), would discover further dramatic possibilities in an exploration of backstage theatrical space.

For Ayckbourn, the transitional play in this movement is *Sisterly Feelings* (1979). Whereas Brecht attempted to turn an audience's thoughts to alternative actions for his characters, Ayckbourn provides those alternatives. Because the play itself illustrates Ayckbourn's theory of comic determinism by exploring the effect of chance or choice on his characters' lives, chance or choice play upon the audience as well. *Sisterly Feelings* is a four-part comedy which inverts the cycle of life by beginning with a funeral and ending with a wedding at which the bride is pregnant. While the first and last scenes remain fixed, Ayckbourn has supplied alternate middle scenes. The toss of a coin at one point and an actress's whim at another dictate the direction the performance will take.

After the funeral which opens the play, two sisters, Abigail and Dorcas, toss a coin to determine who takes the last remaining seat in the last car. The loser is actually the winner, for she gets to walk home with Simon and establish a relationship with him. Later, when a rainstorm disrupts what is either Abigail's or Dorcas's picnic, the actress playing the sister who has ensnared Simon has the choice of prolonging the affair or giving him up to her rival. This leads either to 'A Day at the Races' or 'A Night under Canvas'. These variable scenes initiated by chance or choice do not, however, determine the outcome. *Sisterly Feelings* always ends with the same fourth scene, 'A Wedding', in which the bride is neither Abigail nor Dorcas, but bossy Brenda, who has been having her way with their docile brother Melvin. Neither chance nor choice has interrupted life's flow. As Dorcas says, 'The important thing is for us to *feel* we've made decisions',[4] voicing the play's theme.

According to Ayckbourn the whole scheme 'has the effect of stimulating actors, irritating stage managers and infuriating box office staff' (p. viii). In theory the audience too should be excited by the supposed spontaneity of the performance as they envision what must be taking place back stage – an entire theatre company at the ready to move in one direction or another, to put in place one set or another, one series of props or another, to set in motion one series of actions or its alternates. In actual practice the excitement is diminished by pragmatism. After the first few performances during the London run of *Sisterly Feelings* at the National Theatre, the course of the play was predetermined, chance giving way to choice. The entire company knew beforehand the result of the coin toss, and the actress's whim was in fact dictated. Backstage chaos settled into theatrical routine as audiences, aware that the alternatives were already selected, concentrated on onstage action.

The frenzy of backstage action comes to the fore, however, in *Intimate Exchanges*, first presented in Scarborough in 1982. If, as Ayckbourn says, in *Sisterly Feelings* he 'dipped a tentative toe into alternatives', *Intimate Exchanges* is 'the ultimate in alternatives'.[5] Comprising some thirty scenes and fourteen hours of dialogue, the mammoth comedy, which manages to turn even Shakespeare's history tetralogies and David Edgar's adaptation of Dickens's *Nicholas Nickleby* into theatrical miniatures, is actually eight complete but related plays involving ten characters, six of whom appear in every version.

Each play begins with an identical scene. Alone in her garden, Celia must decide whether or not to have a cigarette before 6 p.m. This trivial decision leads to more and more complex decisions on her part and on the part of the man who joins her shortly afterwards – her husband Toby, the headmaster of the Bilbury Lodge Preparatory School for Boys and Girls; Miles, the director of the school's board; and Lionel, the school's groundskeeper. In various versions Celia either continues or breaks off her relationship with her husband and enters into or discourages a relationship with the other two men. All the men explore further relationships with either Rowena, Miles's wife, or Sylvie, Celia's sometime helper around the house. Other characters who appear briefly but tellingly are Celia's mother, Lionel's father, a chatty clubwoman, and a gentlemanly neighbour. Each version is played in four scenes, all the scenes having alternates based on various decisions. Each time the first two scenes are set in the garden, the third in any one of several places – a cricket field, a golf course, a hotel terrace – and the fourth always in a churchyard during the observance of what may be a happy occasion – a wedding, a christening, the school's anniversary – or a sad one – a memorial service or a funeral.

A small-scale play despite its gargantuan underpinnings, *Intimate Exchanges* avoids the sensational and the melodramatic, but in its examination of the inception and the sometimes disintegration of the tenuous relationship of any two human beings, Ayckbourn continues to ask the question which he first raised in *Sisterly Feelings*: are our lives guided by chance or choice? In *Sisterly Feelings* it seems finally not to matter since each version ends in the same way, suggesting that something within our characters guides us whatever we will. In *Intimate Exchanges* Ayckbourn is not so certain. Chance or choice rules us, but the sixteen separate endings dictate that the terrifying question must finally remain unanswered.

Metaphysics aside, Ayckbourn has by no means lost the knack of entertaining his audience. To do so, in *Intimate Exchanges* he presents his actors with their greatest challenge, which in turn provides yet another dimension for his audience. Although the course of each performance is set in advance – there are eight subtitles to enable returning spectators to seek out a version they have not seen before – all ten characters in all eight versions are played by two performers, one man and one woman. Each time one of the two leaves the stage, the audience is in a state of suspense: will uptight Celia reappear as sophisticated, all-knowing Rowena, as Celia's dowdy mother, as slovenly Sylvie, or overbearing Irene Pridworthy? Will dithering Miles return as angry, drunken Toby, or sullenly arrogant Lionel, or Lionel's doddering father? As in *How the Other Half Loves* the audience is not only caught up in the characters' relationships, but in the mechanics of the performance; but this time they are directed to contemplate what must be happening backstage. How does the performer change costume, wig, even girth so rapidly? How does he or she get from exiting side to opposite entering side? The single female performer must quarrel with herself off stage. The single male performer must even come to blows with himself in a garden shed and a cricket hut.

Ayckbourn has provided a theatre piece with a double focus throughout. In its exploration of relationships *Intimate Exchanges* is recognizable as life; in the frantic activity it demands backstage, it offers its audience some insights into a life in the theatre. One can only wonder how long it will be before Ayckbourn makes use of the space in the theatre lobby, the space outside the theatre. Perhaps one day Ayckbourn will be manipulating the actual traffic jams which occur nightly at curtain time along Shaftesbury Avenue.

What is less apparent but more significant is that while manipulating theatrical space, Ayckbourn is in fact commenting on the classical unities of time, place, and action, the Aristotelian tradition in which he is still immersed. In seeming to flail against that tradition, Ayckbourn actually aligns technique and theme. As Oedipus flailed against his pre-ordained destiny, Ayckbourn's characters desperately make their choices only to learn that chance plays as important a role in the shaping of their lives. Ultimately the playwright himself must play God to his characters, but in arranging alternative possibilities Ayckbourn seemingly forces the actors themselves to have a hand in their characters' destinies. If the Aristotelian tradition itself constrains fate within the bounds of one time, one place, one action, Ayckbourn's alternative scenes adhere to the same unities, but he has expanded them to the unity of the entire theatre – on stage, off stage, and backstage too. In *How the Other Half Loves* two times are one time; in *The Norman Conquests* three plays in three places are one time, one place. In *Intimate Exchanges* eight actions are one action as each character explores all of life's relationships in a single, but expanding, pairing of the male and the female. As long as Ayckbourn's frantic performers manage to avoid a fatal collision in some part of the theatre, he may continue to explore the limits of the Aristotelian tradition leaving his audience, as usual, helpless with laughter as they contemplate the mirrored traffic jams of their own lives.

NOTES

1 *The Norman Conquests* (New York: Grove Press, 1979), p. 10.
2 *Three Plays: Absurd Person Singular, Absent Friends, Bedroom Farce* (New York: Grove Press, 1979), p. 7.
3 Ibid., p. 8.
4 *Sisterly Feelings* and *Taking Steps* (London: Chatto and Windus, 1981), p. 146.
5 *The Times*, 9 June 1984, p. 20.

REVIEW SECTION

Taking farce seriously: recent critical approaches to Plautus

DAVID WILES

In contrast to Terence and Menander, who are generally considered to have written 'comedies', Plautus is often considered to have written 'farce'. Two aspects of Plautus encourage critics to prefer the term 'farce' – the lack of a discernible moral, and the lack of any exploration of character. These lacks are associated with a more general absence of what is referred to as 'illusion', 'realism', or 'mimesis'. My purpose in this review essay is to discuss, not the plays of Plautus, but rather, so far as a distinction is possible, the critical enterprise of Plautine studies.

Let me begin by exploring the simple question of why modern critics should consider that farce, and Plautus as a master of farce, are worth their serious attention. I have been able to discern, in my reading of the critics, three broad reasons for studying Plautus: first, because he is there; second, because we shall be better people as a result of studying or watching Plautus; and third, because Plautus is historically important.

The first is a non-reason. The study of theatre history and the study of classical civilization have alike institutionalized Plautine studies. Writing about Plautus is one respectable way in which academics carry out the job for which they are paid. The second, that we shall be better people, has more substance. It is increasingly hard to argue, in the twentieth century, that Plautus is morally instructive, or a receptable of universal truths – but farce can improve us in other ways also. Eric Bentley's essay on farce[1] is probably the classic modern exposition of why farce is good for us because of its therapeutic or cathartic effects. In practice, Plautine critics make less sophisticated claims than Bentley. They tend to study Plautus because they find the activity pleasurable, and – *pace* Plato – pleasure is accepted as inherently a good thing. The third rationale, that Plautus is historically important, can be subdivided. Plautus' importance may be literary or ideological. On the one hand, Plautus' plays can be seen to have shaped European comedy. Plautus thus matters because he shaped and transmitted a genre later adopted by Shakespeare and Molière, whose importance goes without question. According to the other point of view, the plays are part of an integral system. The ideological function of the plays can be

analysed in relation to a Roman audience poised to conquer and transform
the western world. These, implicit or explicit, are the discernible reasons
why people write about Plautus. The nature of the criticism offered
depends, in any given case, upon the critic's view of his or her own activity.

Before discussing the state of Plautine criticism, I shall sketch in some
necessary background. The discovery of Menander in the twentieth century has had a profound effect upon Plautine studies. The Darwinian model
of theatre history – whereby Plautus was a crude primitive, and Terence his
sophisticated successor pointing the way to the future – is no longer viable.
The discovery of Menander has revealed the inadequacy of Terence vis-à-
vis his Greek models, and has revealed that Plautus, in his drastic
reworking of Greek models, made deliberate aesthetic choices. Plautus'
plays can now be seen as a creative fusion of two distinctive modes: a Greek
tradition and one, or properly several, indigenous traditions. The discovery
of the Cairo Codex in 1905 (the first big Menander discovery) yielded
seventeen years later Fraenkel's monumental attempt to disinter the
Plautinisches im Plautus – the original Roman element in Plautus.[2] Fraenkel
remains the starting point for much current research. To separate out the
Greek original is a favourite game which academics like to play with a
Plautine text. Despite this danger, all the most productive criticism of
Plautus starts from a recognition that Greek drama and Roman drama are
distinctively different forms. The Menander discoveries of the 1950s and
1960s – in particular the discovery of a section of the Greek source for
Plautus' *Bacchides* – broadly confirmed Fraenkel's arguments of 1922.

I shall discuss some examples of recent Plautine scholarship which are
representative of the post-Fraenkel critical enterprise in Britain, the USA
and Italy. The British have made important contributions to philological
research into New Comedy, but have contributed relatively little to literary
studies, perhaps because of a bias against literary studies within Oxford
and Cambridge. I shall take as my example Richard Hunter's *The New
Comedy of Greece and Rome* published by Cambridge University Press in 1985.
This is a conscientious book, breaking little new ground, and it sums up
what I take to be the British concensus view of Plautus. The dust jacket and
preface pay lip-service to the notion of 'pleasure', but within the text there is
little to suggest that Plautus is studied for any other reason than because he
is there. The book starts with the techniques and forms of New Comedy, it
moves through the themes, and finishes with a chapter on 'the didactic
element'. It therefore privileges the idea of a moral purpose in the writing.
Greek poetry, Hunter writes, was 'a powerful medium for the transmission
of ideas'.[3] Plautus is viewed through Hellenic spectacles, and he doesn't
come out very well. In a typical discussion of Plautus, Hunter refers
apologetically to 'comedy's traditional lack of concern with coherent
characterization, particularly when such a virtue would get in the way of

the humour'.[4] *Characterization* is perceived as inherently a virtue in drama: *humour* has to be tolerated. Again: 'Plautus is often less concerned in these scenes with dramatic realism or the preservation of consistent character than with the immediate comic moment'.[5] One deduces that Plautus' plays were ephemeral in comparison with their more *realistic* Greek originals. A value judgement about farce is always present. On the one hand, 'Plautus' use of farce and broad humour hardly requires lengthy illustration';[6] and on the other, there is extended praise for the Hellenic philosophizing of Pseudolus. 'These beautiful verses demand a complex response from the audience', Hunter writes, confident that the farcical context will not affect 'the power of the verses to move us'.[7]

This is Plautus as presented to students at Cambridge, England. It is not the most stimulating of British scholarship on Plautus,[8] but it represents a widely held and entrenched point of view. I shall turn by way of contrast to a production of the university press at Cambridge, Massachusetts – Erich Segal's *Roman Laughter*, published in 1968. This is a book that respectable English classicists love to despise, not so much for the slipperiness of its arguments as for the brashness of its style. Richard Hunter makes his views plain by omitting all mention of the book from his notes and bibliography of recommended reading. Despite his faults, however, Segal in his day did have a distinctively new product to put on the market. The core of Segal's argument is that the plays follow the paradigm of the Saturnalia, the festival in which the normal order of society is inverted. Repressed desires are liberated in the harmless fantasy world of the plays. The exotic Greek setting and costumes certificate the point that the plays are fantasy, and not an imitation of life as it is actually lived. The principal intellectual debts are to *Shakespeare's Festive Comedy*[9] and to psychoanalysis. Segal's argument is a challenging one because it confronts the basic question (which Hunter ignores) of the relationship between Plautus and his Roman audience. Segal has learnt from Freud that the notion of 'escapism' – a term often invoked to foreclose discussion – is never sufficient, and that laughter has its roots in specific and identifiable forms of repression. Segal's book dragged Plautus out of the clutches of philologists into central areas of intellectual debate.

Segal's pleasure in Plautus is related to his own double identity as a professor at Yale on the one hand, as Hollywood scriptwriter and author of *Love Story* on the other. The commercialism of Plautus, which Horace deplored, is a source of joy to him. The Rome that Segal conjures up has a distinctly capitalist flavour. It is a world obsessed with making profits, beneath a veneer of high public morality. One of the chief drawbacks to the book is its casual handling of historical sources. Myths about Plautus' period put about a century and a half later are accepted without questioning. This is a pity because I think that there is more solid evidence available for arguing that Plautus' society was, in contrast to Menander's, repressive, and that the release of repressed impulses is indeed the mechanism that Plautus triggers. The main locus of repression, to Segal's twentieth-century eyes, is the family. He takes no account of public repression. He makes nothing of the fact that a propertied male Roman citizen spent much of his life in the army. During the second Punic war (when Plautus' earlier plays were written) one-third of the adult male citizenry was mobilized, and half of these men died. Soldiers were bound by solemn oath, and discipline was ferocious. Mutinies were not unknown.[10] Segal's claim that the family is the state in miniature[11] is not examined in all its implications.

Segal's exclusive focus upon the family causes him serious problems. He does not know what to make of the father figure. He cites the Roman father's legal power of life and death over his children – although there is no evidence that the *use* of such legal power was deemed morally acceptable in Rome. He describes the conflict of father and son, and identifies a 'parricidal urge' in the comedies. This sits awkwardly with his later argument that fathers in Plautus, in contrast to Terence and Molière, are not agelastic blocking figures. More commonly, fathers indulge their own or their sons' erotic impulses.[12] It is not clear how the theory of the parricidal urge can be accommodated with an audience which included both fathers and sons. Segal's treatment of Roman women is equally unsatisfactory. He describes 'the typical Plautine matron' as 'bitchy' – a doubtful generalization – without any explanation of why 'the Romans' should think this is a good joke. It is not clear whether 'the Romans' is intended to include Roman women.[13] He cites Cato's ideal of decorous womanhood as an example of Roman values, and fails to cite Livy's account of a mass demonstration by Roman women against Cato.[14] In 195 BC, rich women took to the streets and successfully lobbied for a repeal of wartime legislation which restricted their display of jewellery and clothing. Such events would not be conceivable in democratic Athens. Roman women had far more freedom to own property and appear in public than their Athenian counterparts. In respect of marriage, the idea that the family is the state in miniature cannot be sustained.

The link between the play and the Saturnalian festival is not clearly worked out. The precise correlations that Barber makes between Tudor festive practices and Shakespearian texts are not available. The riotous inversionary Saturnalia was a feature of the Empire, and in the middle Republic, when Plautus wrote, such anarchy would not have been tolerated.[15] The idea of the Saturnalia serves merely as a metaphor. It is a misleading metaphor because it implies that the plays invert a stable hierarchical pattern which can be restored at the end of the festive performance. Segal's premise is that of psychoanalysis: once tensions have been released, once proscribed fantasies have been allowed past the censoring superego, then the hierarchical pattern can be restored. This simple inversionary model will not do. As Livy's account of the women's demonstration illustrates, Roman morality was not monolithic. Plautus' Rome was a world in rapid cultural and demographic transition. One reason for the authorities' encouraging theatre as a mode of public con-celebration must have been its inherent controlability in a volatile situation.[16] The Roman invasion of the Greek world opened Rome up to new influences, a new immigrant population. Plautus' plays and (almost certainly) his actors were part of this influx of people and ideas. There is a basic difference between theatre and ritual that Segal does not explore. Ritual always repeats itself, theatre never repeats itself. Plautus' theatre is more than an inversionary ritual.

The liberation of the individual psyche is no longer the answer to the world's problems – as it may have seemed to be, to Segal and to many, in 1968. In the context of present debates about the effect of popular entertainment upon our own society, different questions have to be asked. What, for instance, was the attitude of senators who funded performances of Plautus? We know from Polybius that the Roman nobility were skilled propagandists.[17] If the plays were a public enactment of anti-authoritarian behaviour, does this mean the nobility were trying to satisfy the lower orders with surrogate freedoms? Or were the plays in some sense express-ive, a public display required by people who insisted that their point of view receive public recognition?[18] The status of Plautus and his fellow writers as foreigners on the margins of Roman society perhaps helped them to create plays that were not partisan but somehow satisfactory to all parties.

I shall deal briefly with two recent American books on Plautus which speak of Segal's book in terms of respect. David Konstan's *Roman Comedy* (Cornell University Press, 1983) takes a Marxist slant on Roman comedy. Konstan examines how Plautus' plays function as ideology, broadly affirming the ideal of the city-state as a closed conjugal group, but to a limited extent challenging prevailing social codes. He rejects Segal's saturnalian thesis on the grounds that the principal blocking figures – the mercenary and the slave-dealer – are outsiders and not high-ranking citizens.[19] He does not confront the problem that all the characters are, in a sense, outsiders, because they are Greek and not Roman. Despite some interesting readings, the book is flawed by its failure to differentiate between Greek and Roman modes of New Comedy. Most Greek city-states were indeed closed conjugal groups, but Rome was much bigger, much readier to assimilate foreigners as citizens. Konstan's thesis would have lent itself much better to an analysis of Menander's comedy than it does to Plautus. Konstan's concept of the 'city-state' as a classifiable political system takes no account of the basic divide in the ancient world between oligarchy and democracy, two opposed systems of government which shaped religious and domestic life – not to mention theatre.

Niall Slater's *Plautus in Performance* (Princeton University Press, 1985) develops an idea first put out in 1970 in an influential conference paper by the Italian Marino Barchiesi: 'Plautus and Ancient Metatheatre'.[20] The cue is a speech by the cunning slave Pseudolus in which the slave claims to be the 'poet' of the drama.[21] The plays are termed 'metatheatrical' because, framed by the formal narrative, the principal slave is presented as an improvisator, creating a new play of his own, and allocating roles to other characters who in this new play must each act out a fresh part. Other characters besides the slave sometimes take on this authorial function. The audiences are invited to relish the way in which the actor/author plays fast and loose with the Greek model upon which the narrative is based. This is an attractive thesis which makes good sense of the relationship between Plautine farce and the Greek comedy upon which it is based.

If we return to the original thesis as proposed by Barchiesi we can see how American criticism and Italian criticism have taken Barchiesi's ideas in different directions. The main thrust of Barchiesi's paper is to attack what he calls analytic criticism. He attacks

> the doctrine according to which every individual experience contains within itself its own expression – so that any discussion of forms is reduced to cataloguing, with no intrinsic dialectic or rationale. This doctrine, with its powerful assertion of the uniqueness of individual experience, has received its historical due, and we no longer find it sufficient. Seemingly, formal changes are conditioned by an interior logic of their own, and certain rules can be glimpsed.[22]

Such rules, Barchiesi argues, can be discerned within the development of western dramaturgy, rules operating in complex relation to 'changing historical and existential situations'. Barchiesi argues for the study of forms, in preference to the study of individual works where the parts have to be studied in relation to a unitary whole. The latter procedure cannot work for Plautus, whose method consists precisely in disrupting the organic relationship of the parts to the whole. A striking feature of recent Italian criticism has been its concentration upon the logic of the form. While critics like David Konstan and Niall Slater work from a proposition about form towards an exegesis of individual texts, Italian critics have tended to see an analysis of the form as their final goal. One consequence of the analytic method is that the play can easily be treated as a self-contained, self-referential system. Niall Slater does not escape from this trap when he claims that 'Plautus does not imitiate life but a previous text'.[23] Slater's methodology does not allow him to investigate why the form of New Comedy developed in the particular direction that it did. A complex debate about illusion and non-illusion remains unresolved because Slater does not get to grips with the physical reality of performance in a particular historical situation. Italian criticism has tended to be very interested in the relationship between Plautus and his world, not only because of the general intellectual climate, but also because Plautus is Italy's earliest national playwright, and there is a natural incentive to define what renders him Italian rather than Greek. I am going to focus on two critics who have examined the relationship between Plautus and his world in what seems to me a productive way.

Gianna Petrone's *Morality and Anti-morality in Plautus' Comedies* (1977)[24] can be read as a refinement of Segal's thesis. Petrone accepts that Plautus' audience broadly shared the stern value system of Cato the Censor. She argues that there are two alternative modes in Plautus: the Greek mode of *mimesis* and the Roman mode of *ludus*. The former is inherently moralistic, the latter inverts morality. The inversion is made so clear that the author's own ethical stance is not publicly doubted. The dichotomy between the moral and the anti-moral can be understood as a tension between form and content. The plot is Greek and moral, the action is Bacchanalian and anti-moral. In Plautus' later plays, Petrone discerns a difference between whole plays which are either moral or anti-moral. The focus of her book is Plautus' *Stichus*, where the two modes unusually coexist side by side: a moralistic play about female fidelity merges into an orgiastic romp by slaves on holiday.

Petrone's argument has implications for an understanding of the audience. While Segal's audience passively absorbs fantasies which bypass their censorious superegos, Petrone's audience is actively involved in disentangling two contradictory messages contained within one play. This is a theatre of dreams, but it is holding up dreams for open discussion. In Saussurean terms, New Comedy is seen as a theatrical *langue*, and Plautus' audience consists of competent users of that *langue*. While Segal's audience is conceived as a homogeneous mass (in a typical formulation: 'The Roman was god-fearing, faithful and forthright . . .'[25]), Petrone allows for a variegated audience in which different spectators make different demands. The parasite, for instance, is seen as a spokesman for marginal elements in society. Petrone makes a plausible case for our believing that Plautus was commissioned to write the *Stichus*, which centres on a return from abroad, to celebrate the triumphant return of Scipio's armies. It is an important difference, therefore, that while Segal's audience is essentially concerned with domestic family relationships, *res privata*, Petrone's audience is concerned with *res publica*.

A more recent book by Petrone, *Ancient Theatre and Deceit: Plautine Fictions* (1983),[26] marks a change of direction – from viewing the play as a moral discourse to viewing the play as a structure. Petrone's starting point is

Barchiesi. She expands the metaphor of the picture-frame, and explores the process of induction as the audience are led from the exterior frame of the Greek narrative into the festive *ludus* controlled by the trickster figure. The first part of the book is a synchronic analysis of the genre in terms of three narrative functions: the authorial function of the trickster (usually a slave), the opponent (often a soldier or slave-dealer) and the helper (whose task is to assume a disguise and dupe the opponent). The second part of the book is a diachronic analysis of deceit as a structuring principle in classical drama. Greek tragedy is taken as the inspiration for Plautus' drama. Greek tragedy, Petrone argues, increasingly distanced itself from mythography, from telling the truth about external reality, and used the idea of deceit, the creating of fiction within fiction, to give theatre-making an autonomous self-justifying identity. Petrone portrays Plautine drama as a logical extension of this Greek idea.

Petrone carries through in this book Barchiesi's project of exploring the logic governing the development of forms. Her synchronic analysis enables her to indicate why form changed in response to a clash of ideologies external to the theatre. According to the Greek model, the world is governed by *Tyche* ('Chance' or 'Fate') and *Tyche* therefore governs the plot mechanics. Roman ideology stressed the importance of *virtus*, the absolute power of man to mould the world in accordance with his wishes: hence the plays centre upon a trickster capable of taking a formulaic Greek plot and moulding it into the shape that he chooses.

A more elaborate analysis of narrative functions appears in the last work that I want to discuss, an essay by Maurizio Bettini entitled 'Towards an Anthropology of the Plot: Simple Plot Structures in Plautus' Comedies' published in 1982.[27] This is the work of Plautine criticism that has most excited me since I first encountered Segal's book. Bettini analyses the narrative structures of the whole Plautine corpus according to A. J. Greimas's actantial model.[28] Briefly, the theory is that any narrative can be analysed in terms of six actants: subject and object, helper and opponent, and the untranslatable *destinateur* and *destinataire*. To quote Greimas's own example: in the story of the quest for the Holy Grail, the hero is the subject, the Grail is the object, the *destinateur* is God and the *destinataire* is humanity. Bettini's project is to analyse Plautine narratives, and to clarify which actor, or group of actors, or symbol, marries up with each actantial function.

Bettini sees the core action of the play as the pursuit of the 'object' by the 'subject'. I will give some illustrative examples of how the system works:

The 'object' is either the woman or money: commonly both, in the form of the expensive courtesan, or the dowered bride.

The old man can be sited in a variety of actantial functions: 'destinateur', 'helper', 'opponent'; but the slave-dealer is always an 'opponent'.

The slave may be the 'helper' and he may be the 'subject' of the plot. What he can never be is the 'destinataire'. His sociological position in Roman society prevents his being placed as the concluding point of the narrative.

Bettini ingeniously uncovers certain rules of transformation within the system, such that if one element changes, another must change also, while the relationship between terms remains constant. In a striking example: if the 'object' is to be a married woman, then the 'subject' must be a god – because the transference of a married woman is not acceptable in any other circumstances. Similarly: if the mother is 'helper', the father can be 'opponent', and vice versa. One fixed term implies another. Bettini's study is 'anthropological' because the basic laws of transformation are sociologically determined.

The great strength of this line of research is its wholesale demolition of the barrier between anthropological and literary studies. Plautine farce is conceived as myth. The form is a collective creation which allows the community to sound out possibilities and impossibilities created by the social code. Bettini indicates why Plautus' theatre is necessarily a theatre of types. Any development of character would obscure the important transformational rules which the drama uncovers.

There are obviously massive problems in adapting this kind of narrative analysis to the theatre.[29] Plautus' disruption of the narrative is a fundamental aspect of his art. His plays are full of parasites, cooks and similar figures who make cameo appearances, providing comic turns which have no bearing upon the main plot. The tension between the shell of the plot and what is physically shown on stage is not satisfactorily accounted for by the notion of deep narrative structures. Bettini's method cannot easily deal with a work like the *Stichus*, where the slave usurps the function of 'subject' in the latter part of the play. Bettini does not take account of the basic difference between narrative fiction, controlled by a single narrator's voice, and drama, where there is necessarily a plurality of voices. In respect of this problem, Petrone (1983) rightly notes the importance of Barchiesi's description of the slave as the incarnation of the 'io epico', the 'epic I', the narrative voice.[30] She indicates how the actantial functions change. In the frame, the young man is 'subject' (or 'hero' in Proppian terms) and the slave is 'helper', but in the *ludus* the young man becomes 'helper' and the slave becomes 'destinateur' (or 'sender'). The 'destinataire' in respect of the frame is the slave-dealer, but the 'destinataire' of the *ludus* is the audience.[31]

The structuralist analysis of Plautine farce is as yet in its infancy.

Bettini's neat schema will not do, and there is much further research to be done. The Italian structuralist approach nevertheless seems to be a purposeful adventure, one that makes us read the plays in new ways. English classicists are too cautious – for reasons that are partly institutional (to protect the place of literary studies) and partly cultural in a broader sense (the English seeming less open to innovation than the Americans). Part of the English problem is a failure to confront the question: why study farce anyway?

I will end with a comment on the word 'farce' – a word that has not been much used in this review. The term has a place in Richard Hunter's critical vocabulary, and its use there marks a deficiency: farce is less profound than comedy, just as comedy is less profound than tragedy. The term 'farce' also has a part to play in a psychoanalytic criticism, where it defines a form that by-passes reason and the censoring superego. It does not have an obvious part to play in a structuralist discourse, where the emphasis is not upon the audience's emotions but upon its intellectual ability to read a system of signs. Within structuralist criticism, however, there would be a certain etymological appropriateness in speaking of the Plautine *ludus* as 'farce' inasmuch as it is stuffed – *farci* – into the frame of a Greek plot.

NOTES

1 Eric Bentley, *The Life of the Drama* (London: Methuen, 1969). (See the comments by D. M. MacDowell in his paper on Aristophanes in this volume.)

2 Eduard Fraenkel, *Plautinisches im Plautus* (Berlin: Weidmannsche Buchhandlung, 1922); a revised Italian edition translated by F. Munari has superseded the German edition: *Elementi Plautini in Plauto* (Florence: La Nuova Italia Editore, 1960).

3 R. L. Hunter *The New Comedy of Greece and Rome* (Cambridge University Press, 1985), p. 137.

4 Ibid., p. 126.

5 Ibid., p. 55.

6 Ibid., p. 55.

7 Ibid., p. 142.

8 For a general introduction to Plautus, I would commend A. S. Gratwick's essay on Roman drama in *The Cambridge History of Classical Literature*, vol. II *Latin Literature*, ed. E. J. Kenney (Cambridge University Press, 1982).

9 C. L. Barber, *Shakespeare's Festive Comedy: A Study of Dramatic Form in its Relation to Social Custom* (Princeton, NJ: Princeton University Press, 1959).

10 See Claude Nicolet, *The World of the Citizen in Republican Rome*, trans. P. S. Falla (London: Batsford, 1980), especially pp. 104ff, 111ff, 123ff.

11 Erich Segal, *Roman Laughter: The Comedy of Plautus* (Cambridge, Mass.: Harvard University Press, 1968), p. 13. Expanded edition, Oxford University Press, 1987.

12 Ibid., pp. 18–19, 92–3; for the distinction between legal and moral criteria, see J. A. Crook, 'Patria potestas', *Classical Quarterly*, NS 17 (1967), 113–22.

13 *Roman Laughter*, pp. 23, 26.

14 Livy XXXIV.8.

15 Contrast *Roman Laughter*, pp. 8–9 with pp. 32–3.

16 For problems of control, see E. Frézouls, 'La construction du *theatrum lapideum* et son contexte politique', *Théâtre et spectacles dans l'antiquité*, Actes du Colloque de Strasbourg, 5–7 Nov. 1981 (Leiden: E. J. Brill, 1981), pp. 193–214.

17 Polybius VI.53, VI.56.

18 On the expressivity of a Roman audience, see Keith Hopkins's essay on gladiator fights in *Death and Renewal* (Cambridge University Pres, 1983), pp. 1–30.

19 David Konstan, *Roman Comedy* (Ithaca: Cornell University Press, 1983), pp. 29–31.

20 Marino Barchiesi, 'Plauto e il "metateatro" antico', *Il Verri*, 31 (1970), 113–30.

21 *Pseudolus*, 401–4.

22 'Plauto e il "metateatro" antico', p. 114 – my translation.

23 Niall W. Slater, *Plautus in Performance: The Theatre of the Mind* (Princeton, NJ: Princeton University Press, 1985), p. 144.

24 Gianna Petrone, *Morale e antimorale nelle commedie di Plauto* (Palermo: Palumbo, Editore, 1977).

25 *Roman Laughter*, p. 39.

26 Gianna Petrone, *Teatro antico e inganno: finzioni plautine* (Palermo: Palumbo Editore, 1983).

27 Maurizio Bettini 'Verso un antropologia dell'intreccio. Le strutture semplici della trama nelle commedie di Plauto', *Materiali e discussioni per l'analisi dei testi classici*, 7 (1982), 39–101.

28 A. J. Greimas, *Sémantique structurale* (Paris: Larousse, 1971). For a short description of actantial models, see Patrice Pavis, *Dictionnaire du théâtre* (Paris: Editions Sociales, 1980), pp. 19–23. Bettini and Petrone also owe a debt to a pioneering piece of Proppian analysis by Cesare Questa: *Il ratto dal serraglio: Euripide, Plauto, Mozart Rossini* (Bologna: Patron Editore, 1979).

29 See on this problem two theoretical essays by Cesare Segre: 'A Contribution to the Semiotics of Theater', *Poetics Today* 1:3 (1980), 39–48; and 'Narratology and Theater', *Poetics Today*, 2:3 (1981), 95–104.

30 *Teatro antico e inganno*, p. 5.

31 Ibid., p. 45ff.

Index